INFECTED MOONLIGHT

ERIN KELLY

To Jamie -
Thank you for
the support!! :)
#Pack Mates 4 Life
Your book club buddy,
Amy aka
Erin Kelly

For more information, the latest news, and more on the Tainted Moonlight series, check out the official website: **www.taintedmoonlight.com**

www.TinyDog.me

ISBN: 9781082226465
ISBN-13: 978-1082226465

DEDICATION

This one is dedicated to my brother Kalen, and his many brothers and sisters in arms in the United States Marine Corps. SEMPER FI!

CONTENTS

1: QUARANTINE

Sophie's head throbbed as she stirred and woke from a deep, troubled sleep. She didn't feel rested but instead somehow more drained of energy, as though she hadn't slept at all. The memories of horrible dreams still flashed in her mind until she remembered that the nightmare was real.

Her eyes slowly opened and came to focus on an unfamiliar ceiling. White panels and a pair of long, fluorescent lights were fixed above her. The room had the same stinging, antiseptic smell of a hospital. She went to move her hand to rub her aching forehead, but restraints bound her wrists and ankles to the sides of the bed. She lifted her hand as far as it would go and saw silver chains were carefully weaved around the bindings. They weren't burning her, but it strengthened the straps.

She winced as her pulse seemed to echo the ache in her skull and looked around the room. It was clean and empty, with only her hospital bed and a small, long table and chair that was pushed over against the wall nearby. High, narrow windows lined the one wall and let sunlight stream in through the frosted panels.

Her mouth felt dry and she made a face as she tried to speak in a hoarse voice. "Help," she cleared her throat as best as she could and fought back the wave of nausea that came over her. She managed to roughly yelp out, "Help!"

The door opened like magic, and a nurse stepped in, a surgeon's mask over her nose and mouth and a plastic clipboard in her hands. She peered at Sophie over a pair of safety glasses. The rest of her was covered in long scrubs. "Oh, Mrs. Bane, you're awake. Good."

She scribbled down something and Sophie grimaced, clenched her hands, and stretched them. She sat up as best as she could so she could put herself in a better position, and asked in a gravelly whisper, "Where's Korban?"

The nurse gave her a quizzical look, and a flash of recognition crossed her face. "Oh, Mr. Diego. He's secured in his room. Don't worry; he won't bother you in here." Sophie slowly shook her head, about to protest that he'd saved her life, and wouldn't be a bother at all, when the nurse smiled brightly and continued on. "Besides you have a very special visitor who's been waiting quite a while for you to wake up."

"Visitor?" Sophie hoarsely asked as the nurse opened the door and ushered her guest in. Her heart skipped a beat as time froze and a chill coursed through her entire body. "Lucas."

He stepped into the room looking much like she remembered. Tall, lean, and deviously handsome. His blond hair was a little longer than she remembered and his sky-blue eyes were lined with dark, weary circles. "Sophie," a smile curved his mouth as his voice quivered with emotion, and she could smell it then, amidst the floral perfume of the bouquet in his hands: a deep, sincere relief.

"I'll just… give you two a moment together," the nurse said, and closed the door behind her, leaving them alone.

Her heart pounded in her chest and she tensed. She was trapped and couldn't run from him. He must have been able to read her uneasiness because he tentatively approached her, stopping to set the vase of flowers on the table, his eyes never leaving her. The tension sang in her body and she suppressed the urge to squirm as he moved closer to her. "I brought you your favorites," he began as his eyes met hers again. "There are some more arrangements that have been sent to you, but I asked them to wait to bring them in. I didn't want the… fragrance… to overwhelm you."

She wasn't sure what to say to that at first. It was so strange to see Lucas out of his element. Now that he was closer, she could see the subtle changes in his appearance. A fine line of fair-colored stubble had started to sprout around his chin, his usually crisp, ironed shirt was wrinkled, and his tie loose. "It doesn't bother you, does it? I can have them taken away, if you want," Lucas said, and for a moment she was too distracted by his pulse and the smell of anxiety rolling off him.

She shook her head in disbelief, still wondering if this was a dream. "What?"

"The flowers," Lucas blinked.

"No, they're fine. Thank you," Sophie grimaced, her mind still hazy. She went to rub her temples again and was reminded of her silver-laced bindings.

"I asked them if they would remove those for you, but they insisted that they are necessary for now," Lucas said, sounding apologetic.

Somehow it made her angry, him feigning this apology after everything. "Why are you here, Lucas?"

He blinked and stared at her again. "You're my wife, of course I'd be here for you."

Something inside her snapped. She may have been trapped there but she wouldn't just lay there while he pretended that nothing had happened. "You can't just suddenly decide to be in the picture, Lucas. Not after you betrayed me. Flowers and empty gestures won't even begin to make it right after what you've done."

Her temper flared to a boiling point. "Betrayed…?" Lucas flinched at her words as if she had struck him.

"Stop treating me like I don't know exactly what's going on! I'm not an idiot Lucas!" She glared at him and growled. She may not have been able to move but she would give him a piece of her mind. "You can't just swoop in now and make it right! Not after you and Nikki were screwing each other behind my back!"

Lucas frowned and confusion knit his brow. "What?"

"Damn it, Lucas, I went to law school! I'm not stupid! Do you really think I wouldn't put it all together?" Sophie was venting now but she didn't care. He had it coming, and she wasn't going to let him easily off the hook. "How could you do this to me? With my sister!" Despite herself, tears erupted from her eyes and streamed down her cheeks. "Of all the women in the world that you could have, you had to pick her. You both had to break my heart." She looked away from him, her entire body tense and shaking as her tears fell down her face.

There was a long moment of tense silence, and then he spoke, his voice cracking with emotion. "Sophie you think that… Nikki and

I were having an affair?"

She hated being this vulnerable in front of him, and not able to wipe away the river of hot tears as they flowed freely down her face. "You bastard. You led her on and she wanted me out of the picture. She wanted that Wolven to finish me off! If Korban hadn't been there, I would be dead. She would have you all to herself."

Through the tears, Sophie saw the look in Lucas's eyes and it was… surprising. He was confused and seemed genuinely shocked at her words. "Sophie, I didn't know that she was behind your attack. I don't know what she said to you, but I swear to you, I've never had an affair with Nikki. Whatever she told you was a lie."

"I—" Sophie snarled but her words suddenly escaped her as her vision cleared with every blink away of tears. She'd been prepared to tear into him for betraying her but the look he gave her now… she sniffled and could smell it in the air. He wasn't lying. She couldn't detect even the slightest hint of deception on him. Besides, Lucas was many things, but acting weak was not something that came naturally to him.

She'd never seen him so heartbroken, as she did in that moment. "Sophie, I swear I have never, and would never, do anything with your sister. You're my wife. I love you. I know we had our challenges in the past, but every marriage does. When we… when we thought you were dead, and I thought we would only ever bury that bit of your bloody dress… I never regretted anything so much as not working things out with you. Above everything else, I wished I had one more chance to make things right and to be the husband you deserved."

A fresh lump bloomed in her throat and the raw pain emitting from Lucas couldn't be feigned. He was telling the truth. He hadn't been having an affair with Nikki.

She thought that the truth would set her free. Instead, it somehow made her feel worse. She gazed down at her trapped, trembling hands. "She made it all up, to push me away from you… she lied to me and… the last conversation I ever had with my sister was nothing but more lies."

She could still see the manic look in Nikki's eyes as she revealed her intentions. She could still smell the smoke and the sickening charred smell of burnt flesh.

Lucas gave her another surprised look. "They didn't tell you?"

He frowned and glanced to the door. "I guess there hasn't been enough time to, since they decided to treat you like some animal and tranquilize you." He sounded very perturbed by the situation and the look in his eyes matched his mood.

"Tell me what?" Sophie asked.

Lucas wrung his hands together, a nervous gesture she hadn't seen him make since college. "Nikki's alive, she survived the car accident."

Her jaw dropped open in disbelief. "What… how is that even possible? She survived, she's okay?"

"She's alive, but the driver who was with her, one of my bodyguards… he died in the crash. Nikki is still in the hospital recovering from her injuries. She was very badly burned, and they've managed to keep her alive, but she hasn't woken up yet." He frowned, gave her another apologetic look. "I had no idea that she… I've been making sure she's been taken care of while in a coma because she is your sister. I had no idea that she was responsible for… well, everything that you've been through Sophie."

Sophie only heard part of what Lucas rambled on about. Her attention fixed on the important part.

Nikki was alive. *Alive.*

Sophie felt a brand-new set of conflicting emotions at this revelation. Her heart swelled when she realized her sister was still breathing, and yet a fresh fear came with knowing her sister was still alive. The feeling of being trapped only tightened in her chest and she tried to calm herself, but her heart pounded even louder now. Inside her, she could feel her wolf stir, awakened by her anxiety. The tranquilizer had started to fade and with it her wolf became aware of the situation and found herself cornered by a man who reeked like prey. She began to struggle against her bindings, while inside she fought the sickening hunger that had emerged. "I can't… stay here. She'll try to kill me again if I'm here when she wakes."

"She can't hurt you here, Sophie," Lucas tried to reassure her, "she's in a coma, in a different hospital."

The restraints dug into her wrists as she fought to free herself. "Let me go. Please, Lucas," Sophie pleaded, desperate as her wolf began to claw from the inside out of her ribcage. "You have to go. Leave. Now!"

She gasped and bucked as she felt the deep ache in her stomach begin to radiate through her body. Her eyes must have reflected this, because suddenly Lucas took a step back from her. "I'm getting the nurse," he said as he warily backed up towards the door.

"I don't want the nurse!" Sophie growled out as a wave of pain crashed through her and caused her body to arch up. She grated her teeth together and tried to focus on her breathing. Inhale. Exhale. Inhale. Exhale. Inhale.

She tried to think of something else, to calm herself somehow. Her thoughts went to Korban, but she still felt her wolf scratching to be free within her. She bucked and the entire bed lurched and moved with her. She snarled again through the pain and glared at Lucas. "Korban. I want to see Korban now. I need him. Please!"

~*~

There was only one nightmare worse than quarantine that plagued him before he met Davey and his merry men. Now that he had conquered another layer of hell and survived his twisted game, it really spiced things up and his usual nightmare now had a new flavor of horror to warp his dreams.

It still started in the same old alley. He walked with Ace, who cracked the same joke he always did and gave him that familiar smile. He would never forget that last moment with his best friend. Even if part of him wished he could.

"You can't be afraid of an alley. Not growin' up in the same 'hood as the rest of us. The only thing I'm afraid of is being home late and having to explain to Pops why."

He had a fair point, and though he was still reluctant, Korban nodded. "Yeah, true."

Ace smirked and stepped ahead, deeper into the shadows of the alleyway. "Come on, it's a short cut."

Korban followed Ace like always into the dark shadows. In his nightmare it felt like entering a void, because the moment he stepped into the darkness it seemed to swallow him whole. The rest of the world faded away. Ace turned to him and smirked. "Come on, Korban. Don't be chicken."

The only light ahead, a flickering streetlamp that buzzed like a bug zapper, suddenly illuminated a massive black wolf. It was so surreal then that his brain seemed to only focus on the fact that it couldn't be real, that he saw it all wrong, and someone's massive dog had gotten loose. Something silver glinted along the beast's furry throat, another oddity that made him think *'It must be a dog, see? It even has a license around its neck.'*

But those intense golden eyes were like two glowing suns, and something about the way the beast stared into him— no dog he had ever met before seemed to be able to see right into his soul like that.

Within his memory, he knew in that moment Ace had stopped alongside him and wondered whose dog had suddenly appeared. But in this nightmare, Ace continued to tease him as he strode ahead, completely ignoring the beast as it silently stalked them at the edge of the alley. Ace's words became an odd loop of gibberish mixed into the final words he had spoken, before the attack. Korban could barely hear him over the pounding of his own heartbeat. So many times he screamed to his best friend and begged him to run.

Sometimes Ace would listen. Other times he would not. It never mattered, because the nightmare ended the same every time, despite how the scenario would twist before the punchline.

This time another figure appeared alongside the black wolf. A tall, lean man who was a recent addition to his nightmare fuel. Ace's words were drowned out by Davey's taunting voice. "Korban. You left me to die. Only I didn't die… not like your friend here is about to."

"No! Davey stop!" Korban yelled, but as Davey emerged from the shadows, he knew that he would never stop. "Please."

"Asking so politely, what a shame. Wasted manners on someone like me, Korban," Davey said, and tilted his head to the massive black wolf at his side. "Kill him."

"Nooo!!!" Korban cried out in vain as the wolf lunged for Ace.

He tried to look away, but he would never forget the way Ace looked after, how pale he'd become, his bright blood like red paint splattered all over the alley.

It's just a bad dream.

He sank to his knees, at the mercy of this warped memory, unable to escape it. The wolf's teeth tore into his shoulder, just as hot and like knives as he remembered.

Just a bad dream.

Something burned in his arm and he yelped, the nightmare fading as Davey laughed. The pain in his arm had been real. His vision swam as he blinked his eyes open. The young man in pale blue scrubs who had been examining him gave a surprised yelp and jumped back, the syringe in his hands filled with Korban's freshly drawn blood.

The bright fluorescent lights buzzed and hummed above him. Korban groaned and squinted. It was too much. Too much.

His mouth was dry and his heartbeat too loud. He tried not to gag at the antiseptic smell of the room, the dank reek of his sweat and fear that was soaked into the sheets. He tried to reach up and block out the blinding light above him with his arm, but his hands were bound tightly at his sides. He was trapped in quarantine. He could almost hear Davey's taunting laughter echo in his ear.

The nightmare hadn't ended, it only continued into his waking life. The voices above him seemed to float. He was still disoriented from the tranquilizer, and who knew how many times they had sedated him since then. He attempted to listen while he slowly cracked open his eyes and tried to make sense of what was happening around him.

"What is going on in there?" Another man's voice floated in from outside the room.

"The patient woke when I was drawing his blood," the nurse said anxiously as a brown-skinned man with a white lab coat charged in. "His eyes haven't changed back. They're still like— "

"You didn't read my notes on him? Mr. Diego here is special. His eyes never turn back. It's fine," the other man's voice said, sighing in exasperation. "He isn't going to turn. This man was infected during the initial outbreak, and he's about five, almost six years into dealing with his lycanthropy."

"He relapsed then? Is that why he's back in here?" The nurse still sounded unsure. They both sounded so far away, though slowly Korban's senses were returning to normal.

"No, he was injected with some sort of catalyst that turned him into a Wolven without the full moon. We are just keeping him in here for observation to make sure there aren't any side effects." The sound of a pen scratching into paper made Korban grit his teeth. There was the resounding click of a pen light and Korban winced and closed his eyes tighter when the doctor shone a light directly into his eyes. "Mr. Diego, my apologies, he's new here, and working on his bedside manner. How are you feeling today?"

"Thirsty," Korban croaked.

"Grab him that water over there and put a straw in it. Just keep in mind it's like treating any other patient with an infectious blood borne disease. It isn't as contagious as the media makes it out to be. It's transmitted through blood contacting blood." Korban didn't know who this doctor was, but he already liked him.

The good doctor pushed a button on the side of the bed. There was a grating sound of gears as they moved the bed up, and a moment later he was sitting up. They hovered over him and as his eyes finally adjusted to the brightness, he saw the nurse's trembling hand lower the bottle with a straw in it. "Careful, don't spill it on him, he's already got enough to worry about without having to be soaked and wet."

The moment the straw brushed his mouth, he wrapped his lips around it. The first sip of water was divine; cool, wet, and heavenly against the contrast of his cotton-dry throat. He drank until the bottle was empty and already felt much better. He was so thirsty he could have used more, but at least his mouth felt more like normal once again. "Thanks," he said, gazing to the nurse then to the doctor.

"You're welcome Mr. Diego," the doctor, a middle-eastern young man with dark hair and warm brown eyes, said with a soothing smile. "I am Dr. Hoover. I have been overseeing your care while you've been here."

"How long… have I been out?" Korban asked and tried to sit up again but to no avail.

Dr. Hoover frowned, but it wasn't a gesture aimed at him. "They've kept you under for fifteen days despite my advice. Unfortunately, not all doctors remember that my patients are just as human as most of us are and prefer to work only with a sedated patient. I just find it a little challenging to work with a patient who cannot respond to me. Makes it difficult to treat someone and diagnose what is wrong or not if you keep someone unnecessarily unconscious."

Korban smiled and relaxed a little. He glanced around the empty room and asked, "I know you can't tell me about another patient, but do you know how Sophie is doing?"

"Mrs. Bane?" Dr. Hoover frowned, but maybe something in Korban's expression made him soften with sympathy. "She is… okay."

"She was asking for you, earlier," the nurse interjected, to another glance over the glasses from the doctor. "I mean, she was yelling your name…"

Korban's heart flip-flopped when he mentioned Sophie had been asking for him but sank when he'd added the rest of the details. "Please, is there any way I can see her? At least for a few moments? Or give her a message?"

Dr. Hoover still glowered at the over-sharing nurse but sighed. "I can see what I can do, but first we need to go through a few questions together now that I finally have you conscious."

He gave a small nod, but no matter what, he was worried about Sophie's well-being. Sophie was smart and strong, but he hated knowing what she was going through. Especially since he wasn't able to be there to help her through it.

"All right then," the doctor began, and asked, "When is the last time you remember transforming?"

Korban swallowed. "During the full moon."

"So you were human again prior to the previous full moon, after you had been under the influence of the catalyst serum?" He asked, pen poised to scribble notes.

"Yes. Sophie and I both woke up in the middle of the Adirondacks, at some quiet place deep in the mountains far from civilization. I remember a lot about our time as wolves, even though she only remembered little bits here and there. I know we didn't attack or hurt anyone… human," Korban amended. "There may be a few fallen deer that we left along the trail. Several rabbits and um… maybe one unfortunate cat."

Dr. Hoover peered at him over his glasses and repeated with a bemused expression, "One… cat?"

Korban blushed. "I think… it maybe crossed the wrong path."

Dr. Hoover snorted, then guffawed and shook his head. "I suppose you're lucky I'm a dog person then. Ah… no offense."

Korban smirked. "None taken, Doc."

"So you last transformed as scheduled, and remember your time as a wolf. Were there any other adverse effects, or changes to you besides the obvious, monthly one?" Dr. Hoover scrawled some notes down as he spoke.

"No, well… not changes to me or my wolf," Korban shuddered at the memory. "I was… captured by another werewolf and his two men. They held me in a silver cage and…" Korban trailed off and gazed down.

"Take your time," he said very gently to him.

Korban wasn't even sure how to begin to explain the whole ordeal he'd been through. He hadn't really had much time to process it himself. The last time he'd told this sordid tale was right before the Commissioner had burst in and had him tranquilized before dragging him and Sophie off to quarantine. Here he was once again, after obeying the rules for so long. This was the cost of disobeying the law, and he only hoped that RJ wasn't locked up as well.

He hated this feeling of being trapped. Especially revisiting the real-life nightmare that was Davey's pit of horrors, and not knowing what was going on outside of these four antiseptic walls. "I need to know something before I tell you the rest," Korban began, looking Dr. Hoover in the eye. "Can you please tell me if RJ, my sponsor, is in prison? Because of me?"

Dr. Hoover shook his head and for the second time within a few minutes, Korban felt relieved. "No, there are notes that he has been suspended from being your sponsor, but as far as I know, he is free. He has been here almost every day since you've arrived, trying to see you, but we had orders from the higher ups that no one was to speak to you until we conducted our own personal interview with you. We had to make sure that you were still, well, YOU, and that the serum did not have any long-lasting effects that could put others at risk of infection."

"Oh," Korban wasn't too surprised that RJ had been trying to visit him and felt better knowing that he was at least free. "Is he the only one who's tried to see me?"

"Well…" Dr. Hoover gave him a slow smile. "It seems that you've inspired a bit of a… fan club."

"Fan club?" Korban blinked in confusion at the doctor.

"You've gained some attention for being the werewolf who returned with Mrs. Bane, and… well, maybe it's better I just show you so you can see it for yourself," Dr. Hoover pulled out his cell phone and poked around it for a moment before handing it to him, and showing him a video online.

The clip started outside of Hutchings, with a small crowd gathered around someone wearing a backwards, neon green ball cap and waving a hot pink poster board in one hand. The camera zoomed in and came into focus on the black text on the sign which read "FREE LOBO" in large, blocky letters. A short, curvy young woman with cyan-streaked hair pulled up in a bun approached Alex and spoke into the microphone she carried. "This is Chel from The Roost Podcast, coming to you live outside of the Hutchings quarantine center in Syracuse, New York. We're here live with the Internet's own newest meme, the one man protest, mister…?"

"Alejandro Cyrus, but you can call me Alex," he said, lowering his sign and flashing a grin. Korban couldn't help but also smile at the sight of his friend.

"Even if you are one man, Alex, you've been getting attention and growing support from many online communities around the world. Care to tell us about your cause?" Chel asked.

"Sure, yes," Alex said into the microphone, but looked to the camera. "My friend Korban was taken away after a simple misunderstanding, just because he's a werewolf. He followed the laws, and then something happened, and now he's back in quarantine again. We don't know how long he's going to be in there, but it isn't right! He helped rescue Sophie, and this is the thanks he gets!"

"Sophie? As in Sophie Bane?"

Alex nodded adamantly and glanced from the young reporter to the camera again. "He's in there and I refuse to let them lock him away to be forgotten! I've been out here every day since they took him and I'm not going to stop exercising my first amendment right until they let me see him!"

"A very noble and honorable pursuit. How long have you been out here?"

Alex counted on his fingers for a moment, including the fingers that poked out of his bright, neon orange cast around his one arm and said, "Nine days, and I'll be here nine more, and then more after that, until they let me see him. He's not just my friend. We're family." Korban felt his heart swell at the words, spoken with such conviction by his friend.

"This video has gone viral, and people are talking. Your friend has gotten you a lot of support. It's a step in the right direction, if you ask me," the doctor said.

In the video clip, Alex was holding up a small boom box over his head, one hand still wrapped in bright, neon bandages. There was a small gathering of people behind Alex who were waving signs that also declared, "FREE LOBO" and "JUSTICE FOR LOBO". Korban got choked up but laughed and shook his head. "I can't believe he's doing all this for me."

"You've got some good friends, Korban," Dr. Hoover said and let the video clip end. He pocketed his phone. "I wouldn't be surprised if you were out of this place soon. We really have no reason to hold you here after the full moon has passed."

Korban hoped he was right and asked, "How many more days until then? I'm usually on top of that but they didn't exactly put a calendar up on my wall in here."

The doctor glanced to his phone again. "The full moon is about eight days away, and after that, hopefully it won't take long to get you cleared to return out into society once again. It's my goal to get my patients who are eligible back out there as soon as possible. So as long as you continue to cooperate and show all signs of being mostly human, it shouldn't be too much longer of a stay here for you, Mr. Diego."

"And Sophie, too?" Korban asked, hopeful.

Dr. Hoover frowned, though he smoothed the look over quickly with another warm smile. "We shall see," he said, then turned his attention back on the paper in front of him, "but for now, I have a few more questions for you to answer and then I can let you rest."

Korban slowly nodded. He didn't miss the look but didn't push his luck and press the good doctor for information. He wouldn't be able to tell him much anyway due to the confidentiality laws, and legally speaking, Sophie wasn't connected to him in any way. It was strange that a little piece of paper meant the difference between knowing and not knowing about how the woman he loved was doing right now. It made him sad, especially because of the quick glimpse of concern in the doctor's eye. He worried about just how well Sophie was fairing in quarantine after all.

~*~

Lucas paced in the hall as another nurse yelped and rushed from his wife's room, looking pale and scared. "What is happening to her? It's not even a full moon tonight," Lucas demanded, his hands shaking. He still couldn't believe this. Seeing Sophie alive again was a dream come true. The last time he'd seen her she'd been carried off in the jaws of a bloodthirsty beast. And now…

"Mr. Bane, I'm sorry sir, she's just… she's losing control. We're trying to calm her down but… this happens sometimes, with those infected, they sometimes can't control it," the nurse said in a flustered tone. "We've paged Dr. Hoover and he's on his way."

A half scream, half howl of rage came from Sophie's room and sent a chill down his spine. Everyone within the vicinity stopped and looked at her door. Lucas went over to the door and peered through the small, square window. His heart sank as he watched his wife as she writhed and fought against the bindings on the bed, which had moved a whole foot away from the wall now. Sweat poured down her reddened face, and her long, blond hair clung with dampness to her scalp as she growled an inhuman sound in the struggle to free herself. She looked so frustrated, and in so much pain, that it broke his heart.

A doctor and a couple nurses rushed past him and went into Sophie's room. Lucas lingered by the doorway and helplessly witnessed as they tried to calm her down, but the more people came in, the more she lashed out at them. Her eyes flashed open and Lucas saw they were bright yellow. The doctor drew a needle from his pocket and injected it into Sophie's arm.

She gave a pathetic yelp, then a low growl that faded as her eyelids grew heavy. Her eyes turned back to their lovely sky blue just as the light left them, and her body went limp as she fell unconscious. "What the– what the hell have you done to her?" Lucas demanded angrily as he stepped into her room.

Dr. Hoover sighed heavily. "There was no choice. We couldn't have her transform, and she was clearly under duress and about to lose control. If she turns and it isn't a full moon, Mr. Bane, we can't clear her from quarantine. I had to give her a sedative. She isn't in pain at the moment, at least."

Lucas bristled but nodded grimly in agreement. Ever since the police came to him and told him they'd found Sophie, alive but infected, he'd focused mostly on the fact that she was alive. He'd offered as much help as he could, posting a handsome reward for any information leading to finding Sophie alive. They'd gotten a flood of calls any time there was so much as a stray golden retriever spotted, but there had been no leads. Then, like magic, she had appeared again after so many weeks of fruitless searching. She'd turned herself in to the police station and the Commissioner had her brought to quarantine. He'd asked Commissioner DeRusso if that had been necessary, because he should have been able to take his wife home to care for her properly. She had insisted and persisted to keep her there for observation until they found out more about the serum that had triggered her transformation outside of the full moon. He was thankful now that she had talked him into this arrangement.

Sophie was alive, but she was not herself anymore. He knew that the lycanthropy virus could change a person, literally, into a wolf, but up until that moment he hadn't focused on anything other than the fact that Sophie had survived. When she woke, looking at him with fear in her eyes and treating him like a stranger, it had hurt. When he'd told her about her sister, and she had freaked out, it broke his heart. He still couldn't believe it. It had to be a terrible trauma that she'd gone through, and now…

Lucas ran his hand through his hair. It was longer than he preferred but he didn't care to take the time to get it trimmed. Not when he'd been so focused, day and night, on trying to locate his missing wife. His wife that had been turned Wolven.

Dr. Hoover listened to her heartbeat with his stethoscope and a finger on her limp wrist to count her pulse. He nodded to the nurse, then stood up and turned to Lucas. "She's going to be okay, for now. She has a strong heart."

He knew the man had no idea, but he maintained a cool demeanor now that she was out of the woods, figuratively speaking. "I'd like to know when she's awake again, please."

"Of course, we can keep you updated Mr. Bane," Dr. Hoover said, then frowned as he gazed over her unconscious form. "It takes time for a lot of newly infected patients to gain control over the wolf within them. It may be awhile before she can safely, and comfortably, leave quarantine, but I have high hopes that Sophie will gain control over her wolf and will eventually be able to go home."

Lucas swallowed to force the lump in his throat down as he asked, "And do you know how long that will take, doctor?"

He winced and shook his head. "I honestly cannot say at this time, Mr. Bane. It can take some people a couple months to be cleared, and others… it can take several years. Some people never gain control over it on their own."

Lucas stared hard at the floor. "I see," he said flatly.

"I'm still very hopeful for your wife though, Mr. Bane," Dr.

Hoover tried to reassure him. "From what Mr. Diego has told me, she has been able to maintain her human side before. She will get there again."

He jerked around and glared at the doctor. "What did he say about my wife, exactly?"

Dr. Hoover held up both hands defensively. "Not much yet, Mr. Bane, as he is still recovering himself, but he did give me reassuring information that your wife has been able to control herself before, and that gives me confidence that she will be able to again."

"I see," he repeated, though this time it was more thoughtful.

The werewolf that had run away with his wife had given the doctor hope for Sophie recovering. Perhaps he owed the… man… another gesture of gratitude. "Thank you, doctor."

He nodded and as they walked out of the room he paused and turned to Lucas. "Mr. Bane, I know it's a lot right now for you, but this is going to take some time. I would suggest you also take the time to take care of yourself, too. You've been here pretty much every day and night since she got admitted and sleeping in that chair can't be comfortable. Why don't you go home, get a real night's sleep, a decent meal from somewhere besides the cafeteria, and come back refreshed tomorrow? I promise you, your wife is in good hands here. I can contact you the moment there is an update on her condition, but she's going to be out for the night."

He didn't want to leave her alone here, but as he glanced to her now peaceful, pale form he knew she wouldn't be waking any time soon. He sighed as Dr. Hoover gave him a stern look. "Go home. Rest. Doctor's orders."

He was a little afraid the moment he left she would disappear, but watching her there gave him a new kind of pain. He wanted to have Sophie back the way she was, and seeing her turn so vicious and unlike herself bothered him more than he could admit out loud. Still, he needed to go home and check in on his son, who was no doubt still being spoiled by his grandparents. Sophie's mother and father had gotten on the first flight to Syracuse when he'd called them and told them she'd been found. He had to give them the update, and he didn't look forward to revealing it all just yet. Still, he had to remain strong, and he wouldn't be able to do that if he didn't go home and rest. "Doctor's orders it is then," he said, and as he walked with the doctor towards the exit, he glanced over to him again. "Thank you for everything you have been doing for my wife, doctor. I know you are doing your best to make sure she can return home with me, as soon as possible."

"You're welcome, Mr. Bane. It is my pleasure to help my patients and their family during their recovery and to try to get everyone back to as normal a life as possible," Dr. Hoover said. "We're still learning a lot about how lycanthropy works as a transmitted disease, and every patient brings unique challenges, but I've had a very high success rate in helping my patients through recovery, especially now that we have more resources and a better understanding of the virus."

"I appreciate all your work, Dr. Hoover," Lucas said, and when they reached the doors to the waiting room, he paused. "I know right now, it's a long shot. But still… I would like to start filing the paperwork as soon as possible to become my wife's sponsor."

"Of course, Mr. Bane," Dr. Hoover said and opened the door. "We can get that started tomorrow, if you'd like. As long as you promise you'll go home and take care of yourself tonight."

Lucas nodded, and shook the man's hand. "You've got a deal."

2: SPIRAL

When the door opened again, Korban was yanked from his lingering thoughts about Sophie, and worries about when he would see RJ or Alex again. The person he least expected to visit him stepped in, and suddenly his concerns were focused back on himself. The uneasy feeling was suddenly amplified when Lucas Bane quietly stepped in and closed the door behind him with a very final, resounding click that seemed too loud.

"Mr. Diego, good, you're awake," Lucas' voice was cold and clear and made him jump as far as his bindings would allow him.

Korban straightened himself and tensed, his heart rapidly pounding against his rib cage. Lucas stood back toward the entryway, a stern and studious look in his cold, pale blue eyes. "Lucas Bane… or is that too familiar?" Korban asked and wondered what he wanted. *Why was he allowed into his room to visit when they hadn't even let RJ in?*

"It's fine… Korban," Lucas said his name in a way that made him bristle. "Relax. I'm just here to talk."

Korban clenched his fists and tried to calm himself. He breathed in from his mouth, exhaled from his nose. His heart still raced but being trapped here with Sophie's estranged husband wouldn't slow it down anytime soon. "How can I help you, Lucas?" Korban asked and leveled his gaze to meet Lucas'.

To his credit, Lucas did not even flinch under his stare, unlike many others who couldn't look him in the eye. Lucas barely seemed unnerved by his wolf-like gaze. He wasn't sure what to expect from the billionaire businessman, but when the man drew a heavy breath, what followed only surprised him more. "I need your help."

Korban's brow knit in confusion. "My help… with what exactly?"

"Not what. Who," Lucas said and took another deep breath. "You've become a white knight of sorts to my wife. She trusts you, and with good reason. I am hoping that you can talk to her and convince her that what I am saying is true."

Convince Sophie? Korban frowned. This was the man who betrayed Sophie, her husband who had been cheating on her, yet now he wanted him to convince her that… what exactly? He opened his mouth to shoot back with an angry response, but something caught him off guard. Lucas had squared his jaw, and his hands were clenched at his sides, knuckles white with tension of his own. Yet those cold and calculating blue eyes held a desperate plea in them. As cool as he was trying to play it off, Lucas couldn't mask his scent. An eau of desperation, with a hint of pain. "When I spoke to Sophie, she told me she thought I had been unfaithful to her, which is simply not true. I don't know what Nikki told her or did to her, but when she discovered that her sister was alive, but in a coma, she… she began to freak out. She was even starting to… transform. They had to sedate her and she begged to see you, before she lost consciousness."

Korban listened, but with every word he wanted to go to Sophie even more. He couldn't smell even a whiff of deceit from Lucas, and somehow this honest confession was worse. It meant that not only was Nikki more deceitful to Sophie than they had originally thought, but now… his relationship with Sophie had grown only to discover that her husband hadn't been cheating after all. Their budding romance in the past couple of months had been a steamy love affair.

He felt a warmth radiate from his cheeks even as the realization sent an icy chill through him. Did Lucas know? Was he really here to kill him after all? He wondered if it was too late to push the call button to summon help. How fast could a werewolf be choked to death? He didn't want to find out.

"I… Lucas, we didn't know—" Korban began but the blond man held up his hand.

"I know," he said in a cool, flat tone, "Sophie was misled to believe that I was cheating on her with her sister. I wasn't able to find out much because she had to be sedated. I am hoping that you would fill me in on what happened after the night Sophie was attacked. Why she hates me so much, and why she is so afraid of her sister—someone who is not only family, but also her best friend."

Korban swallowed, his mouth going dry again. Lucas knew… but at the same time he had no idea of the magnitude of this situation. "Did Sergeant McKinnon or Sergeant Ellyk tell you what happened?"

"They revealed only so much, due to it being an ongoing investigation," Lucas stated. "That isn't what I want to know. I want to know what happened before the night Sophie became Wolven. Why she couldn't come to me and tell me that she was still alive after the attack. Why I had to bury a scrap of her dress, then explain to our son that it was all a lie. That his mother wasn't in Heaven." He raised his voice with every word, anger infiltrating through the pain.

Korban wilted. A flash of the news clip he and Sophie had witnessed flickered into his memory. Lucas holding Daniel's hand as they stood over an open grave. A rose gripped in the small boy's hand. It reminded him of himself, slightly older but still young, surrounded by RJ, Alex, and Ace all dressed in black. Ace had put his arm around his shoulders as they lowered his mother into the earth.

"Well?" Lucas snapped at him, glaring.

"We didn't know who had set up Sophie. We had no idea who was behind the attack. I overheard someone talking in the alley while she was bleeding out, and they would have finished her off if I hadn't been there. If that Wolven – Brett Kensington – hadn't done it," Korban explained. "Sophie had told me the night she met me that she'd thought you were cheating on her—"

"I wasn't. I wouldn't," Lucas growled defensively, and Korban could see another flash of anger, and a flicker of his raw hurt.

He hadn't expected this. As uncomfortable as this was, he never imagined this kind of encounter with Lucas. He'd been angry when he believed he was actively hurting Sophie. Hell, he'd believed that he'd been behind the wicked plot of sending a Wolven after her at one point to try to have her killed.

"We didn't know that," Korban repeated gently. He couldn't be angry, as much as maybe he wanted to, if only keep his focus. "RJ wanted to make sure we checked into any leads and rule you out as a suspect if necessary. We wanted to find out the truth behind Sophie's attack. Someone planned to kill her, and the way it had been so public and so violent… we weren't sure what to think. It was Sophie's decision to lay low when she realized she had some challenges when it came to controlling herself after being infected. We made it through the first full moon, and then focused on finding out who was trying to kill her."

"And you found, in your investigation, that Nikki had been the one behind all of it?" Lucas frowned.

Korban nodded. "We thought… incorrectly, that you had a hand in it. Obviously we didn't find enough evidence to blame you for Sophie's attack. We did find your file on her attack and it seemed pretty damning. Until we put our trust in… well, Sophie trusted Nikki, and the first time, she sent a bomb to the garage to finish the job. My friend Alex – the mechanic you met that day you visited Cyrus Autos – almost died. The second time she lured Sophie out and revealed herself, just before she had your bodyguard shoot us with the serum that forced us to transform."

"Matthew Argentino. He was my employee and one of our family guards," Lucas said, frowning deeper and releasing a heavy sigh. "He was killed in the accident that put Nikki into a coma. I had wondered what he had been doing there… and why he had been there when Sophie lost control."

"We told Sergeant McKinnon once we were able to return home, but before we could really find out more, we were taken into quarantine. And now, here we are." Korban did not feel like revisiting his experience with Davey with Lucas, especially as trapped as he felt right now. The echo of Davey's mocking laughter from his nightmare seemed to haunt his memory, but he pushed it away.

Lucas was quiet for a moment. He leaned back against the wall and folded his arms over his chest. "So you spent weeks out in the wilderness as Wolven… yet you were able to return as human and were able to control yourself again… and also help Sophie gain control over herself… her wolf self?"

"Yes," Korban said, shifting and stretching as best as he could. "I don't know how, exactly, but… I am able to help others stay in control." He remembered the rush of power that came when he'd helped Blaze, Hati, and Spike return to their true forms.

"I see," Lucas said, looking thoughtful. Another awkward silence fell around them. The strained quiet spanned for so long that Korban wondered what else Lucas wanted to ask. He really hoped he didn't inquire about his relationship with Sophie. He was certain that would lead to a far more awkward and heated argument.

Finally, Lucas spoke. "I need your help to keep Sophie in control. She got too upset before… they had to sedate her before I could calm her down. They won't let her leave quarantine unless she can prove she won't attack or transform unexpectedly. If you helped her before, do you think you could do it again?"

As conflicted as he was at the conviction and love that still radiated from Lucas, there was no question in how he'd respond. "Of course. I'd do anything for Sophie," Korban said and straightened in the hospital bed.

"I'm glad to hear that you'll help," Lucas said with a nod of his own. "I will see what I can do then. I want Sophie to know she doesn't have to fear me. That… I had no idea how terrible everything she had been through was."

We haven't even scratched the surface, Korban thought, but simply nodded in response. That awkward feeling was only growing and made him feel uneasy. The unspoken questions that hung in the air only made the worry and anxiety worse.

Lucas gave him another pensive and considering look before he moved away from the wall. That cool mask had returned. Perhaps it wasn't just him feeling uncomfortable with this conversation after all. "I'll discuss some options with the doctors then. I appreciate your cooperation, Korban." He paused as he turned for the door. "My wife means more to me than I can say. You've saved her life, at least a couple times that I know of, and… if you are able to help her through this… I'll be in your debt, and beyond grateful." He paused again and gave him a cool glance, his expression becoming unreadable. "I will see you soon, Korban."

This time there was a finality in his tone, and he left the room, leaving Korban alone with an entire new set of troubling thoughts.

He breathed a sigh of relief, though his worries did not completely disappear the moment his rival did. A new and cumbersome problem had developed, one he wasn't sure how to approach.

Lucas had not cheated on Sophie, but as Sophie had confessed to him when they were alone in the wilderness, there had been other problems in their marriage. Perhaps Lucas did not see the issues the way Sophie did, and with her return from the dead, Korban couldn't fault him for entertaining the possibility for reconciliation.

The thought of losing Sophie hurt him beyond comprehension. He loved her, and she loved him. He knew he could help her maintain control, until she was strong enough to deal with other human beings again on her own. He wasn't sure how Sophie was going to respond to this revelation.

As guilty as he felt for even thinking it, he silently prayed that this wouldn't change anything, and that Sophie would stay with him against all odds.

~*~

The good doctor came through, and despite his anxious mind reeling from the news delivered by Lucas, when the door opened again, and RJ stepped into the room, Korban was overcome with relief. It was so good to see a friendly face again.

RJ's expression reflected his feelings and he went over to Korban and clasped on to one of his hands. "It's so good to see you," Korban blurted, then added quickly and sheepishly, "I'm so sorry, RJ. For everything. I couldn't leave Sophie alone as a Wolven. I had to try and help her. I'm sorry for whatever they did to you while I was gone away. I hope I didn't ruin your life more than I already–"

RJ squeezed his hand and shook his head. "Korban stop. I accept your apology, but there is no need for it. You did what was right, even when it wasn't easy. I can forgive that. What you did… it hasn't been simple for either of us, that much is true. But if you didn't go after her from what Tim said… who knows how many more lives would have been lost, or how far the infection would have spread? You didn't just save Sophie that night. Not by a long shot."

Korban felt a lump form in his throat. He hadn't thought of it that way, but now that RJ pointed it out, he was suddenly overcome with emotion. "So much has happened, RJ. I don't even know how to deal with it all," he confessed.

RJ nodded and grabbed the chair from the wall and pulled it over. He sat down, still holding Korban's hand. It was nice to be touched without someone flinching away from him. "I remember everything you said at the police station. The nightmare you went through at the hands of that psychopath," RJ frowned, but his eyes held a steadfast conviction. "You don't have to worry about him. Tim told me that David Bailey was taken out of the picture for good, and he won't be bothering anyone else anymore. His two partners in crime are also behind bars, and from what I've been told, they won't be breathing free air again for a very, very long time."

He exhaled, and the intense feeling of relief left him in the rush of hot air. This news helped calm some of his unspoken worries. "What about his traps?" he asked, hoping that no one else would fall victim to Davey's cruel game, even if it was unmanned now.

"They found four wolf pits around the area, and filled them in. Nobody else will be stuck in that nightmare again," RJ said and squeezed his hand once more. "Again, all thanks to you and Sophie."

Every time he heard her name his heart skipped a beat. His heartache must have shone through his expression because RJ patted his hand. "I miss her so much," Korban said softly. "I want to see her."

Especially after what Lucas had said. If she was losing control of herself because of the stress of quarantine… he wouldn't let that happen if he could help it.

"From what I overheard on the way in, she's been asking for you," RJ reported and leaned back a little in his chair. "Not that I am one to spread gossip, but I did have some concerns when I heard one nurse telling the other how Lucas Bane had snuck into your room and tried to kill you."

Despite himself, Korban smirked. "His assassination attempt was slightly exaggerated, but he did drop in unexpectedly."

"He didn't hurt you, did he?" The feral, protective look in RJ's eyes would rival a wolf's in that moment.

Korban shook his head. "No, he didn't hurt me…" He trailed off and wondered if somehow, he maybe was the one who hurt Lucas. "He came to ask me for my help with Sophie." RJ frowned in suspicion and Korban continued, "He… he didn't have anything to do with what happened to Sophie. It was Nikki all along. He didn't even have an affair."

RJ's frown only deepened at the news. "Are you sure?"

Solemnly, Korban nodded. "As much as I want… I don't know… I shouldn't say that," he sighed heavily. "I can sense when people are lying. It's one of the perks of being a werewolf. I can smell this whole new range of scents, some that I can't even begin to describe. It's not like a sixth sense but more of… an enhanced sense of smell. People can't hide the changes their emotions have on their body, even if they can mask how they express it. I could sense his pain, and it was genuine. He may not have shown it, but I could tell."

RJ scratched under his chin thoughtfully. "I have to admit, that's a pretty useful skill to have. Would be really helpful to have in the classroom, especially with my crew."

"It is, until you're overwhelmed by how many people try to hide their fear of you," Korban said, lowering his gaze. "It's not the only thing I've discovered about myself."

"Oh?" RJ tilted his head slightly at the question.

"I told you guys about what Davey could do… how he could make werewolves do his bidding just by a look or a touch. How he could bend the will of someone not as in control of their wolf side," Korban said and took a breath to steady himself, then looked back up to RJ. "It seems that I am also able to do that. Maybe I've been doing it all along with Sophie."

"Controlling… not only your wolf, but also Sophie's wolf too?" RJ asked gently, his voice filled with wonder.

"Yes," Korban nodded and winced. "What if the only reason Sophie cares about me is because I—"

"Korban Diego, you stop it right there," RJ snapped and scolded him, shaking a finger in his direction. "Maybe she is able to control herself better around you. But you have never forced her to do anything against her will."

"I was able to make three Wolven stop and listen, RJ. They obeyed my every word, like they were trained dogs. I have the power to force someone to turn back… or to turn, like Davey did," Korban said and shuddered. "He has the same eyes like me. Maybe that means that others with Wolven eyes can also do it, too. Have power over other lycanthropes, I mean."

RJ was quiet for a moment but then he sighed and adamantly shook his head. "I've never met David Bailey, but I know one thing for certain. You aren't like him, Korban. Maybe you both have the same eyes and the same abilities, or powers. But you are not a monster. You never have been, and you never will be." He paused and gave him a pointed look. "You can help a lot of people who are struggling with their control, or you can stop someone like Davey who abused his power. It isn't what you can do that makes you evil.

It's how you choose what you do with your powers. And you are choosing to not abuse it."

RJ's words resonated with him and reminded him of Sophie's reassurances on their way back home. He missed her even more, and wordlessly squeezed RJ's hand again.

It was rare for him to be speechless, but in that moment, there wasn't anything he could say and for several moments he simply held RJ's hand.

RJ smiled to him and patted his arm after a long moment. "I'm proud of you, brother. You continue to impress me. It's been a rough ride so far, even before you were attacked, but know that I am always in your corner. Rescuing Sophie was a risk, but you saved her life, and then her humanity. You know if there's anything I can do to help, I got you."

Korban nodded, still unable to speak. RJ had always seemed to be the voice of reason in their small group of friends when they were growing up. When they were young, he had been closest to Alex and Ace. He had lost so much, first his mother and then Ace, but RJ had remained a constant in his life. He had done so much more when he stepped in after he'd been bitten and chosen to risk his own life and freedom to become Korban's legal sponsor. He recalled having this same feeling once before, the first time he'd been released from quarantine. He had come a long way from the shell-shocked werewolf attack survivor that was anxiously released that day. He literally couldn't have done it without RJ by his side, or Alex too for that matter. He pictured Alex out there holding up the boom box in his one-man protest.

Korban suddenly chuckled, the humor breaking the bubble of emotion inside of him. "Sorry," he apologized as his laughter faded. "I just was thinking how lucky I am to have you and Alex in my life and… well, the doctor showed me what Alex has been up to online."

RJ smirked. "I told him if he goes viral, it will be a lot easier to crowd fund his bail money, but he better not end up in jail. He said not to worry. I said that's my job to worry about my boyfriend, especially because he's too pretty for prison."

Korban laughed again and loosened his grip on RJ's hand as he relaxed a little and suddenly felt much better than before. A heavy weight had been lifted from his shoulders.

RJ gripped his hand again and his smile faded when he gazed

down at the bindings that held him down. "I can't wait to get you out of here," he said. "We're going to have one hell of a party. Michael said when we're ready to let him know and he'll reserve some tables at Howl at the Moon for us."

"That will be nice," Korban smiled, though his expression sobered as the thought resurfaced, "to celebrate our freedom together."

"We will," RJ stated firmly. "All of us. Sophie included."

He could picture Sophie's smile, hear her laugh, remember her scent and taste. He missed her and worried about her, especially now that Lucas told him her control was slipping away. If only he could see her, or get a message to her to reassure her that he was there and that there was still hope. It took him months alone to get control, and even then, it had taken years to overcome just some of the obstacles he faced in transition to a somewhat normal life. Only after he'd met her and embraced what he had become had he really, truly healed. She helped him accept himself. He wanted so badly to go to her and hold her, and comfort her the way she comforted him. To remind her that he still loved her, no matter what happened.

The idea struck him suddenly and rekindled his grin. "RJ… you've done so much for me… but I need to ask another favor from you…"

~*~

Strangers came and went quickly from her room. Every time the door opened, and she was conscious, a fresh panic filled her. No one stayed too long with her, though Lucas tried once more, only to result in her being sedated again. He hadn't returned into her room since, though she could sometimes catch a glimpse of his scent out in the hall, and once heard his voice as he argued with the doctor. At least she thought she did. It was beginning to get hard to tell her dreams from reality, especially when they kept her heavily drugged. Her usually sharp and perceptive mind was dulled down to a fuzzy haze. She hated this helpless feeling of not even being able to gather her muddled thoughts. She only knew for certain that she was asleep when she saw Korban in her dreams.

His vivid smile, the way he made her feel complete… she missed him beyond words. She wondered how he was doing in this nightmare known as quarantine. She now knew first-hand why he couldn't even talk about this place, even to her.

I love you. His sincere confession of his feelings echoed in her mind. She took a small measure of comfort in knowing that she had managed to tell him those three words before they had been separated again. Even now, when Lucas revealed his innocence, her feelings for Korban remained unfazed. He met her many times in her dreams, in that place that seemed so far away now, in a time that they were lost but managed to find home with one another.

Just as she would gain her senses, the wolf would stir again inside of her. Angry that she was trapped in this place, only to be poked and prodded by prey. Angry that her Mate was taken away.

She squeezed her eyes shut and tried to breathe through her mouth. Her heart pounded in her head. She hated this, but she loathed the feeling of being sluggish and lethargic even more than being on the brink of losing control. Her hands, still bound to the sides of the hospital bed, clenched the sheets until her knuckles went white. She tried to picture him there, but with wolf growing angrier inside of her, and the memory of her dreams fading as the tranquilizer wore off, it was becoming a struggle to focus.

She tried breathing through her mouth and inhaled the decaying floral scent of the many flower arrangements lined alongside one another on the dresser nearby. It did nothing to calm wolf or herself down. *How long had she been trapped here? When would she be free again? Why couldn't she see her Mate?*

Frustrated, Sophie blinked back tears. She bit back a growl. They would just drug her again if they thought she was on the verge of transforming. Wolf whined inside of her and scratched, desperate to be released. *Let me out,* she seemed to say. *Let me free and we can run. Escape. Find our Mate.*

The door opened and for a moment fear gripped her and she froze. Her heart leapt into her throat and she wondered if her hold would break. "Special delivery," a familiar man's voice said as he stepped into the room with a new bouquet held in his arms.

Her heart skipped a beat when recognition dawned on her. "RJ?" she breathed his name in surprise. "How did you…?"

RJ winked to her. "They really need to improve the security around here. Or not. I was visiting Korban and snuck in to bring you these."

Her mouth formed a round "oh" of surprise when the flowers RJ held glistened and began to spin.

Pinwheels.

Vibrant, multicolored, shiny, and new pinwheels, that were bundled together like a bouquet.

"Korban," she croaked his name as a fresh flood of tears came.

RJ nodded and set them down amongst the others, but in front of the rest so she could see them. "He asked me to bring you these. One for each week that you've been apart. He also wanted me to tell you he would have made it so I brought you one for each day instead, but I was afraid if I snuck in every day I'd get in trouble, and then I wouldn't be able to come visit you or him."

She shook her head. "They're beautiful, it's perfect as is," she sniffled and smiled through her tears. "Thank you. This means more than anything, RJ."

"You're welcome," he said and she watched the dizzying array of sparkling colors spiral around. "I wish I could stay longer, but I will be back as soon as I can. Dr. Hoover is trying to see if Korban can come visit you. But until he gets that cleared, I hope that these help."

She nodded and relaxed against her pillow. "It does help. Thank you so much," she repeated, and watched them slowly spin as RJ headed for the door. "RJ?" she made his name a question as he grabbed the doorknob.

He paused and turned to her again.

"Please tell Korban that I miss him, and I can't wait to see him again," she said softly.

"I know he feels the same," RJ smiled and nodded. "See you soon."

He left quickly, and as the door closed behind him, a small gust of wind sent the small cluster of colorful pinwheels spinning. She leaned back and watched them, and her heart was full again.

For the first time since she'd woken up in that hospital bed, she felt a tiny bloom of hope.

3: INCUBATION

The pinwheels worked their magic. Every time the door opened, they would whirl and spin. The motion would catch her eye even in the tensest of moments. The nurses could walk past, and she managed not to growl. She focused instead on the way the colors blended together. She was instantly reminded of Korban, and his love for her, as well as the strength she had within herself. She wanted to see him, and the only way to leave this dungeon was to regain the control she had lost. He helped her once, and this time even though he wasn't there, the gift was to remind her of his words. It took him awhile to gain control. She could do it, too. She would break free from this curse.

Every day that passed she focused on the baby steps. She made it one day without growling at all the nurses. She made it another day without having to be sedated.

One morning she woke and found a new pinwheel had been added to the collection. She felt sorry that she had missed RJ's visit, but smiled. She only wished there was something she could give to Korban in return.

It was later that day when she got good news. Dr. Hoover and a female nurse came in and set off the pinwheels. He grinned brightly as he approached her bedside with a chart in his hand. "How's my favorite patient doing today?" he asked cheerfully.

"I'm sure you say that to everyone," Sophie teased, "but I am good. A little better each day."

"You've been making incredible progress in maintaining control," Dr. Hoover said. "It's amazing how far you've come in such a short amount of time. I've never seen someone turn around as fast as you have."

She smiled at his words, and watched the pinwheels rotate and shine as they slowed down. She kept them in sight, just out of the corner of her eye. "I'm trying my best. It's difficult but every day I am getting better at staying focused."

"That's good to hear," the doctor said, commending her, "I have some good news of my own to share with you."

She perked up and looked him in the eye. For the first time in a while she felt confident and in control. She didn't see his gaze as an unspoken challenge. Another small step in the right direction.

"With your permission, of course, if you would like, I have been authorized to arrange a visit between you and Korban. You don't have to give your answer now—"

"Yes!" Sophie emphatically exclaimed. "Yes, please. I would like to see him. It would mean so much."

Dr. Hoover smiled. "I know Mr. Diego will be happy with the news too. I'm going to arrange it then. The full moon is coming up, and if you and Korban agree, I would like to observe you both, and test a theory of mine."

"Theory?" Sophie inquired.

"I believe that with the lycanthrope strand of the virus, people will recover faster and be in better control if they are in groups," Dr. Hoover explained. "I've seen your individual progress, but I would like to see if it improves even more if you were to share a room with Mr. Diego. If this virus is like some of the legends, and you transform into a wolf, it makes sense that it is more in your nature to do well as a pack. My theory is that the virus would respond to the genetic coding that is wolf, and wolves are extremely social creatures in the wild. At least, this is something I'd like to observe. We don't usually put Wolven together because of the possibility of them not getting along. It's too risky and may end up costing someone their life. But since you and Korban's wolves stayed together and thrived in the wilderness, I am fairly confident that you will both be fine."

"The first time I transformed under the full moon, I don't remember what happened. But I woke up next to Korban and we were both all right…" Sophie blushed faintly at the memory before she shook her head, and the thought, away. "So yes. If it may help others, I know I am willing to help be a part of your study."

"Thank you, Mrs. Bane," Dr. Hoover beamed. "I'll start the necessary forms and then we'll get a room ready."

She nodded, and then asked, "We won't be chained down for the full moon, will we?"

Dr. Hoover shook his head. "No, I will be making sure we have one of the rooms ready for you both. Don't worry, soon those will be coming off, and it is my hope that it will be for good."

"That sounds amazing, doctor," Sophie sighed wistfully in relief. "I can't wait."

Thankfully she didn't have to wait too long. Dr. Hoover returned with a different nurse, one who was covered head to toe in protective gear. The nurse shuffled over and asked her to hold up her hands. Sophie complied and the nurse snapped on the new bindings and removed the ones that held her to the bed. It felt nice to no longer be tethered to the hospital bed, and even better when she stood up. Finally, she was able to properly stretch; it felt good to walk again.

Now the real challenge was to not run as they escorted her down the corridor. She wanted so badly to see Korban. Her soft, sock-like hospital slippers barely made a sound as she padded anxiously up the hall. When they brought her towards a new door, she caught the familiar scent of forest and wolf. Her heart leapt and when she turned the corner and entered the room, he was standing there.

His name escaped her lips with so much relief that it was more like a breathy sigh than a word. The grin that lit up his face filled her with indescribable joy. She could no longer hold herself back and she ran to him, closing the gap between them. She couldn't throw her arms around him because of the handcuffs, but she leaned into him and held his hands. "I got your 'flowers'," she murmured into his ear with a smile, "I love them so much. But not nearly as much as I love you."

His fingers intertwined with hers as he murmured back, "Love you too. I've missed you. So much."

"Me too," she whispered back. She pulled back a little so she could get a better look at him. Worry filled her eyes. He was still thinner than usual, since Davey had held him captive, and there were red, bruised healing marks around his wrists. "They better be treating you right."

"I've been through a lot worse," Korban said.

Sophie's frown remained. "You may be ready to joke about it but I'm not," she said and paused. "I guess it's good you can."

"How have you been?" Korban asked as his expression sobered and he glanced her over.

"Better, now, thanks to your reminder that I've come a long way." Sophie clutched his hand and wished she could hold him. She gave a frustrated growl and trailed her fingers lightly around the raw marks along his wrists. "I wish I could properly hug you."

"Me too, even though we have an audience watching," Korban said, glancing to the one flat but shiny wall across from the doorway.

She looked over and could feel the eyes upon them now, too. She wondered if Lucas was behind that one-way mirror and she sighed. "Things have gotten… complicated… haven't they?"

"You mean the whole being separated in quarantine, while finding out your boyfriend and husband have been loyal to you?" Korban teased, but when Sophie blushed, he squeezed her hand. "It's been complicated from the beginning. I don't mind, as long as… as long as you're happy."

She saw the emotion fill his expressive eyes and reached up, then cupped his cheek with her bound hands, careful not to brush the silver against his skin. "I am happiest when I'm with you," she confessed and tried to reassure him with a smile. "I'm not going anywhere. Not after what we've been through. Especially now."

He gave her a curious tilt of his head and she added, "Well… when we get out of here, now that we've been through a lot of the bad stuff together, I think the universe owes us some of the good."

Korban smiled. "I hope so," he squeezed her hand back, and she wondered how big their audience was at the moment before she realized that she didn't care and leaned in closer to him.

His kiss was as amazing as she had remembered.

A loud electronic crackle from above made them both jump. "Sorry to interrupt," Dr. Hoover's voice came over the speaker in the ceiling. "I will be in there shortly to release you from your restraints. I wanted to ask how you were feeling first."

It was a little strange to answer a disembodied voice, but considering their unusual circumstance it wasn't the strangest thing they had encountered recently, not by a long shot. Korban exchanged a glance with her and she nodded in reassurance. "I'm good. I can control myself."

"I'm glad to hear that. I will be in there in a moment." The speaker clicked off and left them alone in the silence.

"He's much nicer than my last doctor," Korban said, relieved. "He genuinely wants to help."

"I get the same impression," Sophie nodded, then added softly, "Even so, I can't wait to get out of this place."

"Same here," Korban murmured, and squeezed her hand. "Though I'll be happy just to get my hands free again."

Dr. Hoover walked in as two security guards hovered at the doorway. He went over and carefully unlocked Sophie's bindings first, then Korban's. "All right. The full moon is in about twenty-four hours. We can't put a bed in here, but I can bring you pillows and blankets. I will be monitoring your progress and filming it for research purposes. If I am not in the other room, my intern or an on-call doctor will be there, as a safety net of sorts. I am confident from what you have shared with me that your wolves will get along fine, but it's best to be prepared for the worst." He paused and looked to Sophie. "Your husband has requested to witness your transformation as well. He has applied to become your sponsor and it may be educational for him to see what you go through first-hand."

Sophie looked down and chewed on her bottom lip. Her sweet, mint-like scent was spiked with acrid anxiety, and Korban reached and held her hand again. Dr. Hoover added, "It is entirely up to you, but given his willingness to sponsor you it may be in your best interest for him to be aware of your symptoms as the transformation draws near. This is something that we normally allow to future sponsors so they recognize how severe the transformation is and can prepare to properly accommodate you."

Korban nodded and swallowed, carefully rubbing her arm to comfort her. "RJ had to watch me transform too… it's the final test of someone who wants to sponsor you."

Dr. Hoover flashed an apologetic smile. "The way things are right now, I'm afraid that it is a mandatory step in becoming a sponsor."

"And… Lucas is the only one who can sponsor me?" Sophie asked, unable to hide the dread in her voice at the idea.

"Spouses are the best candidates and are often approved immediately once they've passed the background check. With your husband's record and influence, I don't see any reason why they'd continue to hold you here once you've turned back after the full moon."

"What if… I didn't want Lucas to be my sponsor?" Sophie quietly asked.

"Others may apply on your behalf, but that process can take time. Especially if Lucas decides to challenge it. Parents are a good option for sponsorship, but there is a cutoff age too since the elderly are more prone to most infections. In some case siblings will–"

"No, no thank you," Sophie said and vehemently shook her head, then sighed heavily. "If Lucas is my ticket out of here… then we'll make it work. Somehow." The look she exchanged with him made Korban feel as though that was directed to him more than the good doctor.

"All right, well then, why don't we get you out of those hand cuffs and fill out a few forms before the full moon takes hold?"

~*~

"This may go down in history as one of my most awkward dates," Korban said, his voice strained.

Sophie chuckled, the pressure and pain of their impending transformation briefly alleviated by the release of tension. She moved in closer, his feverish skin hot against hers but oddly soothing to touch. She felt him relax too. It was comforting to know they were together in this, even as stressful as it was knowing they were not alone. "Is it the fact that we have an audience watching us now, including Lucas?" Sophie managed between clenched teeth as a wave of pain coursed through her body.

"Well, that… and the whole wearing nothing but a hospital gown thing… it's not even my color," Korban tensed and shuddered.

Sophie laughed again, her fingers intertwined with his as they both lay stretched out on the floor. It wouldn't be too much longer now. She smiled at him, despite the growing discomfort that roiled inside her. He returned her smile and squeezed her hand. "Even still… I wouldn't trade a minute of it. As long as you're here with me," Korban whispered.

His vibrant yellow eyes seemed to glow. Maybe she was getting used to this, but when the time came the scenery faded away and no longer mattered. She didn't care that they had an audience just beyond the wall. She braced herself against the flood of pain that usually came, but this time it was more like a rush of water flowing through a stream, instead of a wave crashing into a wall. It still hurt and it was intense, but not nearly as bad as the first time, and better than the other times she'd experienced before.

Her bones twisted and stretched as her muscles pulled and burned. Her own pain melted away as the change took hold, and she watched Korban shift under the harsh fluorescent light.

His golden eyes were the only constant stars in the growing night as his handsome features gave way to the wolf within. The wolf emerged, in tandem with her own, and she waited in wonder for the unconsciousness that accompanied this final stage.

Yet the dreamlike darkness didn't come. She blinked and sneezed in surprise as the transformation completed and she didn't pass out. Instead she lay there beside him, her Mate, the massive gray wolf that shook away the shredded remnants of his hospital gown, then carefully prodded her soft blonde fur with his warm, wet nose.

Her ears perked up and it was an odd sensation, which only got weirder when she felt her tail suddenly thump behind her back legs.

Her tail.

Perhaps some things would still require getting used to after all.

~*~

Lucas stared in horrified wonder as the woman he loved literally transformed into a werewolf before his eyes. His jaw hung open in disbelief. Sure, the reports on the news had been visceral and intense. But no movie, no amount of preparation, could ever prepare one for the true terror of witnessing someone you loved becoming a monster.

Worse yet was the helplessness he felt as he watched her contort and twist on the ground in agony. He was unable to do anything to comfort her, and yet he desperately wanted to burst in there and be by her side. When she reached for Korban it was like a dagger had pierced his heart. When the other man – the werewolf – held her close and made her laugh, even through her pain, it hurt more than he could say. He couldn't hear what they said in the viewing room, but he glared coldly at Korban for doing what he could not right now.

He was grateful when finally their transformation had finished because now Korban didn't have arms to hold his wife. His jaw clenched along with his fists. He despised this feeling of jealousy. He wasn't used to it, and it was a bitter pill to swallow.

Sophie was still his wife. *His.*

He watched as she became a wolf, her fur the same color as her soft, blonde hair. He stared as she slowly got to her feet, her legs trembling at first, and then as she grew stronger and began to bound and play with the gray wolf, her companion. Their tails wagged as the preternatural beasts calmed one another, becoming more like friendly dogs than ravenous beasts of the night.

The sour feeling of jealousy turned his stomach. He had hoped to make things right and work things out with Sophie. But seeing her smile the way she used to only smile for him… the look in her eyes as they turned gold, to match *his*… the reality of her now being a werewolf, like *him*… it all sank in and devastated him.

If only his bodyguards had been faster and armed with silver bullets that night. If only she hadn't been bitten and infected. If only she wasn't a werewolf, maybe he would have a chance…

"It's difficult to watch, but it never ceases to amaze me," Dr. Hoover said and Lucas nodded once in agreement. "The human body can really do some incredible things. I've seen late stage cancer patients rally and come back from the brink of death. I've seen all kinds of medical miracles first hand, but nothing quite as amazing as watching people overcome this virus."

Lucas' mouth flattened into a thin line as he watched the two Wolven chase one another playfully. "Overcome?" he repeated in a cautious tone.

"Well, there is no cure, but the way we can adapt to it as human beings is a feat in and of itself, really," Dr. Hoover said. "Treatment, and adaptation. Those are key steps in recovery. And maybe, one day, finding a cure."

Lucas watched his Wolven wife, and a flicker of hope rekindled inside of him. "Tell me, Dr. Hoover… hypothetically, what resources would you need in order to better research and understand my wife's condition?"

4: INNOCULATION

It didn't take the keen senses of being a werewolf to tell that Lucas was upset with the news, the air thick with the almost palpable stench of his distaste. She knew him well enough by now that the moment the corner of his mouth twitched, and he averted his gaze from the Commissioner, that Lucas' mood had soured. Even though it was brief, the motions were familiar, and Sophie knew his discomfort would soon transform into anger. Lucas had never taken "no" at face value, the business man in him didn't accept it. It was one of the reasons he had been so successful.

A resounding quiet had fallen over the room, despite the number of people gathered there. It had been nine days and nights since the full moon, and with no new side effects, they were now in review for release from quarantine. A wonderful prospect, even with the terms that had just been laid out to them.

Sophie felt anxious, and despite her excitement at the mention of upcoming freedom, extremely conflicted by the dilemma at hand. Commissioner DeRusso had a serious but grim expression on her face. Lucas frowned across from her, displeased. To her other side, Korban sat and attempted a neutral expression, while to his right RJ mastered it.

"There is no other way, Commissioner, for my wife to return home with her family?" To his credit, Lucas kept his tone leveled, even while his hands were clenched into fists in his lap.

"I'm sorry, Mr. Bane, but the law is clear on this matter," Commissioner DeRusso said sympathetically, "the risk of infection is higher in the young and the elderly. Until your son is sixteen, I'm afraid that Sophie cannot live under the same roof. It simply isn't safe and so the law is absolute."

"I see," which was another way for Lucas to amicably disagree, Sophie knew, and he squared his jaw to restrain whatever statement followed that. "I suppose we can stay at the lake house for now. Daniel can stay with his grandparents until later."

"Given the… unusual circumstance here, and your wife's fragile control over herself when alone, I normally would not even consider releasing her from quarantine at this time. In fact, I am strongly against it," the Commissioner's gaze narrowed as she frowned, "yet Dr. Hoover has assessed that she is stable enough to be released on a trial basis, as long as she is in the company of Mr. Diego."

Sophie caught the look that her husband shot at her lover, and it was not a friendly one. She felt her cheeks grow warm. She was still processing the fact that she'd been misled, and falsely believed that Lucas had been the one to betray her. Her sister's deception went deeper than she had ever imagined, and even if it hadn't worked in Nikki's favor, it had managed to divide them anyway. Not that she regretted falling in love with Korban. It complicated things now, but she still loved him deeply. It didn't stop the awkward, squirming feeling in her stomach as Lucas glared daggers at Korban.

The Commissioner continued. "I have decided based on what Dr. Hoover has recommended that you have clearance from quarantine and will be granted return to the public on a temporary trial basis. A probation of sorts. I expect that both of you will be reporting in immediately after the full moon by phone to Sergeant McKinnon and Sergeant Ellyk, in person no later than twenty-four hours after the next three full moons, and then forty-eight hours for the following cycles. Until we are one hundred percent certain there are no long-term side effects to the catalyst serum, neither one of you is to leave this city. You cannot break curfew. As you may or may not be aware, a mandatory curfew is in effect in part due to your absence. Any further violations of your probation may result in permanent quarantine at least… termination at the most. It is my job to keep the citizens of Syracuse safe. I cannot have any more incidents of werewolves running amuck."

"Yes, Ma'am," Korban swallowed and nodded.

The Commissioner tensed and turned her gaze to Sophie. "I am releasing you to your sponsor, who will be legally responsible for your actions from this moment on. Anything that you do will result in your sponsor, Lucas Bane, also facing consequences for your actions. Minor infractions may result in permanent quarantine for you, and jail time for your sponsor. Too many minor infractions could result in a suspension of your sponsor, and land you back here in quarantine. More serious penalties will be given should you spread the lycanthropy virus, harm, or kill someone as a wolf, up to and including the death penalty. Do you understand the terms of your release?"

Sophie nodded, then said, "Yes."

"Mr. Bane," the Commissioner turned her gaze upon Lucas, "do you understand your responsibilities as a human sponsor to Sophie Bane? I am releasing Sophie to your sponsorship. This means you agree to provide a safe, secure location for her to transform during the full moon. You agree to provide a residence upon which she can obey the curfew. You are also responsible for monthly check-ins after the full moon, and to be accountable for her location at all times while in her Wolven form. Do you understand the terms of your role as sponsor?"

"Yes," Lucas said without hesitation, "I understand and accept."

There was something about the whole ordeal that vaguely reminded Sophie of their wedding. A different kind of vow was being made between them, a new partnership that maybe would outlast their marriage. It felt more permanent. Guilt twisted in her stomach.

Lucas was still loyal to her, and willing to risk everything for her freedom. She watched as he signed the contract, and her fingers brushed against his when he slid the paper over to her. She met his gaze and the sleepy wolf inside her stirred. Wolf wasn't happy about this. The only one in this small meeting room that didn't smell like prey was her Mate.

She inhaled sharply and lifted the pen. No matter what happened now, Korban would be there to help her. She could do this. She had to do this. The comforting scent of pine forest and musk of wolf calmed her, and she signed the contract.

It didn't take long for RJ and Korban to follow the procedure, which ended RJ's suspension as Korban's sponsor. They were all ready to leave by the time they were finished, but the Commissioner looked at them sharply when Lucas tried to stand up and excuse them. "There's another matter we need to discuss before I allow you to sign your discharge papers and be on your way," she said, glancing to his seat, which Lucas sank back into, and she continued. "With all the media attention your wife's public attack has gathered, the mayor has asked me to hold a public forum. This will hopefully minimize the media frenzy and prevent Sophie from too much anxiety, which may trigger an unscheduled transformation, and will also give you a safe place to share your recent experience without being swamped by the curious hordes."

"What kind of forum, exactly?" RJ asked.

"A televised but closed to the public forum, to have a panel go over some questions and answers with you. Well, with Mr. Diego and Mrs. Bane," the Commissioner steepled her fingers. "The panel will be comprised of several experts and local law makers who want to review the laws that we have currently in place to see if we need to make adjustments after the discovery of this catalyst serum."

"Adjustments?" Korban paled at her words.

The Commissioner shifted and leaned back in her chair. "The mayor is considering some amendments to the current laws in effect. With Mrs. Bane's public attack, then your return well… let's say it has rekindled public interest in the treatment of our infected citizens. Many of the laws passed during the outbreak five years ago were hasty, put in place quickly to prevent the infection from spreading. But the public, as in the voters, are now demanding change. As a courtesy, Mayor Varno has decided to arrange a public forum with our two most famous werewolves."

"So they're trying to save face, to gain votes?" Sophie asked with a frown.

"You know politicians. They look at opportunities like this as a good way to boost their approval. Especially after such a public mess to clean up." Commissioner DeRusso leaned forward again. "It will give you both a chance to show the Mayor and the city – hell, the world – that maybe not all those who are infected are monsters."

Sophie felt dizzy with the weight of the possibilities. "So this forum could lead to change?"

"It'd be a start," she said. "A step in the right direction. After all, it wouldn't be the first time in history that Central New York set the precedent when it comes to the rights of others. Seneca Falls held one of the most successful rallying cries in the women's suffrage movement before women could vote. We became a sanctuary city to protect and aid refugees. We take steps before many others do. Why not in this?"

Sophie saw Korban straighten up in his chair, and that spark had returned in his eyes. She was certain that he felt the same thing that she did in that moment. Hope.

Commissioner DeRusso pulled out a couple other sheets of paper and smiled. "Well then. The forum will be scheduled in a few days, so I will be in touch through Sergeant McKinnon. He'll give you the specific dates and times when the mayor's office contacts us. In the meantime, I need you to lay low and stay out of trouble. I have been assured that you can both do that."

"Yes, yes Ma'am," Korban smiled.

"Good. Then let's get the rest of these papers signed so you can be on your way," she said, and pushed the next set of forms over their way.

~*~

Relief didn't come until he finally stepped outside the metal double doors. He felt the sun on his skin and breathed in the city air. An entire morning now gone, lost to a mountain of paperwork and a series of forms and exit interviews, but it was over. For now, he was a free werewolf. Sophie's warm hand brushed his and he felt the tension leave her too, if only for a moment.

Then chaos was unleashed.

A small group of reporters and onlookers gawked at them from beyond the Hutchings gates. The barrage of questions was punctuated by the bright flares of unnecessary flashing and clicking of cameras and cell phones. All eyes – natural and mechanical – were suddenly focused on them.

"Mrs. Bane!"

"Mrs. Bane!"

"Is it true that you faked your death in order to cover up Bane Corporation's bankruptcy filings?"

"Are you really a werewolf now?"

"Some sources say you're a zombie! Care to comment?"

Sophie tensed and froze, and both Korban and Lucas reached for her hand on each side of her.

Lucas glared at him, but then thankfully a large, black SUV pulled up and blocked some of the media swarm's view. He stepped forward and opened the back door for Sophie with his free hand. "After you, my dear," Lucas said with a plastered on smile.

Though the arrangement had been made inside, it was obvious that Lucas wasn't too happy with it. Sophie had refused to leave quarantine without him, of which Korban was eternally grateful. With the garage at Cyrus Autos under repairs and in need of inspection, it was the only way for him to have a secure, approved place to transform for the next full moon. Lucas had argued it was still weeks away, but the law was clear and Commissioner DeRusso made her point explicit. Korban was to stay with her and help keep her wolf side under control. At an impasse, he had reluctantly agreed to allow Korban to stay at their lake house, and graciously extended the invitation to RJ and Alex as well. More than likely so that there would be extra eyes around to keep him and Sophie from continuing their relationship.

They piled into the SUV and Sophie sat down in the middle row of the spacious vehicle. Lucas brushed past Korban and sat down in the seat next to Sophie. RJ clapped Korban's shoulder and they climbed in and sat in the back together. The driver closed the door when RJ asked, "Mind if we make a quick stop?"

"Sure," Lucas said. "Where to?"

"Just over there to pick up Alex," RJ said, pointing and Lucas raised an eyebrow as his gaze followed his finger.

Lucas shrugged and leaned back in his chair. "Damion, we're going to make a quick stop over there to pick up the protester."

"Which one, boss?" Damion peered over his shoulder.

"The one in the neon green shirt that reads, 'FREE LOBO' on it," RJ supplied.

The driver smirked in amusement and drove the car carefully over to the edge of the crowd. RJ rolled down his window and beckoned to Alex, who lit up and handed his sign over to the girl next to him. He headed over to the vehicle and waved to the others. "We did it guys! We freed him! Lobo's back!" He howled and pumped his fist in the air. "We did it!"

The crowd cheered and clamored around the SUV, but the

police along the perimeter formed a barrier and Lucas opened the door. Alex gave another gleeful whoop and climbed inside. He moved through the two middle seats and into the back, sitting between RJ and Korban. He threw his good arm around Korban and hugged him fiercely. "I'm so glad you're free, Lobo. Sophie too!"

"Me too, brother." Korban hugged him back and then Alex settled into his seat, a wide grin plastered on his face.

A tense silence fell over them as they drove towards the lake house, out of the city and into the green lush countryside. From the bustling streets to a quiet, spacious community near Skaneateles Lake. Korban itched to hold Sophie's hand but with her sitting in front of him, and Lucas' narrowed eyes watching him like a hawk, he doubted that the gesture would go over well. At least RJ and Alex were there.

RJ seemed tense, his posture stiff as he remained alert and on guard, even though they were putting miles between themselves and the quarantine facility. His friend and sponsor glanced his way and asked, "You doing okay?"

Korban nodded. He wondered if this was such a good idea after all. The awkward, tense silence in the car was bad enough. He wanted to be near Sophie but felt an odd sense of guilt now. It didn't diminish his love for her, but with Lucas around… it made things complicated. He wanted to talk to Sophie about it, and watching the back of her head, he wondered how she felt about this whole ordeal. It was a lot to process, without the need to overcome quarantine as well. He could still feel the phantom weight of the restraints that had been on his wrists.

"So… nice ride you have here," Alex was the first to break the silence. "Rich, Corinthian leather. Mind if I try the seat warmer?"

Lucas blinked in surprise and stared at Alex for a long moment, as if he hadn't heard him correctly. Then he nodded. "Yes, go ahead." He watched Alex with a sidelong look as the mechanic adjusted the buttons.

"Ooooh… oh, that is nice! We need to have this in our next car, RJ," Alex sighed contently.

"It is nice, especially during the winter," Lucas agreed after a moment.

"Mmm," Alex leaned back and closed his eyes. "You guys have got to try this."

Korban smirked. Leave it to Alex to help cut the tension. He chit-chatted about the high-end features of the vehicle, and was suggesting some adjustments to improve the fuel efficiency, when the lake house came into view. From the looks of things, Korban hoped the place came with a map.

The lake house was at least two stories high, and it looked large enough to hold two, maybe even three or more of their entire garage comfortably inside. House seemed to be too small a word for it. The place was a mansion. Skaneateles Lake sparkled blue and calm behind the beautiful manor.

Seeing the water reminded him of the blissful, brief time when they were alone in the forest. His cheeks warmed as he remembered skinny dipping in the small lake they had come across.

The car pulled to a stop in front of the entrance at the horseshoe bend of the driveway. "Welcome to Buckingham Palace," Alex murmured and whistled under his breath in appreciation. "Nice digs."

"Thank you," Lucas said crisply, polite in his own way. "Please make yourselves at home. I will show you around, later, but I can give you a brief tour of the guest house where you will be staying."

As they rounded the driveway, another house, closer to the lake and shielded by a small cluster of lush green trees, stood a small house that was more modern in appearance. It appeared to be a spacious, one story ranch house that overlooked the sparkling, deep blue water of the lake. It even had a nice wrap around porch, similar to the main house. "There's a kitchen, one bathroom, and two bedrooms inside. Along with a pull-out couch in the living room. If you make a list for Damion, he can pick up any groceries you may need. There's also a grill you can use out on the deck. I'm sure you may like to get some personal belongings as well, and I can arrange transportation to the garage if you would like. The kitchen is stocked with essentials but if you have any dietary restrictions or food allergies just let us know and we can adjust the shopping list accordingly."

Lucas seemed to keep his cool, level demeanor for the moment while he was in charge. The tension was slightly dispelled by Alex again who cracked, "Well, with my constitution, I have to avoid caviar. Fish gives me gas and no one wants to go through that."

Lucas tried to stare him down, but snorted a laugh and shook his head. "I'll keep that in mind then, Mr. Cyrus— Alex," he corrected, then straightened up again and turned to Sophie. "There's something I'd like to show you, if I could."

"Yes. Of course," Sophie said. She paused by Korban and took his hand again and gave it a squeeze. "I'll be back soon."

He nodded, but the concern must have reflected in his eyes when she gave him a reassuring smile. "I'll be fine."

He trusted her, but the nasty glimpse he caught from Lucas as he turned and lead Sophie away didn't help settle his nerves.

Alex playfully prodded him in the side with a finger on his good hand. "Come on, let's explore. Pick out our rooms and all that fun stuff. I don't think Sophie is gonna eat him, but even if she did… would that really be so bad?"

It was a terrible joke, but Korban cracked a smile anyway and shook his head. "All right. But I call dibs on first shower."

Alex wrinkled his nose and made a face. "I won't fight you on that one, Lobo."

Korban playfully swatted Alex's good arm and teased back, "You only won't fight me on it because I'd mop the floor with you."

"Nah, I don't want to embarrass you in front of RJ by whooping your butt with one good arm and all. You'd lose some street cred with him, then he'd have to return your werewolf butt to the pound." Alex winked and poked him again with his good hand.

"Too soon," Korban groaned, but playfully grabbed Alex and gave him a noogie, before he pulled him into a hug. He gently patted his back and withdrew again, a smirk still plastered on his face. "I missed you, jerk."

"Missed you too, Lobo."

~*~

Sophie followed Lucas outside of the guest house. He stepped down off the porch and headed for the main house. She matched his pace and walked alongside him in silence. She kept her gaze focused on the ground, then the house itself, as they approached it. Every step took her further away from Korban and his soothing presence.

Very human memories stirred as they walked up the path toward the large house. She pictured happier times, sitting out on the porch and overlooking the lake as she held Danny in her arms, when he was just a tiny, pink baby. The porch swing was still there where she spent countless numbers of hours reading, once to herself, then to Daniel as he got older. While it was familiar and home to her human half, the Wolf inside found this place foreign and new, and her senses were suddenly keen and alert as she left the familiar harbor of her Mate's side and waded out into the dark, mysterious depths. She was careful not to look Lucas in the eye, afraid that her fragile control would snap and she would hurt him, or worse. As if the whirlwind of turbulent emotion inside of her wasn't chaotic enough.

They climbed the steps of the porch, and as Lucas reached for the doorknob, she stopped and blurted, "Wait."

He paused and turned his head towards her. Her eyes quickly darted from his icy blue glance and she took a shaky breath. "Let's sit out here on the porch for now. Please. The air… helps."

She caught a glimpse of his mouth as his lips formed a taut line of disapproval, but he sighed and said, "All right."

They sat down together on one of the white benches nearby. Here she could overlook the sprawling green hill that the house was set upon. The dirt path that they had walked on snaked down to the guest house, then further down to the sparkling blue lake. The view of Skaneateles was breathtaking from here. The tightness in her chest lightened up as she took in the enchanting sight of the valley around them. The scent of the trees and water was fresh and filled with the perfume of the wildlife and vegetation that bloomed around the area. The lake was a deep, dark blue that mirrored the darkening sky. It was all a perfect distraction for Wolf, and as a breeze fluttered by, she felt grounded again.

She could do this. She was in control. She chanced a glance over to Lucas, who sat more hunched over than usual, his shoulders and jaw tense as he stared down at the lake – or maybe their guest house. He was downwind of her, but she caught an unusual tinge of something unfamiliar in his scent, that usual confidence weakened and in its place something undefinable.

"Lucas, if this is about Korban–" Sophie began, but he held up his hand and fervently shook his head.

"Please. I don't want to talk about him right now." Lucas' torso heaved with the force of his breath as he inhaled deeply. He clasped his hands together in front of him and Sophie saw his knuckles were white. "I… I'm grateful he was there for you, and that he saved you, and helped you keep your humanity. I can never, ever thank him enough for what he has done for you. For our family. But… I don't want to talk about him right now. I wanted to show you an idea I had, something special to help you through this difficult time," he said, pulled out his phone, and tapped a few buttons.

He held his phone carefully, but she saw a glimpse of his screen and it made her heart ache. It was a shot of the three of them from over a year ago. Lucas, Danny, and herself— all smiles and the picture-perfect family. She didn't get to linger long on the image as the phone rang and seconds later a video screen popped up. It was blank at first, and a familiar, young voice chirped over the line, "Hello, Dad."

Sophie's heart skipped a beat. His voice hadn't changed all that much, yet he seemed to annunciate his words more maturely than she remembered. "Hey buddy," Lucas greeted him warmly, his voice taking that lighter, more gentle tone that was reserved only for their son. "There's someone here who's really missed you."

Lucas turned to her and held up his phone. Sophie's hands went to her face and she tried to shield her gasp. It wasn't only his voice that had grown. Her son was older – of course he would be – but the roundness of youth was starting to fade from his face. Yet when he saw her that bright, familiar smile spread across his face and he yelped out in excitement, "Mommy!"

The image blurred as tears filled her vision. Sophie blinked them away, then quickly brushed them aside with the back of her hand. "Danny… oh baby, I've missed you so much."

"I've missed you too Mom!" He bounced and shook the screen and for a moment there was a pixelated nose, then an eye, and then another familiar voice, ripe with emotion heard over the line. "Daniel, be careful sweetheart. You might accidentally hang up on your mother," a feminine voice gently chastised.

The image refocused on Daniel as he grinned, and two other familiar faces came into the frame. Her mother looked the same as always at first— exactly how she would want it. Her hair styled and perfectly in place, not a wrinkle to be seen in her brand name outfit. Though at a second glance Sophie saw the small glimpses of silver in her usually impeccable blonde hair, and more pronounced laugh lines than she had ever allowed herself to have before.

Her father's bright blue eyes shimmered with unshed tears. He was like she had remembered as well, though his hair was a bit wispier and his complexion paler than she recalled. His familiar white mustache curved when he smiled and greeted her, "Hello, Sweetie."

"Daddy… Mom…" Sophie's heart felt flooded as she realized how her absence had taken a toll on both of her parents.

"You gave us all quite the scare," her mother chided but smiled, relief reflected in her eyes. "Welcome home."

"Thanks," Sophie croaked, her voice choked up with emotion.

"I've been keeping them in the loop while you were in the hospital," Lucas explained.

Hospital seemed such a mundane word for what she had endured, but she didn't correct him. All that mattered right now was the smiling faces on the other end of the line, especially the youngest one, whose bright grin revealed another change in her son that tugged at her heart. "You lost another tooth!"

"Yeah, Gram and Pawpaw made sure I put this one under my pillow for the tooth fairy. I didn't swallow it on accident like the first time," Danny beamed proudly.

Sophie laughed and began to reach for the phone, but stopped herself and put her hands over her heart. "I'm so glad, baby."

"I got two dollars, Pawpaw said it was because I brushed my teeth really well," Danny said and grinned wider, wiggling another loose tooth with his tongue. "See? I have another wiggly tooth, and another one is kinda wiggly too. I'm gonna be rich in no time!"

She laughed again, and this time Lucas joined her. "I want to show you my money, Mommy. Gram got me a bank to put it in and everything. When are you coming to visit Gram and Pawpaw too?"

Her expression sobered at his innocent words. Lucas cleared his throat. "Mommy will see you when she can, buddy. She's getting better every day."

Danny's smile faded. "I want her to be here with me. I miss you Mommy."

"I miss you too. So much." Sophie struggled to find the words to comfort him, especially when her own heart broke.

"Mommy needs her rest, so we'll talk more tomorrow, okay? It's been a very long day," Lucas said. "Say good night for now, buddy."

Danny sighed and frowned. "Okay, Dad." He perked up a little as he waved to the camera. "Bye Mommy! Good night!"

"Talk to you more tomorrow, Sophie. Glad you are back where you belong," she said and blew her a kiss.

"Good night, Sweetie," her father, a man of few words, managed to get out before the call ended.

Sophie's hand scrubbed away the stray tears that fell as Lucas pocketed his phone. They sat in silence again for several minutes when Sophie found her voice again. "Thank you for that, Lucas."

He nodded. "We've all missed you, but he's missed you like crazy. I know the feeling all too well."

He reached then put his hand over hers. She tensed for a brief moment, and turned to him, but didn't pull away. "I don't know what you have been through these past few months. All I know is that I've missed you. I begged, pleaded, and prayed for some way or somehow that I'd get you back. I never imagined it would be possible. But here you are. My wish, miraculously, came true."

She opened her mouth to interject but he shook his head and the look in his eyes made her stop. Raw pain reflected in his usually stormy but stoic eyes and halted her train of thought. "I know we had our challenges before, Sophie. But there must be a reason that you were brought back to me. Whatever happened out there – between you and *him* – I don't care. We're back together again. We have a second chance to make it right. A clean slate. All I ask is that no matter what happens, from here on out, is that you give me and us a fair shot again. I love you, and I'll do what it takes to make this work. Our marriage, our family, and our life together."

She didn't know what to do and had a lot to think about, but for now she offered him a small, brief smile and squeezed his hand. He squeezed hers back, and she looked back down to the lake.

No, she lied to herself. It wasn't the lake she focused on, but the guest house below, where the lights had already begun to glow against the darkening sky.

~*~

It felt nice to stand under the hot water and lose himself for several minutes. The shower in the guest house was huge and would have taken up at least half of the bathroom back home. It took him a few minutes to get the settings the way he wanted, but once he did, the steady stream of water was like heaven. The shampoo was some fancy brand he didn't recognize that smelled pleasantly of tangerines and mint. Korban didn't care if he smelled like some fruity drink, as long as it helped wash away any traces of quarantine. Besides, the sweet mint scent on his skin reminded him of Sophie and just the thought of her made him smile.

A heavy weight was lifted from his shoulders as he rinsed the suds away and the remnants of the hospital stay swirled down the drain. He stood there for a little while longer after the last of the bubbles vanished and closed his eyes. He'd managed to do the impossible. He was out of quarantine again, and he had to take a moment to count his blessings for that miracle.

When they were taken to Hutchings, he was certain that he wouldn't get another chance at freedom. It was simply unheard of. Those who were infected and broke the law knew that any infraction meant either permanent quarantine or death. It was extreme, but it had been necessary to stop the spread of infection. No virus, or whatever this was that changed him, had ever acted like this one.

The law was the law, and the rules were extreme for a reason. It made sense to him when he had first been released from quarantine. He knew the risks, but he wanted some fraction of normalcy despite his world changing forever. He'd risked his life, and RJ's, to help rescue Sophie from a grizzly fate. She'd turned around and returned the favor now more than once. First, she sprung him free from the grasp of a madman, and now she was the reason he'd been spared being locked away for the rest of his life.

He wanted to thank her, somehow and someway. He wasn't sure how he could even begin to repay her for all she had done for him. Right now, he had his freedom, but until the garage was repaired and inspected, he was homeless and dreadfully still unemployed. Yet here he was, as Pops would say, "landed on his feet again".

There was also the matter of meeting with the public forum that Commissioner DeRusso had told them about. The thought of meeting up with the mayor and a group of politicians made his insides squirm with both anxiety and excitement. The crowd outside all were holding signs of support, and like the Commissioner had said, the public was demanding change. Maybe he could bring up ways to amend the laws in a way that would keep the public safe but would grant more freedom to lycanthropes. Maybe there was a way to talk them into letting Sophie see her son before he was old enough to start shaving. The thought filled him with hope, but he cautioned his mind to slow down and not get too far ahead of himself.

He wasn't a lone wolf anymore, though he really never had been truly alone. He should have realized it the night he first transformed, when he heard the chorus of howls as others who had been cursed with the same affliction succumbed to the full moon's embrace. He'd spent so much time running from what he had become, until Sophie came into the picture. Now that she was by his side, they could do this together. The thought filled him with infinite happiness.

He turned off the shower and yanked one of the soft, white towels from the rack. He dried then wrapped the towel around his waist before he padded over to the mirror. A thin layer of steam fogged up the mirror and he scrubbed it away with the side of his hand. From the mist his vibrant yellow eyes appeared and for the first time that he could remember he didn't despise what he saw in his reflection.

He hummed to himself as he stepped out of the steamy bathroom and out into the bedroom, which wasn't the Master bedroom but may as well have been with its king-sized bed. His voice caught in his throat when he realized he wasn't alone, and he grinned. "Hey, I was just thinking about you."

Sophie sat on the edge of the bed and smiled, though it faded fast as her expression turned serious. Before he could even ask, she said the dreaded four words, "We need to talk."

5: FRACTURE

No one liked to hear those words, and Sophie hated herself for starting out their conversation this way. Especially as his trademark smile vanished and in its place his brow crinkled with worry, those expressive yellow eyes filled with sudden concern. "Everything under control?" Korban asked carefully.

"Yeah. I'm doing okay with that, for now. Really." This was even more difficult than she imagined it would be, especially as he stood there and worried about her, his tan skin a lovely contrast to the bleach-white towel draped tantalizingly around his narrow hips.

She felt her cheeks warm and averted her gaze, suddenly focused on her hands clasped down in her lap. "We, um, have some robes hanging in the bathroom closet if you want to use one," she offered.

It was silly, to get so flustered when she'd spent so many days with him where they'd both worn less than a mere towel, and had far more intimate encounters, but this was going to be difficult enough without reminiscing on those times. Korban smirked and joked as if reading her mind, "No foliage to cover up with?"

She gave a small laugh and shook her head. "No, no foliage in there. Though maybe I can get you something off one of the trees outside if you want."

Korban chuckled and vanished into the bathroom. He emerged just moments later with a white terrycloth robe tied around him. His hair was damp and messily clung to him, jet black strands that only emphasized his unique golden eyes. It didn't matter if he was wearing a robe or not. She was sorely tempted to tear the robe off him and forget that she'd ever suggested this conversation to begin with, but that would only further complicate the matter at hand. A matter she really wanted to run away from, but one that they had to deal with now.

He sat down next to her and Sophie steadied herself with a deep breath. His forest and fur scent had a somewhat tropical flare from the shower, but it calmed her just the same as always. Her gaze returned to her hands again as her fingers fidgeted. "I guess there is no more avoiding it," she began with a shaky breath. "Lucas knows. He… he doesn't know all the details of what you and I did. But he knows I cheated. Not him. I don't know why I was so blind at the time. I believed everything I saw, the evidence I found added up and Nikki just… she twisted it even more so that of course I would fall for it. I've never felt so stupid in all my life."

Her voice trembled with the last line of her confession, and Korban reached and took her hand in his. His touch was warm and comforting, like a blanket. "You're not stupid, Sophie. You've never been stupid. You're probably the smartest person I have ever known," he stated firmly, and when she shifted and met his gaze again, she saw that fierce sincerity reflected in his eyes. "Nikki knew you trusted her and she betrayed you. She took advantage of you, knowing that you would believe whatever she told you. That doesn't make you any less intelligent than you are."

Even now he was defending her, and it broke her heart. "You're so sweet," she squeezed his hand, "I don't deserve you. I really don't." She took another shaky breath. "You mean so much to me, Korban, and I love you. I don't want to hurt you. It kills me to even suggest this to you, but… I will always be honest with you. I owe you that much, at least."

"You don't owe me anything, Sophie, if anything, I owe you," Korban began, but she squeezed his hand again and he stopped.

"You and I… we've done a lot for one another. Let's not keep score. Please. You are my best friend and a huge part of my heart. I don't regret anything about our relationship. I love you," she repeated, then sighed heavily, "only… I'm still married to Lucas."

"Yeah," Korban sighed as well and rubbed her hand. His shoulders sagged in guilt as well.

They sat there quietly for a long moment, as Sophie struggled to find the words, anything at all that would make this easier. She was at a loss for words, but Korban sat there patiently. He still kept her hand in his and didn't pull away even now. She gathered her thoughts for a moment before she spoke again. "I saw Danny… and my parents. He's safe at their house. It was just over a video call, but it made me so happy. I miss him even more." She drew another deep breath as her guilt weighed on her even more. "Lucas offered to forgive me, if I go back to him. He is willing to overlook my… our… indiscretions… if I give him a chance again. He was being so sincere and honest when he talked about saving our marriage and staying a family. I… I honestly don't know what I want to do. Part of me is selfish and wants both. I don't want to hurt you, or him, but I'm afraid that I'm just going to end up hurting you both and the truth is… I don't know what to do. I need to make a choice, and reason dictates that I should try to salvage my family. But my heart… it tells me that I shouldn't give up on you either. I love you too much, and after all we've been through you are still here by my side. Being so patient despite the fact that I'm here breaking your heart." She couldn't hold back the tears that formed. "This has all been so much to take in and think about. I just need some time to process it all."

Korban gently put an arm around her and gave her a hug. His frame trembled a little and drawn this close to him she could smell the conflicted emotions going through him. Not that she needed to with the amount of tension that sang through his torso. She wrapped her arms around him and buried her face into his throat. "If you need time to sort through your feelings, I understand," he said softly as they clung to one another. "I know the truth was a shock to me too. I can't imagine what you are feeling right now. If you need time, you know you got it from me."

His words both relieved her and caused her guilt to spike even more at the same time. Even as he hurt he was still so kind to her. She hated herself for doing this to him, but what choice did she have? "Thank you, Korban," she whispered, and her voice choked up with emotion. "My heart feels like it is being torn in two as it is right now. I'm sorry to even have to ask you for this, I just… I just honestly don't know what to do."

He rubbed her back and gently murmured, "Take your time. I'm here if you need me."

His voice was still tight with emotion and she hated herself even more for putting him in this position. When she pulled away from him, she saw a flash of pain in his eyes, but he didn't once complain about her request. "I'm going to stay in the main house, in my own room for now. I've asked Lucas for space too. Between getting control over my impulses as a werewolf and everything else, I think that's the best thing I can do right now for everyone involved."

He gave a small nod and looked like he was at a loss for words. She stood up and sighed again as she despised herself for making it suddenly awkward to be alone in the room with him. "It's getting late, and it's been a long day. I'll see you tomorrow, okay?"

"Okay," Korban said, and to his credit he masked his dejection well. She only caught a small whiff of his pain though and turned away so she couldn't make it worse as her own pain spiked again.

She headed for the door and was almost out of there without bursting into tears, when he suddenly stood up and said, "Wait. Sophie."

She stopped and had to fight back her tears when she glanced over her shoulder to him. He paused and swallowed before he spoke again, "I love you. No matter what you decide to do, I want you to know that. I just want you to be happy. Even if that means… even if it means losing you."

She couldn't stop the tears that escaped now, and she turned away. "I love you too, Korban. Good night." It sounded more like good-bye and she left then, before she lost the nerve to do it.

"Good night," she heard him say, and felt a stab in her heart as his voice cracked.

As she rushed outside to the main house, she dreaded every step that she took away from him. It felt like she was making a huge mistake and her heart grew heavier with every footstep. More than anything she wished she could be the one who would make Korban happy, as happy as he had made her. It was the hardest thing she ever had to do to walk away from him. If this was the right thing to do, she didn't know why it felt so painful.

She managed to make it to her room and lock the door for some privacy before she finally let herself break down. She felt so alone but had only herself to blame for it.

~*~

Korban watched her leave and fought hard not to chase after her, especially when he could smell the raw pain that came from her. It took everything he had not to follow her and comfort her.

She asked for space, and he would respect that no matter how much it hurt. He sat back down on the bed for a long moment and wondered where he had gone wrong. Maybe he'd gotten too comfortable with the idea of being with her. Naturally, finding out that Lucas hadn't cheated would cause her conflict. She had a family that loved her, and why wouldn't she want that back now that they were here? He should have been used to losing those he loved by now, shouldn't he?

A lump formed in his throat that he couldn't swallow down. He tried not to just sit there and feel sorry for himself but was suddenly at a loss of what to do himself. He got up and paced for a moment in the room, but the scent of her lingered in here, full of pain and only made worse when he caught the small hint of mint on his own skin. He had to get out of here.

He headed out into the hall and towards the living room. The opposite direction from where Sophie had headed. RJ was channel surfing on the couch, his feet up on the foot-rest as he reclined back. Alex was passed out alongside him, his head resting on a pillow that was over RJ's lap. His broken arm was draped over his chest and seemed to glow, the neon pink bandage bright even in the dim light of the television. He almost ran back to his room, or darted for the outside door, but the moment RJ saw him he knew it wouldn't do either of them any good. The perceptive look his best friend gave him stopped him in his tracks. Without words RJ gave him a questioning look and beckoned him over without so much as lifting a finger. Korban sighed and shuffled over to sit alongside his best friend. "Tell me what happened," he said softly, his voice low to keep from waking up Alex.

Korban sagged down. "Sophie asked for some space."

RJ nodded and sighed in turn. "I'm sorry, Korban. I wish there was some way I could help you catch a break."

"Me too. I guess that's the downside to dating someone who's married," Korban glanced over to Alex, and both wished he was awake and was grateful for him being passed out at the same time.

Alex's face scrunched up occasionally in his sleep, and as his features smoothed again, he noticed the pain that radiated from him for the first time. It dawned on him then that he had been so wrapped up in what he and Sophie were going through that he'd neglected to ask how his friends had been doing while he was away. Fresh guilt filled him as he asked RJ, "Alex's gonna be okay, right? His arm is healing and everything?"

RJ gazed down affectionately to Alex as he slept and nodded. "He'll be okay. He's just as stubborn as always. He'd be doing better if he was resting more like his doctors have instructed him, but you know him. He won't touch the pain killers, and no one slows him down. Especially when he's on a mission."

Korban gave a small smile at that as he pictured Alex leading the protest. "Getting my sorry butt out of prison."

"He was relentless. Even before you returned, he was out most days searching for you guys. He was posting flyers online, and around the neighborhood," RJ said, chuckling softly and shaking his head. "I asked him what he planned on doing when and if he actually found two werewolves. He insisted that you'd recognize him, but even when I pointed out that Sophie tried to eat him when she was in human form, he just shrugged it off. He was afraid if we didn't find you guys that not only would something bad happen to you, but something bad would happen to me too."

Which was possible, and they both knew it, so Korban gave RJ an apologetic look. RJ merely shrugged. "You did what you had to in order to protect Sophie. I can understand. You've always done what's right for people you love. Even if it's going to hurt you." He reached over with his free hand and patted Korban's shoulder.

"I shouldn't have been so careless when your freedom was at risk, too," Korban sighed. "I'm sorry. Again."

RJ only squeezed his shoulder. "Don't worry about it. Just don't do it again. I got lucky that Tim vouched for me, but he can only do so much if you go running amuck again."

"I'll do my damnedest to not turn into a Wolven and run off any time soon," Korban promised, and then stared blankly at the television. There was something on the news about a wanted terrorist on the screen and he sighed yet again. "The more things change, the more they stay the same."

"The world keeps on spinning," RJ said and removed his hand from Korban's shoulder and picked up the remote to mute the television. "Are you going to be okay?"

Korban gazed down. "I guess so. Eventually. I… I should have seen this coming when we found out about Lucas. I mean… she has a son with him. They're a family. He's her sponsor now. It would be good for them to work things out."

"Yeah, in some ways it would," RJ agreed, "but I still think it's good she takes time to sort out her feelings and thoughts. You have both been through a lot. She clearly cares about you, otherwise it wouldn't be such a difficult decision for her to make. I wouldn't toss out the idea of the two of you being good for each other too. Anyone could see that you've been good for each other, and despite everything that's happened you've made it through together." He threaded his fingers through Alex's hair and smoothed it back. "She compliments you in all the right ways. Just like Alex does to me. I wouldn't give up hope just yet."

"I really, really hope you're right RJ," Korban said, then offered him a genuine smile, even though it faded rapidly as he confessed, "I really, truly love her RJ. I don't know what'll happen if I lose her."

"She hasn't made her choice yet, Korban. Don't rule yourself out." RJ was careful not to disturb Alex he put his hand back on Korban's shoulder again. "You've never been one to give up before. I don't recommend starting now."

"You're right. You're always right." RJ always knew what to say in order to lift his spirits, and while it didn't change the awful situation, it was reassuring to have his support.

For now even if it still hurt, at least his friend's hope fueled his own that maybe, just maybe things would work out.

~*~

"Wakey, wakey Lobo," Alex's voice stirred him from his slumber sometime that next day.

For a brief, blissful moment Korban wondered if everything that happened last night had been just a bad dream. Then Alex jabbed him in the ribs with a finger and caused him to gasp and wriggle away with a jolt. "Hey. You're not gonna sleep all day and feel sorry for yourself." Though at the nasty glare Korban gave him, Alex wilted a little. "Sorry. Too soon. But even still, we've got work to do, and RJ's made breakfast, so it's time to get up."

Korban groaned and rolled over. He really wasn't in the mood for this. The little bit of hope that RJ had given him last night was wearing out. Or maybe it was just too damn early to deal with it. Especially as Alex poked and prodded him awake. He pulled his pillow over his head and gave a muffled, annoyed response. "Go away Alex."

There was the rustle of cloth and he felt Alex's weight shift the mattress, and then the pillow he gripped over his face was lifted. Alex sat alongside him and peered down at him. "Look. I know that things look bad right now. Let's go have some breakfast and then we can begin to plan how you're going to get Sophie back."

"She asked me to give her time, so I'm giving her time, Alex," Korban said, shielding his eyes with his hand then rubbing his forehead.

"Sure you can bench yourself. Do nothing, while Lucas puts all his best moves on her. All while you just sit it out. Or… you can follow my soon to be patented, fool-proof method of winning her heart back," Alex stated in a tone so serious that Korban stared at him for a long moment.

"Alex, I haven't had my coffee yet, and I didn't sleep too well last night," Korban warned him with a growl, but the mechanic wasn't fazed and just poked him in the stomach again.

"All the more reason we need to go have breakfast first," he stated simply. "Caffeinated werewolves are happy werewolves. RJ's put on a fresh pot. He even found a waffle maker in there. This place really does have everything. It's the perfect lair to get our plan under motion."

Korban grunted again but despite his protesting he sat up, much to Alex's delight. "We planned one heist with mixed success, and suddenly you're the guru of planning?"

"Based on many years of watching romantic comedies, despite RJ and you repeatedly giving me crap for it, I have learned a thing or two on how our hero ends up back with his lady love, against all odds," Alex said, holding up his brightly bandaged arm to the sky. "As someone who was almost literally blown up by one of those odds, it is my sworn duty to make sure my best friend ends up with the woman of his dreams. So yes, I have a plan on how you can remind Sophie that you're the man for her. And, on a full moon night, the wolf for her too. But I'm not sharing so much as a word of said plan until you get up, get dressed, and join us for breakfast. Please."

Korban smirked and shook his head, but he relented. "Fine. If it will get you off my back, and out of my bed, I'll get up."

He knew Alex well enough that he really wouldn't give up and would only pester him until he gave in anyway, but he couldn't deny that part of him was genuinely curious about this plan of his. Alex, happy that he'd gotten his way, bounced off the bed and onto his feet. "I'll go pour the coffee then."

"You go do that," Korban said as he went into the bathroom to commence his morning ritual.

When he finished getting dressed back in his clothes and headed into the hall his stomach churned in renewed hunger. Despite the hollow feeling in his chest right now, he still needed to eat. It was hard to feel utterly hopeless when he sat down to a fresh mug of coffee and a waffle with fried eggs for eyes, a bacon smile and two triangular formations of bacon at the top of his waffle, which were ears to resemble a wolf.

He glanced over to RJ who merely pointed to Alex. "He insisted on decorating your breakfast this morning. Don't worry, I cooked it, he only embellished it."

Alex beamed and Korban chuckled and shook his head again. "Thanks guys. Really." He picked up his coffee first and took a long sip before he ate one of the wolf's ears. He took his time chewing, especially since he saw the eagerness in his friend's eyes as he pretended to wait patiently for him to ask. "So what's this plan of yours Alex?"

Excited, Alex perked up then explained, "It's simple, really. We need to set up a recreation of the day you met. Even before all this, you two had a connection. If we remind her of that, she's bound to choose you. Mikey is bartending early tonight, so we can stop by Howl at the Moon later and you can practice a few songs, including a certain Billy Joel hit that is sure to bring back memories. When she's ready, you'll just ask her out for the night, take her there, and woo her with the sultry sound of your voice."

He wasn't sure what he expected, but Alex's plan didn't sound too difficult, and it was simple but meaningful enough to maybe work. He chewed and swallowed a bite of waffle and watched as RJ's eyebrows lifted in genuine surprise when he said in wonder, "You know, that's really not a bad idea."

Alex puffed up a little at that, proud of his idea. "See? Not all my ideas are super outlandish and complicated! You have to respect the classics."

"I still don't agree that your choice in movies are classics, but we've definitely pulled off more complicated stunts than this before." Korban tapped the side of his mug thoughtfully and nodded. "All right. I'm on board. What time is curfew tonight?"

"Curfew is at eleven o' clock tonight, so that gives us plenty of time to get there when they open at five and get back here with time to spare," RJ reported. "I'd like to get to the city early anyway so we can stop by the garage and pick up some things."

"Sounds like a plan to me," Korban said, stabbing his fork into another bite of waffle, which suddenly tasted even better than before.

Maybe this would work. Maybe he could remind Sophie just how much she meant to him. There were still a lot more complications involved in this whole matter, and he knew there were many other hurdles to overcome. Sophie reassured him that she loved him, but she was torn between returning to the safety of her old life and their new life together, which definitely was filled with a lot of uncertainties and unknown factors.

This would be just a small gesture, but it was better than sitting around and doing nothing at all, like Alex had said. Besides, if nothing else it would be nice to get out for a little while and have some kind of normal evening after everything that he'd been through. He was already looking forward to it.

~*~

Michael was ecstatic to see them walk into the bar that evening. "Hey! Welcome back stranger!" He heaved the crate of bottles that he'd been carrying up onto the bar and extended a hand to him.

Korban greeted him warmly with a firm handshake. "You know they don't come stranger than me, Mikey. Your very own friendly, neighborhood werewolf, free at last. How've you been? How's school been treating you?"

"Getting closer to the finish line every day," Michael beamed as he squeezed his hand. "I'm so glad you're back. The first drink is on me to celebrate."

"Thanks man," Korban said, leaned against the bar, and glanced around the room. So far they had the place to themselves. Michael poured a gin and tonic and set it on a coaster in front of him. "You remembered."

"You haven't been gone that long, Korban," he said and poured himself a glass of tonic water, "and besides, it would be bad for business if I forgot my favorite customer's usual poison."

"Hey! I thought I was your favorite customer," Alex pouted as he sat down on the bar stool alongside him.

"Technically he means all three of us anyway, Alex," RJ said with a smirk. "We've covered Korban's tab here more than once or twice."

Michael laughed as he poured out their usual drinks in turn. "Well, you aren't wrong there."

"Geez, and here I was misled that tonight was meant to make me feel better. I didn't realize I'd be dragged out to be roasted by all my friends." Korban attempted to be offended but couldn't hide his amusement, even when he lifted his glass to his lips.

He stopped before he took his first sip and raised his glass again. "A toast to freedom, and friendship."

RJ, Alex, and Michael held their drinks up to that, and clinked their glasses together.

They made small talk and caught up with one another until things began to pick up. As time went by more people filtered in, and soon the three friends departed from the bar and relocated to their usual table in a corner, over near the stage. Tonight's deejay was setting up karaoke and they put in their first round of song requests, then ordered some snacks while they waited their turn.

There were some friendly greetings from some of the regulars, but as the evening moved into the night Korban noticed more strange glances aimed his way. It dawned on him then that he hadn't brought his sunglasses. It had been so long since he'd worn them that he had completely forgotten to put them on. No wonder some people were staring at him.

The attention felt different from before. There weren't too many disgusted expressions aimed at him, but instead more looks of curiosity and recognition. He could hear some whispered mentions of his name, and Sophie's too.

"He's that werewolf who rescued Sophie Bane!"

"Really?"

"Yeah, I'm sure of it."

"Why did she run off with him?"

"Look at him! I mean, he's kinda cute. I wouldn't mind running away with him myself."

"Yeah, but *why* would she? She's married to freaking Lucas Bane! He's dreamy and he's a billionaire."

His stomach suddenly churned, and it probably wasn't because of the order of nachos he was picking at. "Be right back, I gotta take a leak," he said and stood up as casually as he could and headed to the restroom.

When the door closed behind him, and he realized he had the quiet room to himself, he breathed a sigh of relief. He stood by the sink and stared at his reflection for a moment, then down at the drain. Maybe this wasn't such a great plan after all. Romantic comedies rarely were good models for anything when it came to real relationship advice. He twisted the faucet on and splashed his face. The cold water eased the knot in his stomach and he gripped the counter. For a moment he closed his eyes and focused on the sensation of water dripping down his face.

He missed Sophie. Practicing songs for her was a romantic gesture, but it only reminded him of her absence. The hole in his heart was unbearable. Maybe it was time to head back to the lake house. He didn't want to go back if it meant not being with Sophie, but he didn't want to stay and be bombarded with whispers and gossip all night either.

He yanked some pieces of paper towel from the dispenser on the wall then used the rough sheets to dry his face. He froze with a jolt when he caught a pale stranger's reflection standing behind his own.

The tall, lean, and strikingly handsome man stared at him with a calm expression. His pale blue eyes studied him from beneath a shock of long, bleach-blond bangs. His arms were folded over his chest and there was an eerie stillness to his posture. He looked more like a photograph of a Nordic model than an actual person, and out of place with a long, over-sized black coat on in the summer heat.

"So you are the famous Korban Diego," the stranger said, a slight Irish lilt in his voice. "I've been looking for you."

"Who are you and what do you want from me?" Korban blurted

the question, proud of how he kept the fear from entering his voice. Especially since his heart was pounding up near his throat.

The handsome stranger smirked in amusement, though his pale eyes remained cold and flat. "Ye can call me Mikael," he began, his accent providing a warm contrast to his cool demeanor. "Ye don't have t' be nervous. I'm not here to eat ye."

Korban stared at Mikael's pale reflection. His amber eyes widened as Mikael flashed his fangs. No wonder he reminded Korban of some Lost Boys reject. "Okay, Mikael. What does a vampire want from me exactly?" *If not my blood,* he thought but was too afraid to say out loud.

Mikael hesitated for a moment and studied Korban. "Word is that yer able to force Wolven to change." The vampire curiously tilted his head and cautiously asked, "Is that true?"

Korban wasn't sure what to expect, but Mikael's answer only further multiplied his surprise. "How did you… who told you that?"

Sure, he'd helped Hati, Blaze, and Spike transform back after Davey had manipulated them and forced them to transform, but he hadn't told a soul about having that kind of power. No one outside of them, or the people in the interrogation room, knew about his new found ability.

"It doesn't matter now. All that matters is ye come with me." Mikael stepped forward and reached for him.

Before Korban could react, the bathroom door burst open and nearly gave him a heart attack. "Hey Lobo! You're up next!" Alex barged in.

Afraid for his friend, Korban whirled around to warn Alex and face off with Mikael. "Alex, get out of here!"

Alex blinked and stared at him from the doorway, equally confused. "No need to shout, Lobo. I'll give you some privacy. Just thought you'd want to know that you're on deck."

Korban turned to tackle the vampire but found no one there. He swatted where he'd just seen Mikael, but only touched air. "What the…?" Korban frowned, even more perplexed than before.

"Are you okay Lobo?" Alex asked as he cautiously approached him. "You look like you've seen a ghost."

Korban glanced around but there was no trace of Mikael to be seen. "More like a vampire," he murmured and shook his head in disbelief. All he could hear over his own thundering heartbeat was

Alex's pulse echoing his own.

"Vampire?" Alex repeated with a worried look. "Maybe a double gin and tonic was a bit too strong to start the night on after weeks of sobriety. No one's in here, Lobo. Just you and me, and I can assure you, I only sparkle on the stage. Come on, let's go. Practice makes perfect."

Mystified, Korban looked around again, but sure enough no one else was there. Maybe Michael had poured his drink stronger than usual, but alcohol hadn't so much as gotten him buzzed in years. Now it was giving him hallucinations?

Alex patted his shoulder and ushered him out of the bathroom. Korban scanned the bar for any hint of Mikael's presence, but no one there even remotely resembled the man he'd seen. The vampire had disappeared and left more questions than answers, along with the unshakable feeling that someone was watching him from the shadows.

6: REFLECTION

His nightmares had a new flavor to them. When he woke up that morning he could only remember so much, but he knew it involved running away from Davey with vampire fangs. The gentle, warm sunlight greeted him when he opened his eyes and he breathed a weary sigh of relief.

The bed was so soft that he wished he could enjoy a good night's sleep in it, but his brain had other ideas. He couldn't help but wonder if he had imagined the encounter with Mikael last night, or not.

Word is that yer able to force Wolven to change. Is that true?

Despite the warm comforter cocooning him, he felt a chill run through his body. How did he find out about something that Korban only recently discovered about himself? More importantly, what purpose could a vampire want with his ability?

The whole situation was unsettling. He thought about telling RJ, or even making a call to Sergeant McKinnon, but what could he possibly say? "I met a vanishing vampire" was not something that would bode well for him, especially after being recently released from quarantine. This would lock him up and throw away the key.

Maybe it was all a simple misunderstanding. He had gone through hell and back, and now he faced losing Sophie, too. It probably wasn't why he would imagine up a mysterious stranger with an Irish accent, but maybe he could justify it that way. Of course, he couldn't even fool himself with that lame excuse.

He rolled over and grunted in frustration. He was already dealing with enough as it was, and now he couldn't even trust himself.

He'd never even met a vampire before, though the unnatural stillness of his posture along with that scent of death was undeniably real. At least his wolf believed him, and remained just as unnerved as he was by the encounter.

It doesn't matter now. All that matters is you come with me.

He burrowed under the covers to try and stop the shivering cold that coursed through him.

One thing was for certain, imaginary or not, Korban had the sinking feeling that he would learn soon enough if he imagined Mikael up or not.

The thought of a vampire hunting him, like in his dream last night, forced him up out of bed. He tossed the blanket aside and was up on his feet and down the hall before he let the thought finish. He must have looked a sight, because when he arrived in the kitchen RJ sipped his coffee while raising an eyebrow in his direction. Before Korban could speak, his sponsor asked, "Where's the fire?"

"I… just bad dreams again," Korban carefully stated, and went over to the coffee pot. He took a mug from the dish rack and filled it up as he asked, "I take it Alex is sleeping in for once?"

"Yeah," RJ said, still giving him a suspicious look. "Are you sure that you're okay? You seemed a little spooked when you came in."

Korban sighed and sat down across from RJ. He took a long sip before he spoke again. "I'm as good as I'm gonna be for now. I just… I miss home. This place is nice to visit but… I miss the way things were, too."

RJ furrowed his brow in concern and nodded. "I think we're all a little homesick. I'm having a hard time adjusting to waking up in a new place, too," RJ said.

Korban relaxed a little, thankful that his friend wasn't prying into it further. "Yeah," he said in agreement. They sat together in silence for several minutes, though Korban used that word a bit liberally. His heartbeat still thundered in his head.

Were his friends in danger, being around him? He had far more questions than answers. If only Mikael hadn't been so cryptic, maybe then he wouldn't have to be paranoid. His wolf didn't like this feeling of being hunted any more than he did.

"It's okay if you miss her, and if you're upset about this arrangement," RJ gently said, misreading Korban's worried look.

The pain of missing Sophie at least dulled the fear of the unknown, and Korban scratched the back of his head anxiously as the lingering hurt was dialed back up again. "I do miss her…" Korban trailed off and stared down into the dark liquid in his mug. "I want her to be happy more than anything. Even if it means losing her. I wouldn't blame her for trying to make it work with Lucas, especially for her son."

RJ frowned but nodded. "No one would blame her if she does decide to stay with him, but you have been through a lot together, too. I guess we'll see what she decides, but I worry about you. I know it's not a choice she will make lightly, but I do hope she chooses to be with you. Not even because you're my friend, though knowing the man you are, she'd be losing out on one of the best if she left you. You two have been through a lot and watching how happy you both are together… there's no denying that you have chemistry."

"Hey, it's too early for your science teacher puns," Korban said, playfully jabbing him.

RJ chuckled and patted Korban's shoulder. "It's never too early, and I mean it. When I see you and her together, it just seems… right."

Korban smiled. "Kind of like when I see you and Alex."

RJ smirked and nodded. "I'll never forget the night we told you. I was so nervous that you'd get upset with us or wouldn't accept us for some reason."

"You were both like brothers to me, so it was an adjustment at first, but that was on me, not you guys. I was happy you both found someone who loves you," Korban stated and finished up the last dregs of coffee.

"And I will be happy when things settle down for you, too," RJ said and stood up, glancing to Korban's empty mug. "Need a refill?"

"Sure, thanks."

RJ poured him a new cup and returned the coffee pot back to its cradle. "I'm going to start breakfast. Maybe a little home cooking is just what the doctor ordered."

"Sounds good to me," Korban said.

As RJ rummaged through the kitchen and whipped up breakfast, there was a shift in his mood and things did seem a little brighter again. Maybe it was the coffee, or the conversation as RJ cooked, but by the time breakfast was ready Korban felt a weight lifted from his shoulders. Even if it was a little relief for his aching heart, he would take what he could get.

~*~

Sophie found herself the next morning alone in her bed, clutching her tear-stained pillow close to her chest. She hadn't slept well but only had herself to blame.

She was supposed to try and make things work with Lucas. If only for Daniel's sake, she had to try to keep her family together. It was the right thing to do, but why did she have to keep reminding herself of that fact? More importantly, why did this feel so wrong?

She kept seeing Korban's expression as she told him. He'd managed to hide it well, but she knew him by now. His smile may have remained, but his expressive, yellow eyes held only pain.

Lucas had let her take the master bedroom to give her some space while he slept in one of the guest rooms. She was surrounded by so many familiar things from the soft bedsheets to the tasteful wallpaper that lined the walls. She reflected on the small but meaningless creature comforts that came with the return to her home. She touched the collar of her nightgown, the strange and wonderful feeling of wearing her own clothing not enough to shake the dark feeling she had inside. Coming home had never felt this hollow.

She felt empty inside, like hurting him had taken away a part of her soul. Maybe in a way it had. The conflicted hurt was only mended by the bright smile of her son. It did nothing to alleviate her guilt, but she was going to have to live with that.

It took longer to pull herself from the soft, comforting hug of the blankets but she refused to let the pain consume her. It didn't make it any easier to force herself out of bed, but her stubbornness over-powered her depression in the end, and she got up out of bed.

She wasn't ready to face the day and so she paced around the room. There were some new pictures of Daniel lined up along the vanity. She paused and carefully picked up one in an ebony frame. Danny's smile was tarnished, in the photo she could see the hints of a deep sadness in her son. She missed him and wished she could hold him. She couldn't wait to talk to him later and see him again. But how long would this fleeting happiness last?

She set the frame down and resumed her pacing. She kept glancing to the pictures of her son and tried to stay calm. The familiar trappings that surrounded her were foreign to her wolf.

The next challenge was getting dressed. After wearing nothing but borrowed clothes for so long it felt nice to have clothes of her own. It felt a little strange to return to so many choices, and a full wardrobe again. She took her time, and carefully searched through her clothes. She started with the dresser, and then the walk-in closet. She touched the fine fabric of dresses she once wore, and could remember flashes of moments from her life before. The memories were like faded photographs, but most of them made her smile. One dress in particular caught her eye. Tucked deep into the closet was a large, baby blue gown. It was plain and frumpy compared to some of the more designer brands that hung around it, but the memories attached to it were worth more than its fancy neighbors. She took the hanger from the rack and smiled as the bittersweet nostalgia took hold.

Sophie stared at the tiny strip of plastic in her hand. Eons of creation had yielded the materials to make that bit of plastic in her hand, just as generations of her family had led to her sitting there in that moment as the tiny plus symbol appeared. All the signs had been there; the constant queasiness in her stomach, the late menstrual cycle, and the sudden, insatiable craving for tomatoes, pineapple pizza, and strawberry milkshakes. It was all as obvious as the proof in her hand, yet she still stared in disbelief. All of the pieces had come together, yet nothing would be the same.

I'm pregnant.

She was elated and scared at the same time. She'd been trying with Lucas for a couple years now, and finally their little miracle had come into existence. She made Lucas' favorite that night for dinner, homemade chicken enchiladas, but as she chopped up the cilantro for the salsa the smell had turned her stomach. She accidentally threw up over her creation, much to her dismay, right as Lucas walked in after class.

They ended up ordering pizza instead, and Sophie broke the news as Lucas picked the pineapple off of his slice. "I'm pregnant," Sophie said for the first time out loud.

Lucas dropped his jaw, and his piece of pizza. The weight of the news was now on his shoulders too, and he stared in awe of her. "You're… we're…"

"We're gonna be parents!" Sophie exclaimed with manic exhilaration.

Lucas' smile spread and she found herself in his arms. All her existence, and his, had come to this pivotal moment and time. She never imagined feeling more love than in that moment. She remembered the pure, unadulterated happiness.

Then came the tail end of it all. What felt so right had also quickly soured. Pregnancy was not kind to Sophie. After the excitement of sharing the news to their family and friends, the pains in her stomach only worsened and as the elation petered down, her fear that something went wrong escalated. She was diagnosed with preeclampsia and ended up having to drop her studies while on bed rest. The review books started to gather dust as she turned to pregnancy books and articles; any information that would help her bring her baby safely into the world. It was eight and a half months of feeling sick and weak, but there were even spots of sunshine during those dark times. Lucas would massage her shoulders and help shave her legs. Even as his own finals week came around, he doted on her, bringing her daily craving and pampering her any moment he could.

When she grew out of her usual sized clothes, her Nana brought her this frumpy, faded blue dress. It was like wearing a comforting hug from her, and at the time even smelled of her favorite rose perfume.

Even now when Sophie held it, she could faintly catch that floral scent as if it were woven into the fabric, along with a mint and strawberry fragrance that surprised her. She wrinkled her nose at the strange combination, faded by a more pungent detergent, but still there. Her human scent lingered on her old clothes, like a phantom of her former life.

When I was human, and after… It was strange to think of her life in pieces, before and after the attack.

As she picked out her outfit, she couldn't help but wonder if she ever could go back to how things were before. It made her sad as she sorted through the hangers of clothes. She mourned her old life and grieved her new one too. She ended up in this odd precipice between the two, where she was now left with the choice of putting her shattered life together as it was, or to make something new with what remained.

She ended up choosing a simple sundress that was a shade darker than the one that evoked memories of long ago. As she stepped outside onto the balcony, she could see the warm colors of fall beginning to emerge along the tree tops. Nature itself was beginning to change along with her.

She tried not to, but her gaze wandered down towards the guest house. She wondered if Korban was awake yet, maybe joking at the kitchen table with Alex. She could faintly smell coffee brewing and imagined that RJ was up and making breakfast. Her own stomach rumbled, but she didn't feel hungry.

She took a deep breath and inhaled the autumn air. The world was moving on, the end of summer bringing the feelings inside of her out like the reds and golds of the leaves. Unfortunately, she was the one with the burden of deciding what happened next; if she went back to the warmth of summer, or if she returned to the cycle of fall.

~*~

After the second cup of coffee, some breakfast and a little more venting, Korban felt much better. Alex joined them, lured out of his bed by the smell of breakfast, and for a brief moment it felt like old times again.

By the time the afternoon rolled around, they were taking a walk around the edge of the lake and Korban's worries were focused on more pressing things than his strange encounter last night. Even as he relaxed, he still had the feeling that he was being watched as they explored the property.

He turned and stared back at the mansion and spotted a shadowy figure spying on them from a window on the second floor. For a second he tensed, until he recognized that it was Lucas.

Korban clenched his fists and his jaw, but turned away to not give his rival the pleasure of seeing him as he was unnerved.

~*~

Lucas frowned as he watched the trio strolling along the lake. He turned away from the window and let the curtain fall into place. This wasn't an ideal situation for any of them, really. The ultimatum given to him by both the Commissioner and Sophie was bad enough. His wife's refusal to abandon her savior in quarantine, and the added complication of him being required to stay near Sophie to keep her from going berserk, was frustrating to say the least. She hadn't said it out loud yet, but he had his suspicions about her relationship with Korban. He refused to let himself dwell too long on it, though. For the moment, Sophie was keeping her distance from both of them. It was fair enough for now, but she was still his wife, and he had every intention of keeping it that way.

He paced the room for a moment, a pensive frown curving his mouth. Sophie had been through so much, it was no wonder she needed time to sort out her feelings. The way she had struggled and writhed on the hospital bed still gave him the chills. It was like she was possessed, with that wild, strange look in her eyes. He despised feeling helpless while his wife became out of control. He loathed Korban even more because she could be herself around the werewolf. He resisted the urge to throw something at the wall, but his hands clenched into fists at his sides. If there was one thing he couldn't stand, it was not being able to control this impossible situation.

Maybe things would change soon, if he could remind Sophie about the better times. He wasn't stupid, he knew things were tense between Sophie and him before she'd been viciously attacked. He'd fallen into the same trap many others had, and thought there would always be more time to patch things up. Once Sophie had been attacked and he believed her to be gone, he realized his mistake, and thought he would spend the rest of his life regretting not making things right between them.

Now he had the miraculous chance of repairing things between them, but there were complications. Complications that were walking down along the edge of his property as he paced in his office.

He couldn't let his anger and frustration get the best of him. He had to figure out a way to remind Sophie of the good times. Because the way he saw it, there were far more good times than bad. He paused and glanced over to the picture of the three of them on his desk. He would do what he could to make it up to her. Maybe a small gesture would be a step in the right direction.

As the idea formed, he headed out of his office and down the hall. He wouldn't lose again to the hands of time. When he reached the door to the master bedroom, he paused for a moment, then took a breath and knocked.

It was quiet for a moment, and then her voice came, "Yes, Lucas?"

Hearing her voice still filled him with inexplicable joy. He'd nearly lost her once, he wasn't going to make the same mistake again. "May I come in?"

She didn't respond until the door opened and she appeared, wearing a blue sundress that brought out the color of her eyes. She tilted her head curiously at him and asked, "What do you want?"

Her hand gripped the door like a shield, and he could see her tense up. It hurt to see her become so defensive against him, but he managed to mask his pain. "I just wanted to talk, though if you are busy right now…"

She glanced away, unable to meet his eyes for long. The doctor had told him that was normal for werewolves, since their wolf deemed it a challenge if they stared too long. With Sophie's fragile control over her wolf, it was no wonder she was clutching the door like it was her last defense. Maybe it wasn't to keep him out, but to keep her in. "I don't know if now is a good time."

He nodded. "All right… if not now, how about over dinner later? I'll order some takeout and we can catch up."

She hesitated, anxiously looking down at his suggestion. He reached for her white-knuckled hand as it curled around the door. Her skin was so feverish he couldn't hide the look of concern. "Are you ill? I can call Dr. Hoover…"

"No, no I'm fine… I just… I'm always warm now," Sophie said, and glanced up to him. "Dinner would be good. But you should go now. Please."

He caught a glimpse of fear in her eyes. She moved her hand down the side of the door, away from his hand, and the corner of her mouth twitched. He nodded, understanding that she was trying not to attack him, and to be civil. At least she agreed to supper, and he would have a chance then to talk more with her. "All right," he said with a nod as he stepped back into the hall. "I'm looking forward to it. If you need anything in the meantime…"

She nodded and gave him another pleading look before she softly shut the door. It seemed to take all her strength not to slam the door and bolt away.

Lucas sighed as he stood alone in the corridor. If anything, at least he had later to talk with her. Maybe food would help keep her mind off him being her prey, or so he hoped. He headed back to his study and opened his laptop. He had several hours to kill; it was time to start doing some research.

~*~

Korban spent most of the day looking over his shoulder. Between Lucas and Mikael lurking it was difficult not to, even when his mood lightened as he spent time catching up with RJ and Alex. It was difficult to keep his mind from wandering, but it did always return to the feeling of gratitude. He was grateful to be free from quarantine, if nothing else, and that put things in perspective. No matter what happened next, he would do everything he could to keep himself and Sophie from ever returning to that place again.

As the sun sank and the sky began to darken, they headed back to the guest house. "Ugh, I hate how early it gets dark," Alex complained as they gathered in the kitchen. "It was pretty nice out there."

"Yeah, it was," Korban said, unable to deny it, but thankful for the bright fluorescent lights that chased any shadows out of the kitchen. It provided some false sense of protection as the darkness fell outside. "It's good we got back when we did though, I wouldn't want you to get lost out in the woods and have to go looking for you."

"City wolf, lost out in the big woods," Alex cracked back with a smile. "I suppose you wouldn't want to try and scent me out tonight, huh?"

"Not after you had tacos for lunch. I'd be better off leaving you to the forest," Korban said, playfully patting his good arm. "Though I guess it isn't too late to get rid of you before that storm hits, huh?"

Alex laughed and playfully nudged him back. "I'm gonna go shower. Care to join me, RJ?"

"You just want me to make sure your cast doesn't get soaked, but I'll bite," RJ said with a smirk.

"Better you than Lobo," Alex said with a wink and then the two headed off to the bathroom.

"Hey, keep it down in there, would you? I don't need any more fuel for my nightmares." Korban protested as he plopped down on the couch.

"You better just learn to turn up the TV, Lobo. Wolves aren't the only thing that will be howling tonight in this house," Alex teased before closing the door.

Korban shook his head but realized that wasn't the worst advice and turned on the television, turning up the volume before he began to channel surf. He heard the water turn on in the other room and changed his mind about trying to drown out his roommates. Before he could hear anything too intimate between the two men he loved like brothers, he got up, abandoning the TV at its current volume, and walked out to the porch. He took in a deep breath of the chilly night air as he leaned on the railing and looked up at the main house.

The large mansion's windows were all lit up, making it look like a dollhouse against the darkening sky. He wondered what Sophie was up to in that huge house. He missed her and wanted to go talk to her. She had asked for space, but would it really hurt to go and check in on her fast?

His legs moved before his brain caught up with the thought, and before he knew it, he was heading across the sprawling lawn, towards the porch of the main house. He strode up the small staircase and could smell something divine being served. Rare steaks, freshly baked bread, buttery mashed potatoes, and the steamed scent of some mixed vegetables. His mouth watered, but he froze and soon forgot the delicious scents that were bombarding his senses.

From the window he could see the dining room table, where the food he'd smelled was served on expensive flatware. Sophie was sitting across from Lucas, her lips curved into a smile. "You always had a way to calm my nerves when it came to dealing with the cameras and the crowds," she said.

Lucas chuckled. "Yes, I have to admit, I've never understood your fear of cameras, but I suppose if I grew up with the lens constantly on me, I would get bothered by it too. Especially now."

It was like watching a train wreck. Korban couldn't tear his eyes away, as much as he felt he should go back. Part of him wanted to run away from this scene. The other half wanted to smash through the window. His hands clenched into fists at his sides and he watched on. He felt like some kind of twisted voyeur, but he couldn't pull away just yet.

Sophie held up her wine glass, took a sip, and then gave a small shrug. "You know how my mother is. There's a lot of pressure to make everything picture perfect. If I'm not in the picture, I don't have to worry about it."

"You shouldn't be afraid, Sophie, you've always been a natural beauty," Lucas said and sipped his wine. "I'm not saying that just because I'm your husband. I knew that the moment I met you."

Korban knew he should go. But he remained there, transfixed.

"Lucas…" Sophie began, but Lucas held up his hand.

"Please, Sophie, let me finish. I know you are dealing with a lot right now. I can't even begin to imagine all that you have gone through since that beast attacked you at the gala. I have been out of my mind, worried sick about you. I thought I had lost you forever. It was one of the darkest moments of my life, to think I had lost my chance to make things right with you. That's all I'm asking for, Sophie. I just want a fair chance to do right by you." He paused, and Sophie gazed down at her plate as she listened. "I'm willing to do whatever it takes. I want to make this work. I want to help you through this, too. I know that… Korban… he is able to help you stay in control. But I want to be able to help you, too."

The way he said his name, Korban knew Lucas was not happy about this situation. Still, his tone was genuine, and he was desperate to help Sophie just like he was. Why did that make this even worse? Guilt gnawed at his stomach, and he could tell by Sophie's expression, her emotions mirrored his own in that moment.

"Lucas, I don't know if we can go back to the way things were before. I'm not the same person I was back then. Literally, and otherwise," Sophie said.

"I know that. Of course I know that, Sophie," Lucas said, then folded his hands in front of him on the table. "I respect your need for space, and time. I understand how difficult this has been for you, as it has been a whole other challenge for myself, too. I just… I want a fair chance of having my wife back. The woman I have loved for so long and will always love."

"I know you love me, Lucas," Sophie said, with a sigh as she looked down again. "I just don't think I'm quite ready yet to go back to all this…"

"Please, just consider it. I can see how tense you are right now, sitting with me. Join me for breakfast tomorrow. Maybe if your wolf side gets more comfortable around me, it will be easier for you to be around other people. Maybe then we can convince them that it would be all right for Daniel to visit you. I know how much it means to both you and him for that to happen. I want it to happen too."

Sophie glanced up from her plate and over at him. Korban hated Lucas for using her weakness against her and wanted to punch the window, but he stopped when her voice cracked, a heartbreaking hopefulness entering her voice. "I want that more than anything right now. To hold Danny again."

Korban couldn't stand by anymore and watch this, or he would be tempted to do something irreversible. He turned and headed back down to the guest house and paced on the porch. There had to be something, anything, that he could do to help Sophie. He wasn't sure what he could do. Compared to what Lucas could offer, what Sophie wanted more than anything… what chance did he have?

"Pacin' must be a wolf thing." Mikael's Irish lilt came from the shadows and Korban froze.

He whirled around and sure enough the vampire was standing on the railing and leaning against one of the pillars of the porch. He was wearing the same dark, leather duster and sly smirk on his face. His pale shock of hair seemed brighter tonight against the night sky. He gracefully leapt down; his movements similar to a cat as he circled around Korban. "What the– what are you doing here?" Korban squeaked out, his heart suddenly up in his throat again. "How did you find me here?"

"Followed yer ride back from Howl at the Moon, of course. Laid low during the day, thankfully the forest is a dark place." Mikael studied him as he had in the bathroom, his eyes roaming up and down his body. "I'm not here to hurt ye. Like I said before, I need yer help."

It took a moment for the words to make sense as fear took hold. Adrenaline coursed through him and was screaming at his body to run, yet he remained still. Running would only make the vampire chase, and he wasn't sure he could outrun someone like Mikael. The power that radiated from the undead man thrummed against his skin like some invisible force. He'd felt something similar to this power before when he met Davey, but there was something different with this sensation. Instead of the power feeling like insects marching over his skin, it felt more like a cold, winter wind. It wasn't trying to push him like that last power had, but instead seemed to be shielding him from something.

"You know, you don't have to be all creepy and stalk me from the shadows. Or vanish from the bathroom just when my roommate appears and make me question my sanity for most of the day." Korban frowned at him, then took a step back, before continuing. "I don't know what it is you want, but I would prefer you don't just take off like that again. If you need my help so damn much then you should stop trying to give me a heart attack by popping in and out of the shadows."

Mikael smirked at that and gave a small playful bow. "My apologies, Korban. When ye've been on the run as long as we 'ave, sometimes ye forget basic things like proper greetin's and manners."

"We?" Korban asked, glancing around anxiously.

Mikael nodded. "My… Mate, the one whom needs yer help. We 'eard through the grapevine that ye were able to help Wolven. We were hopin' ye could work yer magic and turn 'im back. I wasn't sure how he'd respond with such… tempting scents around, like that of yer roommate. I asked him to wait near the edge of the forest for us."

"Tempting scents?" Korban repeated and realized he was referring to RJ and Alex.

"Mmm hmm," Mikael nodded grimly. "One reason I had to dash away from our conversation. I'm afraid it's been some time since I've smelled someone as tantalizin' as yer friend. I don't believe ye would want to help me if I happened to eat 'im."

Well, there was another disturbing thought for the evening. Korban coughed and changed the subject, so that the vampire wouldn't get any further ideas with his roommates nearby. "You're right about that, at least." He wasn't sure wandering off into the woods alone with a vampire was the wisest decision right now, but what choice did he have? "All right. Let me see if I can help your friend." If he gave the vampire what he wanted, then Mikael would be on his way. Surely once he'd turned back his friend, he would be happy, and they could go on with their lives.

The vampire looked relieved, though his stoic mask returned quickly as he nodded. "Thank ye," he said simply, then headed off the porch. "Follow me. He isn't too far away."

Korban reluctantly followed, his gut still questioning his decision. This could be some kind of trap. He knew little to nothing about this man, and it was difficult for him to read any of the emotions that rolled off the vampire. His face was a stoic mask, and his emotions were even more hidden. His scent remained just as difficult to decipher. Unlike the living, who tended to give off cues to their change in emotions, he couldn't read what Mikael was feeling, or if he was lying to him. He had to take the vampire at his word, and how far that would go… well, only time would tell.

They moved silently down the winding path that edged near the forest and there, some distance from the guest house, Mikael turned to him as they walked. "I hope yer as good as they say ye are," he said, his pale blue eyes bright in the moonlight.

"How did you find out about my… ability?" Korban asked, hoping maybe to at least discover who had recommended him. Maybe then he would feel more at ease around the vampire.

"I suppose that's a fair question," Mikael said, with a small smile. "I can't reveal me sources, but let's just say that word travels fast in the Underground, and ye've got the rumor mill spinning. We were hoping that it was true. Some rumors are more reliable than others. I wouldn't know exactly who started to spread the word about ye. Most people don't snitch out one another. Not when everyone's life ends up on the line."

"What exactly is the Underground?" Korban asked, not satisfied with the non-answer that he had given, but at least he was talking.

Mikael hesitated for a moment, as though to consider his words carefully before he continued. "Of course ye wouldn't know what it is… ye've been following their human system since ye were infected." Mikael paused again, and they stopped just within the sanctuary of the trees. "We don't usually discuss it with outsiders, but given that yer willin' t' help, and ye haven't told anyone else about me yet… I think ye can be trusted. Once ye help Naraka, then I can tell ye more. He's been waitin' long enough."

Before Korban could ask who, the shadows behind Mikael seemed to ripple as they moved, and suddenly a massive black wolf stepped out of the darkness. Korban forgot to breathe and stared. His jaw dropped open and his heart was suddenly pulsing in his throat. This was the same wolf he'd been having nightmares of since the night of his attack. He wasn't as big as he remembered, but then again he had seen some more Wolven since then, including Spike who was massive in size. Those haunting, yellow eyes glowed with an intelligence that sent a shiver through Korban. Did this Wolven recognize him too? Was he here to finish him off now?

He'd be easy prey, even as a werewolf. Korban couldn't move, but wished he could turn and run. Not that it would do him much good on two legs versus four. Korban took a step back and held up a hand. "Wait. Stop." His voice croaked as he pleaded the two words, and graciously, the black wolf complied which helped somewhat to calm his nerves, though his body remained tense.

Maybe it was some strange coincidence, though the fear remained as Mikael reached down and scratched the back of the wolf's ears, as though he were nothing more than a gigantic dog. "This is Naraka. He's been stuck like this for some time now. If ye can help him turn back, we can both answer all yer questions."

"Hello, Naraka," Korban greeted him, his voice still taut with fear as he tried to speak around his heart, which currently felt as if it had relocated into his throat.

The dark wolf gave a small grunt in greeting and leaned into the vampire's touch. Mikael smiled, and for the first time the emotion that he revealed seemed genuine. "What do ye need t' do it? To turn 'im back?"

"Just… uh…" Korban struggled to think for a moment, then it came back together as he looked into the vibrant, expressive eyes of the wolf before him. "I need eye contact, and it helps to touch him… not that it matters too much, but he won't bite, will he?"

Mikael scratched under his dark chin and looked Naraka in the eye. "He'd better not if he wants t' make friends," Mikael said, and Naraka gave a slow wag of his tail. "Go on then, furball."

Naraka prodded the vampire with his nose, then cautiously padded over to Korban. He kept his tail low, and his posture as non-threatening as possible. These were cues that Korban's wolf understood more than him, but somehow they did help make his human side feel relieved. He knelt, remembering how he'd helped Blaze, Spike, and Hati. As difficult as it was to meet the other wolf's gaze, he focused his eyes onto those golden orbs as his hands reached and gently rested along the soft, dark fur of the werewolf's muzzle. This close, the vibrant yellow held hundreds of hues, ranging from the bright yellow of the sun to dark amber that was similar to brown. Naraka's power thrummed against him, and nearly took his breath away when his ability connected to it. It was like plugging a fork into an outlet, and electricity coursed through him.

It didn't knock him down, but it did send the air rushing from his lungs as he gasped. That unsettling feeling of weightlessness made him feel like he was floating. He knew the images would come, but he couldn't prepare himself for what he saw next.

It wasn't like when Davey had shared his vision, or like when he had helped the other wolves out. When the bright light around him faded this time, he knew exactly where he was, because he had the same memory.

He'd dreamed of this moment hundreds of times over the past year, though parts had always remained fuzzy in his memory. Those were parts he was trying to block out, his doctor had said. The human mind wanted to shield itself from pain, and trauma. Nothing could be more traumatic than watching your best friend die in a violent attack. Yet he knew what was about to occur the moment he appeared in that all too familiar alley.

Only this time, he was strangely out of his own body, watching as his younger self stumbled around the corner with Ace at his side. Younger Korban's laugh seemed much more innocent, even though it had been only five years ago. It was surreal to see his brown eyes filled with laughter as the pair stumbled around the corner.

From this vantage point Korban could hear his last words exchanged with his best friend. He'd replayed the familiar conversation in his nightmares and had most of it memorized. This piece fit like a new part of the puzzle of his terrible, fractured memory. The shadow next to him moved and a great, black wolf who had been waiting around that corner revealed himself. Korban opened his mouth to scream a warning, but it was too late as his past-self saw the same black wolf as it lunged toward him.

Korban scrambled back, away from Naraka. He moved so forcefully that for a moment time was lost to him. He could still feel the fangs in his shoulder and his scar seemed to throb. He was briefly disoriented, seeing both the alley sprayed with his blood, and the dense forest around him. The thing that connected both was the wolf that stood before him, his yellow eyes bright and round with surprise. He hadn't expected this either.

"It's you. You're the one who bit me," Korban said in disbelief, his body shaking. The memory did one thing, it had warped his fear into anger. "You're the one who killed my best friend!"

Naraka's ears drooped in response. Mikael moved to the Wolven's side again and rested a pale hand upon his furry shoulder. "He may have been the one who bit ye boyo, but he didn't kill yer friend. Naraka doesn't kill civilians."

"Tell that to Ace, you fucking monster!" Korban angrily snarled.

That made Naraka's ears perk up and the wolf and vampire exchanged a glance. Korban had enough of their games and was in a way thankful he could feel something other than fear or pain. Rage was a refreshing change of pace. He stood up, his hands clenching into fists. He turned to leave without another word before he did something he would probably regret later.

"Wait! Please," Mikael's tone made Korban pause. He sounded desperate, and pleaded, "Please, yer the only one who can help 'im. I don't know what ye saw, and I know it was bad, but if yer talkin' about the same Ace then ye need t' listen"

"I don't have to do anything more for either one of you!" Korban growled and turned, his fists shaking at his sides. "Naraka's done more than enough to ruin my life. Ace is dead because of you!"

"Ace is a vampire because of me!" Mikael blurted.

"I don't want to hear your–" Korban began to yell back, but then the words registered, and his brow knit in confusion. "What?"

Mikael held up his hands defensively. He opened his mouth to speak but Korban strode over to him, anger radiating from every fiber of his being. "You better start talkin' fast, ***boyo***. I'm done with the games. You want my help, you'd better start being honest."

Naraka gave a warning growl and stepped in front of Mikael, but Korban ignored him. Mikael put a hand in front of Naraka. "All right. Ye connected with Naraka, right? Ye can see fer yerself. Like I said, Naraka doesn't kill civilians. Not if he can help it. I however… I've made some mistakes." Mikael kept his hands up like a shield. "But Ace isn't gone. He's just… a vampire now."

Korban glared at Mikael. "If he was still around, he would have told me long ago. Stop lying and confess! You murdered him!"

"Ye know, yer really gettin' on m'nerves with yer accusations and shite." The vampire grumbled back, and his eyes narrowed. "Did ye think maybe that he couldn't come back? That once yer livin' in the shadows, it's difficult t' come out in the light again? Maybe he had t' leave ye behind."

"He wouldn't do that to me! Liar!" Korban snarled back, but a small note of hesitation entered his tone. What Mikael said was possible, after all…

"I'm not lyin' t' ye!" Mikael snapped back in frustration. "I've no reason to feckin' lie t' ye! I can take ye to 'im and ye can see fer yerself! But it'd be a lot feckin' easier if ye just helped Naraka shift back first!"

As angry as he was, Korban couldn't deny that it would be difficult to go anywhere with a giant Wolven in tow. He never even remotely entertained this impossible idea. Not after seeing Ace so pale and lying motionless on the concrete. He never imagined seeing his best friend alive again. He still wasn't sure he trusted either one of them, but at least when it came to Naraka he could see if there was any truth to all of this. He focused on the Wolven who stood there, giving him a patient, expecting look. He could smell the anxiety in the powerful beast. While he couldn't get a reading on Mikael, there was no way that Naraka could hide his emotions from a fellow werewolf. Especially one with Korban's talent.

He took a deep breath and knelt back down again, meeting Naraka's intense gaze with his own. The lights became brighter as his power took hold, and Korban braced himself to relive one of the worst moments of his life.

7: FATE

"I can't believe you did that!" Ace snickered as he slid his arm around Korban's to catch him as he tripped over his own two feet. "Damn, man, how are you supposed to help me get home if you're drunker than me?"

"I'm not drunk!" Korban slurred, and then laughed at his own voice. "You're drunk!"

Ace sighed and shook his head, his blond, curly hair bouncing as he moved. "I'm buzzed, you're barely able to stand on your own two feet." He shifted Korban up so he could get a better footing, and they continued up the alley. "You're hopeless. What would you do without me?"

Korban's throat tightened at that, as he watched his younger self merely brush off the terribly ironic words. It had been a joke to his younger, more carefree self. "Pffft, you're not going anywhere, and you know it."

Ace smiled at him. "Maybe. Maybe then you'd appreciate me more, and not try to out drink Alex."

"*Alex*, he wishes he could hold his liquor like I can!" Korban said and hiccupped.

"I see," Ace grunted as Korban nearly tripped over his own two feet and hauled him over along the wall. "Hang on a second… let's wait a minute. I can't keep both of us upright if you keep getting tangled with me."

"Yeah, probably a good idea to stop. I'm kinda dizzy," Korban said, sagging against the wall and drew Ace closer to him. "You should stop moving too Ace."

"Heh," Ace snorted, and then poked him in the ribs. "I am stopped, silly."

He smiled at that and rested his head against Ace's shoulder with a sigh. "It was a good party, wasn't it?"

"Yeah," Ace said, though he seemed distracted, "it was."

Korban watched as Ace glanced up and down the alley, as though he could sense they weren't alone. Maybe he could have. A lump began to form in his throat. He remembered parts about this, but watching it from the outside… it was surreal, and terrifying. He knew what was coming, but the before was a bit hazy. He remembered stumbling in the alley with Ace, and then the pain of the attack.

Ace's look sobered and he gave Korban a serious expression. "Hey… you okay man? Really? I mean… with RJ and Alex coming out like that?"

Korban stared at Ace, and then tilted his head as he blinked in confusion at the question. "Why wouldn't I be?" The question seemed to sober him up as his brain worked around Ace's inquiry.

"I don't mean... well… it's just… they're like brothers to me. You don't think this changes everything… do you?" Ace asked, his cheeks turning pink as he got flustered on his own words.

"Well… yeah it changes things but… I don't know. I'm happy that they're happy," Korban said, shrugging. "I don't want to picture either one of them with someone anyway, so… I guess I just don't think about it too much."

"Oh," Ace said, then looked down thoughtfully.

"Why, does it bother you?" Korban teased him playfully.

"N-no! I just… I just was wondering if it upset you that they're gay," Ace stammered as his cheeks darkened to a deep pink.

"Naw, man. They're my brothers, just like you. I'd love all of you guys, no matter who you were in love with." Korban pushed himself up from against the wall. "Let's get home, they're probably gonna beat us there and then we'll never hear the end of it."

"Yeah," Ace nodded, but he suddenly reached for Korban's arm, and stopped him from pulling away. "Just… wait."

Young Korban blinked his brown eyes in confusion.

Korban watched on, his mouth dry. He didn't remember this part, but something about this scene was achingly familiar.

He could hear Ace's heart racing in his chest, his own heartbeat echoing his friend's. How his heart skipped a beat as Ace leaned in and pressed his mouth against his…

Time seemed to stop. As suddenly as he pulled him in for the kiss, Ace quickly shoved him away. "I'm sorry, I shouldn't have–"

Young Korban hadn't gotten the chance to respond, because as his mouth flopped open in response, a menacing growl grumbled from the shadows.

"No!" Korban gasped, knowing what came next all too well, and wanting to run away now more than ever.

The massive, black wolf stepped out of the shadows, his dark lips curled back and his fangs sharp, white shards that were bared viciously into a snarl. There was a silvery object that glinted around the beast's neck that resembled a dog's license, which is what Korban believed it to be back then. From the angle he was at now, however, he could see it better. Several military tags hung heavily around Naraka's neck and glistened like silver in the dimly lit alley.

Even as flustered as he was, Korban watched his younger self quickly assess the situation. He stepped in front of his best friend and shielded him, his brown eyes narrowed in challenge to the growling beast before him. "Go away mutt! Get outta here!"

For a split second, the beast seemed to consider, and then, a black rush of fur and muscle struck him down, his fangs tearing into his collar. Korban's screams echoed through the alley, and Ace tried to strike the wolf to get it off his best friend. "Leave him alone!"

The dark wolf only tore into young Korban's collar and shook him like a rag doll. Ace lunged for the wolf and wrapped his arms around the beast's neck in a desperate effort to save him. Korban watched as his younger self's eyes rolled back in pain and his cries were muffled into a low moan as he passed out.

Korban's heart thundered so hard it felt as though it would burst through his chest. He couldn't breathe. He knew what would happen next, but he didn't want to see it happen.

Ace struggled to keep his balance as he tried to pry the wolf's jaws from young Korban's collar. The wolf seemed unfazed, until something made Naraka yelp and cry out in pain. He bucked wildly and sent Ace flying through the air.

Ace struck the brick wall nearby and fell to the ground. He was panting and blood trickled down his chin, but he was still alive. His bright, blue eyes were round, equally surprised by the wolf's sudden change of attitude as he scrambled to get back on his feet and put himself between the beast and Korban. The silver cross that hung from Ace's neck was illuminated and Naraka backed away slowly with a soft whine, still growling between breaths as he kept his yellow gaze on the small, blond boy.

Ace's hands shook as he turned to go help his fallen friend, but the shadow behind Naraka moved and a familiar looking stranger descended upon him from the darkness. He gripped Ace's throat with his pale hand and his eyes burned red, like smoldering coals. "Ye shouldn't 'ave hurt him with that." The Irish accent only emphasized the irritation in the vampire's words. Though his hair wasn't the shock of white it was now, and his eyes glowed like a demon's, there was no mistaking Mikael. Especially as his mouth opened wide, and his face twisted into a monstrous expression as he tore into Ace's throat and began to feed on his blood.

Ace screamed and struggled in vain against the vampire, but this time he wasn't as lucky. Korban's heart ached as he watched his friend's hands go from punching and pushing away at Mikael, to falling limp at his sides. His fists uncurled as his skin went pale, and Mikael dropped him to the ground like a doll.

The vampire's mouth was dripping red with Ace's blood as he turned to the dark wolf and approached him. "Are ye all right?"

Naraka only gave a short nod of his head in response, and Mikael turned around and motioned with a hand for him to follow as the sirens began to sound in the distance. "Let's get out of here."

Korban felt sick to his stomach as the pair left the alley, and he watched as Ace struggled to breathe, and bled out on the filthy ground of the alley. Ace reached out for Young Korban, who hadn't moved in a long time, but he was too weak to move closer to his friend. Ace's tears were tinged pink with blood as they ran down his face. Korban couldn't watch any more. He pulled back, as fast as he could, shaken to his core. He'd seen enough.

Trembling with an unshakable, icy feeling coursing through him, Korban found himself once again at the edge of the forest. The smells of the lake nearby and the trees of the forest were welcome and fresh, compared to the memories of all the blood that had spilled in the alley that fateful night.

He glared at Mikael with venomous hatred that radiated through the air. "You're right that Naraka didn't kill Ace. You killed him. You're the one who murdered my best friend."

"I thought I'd killed him back then. But turns out vampire bites are a wee bit more infectious than I knew. He's alive and kickin' and he's seemed t' move on with the whole bein' turned thing. Kinda like ye have," Mikael said.

"I want to see him. Take me to him." Korban didn't care if it was a trap at this point. He still didn't trust the vampire, but the feelings he had gotten from Naraka were genuine. He'd been caught up in his own emotions during the shared memory, but the pain was echoed by the other werewolf. The thick scent of remorse still radiated from the large wolf in front of him as his head hung low, and his amber eyes were filled with regret.

Whatever had happened in the past couldn't be changed, no matter what he wanted. Right now, all that mattered was seeing Ace again. A miracle he never expected to happen.

"I will help you, Naraka. But then you're taking me to where Ace is. Deal?" Korban's eyes locked with the black wolf's again, and the large creature bobbed his head in affirmation.

Korban took in a deep breath and steadied himself. This time when he locked eyes with Naraka, he drew upon that latent power within himself. The same power that emerged with the full moon coursed through him, and his wolf stirred and stretched. He flexed his fingers and touched the beast before him, his fingers crackling with unseen energy as he touched the sides of Naraka's muzzle, then focused on pouring that energy into the other werewolf, coaxing the other wolf back the same way he'd done to Hati, Spike, and Blaze. "Rest now. Until the moon calls you again," he said out loud, urging the black wolf back with power and authority in his words.

The great wolf stared back at him, and after a moment, began to tremble and stepped backward, away from his touch. The power had taken hold, however, and though he moved away, Naraka began to shift back. His onyx-colored fur began to recede, and his bones cracked back into place. Naraka's muscles pulsed and a low, pained moan escaped the wolf that was more man than animal. Korban took a step back as the wolf curled into itself, and soon transformed back to a man huddled in fetal position.

The man who now appeared before him had a sickly gray tinge to his pale, brown skin at first, until his body began to adjust to being human again. His toned body was something to be envied and admired. Shaggy, shoulder-length, dark hair was tangled on his head and soaked with sweat, giving him the grizzled appearance of a hermit. He peered up at Korban from under the long, unruly locks of his hair with intense, yellow eyes that seemed brighter against his dark beard. A twisted smile curved his mouth, and there was relief reflected in those wild eyes. "Thanks," he said gruffly, his sultry voice deeper and smoother than expected.

Korban gave him a small nod, the wave of gratitude from the rugged, stunning man causing his cheeks to warm. The rush that came from using his ability sent his pulse racing, and the look in the other man's eyes made him glad he had been able to help.

Mikael swore under his breath, something in Irish, his unintelligible words filled with disbelief. He walked over, removing the long leather duster from himself and gently draping it over Naraka's bare shoulders. He knelt and helped the naked werewolf to his feet, wrapping the long coat around his trembling frame. Naraka didn't give any other outward signs of hurting, the relief in his gaze outweighing any other emotions that perfumed the air around them. Mikael whispered something so softly into his ear that even Korban's keen sense of hearing couldn't pick up, and Naraka smiled. "How do ye feel?" Mikael asked softly, loud enough for Korban to hear this time.

Naraka's weary gaze remained lowered, careful not to reconnect with Korban's eyes as he cleared his throat and cautiously studied him. "Tired," he said, then added with a soft sigh, "Calm."

"Good," Mikael said, then glanced over to Korban, the vampire unafraid of meeting his gaze. "Ye actually did it. Thank you." He emphasized the two words and gave Korban a genuine smile, careful not to flash his fangs.

Korban nodded, the rush of power still flowing through him. He felt invigorated, on a physical and metaphysical level. His fingers tingled with energy and he marveled at the possibilities. It had worked again. He was able to help someone else turn back to normal again. His mind was still spinning from the rush of memories, but the elation and the endorphins that came with using his ability were giving him a good feeling that he couldn't shake. He was glad to help

Naraka, and now that he was human again, he hoped for answers.

Hundreds of questions whirled around his brain. He wanted to know why Naraka had attacked them to begin with. He wanted answers to why they had no choice but to bite them both back in that alley five years ago. *Where had they come from? Why had they returned now for his help?*

He wanted to be angry at them both. Naraka had bitten him, infected and cursed him to a life where he'd lost his rights and freedom. Mikael had murdered his best friend, though supposedly he was now among the infected vampires. He wanted to scream and rage at them both for what they had done. Yet as he watched them, it was hard to be angry. Naraka's legs were still buckling beneath him as he adjusted from being on four legs to two again. He remembered how strange it had been for him in the forest after a few weeks. He had no idea how long he had been stuck like this. Mikael, though cold and difficult to read, continued to gently aid the newly transformed man in a way that seemed genuine. Whatever they had done in the past couldn't be helped now, Korban reminded himself, and unclenched his fists.

"You're welcome for the help, but what happened? How did you get stuck like that to begin with?" Korban asked as he finally settled on a question, wondering if maybe he'd been hit with that same serum that Sophie and he had endured.

Naraka gave him a sheepish look and glanced down to the forest floor. When he spoke, his voice remained heavy with exhaustion, as if every word he uttered took more precious energy than he had left in him. "I have trouble… keeping control."

Mikael nodded in agreement, a small smirk curving his mouth. "Ye could say that again. Unless it's 'round a new moon, ye spend most of yer time these days big, furry and four-legged."

"I'm always big, for your information, even if I can't always keep control," Naraka winked playfully as his weary words dripped with innuendo.

Mikael gave an exasperated sigh. "Sure, ye can joke about it now, but yer not the one who has to make sure we keep duckin' in the shadows. Not everyone buys the whole friendly dog routine when yer waltzin' around as a wolf."

"So you sometimes shift, even when it's not a full moon?" Korban asked with a frown. "Without any warning?"

Naraka shrugged and though there was a flicker of something in his eyes, he played it off with a cool smile. "It's okay now, you were able to change me back. That's all that matters, right?"

"No," chorused Korban and Mikael at the same time. Something they could both agree on.

Naraka sighed, and looked up to the moon in the sky. "I don't even have the strength right now to argue, never mind transform again. I'm pretty sure I'm good for now."

Korban opened his mouth to ask another question, when Mikael spoke up and interrupted his thoughts. "Ye kept up yer part of the deal, so I'll keep m' word. I'll take ye to where Ace is."

Korban frowned. "You can just tell me where he is, and I'll go from there. No offense but I don't know either one of you enough to trust you." Plus, the last time he'd encountered these two, he'd been bitten and nearly killed, but that went without saying.

It was Mikael's turn to frown. "The deal was to take ye to Ace. We will keep our word. We haven't steered ye wrong yet. Besides, it's not a place ye want to go alone. Strangers aren't welcome in the Underground, even famous ones like ye, and it's easy to get lost in an unfamiliar territory."

The vampire's cryptic response was frustrating, but Korban couldn't deny that he probably had a point. It was already well past curfew, and to be wandering around after hours in an area he wasn't familiar with could cost him, RJ, and possibly Sophie, their freedom or their lives. "All right, then we stick together. Let's head back to the guest house and I'll see about getting us a ride to… wherever we are headed."

Mikael bristled. "I don't think it's a good idea to be around humans," he said. "Yer friends or anyone else. Humans can't be trusted. Not when they get rewarded fer turning in people like us."

Korban was about to protest that RJ and Alex wouldn't snitch on them, but he stopped himself. If they were afraid that associating with these two would lead to Korban's return to quarantine, or worse, they would blow the whistle in an instant. They wouldn't do it to be malicious toward Naraka or Mikael, but they would do it to protect Korban.

He watched as Naraka leaned against Mikael as they walked along the path, his legs stiff as he took tentative steps, still not used to being upright. It was getting late, and it didn't look like either one of the men he walked with were up to heading anywhere for the evening. He wanted desperately to see Ace, to have something go right when everything else seemed to be going wrong. He watched as Naraka limped along on two legs, his bare feet carefully navigating around the roots that emerged along the path. He hid his pain well, but the tension sang in his every movement. "How long were you stuck as a wolf?"

"This time?" Naraka smiled to him as he made it a question, but the expression was a mask as he tried to appear upbeat. His anxiety rolled off him like a cologne, and he sighed and added, "Since a few days after the last new moon."

Korban did the math and frowned. That was a long time to be stuck as a wolf. "No wonder you're exhausted," Korban commented softly as he watched the odd couple walking along.

The weary werewolf, wearing only a long trench coat and a smile, gave a small chuckle in response, and leaned against the serious, worried looking vampire as they continued along the path.

They were putting a lot of trust in him, coming to him for help to begin with, he realized. Naraka was weak and vulnerable right now, and though they didn't outright say it, he wondered if there was more than one reason why they avoided human beings. Infected people without sponsors got a one-way ticket to quarantine, unless the officer on duty wasn't feeling so generous and decided a silver bullet was less hassle than dealing with the arrest of a supernatural being. Rewards were often given to any human citizen who came forward with information that lead to the capture of an infected person, as a thank you for keeping the infection from spreading. While some people were more than happy to assist with the witch hunt, now Korban wasn't so sure. He'd blown the whistle himself on Davey, but he had been a literal monster, in every sense of the word. While Mikael was a little shady and he barely knew Naraka, he didn't get the feeling in his gut that they meant to harm him. And if they were telling the truth about Ace, and Ace trusted them…

Naraka stumbled and Mikael caught him, though he nearly fell under the bulk of the larger man. "Sorry," he apologized to the vampire.

As much as he wanted to see Ace, he felt a surge of guilt. Naraka wasn't up to take him anywhere tonight. Besides, it was after curfew. It was already risky enough to be out after hours and on private property. It would be a whole other problem to be back in Syracuse, or wherever they met for the Underground.

"Look," Korban said as he approached the pair, "Naraka, you're not in any shape to go anywhere tonight. You can stay in my room at the guest house and rest, and we can go first thing tomorrow night to see Ace."

Naraka and Mikael looked to one another, and the werewolf turned to Korban. "Are you sure? You'd really give up your bed for us?"

"Yeah, it's fine. I shouldn't be running around after curfew, anyway, especially since I just got out of quarantine. I can take the couch for the night, and you can lock yourselves in my room for the day. It shouldn't be too difficult to hide the sunlight either, there are black out curtains in my room." All the amenities one would need for a vampire to shack up in there, of course, except for one thing. "The only thing I don't know how to get you is blood."

The word hung heavy in the air, but Naraka only chuckled again. "You're taking care of enough for us, Korban. I can help feed Kael, especially now that he won't be getting fur in his fangs."

There was something darkly intimate about the word 'feed,' but Korban brushed it off and nodded. Once they were inside and locked safely away from Alex and RJ, he didn't care what the pair did together. "All right then," Korban said as they approached the guest house. "Just… stay quiet and hidden for a moment. I'll make sure it's clear and bring you guys in around the back." That way no one from the main house would see them enter either, just in case Lucas had returned to his post and was glaring down at him as they spoke.

Naraka and Mikael nodded, and waited on the edge of the forest as Korban went up to the porch, studying the main house carefully as he approached the guest house. The lights were still on but no silhouettes were illuminated in the windows this time. He headed up to the door and entered the guest house, finding the kitchen empty, and the living room as well. When he passed their bedroom, he could still hear the shower running in Alex and RJ's bathroom. How much time had passed? He felt like he'd spent hours away, but maybe he hadn't been away that long after all. Either way he had to act quickly. He would already have to explain a lot to RJ and Alex tomorrow as it was, and he didn't want to get caught sneaking in his new… allies, for lack of a better word.

Korban returned to the back-porch door and motioned to Mikael and Naraka. The vampire was hindered by assisting the werewolf, but they otherwise moved silently and as swiftly as they could over to where Korban stood. "Follow me, as quickly as you can. I'm not sure how much longer we have until my roommates get out of the shower."

"Kinky," Naraka smirked as he spoke, and Mikael frowned and ushered him forward into the kitchen.

They made it down the hall when Korban could hear the faucet turn off. His heart raced again as they went past RJ and Alex's room and he quickly ushered the pair to his room. He could hear RJ and Alex's voices, muffled by the walls, as they talked about something in the other room. They didn't have much time left. "All right, anything you need is in here for tonight. Just lock the door behind me and have a good night. I'll see you tomorrow."

"We'll keep it down, don't worry," Naraka teased Korban with another playful wink as Korban headed backwards towards the door. He leaned in as he clutched the doorknob, the dark circles under his eyes noticeable as he leaned in close and added, "Thank you again, Korban. We owe you for this kindness."

"You're welcome," Korban said.

Mikael approached and handed Korban a pillow and blanket, which he gratefully accepted. He gave him an approving nod before he closed the door, and Korban heard the tell-tale click of the lock.

His own exhaustion set in. So much was happening, and it hit him as he stood in the empty hall, finding himself alone. He wished he could talk to Sophie and share with her all he'd learned just now. To see if she thought this was a good idea, trusting these strangers, or if he was being reckless and foolish. Maybe she'd get angry and scold him, or more likely she would shake her head at him and laugh. He wouldn't care either way, because at least then she would be there with him. He missed her voice, her scent, her touch… everything about her. He squeezed the pillow in his hand and took a deep breath, slow and steady. He was coming down from that high that came with using his power and his mood had begun to plummet again.

As if sensing he was upset, the door opened and Alex popped out, his hair still damp from the shower, and a fluffy robe wrapped around him. One sleeve flapped around loosely as he had his arm in the sling for the night, and had draped the robe over his shoulder, most likely with RJ's help. His smile upon seeing Korban faded quickly as he caught the dark look in his eyes. "You okay, Korban?" he asked in concern.

"I'll be okay, eventually," Korban sighed. "I can't sleep, so I figured I would try to binge watch something until I could."

"Oh," Alex said, then smiled and reached out with his good arm, patting his shoulder. "Me either. I'll go make popcorn."

"You don't have to," Korban began to protest, but Alex just widened his grin.

"I know. I want to," Alex said.

"Oh no you don't," RJ interjected as he emerged from their bedroom, wearing an identical robe. "We can't afford replacing a single tile in this place, never mind the entire kitchen if you set it on fire. I can handle the popcorn, if you will grab us some beers out of the fridge?"

Alex took the jab in stride and beamed. Korban shook his head and laughed, feeling better already. The three of them ended up camping out together in the living room, critiquing some terrible made for TV movies. The entire time Korban wanted to tell them both what he'd found out, that Ace was alive, sort of, and a vampire somewhere nearby. He held that information though, in case that small bit of doubt in him was right. He couldn't break RJ and Alex's hearts if it ended up being not true. As they joked and snacked, he felt better, and they continued to watch until they finally succumbed to sleep.

He didn't remember exactly what he dreamt of that night, but it involved bittersweet memories of Sophie and Ace.

~*~

When she woke up the next morning, Sophie could smell something delicious that made her mouth water, even before she opened her eyes. She stretched, finding herself alone in her bedroom again. She got up, sniffing the air as she did. There was the faint scent of eggs, buttered toast, and bacon in the air, but something else, much closer, caught her attention. She slid off the bed, and headed down the hall, her stomach grumbling with every step. The smell of breakfast was stronger out of her room, but so was the mystery spice.

Something familiar lingered and she licked her lips as she found herself outside of the nearby guest room. She could smell Lucas there, his clean, crisp, and prey-like scent familiar to her sensitive nose. She opened the door, her curiosity outweighing her control. She could hear him in the bathroom, his door ajar, and saw his reflection in the steamed mirror.

Lucas' blond hair was still damp from the shower, and he was naked from the waist up, a towel wrapped around him. He was dabbing his chin carefully with a sheet of toilet paper, and she saw the crimson spots bloom on the white and she froze. He'd cut himself shaving, and she'd smelled it, and began to drool.

It took all her strength to turn away, even as her stomach churned and she was disgusted with herself. She hurriedly left the room, raced down the stairs, and out onto the porch. She didn't realize she had been holding her breath until she gasped there, her breath coming out in a puff of warm steam into the cool morning air. She fought back tears as her body shook. She'd come so close to losing control. Even last night, as she tried to pay attention to Lucas' words, it had been difficult to concentrate. Even with the distraction of a delicious meal before her, all her senses were on overdrive. Worse, everything seemed to only remind her that despite the tender, rare steak on her plate, her husband would be even fresher, more tantalizing prey.

Even now as she stood there, clutching onto the porch railing, she wanted nothing more than to turn around, rush back upstairs, and sink her teeth into Lucas. She gripped onto the wooden railing, inhaled deeply, and stared down at the guest house. Salvation was so incredibly near. Her wolf wanted meat, or her Mate. There was no other option.

She heard the wood groan under her grip and exhaled slowly before taking a deep breath to steady herself. The fresh air helped the tempting scent of Lucas' blood fade away. She closed her eyes and concentrated for a moment, but the darkness made her wolf stir and her eyes flashed open. She focused her gaze down at the guest house. It was so tempting to run to Korban for help, but it wouldn't be fair to go running back to him the moment she felt weak. Not after she had asked for space.

She wanted to, no, she needed to do this on her own. It was part of the reason she asked him for space. She had to learn how to control this without him. If she wanted a chance to see her son again, she had to prove she could do it alone.

She let go of the wood and saw that there were finger-shaped indentations left behind. She walked around the porch and paced for several minutes as she collected herself.

Every breath and every step made the tension dissolve within her, and as she reigned in her wolf, she tried to think of who she could reach out to if she became weak again. It would be cruel to reach out to Korban, but who else did she have right now? Freki and Valkyrie came to mind, but she didn't want to risk them getting caught if she contacted them. She didn't want them to come around to help her and end up in quarantine, or worse.

It dawned on her then who she could rely on, and a fresh pang of guilt filled her since they hadn't come to her mind right away. Her parents. While she couldn't turn to them before, she was home now. She had her family, or what was left of it anyway.

She returned inside and hurried back to her bedroom, holding her breath as she passed near the guest room. She closed the door and locked it, just in case, then picked up her phone. She dialed the one number she had memorized, even after all this time, and sat down on the edge of her bed.

The phone rang three times, and then someone picked up the other line. "Hello?" her mother's voice answered.

"Hello, Mother," Sophie said, her voice taut with emotion.

"Good morning Sophie. I was wondering when you'd call," her mother began, and at first Sophie was afraid that a lecture would be incoming for not calling sooner, but her mother surprised her as she continued on, "I've missed you. It's good to hear your voice again."

Sophie felt tears run down her cheeks, and an overwhelming sense of relief. "I've missed you too."

~*~

Somewhere on the nearby coffee table, Korban's phone began to vibrate and blare Duran Duran's "Hungry Like the Wolf." He groaned as he woke up, a little stiff and sore from sleeping on the couch. "Seriously, Alex?" he scooped up his cell phone, and rubbed the sleep from his eyes.

Sergeant McKinnon's name glowed on his caller ID, and he

answered it as he heard Alex's sleepy chuckle of amusement on the other half of the couch. "Good morning, Korban. I've got some good news. Clear your busy schedule, and get your best suit pressed. The mayor's set the forum for tomorrow."

"That's good news," Korban said as he sat up, trying to keep his voice down as he glanced over to his two roommates, who were still dozing on their end of the couch. "Is there anything else I should bring with me?"

"Just your dazzling personality, though I suspect they'll be asking a lot of prying questions, so brace yourself as best as you can. I'm not saying you should get a drink before the forum, but it may not hurt to have one tonight. Which reminds me, you'll want to make sure you stick to curfew. I know you're doing it anyway, but it will make you look even better if you're sticking to the rules. Upstanding werewolf citizen." There was something in Tim's tone that raised some questions.

"Is everything okay? It sounds like there is more to this then you're letting on."

"Yeah, we're just on high alert down here at the station. We're getting alerts that some Wolven has been spotted around the city and so we're enforcing an earlier curfew. It's good you're taking a bit of a vacation over in Skaneateles. It's getting a bit tense downtown."

Korban had his suspicions about who exactly they had seen running around Syracuse, and glanced down the hall towards his room, thankful that this wasn't a video call. "Wow… I'm sorry Tim," he said, uncertain of what to say to that.

"No need for you to apologize. It's not like this time it's you running amuck as a Wolven. Just make sure you're early tomorrow, the judge they have tentatively assigned to moderate is a stickler for the rules. He follows the law as it was written, with every crossed 'T' and dotted 'I' taken as literally as possible, and he doesn't do well with tardiness."

Korban felt a small pang of guilt. Once again, he was keeping something from Tim, but right now, it was all he could do. "I'll keep that in mind. Thanks for the heads up."

Tim grunted in response and then asked, a bit more grimly, "You doing okay out there, Korban? At Chateau Bane?"

"As good as can be expected," Korban said with a sigh. "Just glad to be out of quarantine." That much was true.

"Good. Keep a low profile, and I'll see you at the courthouse tomorrow," Tim said.

"See you there." Korban hung up as Tim bid him farewell.

He leaned back against the couch again with a heavy sigh. He spared another quick glance to RJ and Alex, but Alex had drifted back to sleep. He was thankful for the quiet moment, though he wished he could share the news with them. When they woke up, he'd fill them in, but there was someone else he could share this with in the meantime.

He sent a text message to Sophie to let her know that the forum was happening the following day, and her brief but enthusiastic response of, "Awesome news! Thanks Korban. I look forward to seeing you tomorrow. I'll make sure we have a ride to get there early." He read it a few times, and it made him smile. He wished he could have seen her face light up in person, but his thoughts didn't wallow on missing her for too long as the weight of the situation fell on his shoulders.

Keeping a low profile went against his plan to go meet Ace later that night. He would have to talk to Naraka and Mikael later, and see what they could work out. Of course, hiding two, unsponsored, infected men in his bedroom wasn't exactly following the rules either.

He gritted his teeth together in frustration. If he wasn't cautious, helping those two would cost him and Sophie the chance to turn things around for everyone. Yet, he couldn't be too upset by his choices. He pictured how weak Naraka was as they walked, how grateful the look in his yellow eyes had been, and it still felt like the right thing to do. He would have to be extra careful, which meant postponing his reunion with Ace for just a little while longer.

What was another day after five long years anyway?

8: CONSULTATION

Sophie read Korban's text message over and over. She could almost hear his voice in her head as her eyes scanned it over for the hundredth time. "Tim called. The public forum is tomorrow and starts at 9 AM. He says we should show up early, and dress to impress. Not even a challenge for you."

Her cheeks warmed at his little bit of flirting, but it was the news of the forum happening that had her brain spinning with ideas. They would have the chance to tell their story. Her stomach squirmed at the thought of being in front of the cameras again. She knew she would have to face the crowd sooner or later, but that didn't make the dread she felt fade away. It had been something she faced most of her life, being the heiress to the Winters family long before Lucas' success. She managed to keep a low profile for awhile but returning from the dead was definitely a curiosity to the public at large. She tried not to think too hard on how many people would be watching beyond the cameras, and instead began to think about what she would say in order to steer those eyes, and minds, towards change. Ever since she'd been attacked and turned, Sophie had been in survival mode. Now that things were starting to settle down, the issue wasn't just to live, but to have a life again. Even with her fragile control, she knew she was getting stronger every day. She knew how difficult it was to keep the wolf at bay, but it could be done. She pictured Valkyrie and her three kids together. She wanted to show the world that it could be done. She wanted to hold her son again and reassure him after the chaos of her attack. She knew she could do it, and others could, too. She just had to show all those thousands of peering, watchful eyes that it was safe to be around werewolves.

No pressure at all.

She took a deep breath and paced as she tried to collect her thoughts and bottle up the panic that began building within. There had to be something she could do. Instinctively, she went over to her bookshelf. If she couldn't gather her erratic thoughts, maybe she could round up her knowledge instead. She pulled one of the leather-bound law books from the shelf and flipped to the index. Maybe if she poured over the existing laws, she could find a solution. The initial laws in place were rushed. Surely there had to be something that could prove to be a loophole.

A new hunt had just begun, and it pleased both her and her wolf to have a new target. Best of all, it shoved those lingering worries aside. At least for now, she could distract herself with this purpose. If nothing else, she would be prepared to make her argument during the forum tomorrow.

~*~

Korban spent the rest of the day anxious for a different rotation of reasons. The upcoming forum aside, every little out of place bump or sound seemed to have him on edge. Of course, he was worried that RJ or Alex would discover their hidden guests. He hated keeping secrets like this, especially from them, but given that he was housing an unregistered vampire, and an out of control werewolf, he didn't have too many options. It was easy enough to keep them away from his current bedroom, especially since the rainy day turned into binge watching several series of shows. They all were a little homesick, even with these creature comforts around them. Korban was thankful that it wasn't too much of a challenge to distract his friends, but the double-edged sword came with a heavy dose of guilt for feeling that way. There was still the absence of Sophie weighing on his heart, and while Alex and RJ were invested in whatever was on the plasma television his mind would often wander to what she was up to in the main house.

As the sun began to set, a new kind of anxiety was building up inside of him. Would Mikael wake up hungry and come out of the bedroom and attack RJ or Alex? He became a bit more tense, and when either one of his friends brought it up, he managed to play it off as nerves. They didn't pry all that much and accepted that he was still dealing with his breakup. The only silver lining in this whole ordeal was the timing of all these complications. Of course, even that kind of silver would sting a little. Korban almost laughed about it, but kept the bad joke to himself.

RJ put a frozen pizza in the oven, and the living room smelled amazing not too long after. Night fell, and with it came another concern. Naraka would be hungry, too. The perfect opportunity came as RJ went into the kitchen and sliced up some pizza, while Alex excused himself to go use the restroom. Korban went and grabbed a plate with a couple slices before sneaking back to his room while RJ searched the fridge for some hot sauce.

He was about to knock on the bedroom door when it opened a crack. Mikael peered out cautiously before he stepped back and let Korban into the room, closing the door behind him. "Room service, how nice," Naraka greeted him in a quiet voice, smirking from where he sat on the bed.

"I thought you might be hungry," Korban said, though he kept a sidelong glance towards Mikael as he approached the werewolf.

"Yes. Thank you," Naraka said, and gratefully accepted the plate from him.

Korban noticed that the recovering werewolf's complexion had improved a little, but his frame still seemed thin, and his cheeks were a little sunken and gaunt. Korban tried not to stare as Naraka wolfed down the two slices of pizza and wondered if he could sneak him something more. He knew what it was like to be stuck somewhere and not be fed all day, unfortunately all too well. "Sorry, I couldn't sneak away sooner. I'm trying my best to keep my friends out of this. They've already been through enough for me."

"We appreciate yer discretion," Mikael said softly. "We'll be out o' yer hair soon enough. Once we take ye to Ace, our part o' the bargain is complete."

Korban winced. "Uh yeah… about that. I can't go out tonight. We've been invited to a public forum and they're keeping a closer watch on us both as a result. Sophie and I have to stick to curfew and it's already in effect tonight."

Mikael frowned at this revelation and walked over next to the bed as Naraka polished off the crust of his second slice. "Well that certainly complicates things, doesn't it?"

Korban nodded and sighed, running a hand through his hair in frustration. "Yeah, it does."

The vampire folded his arms over his chest, and a chill ran through Korban as his face became a blank mask for a long moment. There was something unnatural and disturbing about watching a man go so motionless, like a mannequin. Mikael's stillness broke just before he spoke again, "We could go and speak to Ace, arrange a meeting time and place with him, and then return tomorrow night to let you know."

It was Korban's turn to frown. He still couldn't get a sense of the vampire's motives. If this was all some elaborate trick they were pulling, they could vanish after they left and he would never get a chance to see Ace again. If Ace was still in existence.

Naraka set the plate down on the nightstand and picked up the half empty glass of water that sat there. "It wouldn't take us that long even. We could go and come back later tonight as long as we were careful," he said and drank down the rest of the water in the glass.

"Why can't you just call him and arrange it? Better yet, why can't you call him and I could hear this directly from Ace?" Korban asked.

"Some places in the Underground are too deep for cell phone reception. And the places that aren't could be possibly traced. We use technology sparingly in our places. It's one reason we have been able to stay in hiding as long as we have," Mikael explained.

"I don't know," Korban said, the feeling that he was being duped nagging him again.

"It'll be fine, you'll see," Naraka said in attempt to soothe him.

The werewolf who bit him stood up with his empty glass in hand and started for the bathroom to refill the cup with more water, or maybe put it back. He made it three steps before he stumbled and nearly fell, the glass in his hand thankfully not shattering as it rolled across the carpeted floor. Korban was fast and made it to the werewolf's side, but Mikael moved like lightning and caught him. For a moment, this close to him, Korban saw that stoic mask crack with concern. Just as quickly the look was gone, and Naraka chuckled. "My hero. I've become rather clumsy on two legs, it seems."

"Yer still shaking. Are ye cold?" Mikael asked.

"No, I'm fine. Just… got up too fast, I think," Naraka said, looking a little embarrassed.

"He's not in any state to run around Syracuse. Not like this," Korban offered him a hand up, even though the vampire could have easily lifted him with so much as his pinky.

Naraka took his hand anyway, and with Mikael's help got back on his feet. He leaned against the vampire once he regained his balance. "Well, we can't stay here either. So what do ye suggest we do, Korban?" Mikael asked.

Korban mentally cursed and knew he didn't have much time left to think of a solution. Any minute Alex could come barging in and this whole situation would get even muddier than it already was. "Naraka can stay and rest another night," Korban blurted before he could overthink it, and rambled on as his brain suddenly clicked a plan into place. "I can handle another night out on the couch, and we'll all be out tomorrow so you'll have a quiet place to recover. Mikael can go and set up the meeting with Ace, and return later, or tomorrow, with that information."

Mikael's eyes narrowed. He didn't like this, and he let Korban know with that look. He exchanged a quick glance with Naraka, who just nodded. "Fine. I suppose that's as good of a plan as we got. Nothing better happen t' him while I'm gone. Ye got it?"

"I'll be okay, Mikael." Naraka reassured him with a smile. "Korban's right. If you go tell Ace what's happened, and work out a time and place to meet, it won't take you that long at all. I'd just slow you down right now. So go. And come back later. I don't like sleeping alone."

Mikael shook his head, but wrapped an arm around the dark-haired werewolf. Korban can't see Mikael's expression, but he can hear the emotion cracking in the vampire's voice as he whispered to Naraka, "I will be back as soon as I can for ye."

Mikael hugged Naraka fiercely, and held him for a long moment. Korban glanced away to give them some semblance of privacy, but also because their interaction reminded him of his current state of loneliness. When they released one another, Mikael led Naraka over to the bed and made sure he sat down again before he headed for the window. "Ye better behave yerself while I'm gone," he said as he opened the window.

"Oh, believe me, I will," Korban responded.

Mikael glanced over his shoulder as he crouched to climb out the window and smirked. "That wasn't aimed at ye, Korban," he said, and then with a rush of wind that left the curtains rippling in his wake, the vampire vanished.

A quiet fell over the room that seemed to emphasize the growling of Naraka's stomach. The dark-haired werewolf only grinned to Korban. "Do you think maybe you could sneak me some seconds?"

~*~

In the main house, Lucas had spent most of the day giving Sophie what she had asked for: space. He spent his day returning some calls and e-mails from his company. Even if he was taking some personal time away to help his wife, there was still work to be done. It was one of the drawbacks of being at the top. He was thankful to have the reliable and hard-working people he employed, including his heaven-sent public relations team, who were pretty much fielding all the questions that he wasn't quite ready to face.

As dinner time rolled around again, even he had to take a break. He got up from his desk and stretched, and for probably the hundredth or so time that day, wondered how Sophie was doing. He hadn't seen her since she swiftly headed back to her room during lunch with a plate of sandwiches in one hand, and a thick book tucked under her arm. She'd told him that the public forum would be held tomorrow, and she would be getting ready for it. He'd offered then to call one of his lawyers, and the dirty look she'd given him was more human than wolf. He'd wisely dropped the idea, for now, but spent some of the afternoon reaching out to one of his trusted business lawyers and putting them on standby, just in case.

He headed from his study and up the hall towards the master bedroom. The door was closed but through the crack along the floor he could see the lights were on inside the room. He took a deep breath and knocked on the door. To his surprise, her voice came almost immediately, as though she had anticipated him before he had even lifted his hand. "Come in, Lucas."

He opened the door, and found her sitting on the bed, her legs crossed, and piles of books circled around her. Her hair was pulled back into a practical ponytail, and she had a yellow notepad rested on one knee as she scribbled down some notes with one hand and turned pages of the book in front of her with the other. The sight made memories of many long-ago nights resurface, and he couldn't help but smile. She had the same intense look he remembered when she was studying. "Hard at work I see. So this is what you've been up to all day."

"You know me. I can't be too prepared," Sophie said. "What do you want?"

It still stung a little to be treated like a stranger by his own wife, even though she did tend to get tense while studying in the past as well. He didn't move too close to her and chose to stay near the door just in case. Time healed all wounds, as the old saying went, and right now she needed time to adjust back to the way things were. He pushed aside his pain and answered her question, "I just thought maybe you'd be hungry. I was thinking of ordering something for delivery tonight, and wanted to ask what you were in the mood for."

She glanced up at him and her look softened. "Pizza would be nice," she said.

"Maybe a meat lover's with pineapple added?" Lucas asked.

She gave him a small smile and nodded. "That sounds good. Oh and maybe some garlic bread crust, please."

"All right, I'll order it up. In the meantime, would you like some help with anything?" Lucas offered as he punched the order in on his phone.

She considered his suggestion, and for a moment he wondered if he'd pushed his luck too far. He was about to say something to deflect the entire idea, when she gestured to the pile of books to her right. "I am finished going through these ones, if you wouldn't mind helping put them back that would help. They go over there on the second shelf."

"Of course," Lucas went over and gathered the books into his arms and carefully began to place them back, alphabetically, as she preferred to have them as far as he remembered. "Anything else?"

"When you're done, maybe… can I borrow your laptop? I need to look up the more recent laws and most of these are out of date."

"Sure," Lucas said, and after he had the shelf in order, he went to go get his computer from the office.

He sat down on the bed, careful to keep some space between them when he returned. Her breath hitched for a moment when he did, but he didn't react to it. Instead he turned on the computer and logged in, before he handed her the laptop. She thanked him and sat it on her lap, and then began to quickly type some keywords into the search engine. They sat together in silence as she got that intense look once again, but this time she didn't chase him away. "Can you see if that book on family law has anything about the state taking custody?"

He nodded and picked up on of the books on her left and began to pour over the index. He helped sort through the information as best as he could, until the pizza arrived. They continued their search together, the pizza box between them. He carefully picked the chunks of pineapple off his own slices and set them down on the open box, and Sophie scooped them up and popped them in her mouth as she continued her online hunt.

Just like old times, he thought but did not add out loud, afraid he would break the magic of the moment.

~*~

RJ and Alex headed to bed earlier than usual, since they planned on going to help support Korban and Sophie tomorrow during the forum. As his sponsor, Korban had assumed that RJ would want to go with him anyway, but knowing Alex would be there too made him feel more at ease. He could get through anything with his friends by his side. They made tentative plans to stop by the garage to check in and pick up some things after tomorrow's meeting. Alex gave him a playful wink as they left the living room for the night. "Don't be up too late binging *Supernatural* without us, nerd."

Korban smirked and pulled his blanket up a little closer as he settled onto the couch. "See you in the morning."

"Good night, Korban," RJ said, and gently guided Alex down the hall.

Once they were in their room, Korban put something on and headed for the kitchen. He rummaged through the fridge and pulled out some leftovers, arranging them as artfully as possible on a plate. Some spaghetti with meat sauce, a thick slice of meatloaf, and fried rice from some take out they'd ordered for lunch. He wasn't sure what Naraka liked, but certainly one of those things would at least help satisfy his hunger. He heated up the plate in the microwave and then headed to his bedroom, leaving the television on to keep some quiet noise running. If Naraka was feeling talkative, Korban had some questions for him, and it would be the perfect background noise to cover it up, as so far out of the city the quiet was resounding.

Korban opened the door and quietly slipped into the room with the plate. Naraka was sitting up on the bed and his face lit up when he laid eyes on the left overs. Korban was careful to look without making direct eye contact, just in case. "The room service here may be slow, but it certainly doesn't disappoint," Naraka said quietly as he accepted the plate and fork.

"I'm glad you like it… sorry it's not much, I wasn't sure what you would like or not but… seems you're not too picky anyway," Korban said as Naraka began to enthusiastically dig in.

"This is great," Naraka said between bites. Once he had polished off the meatloaf, he paused to add, "Once you've lived on a diet of MRE's, you don't complain about food much. Especially when it comes to home cooking. Did you make this? I may need to forsake Mikael and marry you myself."

"Er… no, I'm not a very good cook. The sauce and meatloaf were RJ's creations," Korban said, giving credit where it was due.

"Well, please give my compliments to the chef."

Korban nodded, and Naraka slowed down as he twirled the spaghetti around his fork. "I'll be sure to do that."

While the other werewolf ate, Korban glanced over to the window. Mikael hadn't returned, but he suspected the moment he did he'd probably jump scare his way in like he always did. He felt a shiver run down his spine. "It takes some getting used to, being around vampires, doesn't it?" Korban asked.

Naraka grinned between bites. "I suppose it does. They have a tendency to be… very still."

That was an understatement. Korban let Naraka finish his meal and thought about what it would be like to see Ace again, this time as a vampire. *How would he react? Would Ace have that same unnatural feeling that Mikael did?*

He tried not to linger too long on those thoughts and shook himself back to the moment when he noticed more color returning to Naraka's face. The werewolf's hands were also holding the fork much steadier as he started on the fried rice. "Can I get you a drink?"

"I'm fine with water, thank you," Naraka responded after

swallowing another bite. "I appreciate all of this. We both do. I know the risk you're taking by doing this. We won't soon forget it." He paused and finished off the last few bites of his rice before he spoke again. "Not to sound ungrateful… but why are you being so kind? After what I did to you, I'm surprised you would even give me the time of day. Never mind help me turn back when I was stuck as a wolf, and then… all of this." He gestured to the empty plate, the bed, and the room with a sweep of his hand.

Korban looked down at his lap and clasped his hands together. He began to shrug, but wondered the question himself. "I don't know," he answered honestly, and gave him a sidelong glance. "I guess I just… I've been through a lot lately, and I wouldn't be here now if it wasn't for the kindness of strangers. Maybe this is just my way of paying it back."

"Maybe," Naraka repeated and offered another smile as he gazed down. "Whatever the case may be, thank you Korban. I know I wouldn't be as forgiving as you, if I were in your shoes." He paused for a long moment and sighed. "If I was you, I'd hate me for attacking you, and ruining my life."

Korban opened his mouth, then closed it. He considered his words carefully before he spoke. "I was angry when I realized who you were, and yeah, I hated you for a long time after the attack. I've hated myself for things I've done. But I can't hold on to that, because everything that has happened made me the man I am today. It doesn't mean I'm not still angry at you. Part of me may always be angry. But… I don't know you well enough to hate you."

Naraka gave a short, mirthless laugh. "Give it time then. You'll hate me soon enough."

Korban turned to him and frowned. "What makes you say that?"

"I've done some terrible things. Most of those things were done when I was on two legs, not four. I'm not like you, Korban. I'm not a good person." Naraka cautiously glanced his way. "I hurt you and turned you. I don't deserve your kindness. Yet here you are, feeding me, giving me your own bed and clothes. I can never make this up to you, let alone the fact that I infected you. I don't just owe you one. I owe you everything. I don't know how I can pay you back for this, but somehow, someway, I will."

"You don't have to," Korban began, but Naraka shook his head.

"I do."

Korban caught a glimpse of the pain in Naraka's amber eyes.

"I will make it right, somehow, Korban. I don't attack civilians. Not if I can help it. Never again." Naraka's voice sounded strained with emotion, and the air around him had changed.

Korban could smell Naraka's wolf then, a woodsy, fur-like scent similar to his own but with distinctive notes of something far away and exotic, like sandalwood and spice. He saw the other werewolf's body begin to tremble and he wondered if he was going to turn again. If so, he had to distract him, otherwise there was bound to be a few sounds that the television wouldn't be able to cover up. "Civilians, and you mentioned MRE's before… were you a soldier before you were bitten?"

The question raised Naraka's eyebrows and the werewolf's mouth curved in an amused smirk. "How observant of you, Korban," Naraka began, but that wolf-like scent had begun to fade, and it seemed to be working. "Yes, I used to be a soldier, once."

"Thank you for your service. Which branch of the military were you in?" Korban asked.

Just as quickly Naraka's smile faded away. "I don't like to talk about it," he said, then turned the question back to Korban, "If you have a thing for a certain kind of uniform, though, I'll be whatever kind of soldier you want me to be."

Korban felt his cheeks warm as the werewolf leaned a little closer to him, and he cleared his throat. "That's okay, we don't have to talk about it if you don't want to."

Naraka's mischievous grin returned. "You're cute when you blush."

His words only prompted his face to go from warm to hot and Korban stood up, a little flustered as he collected the fork and plate. "Um, thanks. Is there anything else I can get you? I should try and get some sleep. Tomorrow's an early day."

Naraka gave him a sultry smirk and patted the spot on the bed alongside him with his hand. "You don't have to go. I won't bite… again. Unless maybe you're into that sort of thing."

"On that note, good night, Naraka," Korban said and headed for the door.

"Korban?" Naraka made his name a soft question as he reached for the doorknob, any of that flirty confidence he'd had just moments before evaporating and making him sound unsure.

He paused and tilted his ear towards him. "Yes?"

"Would you… stay a little longer? Until Mikael comes back? I promise I will behave myself. I just… I just don't like being left alone for long," Naraka's voice went softer as he spoke.

Korban gave a heavy sigh and wondered just how much patience he could muster for the night. "Will you cool it down with the flirting? I'd rather not be murdered by your vampire boyfriend when he comes crawling back through the window."

"Yes. Sorry. I sometimes try to distract myself when I feel myself losing control by flirting. Which is obviously much easier when Mikael is around," Naraka explained. "I'll stop it if it makes you uncomfortable. Just please stay."

Korban wasn't sure what to think of that, but he supposed whatever worked for him was fine, as long as he didn't push it. He sighed again and glanced to Naraka. "All right. I'll stay for a little longer, but I'd like to at least get a few more answers."

"Deal," Naraka said and nodded in agreement.

"How did you find out about me?" Korban asked, setting the plate and fork down on the dresser closest to the door.

"You kidding? You've become quite the famous werewolf. I think the first report I remember hearing about you was the one where you and Sophie Bane ran off together as Wolven. Then with your triumphant return together… I guess you wouldn't have heard all the buzz. I know how they aren't exactly forthcoming with information when you're in quarantine."

Korban raised an eyebrow in surprise. "You've been in quarantine too? How did you escape without needing a sponsor?"

Naraka gave him a sad smile. "That is a long story for another time, but the short version is, I wouldn't have gotten out if it wasn't for Mikael's help. We've been laying low in the Underground since our escape from quarantine over five years ago— the night that I bit and infected you."

A cold chill coursed down his spine and Korban frowned. "Why did you attack me?" Korban cautiously asked.

Naraka hung his head down in shame. "Like I said, I don't usually attack civilians. I didn't have control over myself that night… I still don't have much control now. But back then the full moon was the worst time for me. We didn't realize it was the full moon when we escaped until it was too late. When I saw you, we'd just broken free and… it was the wrong place, wrong time."

He could smell the sorrow and guilt that radiated from Naraka, and the look he gave him, while still careful not to let their eyes connect, was one of genuine remorse. Korban wasn't sure what to say to him, but Naraka continued on, "Like I said before, I don't know how I will ever make it up to you. I don't know if I even can. But somehow, someway, I will make it right. Or I'll spend the rest of my life trying."

"When you help me reunite with Ace, that's a step in the right direction," Korban said with a smile, though he frowned thoughtfully as a realization formed in his mind. "I'm the only one you attacked that night of the outbreak?"

Naraka nodded. "We ran into hiding afterward. I thought I'd killed you, and Mikael believed he had murdered Ace. We didn't want to leave a trail of bodies behind us, for more than one reason. I already felt awful about what I'd done. When we found out later that you had turned, I felt some small amount of relief. I hope that it hasn't been completely awful for you to become a werewolf."

Korban scratched the back of his head anxiously and sighed. He went back over to the bed and sat down on the opposite end, giving Naraka some space. "It's had its ups and downs. More downs lately."

Naraka didn't pry, or maybe didn't know what to say. Korban glanced over to him. "If I'm the only one that you attacked that night, then how did the outbreak occur?"

"We're not sure. Everyone in the Underground has their own theories as to what happened to cause the virus to spread. The only truth we have is our own making," Naraka said.

"Do you know who bit you?" Korban asked.

"I know who infected me," Naraka answered, "and not all who are infected were bitten. I'll have to share that story with you sometime."

Korban paled a little, recalling one of the more colorful memories given to him by Davey. "Er…. you've never… eaten anybody, have you?"

Naraka tilted his head at that, and a sly smirk curved the corner of his mouth. "Like Big, Bad Wolf style? No, I'm not a cannibal. I've never eaten someone who hasn't wanted it."

Well, there went any chance of his blush going away for the evening. The look on his face must have been an amusing sight, as

Naraka began to chuckle, covering his mouth to muffle the sound.

He looked so much younger when he laughed, and the mood was rather infectious. Korban couldn't help but join in his laughter. It was still a bit of an inward struggle to wrap his mind around the fact that this man had been the one who attacked him, but there was more to this story. He didn't get the same feeling from Naraka as he did with Davey. Perhaps his wolf recognized him, or maybe it was his own sixth sense when it came to people. Naraka was here to heal, and maybe to atone for what he'd done. Maybe one day he could even look upon this man as a friend. Stranger things had happened, after all. "Well, on that note," Korban said when he trusted his voice wouldn't stammer too much from his own embarrassment. "I'd better try to get some sleep."

"There's plenty of room in this big, old bed if you'd like to join me. Just saying," Naraka winked at him.

Korban ignored the look and grabbed a couple pillows. "No thanks. You should try to rest while you can as well. Tomorrow is going to be a busy day."

"And when we go and meet with Ace in the Underground, an even busier night," Naraka agreed, stretching as he laid back against the remaining pillows.

Trying to keep Naraka on a topic that didn't involve inserting his innuendo, Korban asked as he laid out the pillows near the doorway, "What's the Underground like?"

"It sounds a lot cooler than it really is," Naraka said, tossing a blanket over to him.

Korban caught it. "Thanks."

Naraka nodded and turned off the lights, though they both could easily see in the dark. The television was still running out in the living room, but it would shut itself off eventually. Korban settled in and the floor actually wasn't too bad thanks to the plush carpet beneath him. He closed his eyes and listened to his heartbeat, and Naraka's. He heard his breath catch a moment, and to his surprise, Naraka continued in a hushed tone. "The Underground isn't just a place, but a group of infected people who have chosen to live on the outskirts of society. Most people in the Underground are scared. There's a lot of uncertainty there. We're all displaced people, infected with our various ailments. Some are easier to manage. Others, like me, have to deal with it ourselves, as best as we can. We don't have people in our lives who can sponsor us. We can't follow their rules, or we end up stuck in quarantine. You know how it is there. I can't go back there again." His voice had become so soft that Korban had to strain to hear him now. Naraka's heartbeat sped up a little as he continued on. "We rely on one another in the Underground. We take care of our own, and follow our own rules. Not the ones that are set up by human courts and governments, but our own. Mikael and I, we take care of the ones who decide to go rogue. Which I suppose is somewhat ironic, given my weak control. But the truth of the matter is, I feel more confident and stronger on four legs rather than two now. My wolf has learned to deal with this world much better than my human half. Maybe I'll be able to find a better balance someday. Until then, though, I do my part to help keep those poor, lost souls in the Underground protected, and help weed out the bad ones. One by one."

Korban felt a shiver course through him and pulled his blanket closer around him. So there were others, like Odin's Pack, within the heart of Syracuse and other places. People who were risking their lives for a chance at freedom. He couldn't blame them. There were only absolutes in the law as it was written now, but maybe tomorrow at the forum he could start changing minds. "People need reassurance that there will be a normal for them, after they've been infected. If they don't have a sponsor… there must be some other way they can be free. Especially if they are able to keep control. Or in your case, keep from spreading the infection," Korban said.

He could hear the rustle of blankets as Naraka turned to face him, and in the darkness, he saw those familiar and haunting yellow eyes glisten. "Maybe they will listen to you, but be careful Korban. Some people don't like change."

Naraka's words rang true. Korban knew better than anyone that change didn't come easy. His mind went to what would happen tomorrow. The possibilities of making a change, even if some didn't like it, gave him a small amount of hope. Maybe if nothing else this would start a conversation and give a more human element to a terrible epidemic. No matter what happened, he at least took a small amount of comfort in the fact that he would be spending the day with Sophie. That wonderful feeling, along with the thought of being reunited with his best friend following that, helped lull Korban into a peaceful sleep.

9: PANEL

The court house was mobbed when they arrived, with camera crews and eager reporters in their best on-camera outfits, as well as clusters of protestors sporting a variety of opinionated signs. While it was somewhat reassuring to see a lot of signs with "FREE LOBO" and "WEREWOLVES ARE PEOPLE TOO," there were some signs in the crowd that made Sophie's skin crawl. She didn't let her gaze linger on them too long, but the few hurtful words she did read stung bad enough. She pushed her sunglasses up further over her eyes as the flashes of lights burst from the crowd, and she kept her gaze down on the stairs and at her feet so she wouldn't trip. They went through security and the metal detectors single file, into the shelter of the building, and past the barrage of questions and comments that came from the gathering crowd.

Her heart was racing and she felt a bead of sweat run down her back as they headed down the hall. She lost count of how many eyes had been on her out there, and she tried to keep her breathing as even as possible to keep from hyperventilating. Lucas was on one side of her, and he glanced her way, seeing her anxious look and reaching for her hand. She accepted it, and he tenderly squeezed it as they walked along. She glanced over to Korban, who was near her other side, and could smell his anxiety as well. She didn't think, only reacted, and reached for his hand too. He flashed her a quick smile and his warm touch soothed her. She didn't hold his hand for long, but the few moments she did lifted her spirits.

They were ushered through the metal detector, then down the hall to a bench outside a set of double doors and were asked to wait. They'd arrived extra early, per Sergeant McKinnon's warning. Korban was wearing a dark gray suit that had been neatly pressed, along with a matching shade for his tie, upon lighter gray shirt. He had dark rings under his vibrant yellow eyes, and she worried that he hadn't slept too well. Guilt formed a lump in her throat. Of course he wasn't sleeping well, and no doubt she was to blame for it.

RJ wore a similar suit as Korban, only the colors were warm, reddish hues of brown that reminded her of the autumn leaves outside. Alex seemed the most uncomfortable by the professional-looking attire. She'd never seen him dressed up before, and even with his vibrant, neon pink cast poking through, he looked handsome in his black and white suit. She wondered if maybe that was the only suit the mechanic had in his closet, reserved for more rare and somber occasions. Even as cleaned up and pressed as the suit was, she could smell the lingering sadness and grief in the fabric, and it broke her heart.

Lucas gently patted her hand and she glanced his way. He always dressed to impress, and his charcoal gray suit complimented his stormy blue eyes. "You doing okay, honey?" Lucas asked her, and she nodded in response, not quite trusting her voice to match the fragile façade of her brave face.

Thankfully, they didn't have to wait too long for the others to arrive. Sergeant McKinnon and his partner, Sergeant Ellyk, walked up alongside Commissioner DeRusso. The two men were wearing their police uniforms, including their official hats, which looked unusual in lieu of Tim's usual black cowboy hat. Sophie missed the black cowboy hat that Tim usually wore, but it seemed everyone there was dressed to impress. Commissioner DeRusso wore her badge on a stylish, navy blue dress suit, her dark brown hair pulled back into a tight, neat bun that was carefully tucked under her dress hat. Her mouth was pressed into a flat, thin line and she carried her usual air of authority, and a slight tick of annoyance slightly curved the corner of her mouth. "Vultures out there. All of them," she murmured as they walked up, then much louder and with a warm smile she greeted them. "Good morning everyone."

Korban and RJ stood up, quickly followed by Lucas, and

exchanged firm handshakes in turn, greeting the two Sergeants and the Commissioner. Tim clapped a friendly hand on Korban's shoulder in greeting. "You two holding up okay?" he asked, glancing between the two werewolves.

Korban gave a small nod, sparing a quick glance to the Commissioner when he said, "We've been adjusting well. Every day is better than the last."

"I'm glad to hear that," Commissioner DeRusso said with a smile. "Today is bound to be a circus. A small group of reporters will be allowed in to record and ask a few questions, but to make sure they don't overwhelm you, we've prescreened the things both the Council and the press will be asking. I'll warn you, even with us skimming through their pool, there are some things that may be asked that are a bit personal and invasive. You can always politely decline to answer things, but I would encourage you both to be as open and honest with your answers as you can be. Most of the questioning will be done by the Council anyway, but I wanted to prepare you that they have agreed to have some questions open to the public."

"Will there be many cameras in there?" Sophie asked softly, trying to keep her voice as calm and flat as possible, but there was a slight tremor to her tone.

"Only one, Mrs. Bane, in both of your best interest, as well as to allow room for more reporters. We'll have the room set up similar to a court, with the reporters in the gallery and the council will be sitting in the jury box. We've only allowed a limited number of reporters, one from each major network and a handful from local news agencies, so we don't overcrowd either one of you. I insisted we make this a comfortable process for both of you. I won't have anyone risking the safety of Syracuse for this wolf and pony show. No offense meant, of course," Commissioner DeRusso said.

"Who will be on this Council?" Korban asked.

"There are six of us. Judge Affleck who will be moderating the forum, Mayor Varno, and myself. General Kane, who is a military representative sent from Fort Drum. Dr. Hoover, who you have met, of course, is here to field some medical questions for his research, and Senator Hunter has flown in from D.C. to represent Congress." Korban's expression went from amiable to unreadable at mention of the man, and Sophie could hear his pulse quicken as anxiety soured his forest-like scent. At his change, the Commissioner merely frowned and added, "No doubt it's a publicity move since re-election is a couple months away. I'm not the biggest fan of these tactics myself, but I suppose Congress could have sent us much worse."

"Y-yeah," Korban agreed out loud, and plastered on a smile that made Sophie frown in concern.

The double doors opened then, and a plump, cheerful woman in uniform greeted them. "Welcome, everyone. Commissioner DeRusso, Judge Affleck said he is ready to have them come in, before we allow the media inside."

Commissioner DeRusso nodded and then gestured with a sweep of her hand. "After you," she said as she ushered them in.

The room was spacious and did resemble a court room, which at least helped with the feeling of being surrounded by so many strangers. If there was one place she felt confident in, it was the court room. Lucas' hand tightened a little around hers, giving her a squeeze of reassurance as they walked up to the front, then they took their seats together on the left side of the court, close to where the Council awaited them. Lucas sat to her left side, while Korban took the place to her right, followed by RJ and Alex. Commissioner DeRusso gave them a smile before going to join the Council in the jury box, while Sergeant McKinnon and Sergeant Ellyk took seats behind them, Tim patting Korban's shoulder again before sitting back and keeping a watchful eye behind them. A small camera crew was setting up on the opposite side, and Sophie turned her attention to the members of the Council, to keep from thinking too hard about that mechanical eye that recorded them.

The Council that had gathered included the familiar faces she recognized, along with some new ones. She recognized the mayor from before she'd been bitten, as she had met her at countless parties and social events Lucas had hosted and attended. Mayor Varno was just as she remembered from before, with her medium-length brunette hair, clean and natural looking make-up, and warm, friendly smile. Mayor Varno sat on the far left of the jury box, and was chatting with a large, grim-looking man in a decorated military uniform that must have been General Kane. His piercing, gray eyes shot a studious, cautious look in their direction as they walked in, and he squared his jaw. The hair that wasn't covered by his hat was salt and pepper-colored, trimmed short, though the grays were starting to outnumber the dark original color.

To the General's right sat Dr. Hoover, who had a tablet and electronic pen poised in his hand. He flashed them a friendly smile that gave her some reassurance they at least had one ally on the Council. He was animatedly sharing something on his screen with the young man alongside him, who Sophie also did not recognize. He wore an expensive, navy blue, tailored suit with a tiny, enamel American flag and a round button reading "RE-ELECT HUNTER FOR SENATE" pinned to his suit jacket. His light brown hair was neatly brushed back in a professional style, and his blue eyes bright. This wasn't the same Senator Hunter she'd seen at campaign parties or in posters, but then realized that this must be one of his interns. She spared a glance around the room, but didn't spot the Senator.

Not far from the jury box sat the final member of the council, an older, thin man who was maybe in his seventies. He had cold, calculating eyes and graying wisps of hair that were almost white. He wore a dark gray suit and sat behind a copper name plate glistening with his title, "Judge M. Affleck," in a crisp, professional font. He folded his pale hands in front of himself as they approached the bench. "Good morning," he said in greeting, though his words held little warmth. A straight to business, no-nonsense judge, as promised. "Before I let the press in, I'd like to have you state your names for the record. This may be a public forum, but I would like to keep some formalities in order, if only to keep these questions and answers on topic. I'm not here to oversee some gossip and rumor mill."

"Thank you, your Honor," Sophie said. "We certainly appreciate that. I am Sophie Diana Bane."

"Lucas Christopher Bane, Sophie's husband and sponsor."

"Korban Miguel Diego."

"Ramiel James Ramirez, Korban's sponsor."

"Alejandro Emmanuel Cyrus, roommate and friend to Korban and Ramiel. Friends call me Alex."

"Manny Cyrus's boy?" The judge raised an eyebrow.

"His grandson, yes. The one and only," Alex beamed.

"I'm sorry to hear about the explosion at your garage. Your grandfather was a good man. I took my car there for years," the judge said, then smoothed his expression back to a serious one as he glanced to the court recorder who was typing away. "An important note, but not necessary for public record."

"Yes, sir," the stenographer said.

Judge Affleck cleared his throat before he continued on. "Before we begin and open this court room to the public, is there anything that you would ask we limit in our questioning?"

Sophie exchanged a glance with Korban, but his amber eyes were focused down at his hands as he shook his head. She shook her head in turn, then said out loud, "No. We wish to address as many of the Council's questions in order to offer transparency to the public. As much as we possibly can, we will answer the questions that you have today. We hope that by doing so, we can help reassure to the city of Syracuse, as well as everyone who is watching, that we shouldn't be as feared."

"Very well," the judge said gruffly, then nodded to the woman in uniform who had ushered them in. "Bailiff, you may let the press in so we can begin."

The waiting crowd of reporters came in, a quiet murmur rippling through the crowd as they stepped into the room and settled into their seats. Sophie tensed, but focused on breathing, while Lucas gently squeezed her left hand, and Korban reclaimed the one on her right. She could do this. She released both of their hands and opened up the small portfolio of notes she'd carried in. The crinkle of paper and the click of her pen helped her stay focused on what she'd prepared. She didn't know what questions to expect, but she had prepared a statement for them all to hear. Once the time was right, she would make her argument. Hopefully then they would listen to her words, and take them to heart.

It maybe wouldn't change the world, or the laws right away, but maybe it would change the minds of those who could do something.

~*~

Korban couldn't help but feel a small amount of pride as Sophie collected herself, and began to prepare for what was to come. She was doing this her way, and though he felt the tension ebb when he'd held her hand, there was something even more admirable when she released his hand, and her husband's as well, and prepared to get down to business. Her neat handwriting was scrawled over pages of notes on the yellow legal pad.

Spending the day alongside her, even in this arena, made him feel better. He'd missed her so much, and seeing that fire in her eye again was reassuring. The judge actually banged a gavel to hush the crowd, and the sudden bang made Korban jump. He tried to play it off, and straightened up in his chair. He caught a glimpse of the many eyes behind him. His wolf hated to be this closely inspected, like some specimen at a dog show. Even now he could feel the wolf's hackles raise, teeth baring, just waiting for a challenging eye to glance his way... and then the soft brush of Sophie's hand, and the wolf's Mate called to him, calmed him. He was not alone here. He had his pack members there for support.

The judge cleared his throat, and all attention was brought back to him. "As you may know, this Council has summoned you both after the public attack of Mrs. Bane, followed by her mysterious return from the grave. The citizens of Syracuse, and throughout the country, have all been curious to meet you, and speak to you in person to recount these events. As well as to calm some of the rumors that you were both still prowling around as Wolven. You have become a celebrity of sorts, and as a status figure to this new... epidemic, we figured it was a good idea to bring you in and speak to you about some compromises that would best work to help prevent the spread of lycanthropy and to better the supernatural community at large."

The judge nodded and smiled briefly before resuming his blank, professional expression once more. "All questions today have been pre-approved by the Council prior to our meeting." He went through the formalities of introducing the members of the Council, the young man on the end introducing himself as Cory Carter, who was there in place of Senator Hunter who had "pressing business with the Senate to attend to" and would not be making it for the forum today. Korban was just glad he wasn't there. The judge continued on, "Now that we've gotten through introductions, I will begin with a drawing to determine which of the council's questions shall be addressed first. We will continue from the selected person counter clockwise around the panel, after the questions have been answered in turn."

"Very good. Well then, without further ado, Mrs. Jackson?" He glanced from his desk to the bailiff, who approached with a hat. The judge reached in and pulled out a tiny slip of paper from the hat, then brought out his reading glasses to read the tiny print. His lips pursed and then went immediately into a thin line. "Very well. Our first question will be from General Kane." He set the paper down and glanced to the general as if to warn him without words to stick to the script.

"Thank you, your Honor." General Kane glanced down at the papers before him. "Mr. Diego, how long have you been diagnosed with lycanthropy?"

Hardly the type of question he'd expected that he would begin with, but the General was a military man. Everything was tactics, building up from the beginning in order to prepare for the final attack. He was starting with the basics. Though it was possible too that a harsh looking man could be easily misread, and the General really wasn't that bad a guy once you got past the grainy exterior. Or maybe he was just sticking to the script. "I was bitten five, almost six, years ago this coming November fifteenth. I was nearly killed but by some miracle I survived the attack. At the time my best friend was also killed." He'd thought Ace was dead, but that was another story. He still wouldn't believe it himself, until he laid eyes on his best friend.

"Interesting." He paused thoughtfully, then looked down at the sheet. "So you survived the attack, rather, one of you did anyway. This was during the first outbreak. Can you describe the wolf that attacked you, Korban?"

Korban hesitated for a moment and frowned. He now knew exactly who attacked him, and had to choose his words carefully as to not reveal too much, but he wondered what this question had to do with anything.

"Well?" The General was still polite, though impatient.

"It was a huge wolf, black. Solid black, except... he had some sort of silver object around his neck..." The General's lip twitched at that, and Korban hesitated from continuing. The rest of the council was either oblivious to the mind games or did not notice the look the general gave him, instead frowning worriedly about possible post-traumatic stress disorder or the like. He was at heart a victim, they realized. Maybe that was his best angle in this, really.

"So you survived the attack. What happened after? Did the beast just leave you?"

"Yes, by some miracle he left me there to die, but I passed out for a while instead. They told me when I woke up that they had attempted blood transfusions but my skin kept breaking the needles. The EMTs knew then that something was up, that this wasn't just some stray dog attack." He paused, squeezing Sophie's hand before continuing. "They brought me to quarantine for observation for a long time. There was more testing done, more doctors and scientists looking me over. I don't think there is a part of me that they did not check, really." He winced at the memory. "When it was all said and done, they admitted at last what I couldn't comprehend. I mean, werewolves weren't real back then, they were just in old stories and special effects in horror movies."

Dr. Hoover interjected with a question, "What was it like for you, as your transition began from man to werewolf?"

"Well… at first, I had strange symptoms. I wasn't sure if I had rabies, or if I'd gone mad, but overall I felt... amazing. Like a million bucks, which made me frustrated because they kept me locked up in the hospital like I really was going out of my mind. I felt so much stronger, and healthier, than I'd ever been. I could hear things, like the gears of a wrist watch, as if I had a microphone to it, from across the room. I could see every fleck of stucco in the ceiling, every speck of dust, as if it were enhanced and in high definition. Even my sense of taste... I can vouch that the best pizza in Syracuse comes from Paladino's." There were a couple small laughs at that from the crowd behind him, and he smiled. Never before had anyone asked him his story, and Korban wanted to tell all now. "The best sense of all though, was my sense of smell. I could smell everything, even things I couldn't yet identify with words. Things I suppose I could not even get a hint of when I was human. It took me awhile to figure it out, because no one knew what it was. I was smelling emotions."

When he looked up again, every eye of the Council was still upon him, and he could feel the eyes of the crowd focused on him from behind. Only this time they weren't staring at the big bad wolf in fear. They were all amazed, and the air was perfumed by the wonder they all felt. It felt... good. He never thought he'd like being the center of attention, used to being in the negative light. But this... this was something else.

"Then, the night of the full moon it all came crashing down. I was so scared at first. I'd been feeling so great after the attack, and then towards the middle of the day I began to feel sick... when the first cramps came I thought I was going to die. I was sure I would just fall apart and never be whole again. No one told me what was happening. They didn't treat me like I was human since I'd gotten there, and I was all alone. That was the worst part, besides the pain. No one would look at me, they only hurriedly dropped off food or water and were on their way. No one talked to me to explain what was going on then. I didn't even know my eyes had turned yellow until after my first transformation, when I saw my own reflection in the glass of the door." He remembered screaming until his throat was raw at the sight of himself then, but he kept that part to himself. His story had their attention, and he could catch the emotions in the air. Not fear towards him, but sympathy, and horrified wonder at his tale.

The cold, calculating eyes of the General remained on him though, unmoved by his story. "It wasn't until around the fifth full moon that after the change I began to remember things, though it was hazy memories then," Korban continued. "Kinda like a faded, old movie. I could see the massive paws that had been my hands. I could feel the power the moon had on my blood, running so rapidly through me, my heart loud and booming in my ears. It was the first time through the whole ordeal that I felt like things wouldn't be so bad... that I wouldn't lose myself to the curse." He saw some of the council consider this, and added, "Some call it an infection. Some call it a diagnosis. Hell, I sometimes called it a curse. But it's more than any of those things. It's a huge change to your life. One day you're normal and going about your business. The next you're being told that you can't do things that you used to do, like going to work or school because of something you can't control. Something that only happens once a month, and if you're careful about it, can be controlled."

"Not everyone can control themselves, though," the General commented.

A chill ran through Korban as he thought of Naraka. "That may be true, especially at first. Everyone is different. For example in my case, my eyes used to be brown. After my first transformation they never turned back. I was a walking example of what people could fear. It was hard for me, and still is in some ways. It doesn't bother me as much as it used to, but there are disadvantages of self-advertising that I'm a lycanthrope, as you can imagine."

"Yes, I suppose it would be challenging. Trying to hide yourself in plain sight," General Kane murmured. "Especially with eyes like that."

"You mention being able to control it. What are some measure you have taken to help yourself transition with this affliction?" Judge Affleck interrupted.

"Yes. While sometimes the curfews help with time management, I keep to my own strict schedule as much as possible. I'm usually cautious around the days of the full moon and I keep a pretty good eye on the calendar and almanacs to make sure I stick to that schedule, in order to prevent any chance of me, or my wolf, breaking free and causing harm to anyone else."

"Scheduled, you say... so this becomes almost a routine for you, then?" Mayor Varno piped in.

"You adjust... that's what they say, anyway. Humans are the most adaptable beings on this planet, after all. I may go wolf once a month, but the rest of the days I'm as human as the rest of you." Though as the cold eyes of the general stared into him, Korban wondered if he was more human than some of the members on the panel.

The mayor smiled brightly in response, and asked, "What are some challenges you both face when it comes to the mandated curfews?"

"I can understand for safety reasons having a curfew on full moon nights. It's safer for everyone to have that in place, for the transformation. But arbitrary nights don't usually help. It limits what kind of work we can do while we are human the rest of the month. People can lose their job if they aren't available to work or have to call out sick every time there is a curfew in effect. It impacts their livelihood if they are even able to keep a job. I'm fortunate now, but trying to find work on my own was very limiting for a long time."

"What is your current line of work, Mr. Diego?" the mayor asked.

"I was helping out when I could around Alex's garage, Cyrus Autos, before the explosion. Business was fairly steady the past few years, and with some people coming and seeing I was a werewolf… it sort of hurt business. I started looking to find work around Syracuse, but for obvious reasons I kind of stick out from most infected people," Korban said, and gestured to his eyes. "I didn't want to be the reason my best friend's business went under, so I tried to find work of my own. I was fortunate enough that one night I ran into Sophie, and as a result of my standing up for her, she…" he trailed off for a moment and glanced to her. He couldn't explain fully to the court that he'd immediately fallen into a crush with her, though maybe his pause and the warmth that radiated from his cheeks in that moment were enough clues for them to put the silence together. He cleared his throat and continued on, trying to suppress his blush. "She recommended me to her husband, and Mr. Bane was willing to take a chance and hired me to work for his company."

"So it is true that you were associated with Mrs. Bane prior to the Wolven attack that infected her?" General Kane piped in, giving them both a stern and calculating look.

"Yes, it is true." Korban answered cautiously.

The general continued on. "Is it true as well then, Mrs. Bane, that Mr. Diego was present the night you were attacked?"

"Yes, he was at the charity ball. He saved me from the Wolven that attacked and infected me. Brett Kensington," Sophie said, a shiver coursing through her. She still felt cold at the thought of this stranger who'd attacked her so violently, and changed her life as she knew it.

"Oh really?" He seemed amused by this tidbit of information. "Would you care to explain why Mr. Diego was there that night?"

Before Sophie could speak, Lucas interjected. "Mr. Diego was there because I had sent him a personal invitation." There was a collective gasp of surprise from the crowd, and several genuine looks of surprise from the Council members, including the stoic General. "I had extended an invitation to Mr. Diego to attend the gala, in order to help him introduce himself to some of my employees. He had just accepted a job offer with my company and I wanted to help him feel more at home with Bane Corporation. When I met him the first time I'd been a bit taken aback by his appearance, so I wanted to give him a chance to meet some of the people he would be working with, an ice breaker of sorts."

General Kane frowned. "Definitely an unorthodox way to handle a new hire in such a large company."

"Yes, well, Bane Corporation didn't get to be the Fortune 500 company it is today by doing things in a traditional manner," Lucas said with a cool smile. "Mr. Diego and I may have our differences, but I do not regret him being at that gala. He saved Sophie's life."

"You sure about that, Mr. Bane?" General Kane steepled his fingertips together and stared him down. "Sure, the videos from that night show him racing through the crowd to chase after the Wolven. But then Mr. Diego hid her away from the police, media, and her family while she transitioned from human to a werewolf. It was an extremely risky and illegal move, according to the laws we have in effect for infected individuals. During that time not only did you and your family believe Mrs. Bane to be deceased, but Mr. Diego potentially risked the lives and safety of others by housing a newly infected lycanthrope. We're lucky that no one else was bitten by Mrs. Bane and infected, or killed, because of Mr. Diego's irresponsible actions."

Sophie gave a small growl, which turned several heads towards her as she stood up. "You're wrong, General," she began. "Korban did what he had to in order to protect me. Brett Kensington was set up to attack me that night. In a crowded room with hundreds of people in attendance, a rogue Wolven only attacked one person there. Me. Don't you find that raises more important questions?"

"Why did you vanish then, Mrs. Bane? What did you have to hide for so long after being attacked? Why not follow the law and be put in the hospital for treatment?" General Kane pressed.

"I had no choice, I was being hunted. My own choice was to run at the time, because I didn't know who or what would come after me next. Korban helped me get through my first transformation, which was only three days after I had been attacked. It was the most excruciating thing I have ever been through, but he kept me safe, and helped me stay strong, and sane, through it all." Sophie gave Korban a smile that made his heart flutter.

General Kane wasn't buying it, even though the emotions that ran through the crowd proved they were sold. "How noble of Mr. Diego. It still doesn't excuse his blatant disregard to the law. Or do you believe you are above the law yourself, Mrs. Bane? The privilege of being a woman who grew up in wealth. Surely you don't believe yourself to be above following the rules set for those who have been infected?"

Sophie squared her jaw at that, and the sharp look the gave the General would have made a lesser man squirm. "No, General. Like I said, there were extenuating circumstances that made it necessary for me to remain in hiding, until we found out who was behind my attack."

"And did you find out who attacked you, Mrs. Bane? This strange, mystery hand who was behind unleashing Mr. Kensington upon you that night?" General Kane asked with a twisted grin, akin to baring his own fangs back at her.

Korban could hear Sophie's heart beat faster, and saw her fist clench on the table. He wondered if he would have to stop her from pouncing on him, especially when she shook with anger. "Yes, actually, I did," Sophie snapped back. "My sister, Nikki Winters. She is the one who sent a Wolven after me to die."

Stunned gasps suddenly filled the air. Mayor Varno's jaw fell open, and even General Kane's eyes widened at this revelation. Commissioner DeRusso interjected, "Ladies and gentlemen of the Council, and the media, this is still an open investigation, and my officers are looking into all possible leads. All that I can tell you is we have Nicolette Winters on our list of suspects for the attack on Mrs. Bane. Given that Mr. Kensington is deceased, and Miss Winters is in a coma, we haven't had any further developments in this case, and would ask kindly to move the questioning away from this open investigation."

General Kane frowned. "Given this development, surely we can discuss this detail—"

The judge interrupted with a loud bang of his gavel. "I will have order in this court, even if this isn't technically a hearing, General. Commissioner DeRusso is right, and General Kane this is not a formal court hearing. This is an open forum to allow questions that we have already deemed appropriate. Let's get back to the approved questions, please. Why don't you pick up the next question, Commissioner?"

"Yes, your honor, I'd be happy to. We all have been wondering what happened after your forced transformation. Where did you go all that time, while you were both on the run?"

"After we were hit with the tranquilizer darts and forced to turn, I don't remember much. Just the feeling of being betrayed, and rage. I was devastated, and that feeling didn't leave me even after I turned. I don't recall the details of what happened, until I found myself, and Korban, lost in the wilderness. It was as if the Wolven were called to the wild. We ended up somewhere in the Adirondacks together. Korban can recall every moment we were Wolven, but to me it is like a distant dream at best." Sophie explained, and Korban nodded in agreement as she continued on. "The moment we turned back, we started to look for help, and find a way back home. We were so far from civilization that it took us a day just to find an abandoned camp, and we were lucky to find shelter there. We tried to find out where the camp was, and looked every day for a way home."

She paused and looked over to Korban, causing his heart to do a small flip. He knew what was coming up, and she reached and held his hand to give it a comforting squeeze. "We were there during the full moon, and we turned Wolven again. I could remember some things from that transformation, thankfully, as Korban was caught in a hunter's trap, and if I didn't remember that… I could have lost him." Her eyes glistened with emotion as she said the words.

The council and reporters were hooked on this version of the story. It was intensely sanitized for the public, but neither Sophie nor Korban wanted to give notoriety to the Bailey brothers and the horrors they committed in their cabin in the woods. While this story definitely left out a lot of personal information, it also wouldn't inspire any copycats who maybe would follow Davey's model. It also would protect their friends who rescued them. Sergeant McKinnon had given them permission to leave out those key elements, especially since that case was now closed and Davey was no longer a threat to the public. *Thankfully,* Korban thought with infinite relief.

Sophie squeezed his hand as if sensing his thoughts as she continued the tale. "Korban was badly injured, and though we heal quickly, it took a few more days for him to recover, and to find some helpful strangers who could help us get back home."

Korban squeezed her hand back, and he caught Lucas curl his free hand into a fist, but his expression remained calm and neutral. There was a mixture of emotion in the air that made his reaction blend in with the others, so Korban avoided eye contact with the man. Sophie released his hand after a moment and stood up, taking a breath to steady herself as she looked to the panel of people before them, and then spared a look to the gathered group of reporters behind them as well. "We didn't choose to transform that night. We only lost control after being hit with the serum. We didn't hurt anyone while we were out in the wild. Our Wolven took us someplace far away from what they perceived as a threat. I haven't been a werewolf that long, but from what I have experienced so far, I can tell you all that it's a challenge that I deal with every day. Some days it is easier than others, but isn't that the way it is for anyone dealing with a disease? I can understand some of the laws in place, to help protect the public, but what about us? What are we supposed to do with our lives, our families, after we've suffered from a sudden and vicious attack? I think it's time we consider a change… no, we start to make changes for those of us who are victims of circumstance. We didn't choose to become infected. We want a chance to have a normal life, just like the rest of you. We want to be able to put the pieces of our family back together. We want to be able to hold our children while we are human. We want our lives back. We are infected, but we are still human most of the month. I hope that these words will move you, and if nothing else make you think, and challenge what you believe. Treat us for the infection, but don't forget that we need compassion."

Her hands were trembling a little at her sides, but she held her head high. Korban's heart swelled with pride at her words.

"That was a pretty speech, Mrs. Bane, but it doesn't change the fact that once a month you become a deadly beast that can spread the infection to others, effectively ruining their lives. Or worse, ending them with one bite," General Kane interjected.

Her eyes narrowed as she turned his way. "I'm not saying we aren't dangerous, General. I realize that many of those laws were passed because we can potentially be a threat if left unchecked. Brett Kensington wasn't able to control himself, and as a result of that I'm standing before you now with lycanthropy. But tearing us away from our family and friends isn't the answer. Locking us away and confining us to quarantine, until someone is willing to risk it all in order to sponsor us, isn't the answer. We're infected, but we are still human, and we deserve the same rights as everyone else to freedom, and the pursuit of happiness."

The general opened his mouth to say something more, when Judge Affleck struck his gavel down again. "Thank you for that insight, Mrs. Bane. Before we wrap this up for the day, I think I speak for everyone when I say that you've given us all something to think about. At the very least, I know there are several new questions I think we should be addressing. I would like to propose a more organized and formal hearing in the near future, perhaps one involving the city council and some other law makers. We would invite both you and Mr. Diego back to share your experience and propose more formal changes to the laws that are currently in effect. If the mayor or perhaps the Senator could consider joining us for such an event?"

The mayor nodded emphatically. "I will definitely look into holding something like that, and I will speak to the city council about arranging it and putting it on the calendar. It's a complicated issue, but we definitely need to look into ways to make it better for all of our citizens."

"I can definitely relay the information to Senator Hunter as well. He stands firmly on the side of all human rights, and I'm sure he would be grateful for the opportunity to be a part of such an historic stance," the intern said.

"Very well," the judge said, satisfied with this response and folding his hands in front of him continued, "that being said, I think we have taken enough of your time for today. Thank you for coming to speak with us today and shine light on what happened to the public. We will convene again, perhaps in a week or so, to further discuss changes in the laws, with people who can certainly help make a difference. I kindly ask in lieu of further questioning today that our reporters please return for a press conference that will be held in conjunction with our deliberation on that day, to be announced soon. Thank you all for coming."

He struck his gavel down once more, a sense of finality in the sound this time. Everyone stood as the judge departed and began to gather up their belongings. As they waited for the reporter to disperse, the mayor approached them. "Thank you both for coming and telling us your story," he said. "I'd like to invite all of you to lunch as a thank you for attending this panel today."

"You sure that we could get anywhere in town today without a media circus parading behind us?" Lucas asked.

"One step ahead of you," the mayor said, beaming. "I've maybe had this in my plans since I spoke with the Commissioner. We've got the room next door set up for lunch and you're not going to want to miss it. Dinosaur Barbeque is catering." Just then the doors to the side room were opened, and like magic, the tangy barbeque scent filled the air. It wasn't just the werewolves whose stomachs were growling. "I hope you'll consider joining us?"

"If you're pandering for the werewolf vote, well, you've just got two of us on board," Korban said.

As they followed the others into the next room, Alex quipped, "Well, you guys may be easily bought, but I'm not going to be convinced until I see there are ribs involved."

There was a mutual sense of relief as they stepped into the room and joined the line that wound around the barbeque spread before them, which to Alex's delight included racks of ribs. It was a well-earned break after the grueling round of questions. Plus the amazing scent of barbequed pork had his mouth watering, and Korban couldn't wait to dig in.

"You did pretty good out there, Korban," RJ said, praising him as they got in line and piled food up on their paper plates. He had grabbed two, one for himself and one for Alex. "And Sophie nailed it, like my students would say. She handled her questions very well. Even the ones that got her stirred up." He glanced meaningfully over to General Kane, who was already chatting at a table with Dr. Hoover and Mayor Varno as he ate.

"Yeah, I learned from a really wise teacher once that it's better to not let the bullies get too much of a rise out of you," Korban said.

RJ laughed at that and winked to him. "Glad you followed that handsome and smart teacher's advice," he said, then carried the two plates over to the small table that Alex had scouted out, and was next to the table where Lucas and Sophie sat.

He was about to pile some barbeque ribs onto his plate when the intern, Cory Carter, approached his side and whispered to him, "Mr. Diego? I realize you're about to eat lunch, but would you mind if I had a word with you, in private? It won't take very long."

Korban kept a carefully neutral expression on his face, though his own curiosity was getting the better of him. "Okay, sure."

"Thanks," the young intern answered nervously, then glanced over to the table of the other Council members. "Meet me in the restroom in about ten minutes. Come alone."

Korban frowned but nodded. "All right," he said.

Cory reeked of anxiety and determination, but he didn't smell like a threat. Besides, he was human. He doubted if it came down to it that he would have a problem with this kid, and his curiosity was piqued. He sat down at the table with his friends and grinned over to Sophie. "I've never seen you in action before but you really were in your element out there," he said to her as he sat down. "Some people may be afraid to face you as a wolf, but I think I'd be more afraid of facing off with you in the court room."

"Thanks, Korban," she said, brightening at his words.

Lucas bristled alongside her and shot Korban a dirty look, but he ignored it. After having so many eyes on him that day, he honestly didn't care what the billionaire thought of him. Sophie had earned her compliment and he didn't care about Lucas' jealousy. His sympathy toward the man was wearing thin with each day that passed in which he couldn't be with Sophie. The thought made his stomach squirm a little. Maybe he was a homewrecker after all for thinking this way. He distracted himself with the first bite of rib meat, which melted off the bone into his mouth.

After getting some meat in his belly, he felt much better. He kept an eye on the clock as they settled in and enjoyed lunch. Once ten minutes had passed, he saw Cory Carter step out of the room and go into the men's room. "Be right back, nature's calling," he said to RJ, who nodded to him between bites of his barbeque pork sandwich.

He hurriedly headed to the restroom and closed the door behind him. Cory was waiting there for him, and gave him a meaningful look. "Lock the door. We can't have anyone overhear this conversation. It never happened."

Korban complied and clicked the lock into place, then frowned at Cory, folding his arms over his chest. "All right, so why the cliché incognito tactics?" Korban asked, trying to be polite but a bit of his annoyance slipped into his tone.

"The Senator wanted me to deliver a message to you personally, and he stressed that I was not to tell you this when others were nearby," Cory said.

Korban scoffed and shook his head. "Unbelievable. He couldn't even come to this and tell me himself?"

Cory frowned, and looked confused.

Korban sighed again. "Okay, let's hear it."

"The Senator asked me to remind you to remember your promise," Cory whispered with a serious, pointed look.

Korban froze at that, and tensed, but didn't say anything.

Cory misunderstood the look in his eyes and nervously added, "Look, I don't even understand what that means. I'm just the messenger, and he asked me to come here and do his part while he is out on the campaign trail. Re-election is coming up soon and the Senator is a very busy man."

Korban sneered at that, but turned away from Cory. The look wasn't meant for him. "Some things never change." He was always too busy to be bothered. "Is that all he asked you to tell me?"

"That's all," Cory said, and took a step towards the door. "Now if you'll excuse me."

Korban stepped in front of Cory and met his eyes. The intern swallowed anxiously and averted his gaze. "You tell the *Good* Senator that I'm not like him. I don't forget my promises. I keep them."

That being said, Korban turned and unlocked the door, and quickly headed out to finish his lunch.

10: PLACEBO

When they all had their fill of barbeque and mingling, Lucas called Damion and had him bring the car around. There were still a lot of people in the front of the court house, so they went through the less swamped side door and quickly piled into the car, dodging a few lingering questions from the reporters who were on the fringes of the crowd. "You really were incredible out there today, Sophie," Korban said, complimenting her from the backseat when they finally settled into their seatbelts and were on the move.

"You weren't too bad yourself," she said, turning in his direction and flashing him a smile.

"Is there anywhere you need to stop before we head back to Skaneateles?" Lucas asked, keeping his tone as neutral as possible, even though he was becoming agitated.

"Actually, would you mind if we stopped by the garage? I need to pick up a few things, and we'd like to check in on the place," Korban responded.

"Of course," Lucas said, and gave a nod to Damion, whose reflection bobbed his head in confirmation as they turned onto Adams Street, and headed towards the highway in order to break through the traffic. "You really were amazing out there, Sophie. I'm glad that you had them thinking about what these laws are doing to our family. I know Danny would be proud of his mother for standing up for what's right."

Sophie blushed and turned her smile to him. "Thank you, that means a lot. I just hope that maybe it will lead to real change."

"The judge and mayor seemed pretty optimistic about it," RJ said. "I'm hoping that ends up being the case, and we do hear back from them soon to discuss the laws. Soon being the keyword, as who knows how long it's going to take to get this organized and get everyone who should be there on board."

"Who knows when it comes to politicians?" Korban said in an agitated tone, though he quickly added, "Sorry. I don't mean to kill the vibe, just… trying to be realistic."

Lucas turned away to keep from smirking in satisfaction. Most likely the werewolf was annoyed that Sophie's attention had been turned back to its rightful place. Perhaps it was a little juvenile of him to think that he was rubbing his rival the wrong way, but he couldn't help but feel some small amount of smugness at the other man's irritation.

"Well, with the mayor on board, and how fast they put this together, I'm still feeling good about it," Sophie said. "I maybe haven't found the loopholes yet in the laws, but I started looking into it, and when I get back to the lake house, I plan on diving back into my research. I won't stop until I find a solution."

Lucas smiled at that and reached out to take her hand again, and she let him. "That's my girl," he said.

~*~

Korban gritted his teeth together in silence for the rest of the ride, and was glad when the car pulled up to the curb by Cyrus Autos. He was already on edge after the interruption during lunch. He was glad that he got to enjoy at least half of his lunch, because after his secret meeting with Senator Hunter's intern he lost his appetite and only finished it in order to keep up appearances. The food now sat in his stomach like heavy rocks instead of delicious, grilled meat. To top it off, now Lucas was gloating and it was taking all his energy to not snap at the man.

The garage was still under repair, with large, heavy plastic flaps covering the new framework of the place and protecting it. There was still the lingering scent of burnt wood and insulation, but the newer smells of fresh concrete and plaster were stronger than before.

Lucas frowned at the state of the garage. Korban realized this must be the first time Lucas had seen the amount of damage in person. "That blast really did a number here, didn't it?"

Alex swallowed and nodded, the pained look in his eyes returning. "Yeah," he said in a soft voice. "I'll be glad when they finish with the construction, and everything gets back to normal again." He glanced at his cast while he said it, and then reached into his pocket with his good arm to pull out his keys. He tossed the keyring to Korban, who caught them. "Go ahead inside, just be careful. There have been a few delays in the construction while they figure out the insurance, so I'm not sure what to expect in there. I… I don't want to go in there and see it like that again. I'm gonna wait out here, if that's okay."

"Yeah, of course Alex. I just need to pick up a couple things anyway. I won't be too long," Korban reassured his friend, then glanced to RJ. "Do you need anything in there?"

"Maybe grab my briefcase and laptop bag. I may as well revise my lesson plans while I still have some summer break left," RJ said.

"You got it," Korban said, then hurried out of the SUV.

He couldn't get out of the car fast enough, and was happy to breathe air that wasn't so closely shared with the smug billionaire. He tried not to stare too much at the painful amount of damage that had been done to their home. There was definite improvement compared to when he'd first returned home, but it had been a few weeks since he'd been in quarantine. He tried not to let that thought linger as he stepped carefully through the cut flap in the plastic, and cautiously entered the dark, gaping maw of the garage. His eyes quickly adjusted to the darkness and he headed over to the small stairway that lead up to the apartment entrance. The new door easily opened with the key, and he smiled a little when he noticed the heart-shaped Backstreet Boys key chain on the key ring.

Inside the apartment upstairs, it was dark and eerie without the usual life that Alex, RJ, and himself gave to it. *Get a grip, Korban, you're a werewolf, you can't be afraid of ghosts,* he chided himself as he walked in and headed towards his old room. He walked carefully around the caution tape that blocked him from the living room and half of the kitchen, then headed up the hall and into his old room. This area was mostly the same, thankfully, and he found his backpack in his closet and began to stuff some of his clothes into it. He wanted something that was his own again, and not borrowed from Lucas Bane.

He stuffed his clothes into the bag a bit more forcefully than he should have and almost ripped it. He stopped, closed his eyes, and took a deep breath. *Calm down, Korban,* he told himself, though his hands were still shaking around the pair of socks he had gripped in them. He opened his eyes, and something caught his eye hanging behind his door. It was a black, leather jacket with *Valhalla Knights* carefully stitched onto it. Sophie's jacket, and a token of appreciation given to her by Valkyrie and Odin's Pack. He went over and picked it up to return it to her. Even now, she helped calm him down as her lingering mint, vanilla, and wolf scent, tinged with his favorite smell of leather, wafted into his nostrils.

He resumed his packing with less vigor as he carefully folded and tucked Sophie's jacket into his bag, and then went over to his nightstand. He opened up the drawer and pulled out a small, worn photo album, thankful that it hadn't been destroyed in the explosion or the fire that followed. He carefully opened it, flipping through to the last page where he had a picture of him and his mother on one side, and a group photo of himself with Alex, RJ, and Ace on the other. The picture was only from five and a half years ago, but they all seemed so much younger and more innocent back then. The picture was taken outside the garage during what he thought was Ace's last birthday party. He smiled at the memory as he carefully closed and tucked the album into his bag. It calmed him to know that soon he would be reunited with his old friend.

Satisfied with his packing, he zipped up his back pack, pulled it over one shoulder, and then headed over to the master bedroom to get RJ's briefcase and laptop.

Their bedroom was still as neat and orderly as he remembered, though there were a bunch of boxes lined up along one of the walls that were labeled "TOOLS" in Alex's handwriting. He went over to the small desk that was neatly arranged, and sure enough, his things were there. He packed up RJ's laptop and charger into the laptop bag that hung behind his desk chair and checked the lock on his worn briefcase to make sure it was closed before he picked it up and headed for the exit.

He gave the apartment a final look before he closed the door. They would be home again soon, and things would get back to as normal as they could be. The future was so uncertain, but wasn't it always like that? There were highlights to some of the surprises that came with not knowing what to expect.

And then there was turning around, after locking the door, to come face to face with a familiar vampire, who was pale as a ghost in the dark of the garage in his dark trench coat.

"*Mikael*, you have *got* to stop sneaking up on me like that!" Korban yelped in a hushed, irritated tone as he nearly dropped RJ's briefcase. "What is it with you and sneaking up on people?"

"Stealth is an important trait to master," Mikael said cryptically, his face a flat mask. "I don't have much time. The long story short is Ace cannot meet with you tonight. He asks that you return here tomorrow at dusk."

Korban's heart skipped a beat, any of his earlier gripes or worries suddenly vanished. "Tell him I'll be here. I wouldn't miss it for the world."

Mikael nodded, then tilted his head a little as he asked, "How is Naraka?"

"Behaving himself, or so I hope. We've been gone all day at the public forum answering questions. We're headed back now, and I saved him some ribs from our lunch," Korban said, shifting the weight of the backpack and laptop bag on his shoulder. "I'll be sure to tell him I saw you."

"Please do that," Mikael said, then glanced around the garage, pausing to tilt his ear again as if he was hearing something that Korban could not. "See you soon, Korban."

Just as quickly as he appeared, Mikael vanished and caused Korban to jump, his pounding heart racing even faster than before. The only hint that the vampire had been there was the slight rustle of plastic as he passed through it, something that easily could be brushed off as just a slight breeze. He took a moment to calm his heart down, but was still spooked when he emerged from the garage and hurried to the vehicle. Sophie gave him a worried look as he came in and was the first to ask him, "Are you okay, Korban?"

He just nodded, handing RJ his briefcase and laptop bag before settling into his seat and buckling up his seatbelt. "Yeah, it's just kinda spooky in there with it being so quiet and empty."

"Aww, I didn't know you missed me that much, Lobo," Alex said and Korban was grateful that he was back to himself, though he felt guilty that no one questioned it further and took his word for it.

~*~

Sophie wasn't buying Korban's answer, but she didn't want to call him out either. Ever since the forum he'd been on edge. Not that she could blame him. With the recent turn of events, he had every reason to be unhappy. Though he had hidden that pain rather well, until that afternoon. He still seemed on edge when he emerged from the garage, looking as though he'd seen a ghost. The others maybe brushed it off as him being shaken up by the state of the garage repairs, but she had a feeling in the pit of her stomach that there was something more on his mind. She decided then and there that she would talk to him about it later, or maybe tomorrow after he had a chance to cool off.

On the long drive to the lake house, Lucas surprised her by turning to the men in the backseat after they'd all gone quiet for several minutes and said, "I've been thinking for a while now, but I never properly thanked you all for returning Sophie home safely. I had offered a pretty hefty reward for any information leading to her, and since you all technically delivered, I'd like to help. I want to pay to get your garage up and running again. It may be a little more than the original offer, but I don't mind."

Alex blinked in surprise and his jaw fell open. "Really? I mean… that's very generous of you, Lucas."

"I insist. I saw how much your garage means to you. I'll make some phone calls in the morning and there won't be any further delays on the construction. Not with the money I'll be putting into improving your garage. Maybe give me a wish list of upgrades while we're at it," Lucas said.

Alex's eyes sparkled like Christmas had come early, and by the time they pulled up to the lake house even Korban's grim mood had been lifted. They exchanged their good-byes for the evening, and Lucas walked with her to the main house. "That was very sweet of you, Lucas," she told him as they walked up the porch steps.

"Well, given that you are here with me now, home safe and sound, it's the very least that I can do for your new friends," Lucas said, pausing in front of her to reach up and run his hand through her hair.

She froze, and her heart fluttered in her chest. She didn't know if this was what she wanted or not, but he was her husband, and they were trying to reconcile. Before she could protest, he leaned in and pressed his mouth onto hers.

His kiss was just as she remembered; soft, warm, and pleasant enough. She closed her eyes and tried to let herself get swept up in the moment, but to no avail. She could go through the motions, but she didn't feel the same spark of passion she did before, and after a moment it felt awkward, and wrong. It wasn't like this before, and even when he put his arms around her, she tensed, feeling not enraptured, but trapped. When he finally pulled away, she felt relieved it was over.

Lucas smiled, and kept an arm around her as he opened the door and ushered her inside. She didn't trust her voice in that moment so she remained silent as they walked in. "Why don't I order us some dinner, and you can give Danny a call? I'll see if Damion is up for a run to Doug's."

Her stomach felt a little queasy, and she didn't know what she wanted for dinner, never mind what she wanted to do with these conflicted feelings. "That would be nice. A fish sandwich with fries sounds good," she said, ordering her favorite, and turning her attention towards making the video call.

The phone screen showed the call connecting, and it began to ring. She stared at her image on the screen and saw how watery her eyes had become, and quickly, carefully, wiped the corners of her eyes with the side of her fingertip. It rang once, and she forced a smile. Everything would be fine once her son came on the screen.

She could do this.

The phone rang a second time. Sure, her feelings had changed for her husband, but saving her marriage wasn't just for her sake, or for Lucas. It was for her son too. After all he'd been through, he needed both of them. He needed them to get back to normal again.

Why do I suddenly want to cry? Sophie wondered, and it dawned on her as the ringing stopped, and her son's smiling face appeared, and he enthusiastically greeted her, "Mommy!"

"Hi Sweetie," Sophie said softly, her voice cracking a little with emotion at the sight of him.

"You look sad, are you okay Mommy?" Danny asked, his brow furrowed with worry.

"I'm okay, honey. I just miss you so much," she said, taking a breath to steel herself. "How are you doing tonight?"

Danny's worried look remained. "I miss you too Mommy. Grandma and Grandpa do too. When can I come visit?"

A fresh lump formed in her throat, but she spoke around it in a strained voice, "I'm not sure when. I hope soon."

"Me too," Danny said, looking sad for a moment, but then he brightened up. "I drew you a picture today Mommy. Grandpa said it's really good and that he thinks you'll like it."

His smile was infectious. "You did? Can I see it?"

"I don't want to ruin the surprise but… okay. I'll go get it. Grandma said she wanted to talk to you when you called anyway so I'll go put final touches on it and show you." Daniel's image was momentarily pixelated as he ran from the living room, which she recognized in the background. "Grandma! Mommy's on the phone."

"Thank you, Daniel," Sophie heard her mother's voice as he handed the phone off. There was a moment where the screen went black and she thought the phone disconnected, and then her mother was peering down at the screen with a grim expression on her face.

Sophie knew that look, and before she could say anything, she knew that she was in for an earful. "Sophie Diana, I realize you've been through quite an ordeal, but why must you drag our family's name in the mud like that? It's not bad enough that you're literally running around with wolves, but now you're blaming your sister for it? Hasn't our family suffered enough?"

Sophie's jaw dropped open, her mother's words like a punch to the gut. "What?" she squeaked in disbelief, for a moment uncertain she had heard her mother right.

"It's all over the news, they're having a field day with it! I'm just thankful they don't have a television set up in her room right now, or your poor sister would be beside herself at this slander!" Her mother rambled on emphatically, "Oh, to think of all days you could do this. Nikki shouldn't have to hear all this nonsense! She just woke up, the poor dear, and this is the kind of news she has to read?"

Sophie froze, her eyes widening as fear gripped her so hard and fast that her heartbeat suddenly thundered in her head. "Nikki's… awake?" she whispered in a terrified tone.

"Yes, she woke up this afternoon, and your father went to go be with her. Oh, Sophie," her mother implored her. "Why did you tell them those awful stories about your sister?"

"Because they're true, Mother! It's the truth! Nikki is the one who sent the Wolven after me. She blew up Alex's garage and nearly killed him! She had one of Lucas' own bodyguards shoot me with something in order to turn me into a Wolven so I would never turn back or be hunted down and killed!" Sophie was shaking, though she wasn't sure if it was from the fear or the anger she felt in that moment.

"Oh, Sophie, listen to yourself. How could Nikki even do all of those things? I think being a Wolven mixed up your memories. There's no way your sister would be capable of those things," her mother insisted. "Please, Sophie, just tell them you were confused and let's put this behind our family once and for all. For your sister's sake, and for our family."

"I c-can't believe you!" Sophie sputtered as her anger began to outweigh her fear. "*Put it behind me?* How am I supposed to do that, mother? I can't even be in the same room as my own son because of Nikki! I can't feel anything when I kiss Lucas, because she made me think he was cheating on me! She wanted to steal my family away from me, and she did!"

"Sophie, please, be reasonable. She's been through enough, and when you see her, you'll see for yourself. It's for the best we put this all behind us and—"

"See her? I don't ever want to see her again!" Sophie yelled, shaking so hard she could barely hold the phone. "I don't give a damn about our family's appearances! Nikki is going to pay for what she did to me, to Korban, Alex, Lucas, Danny, and to the Kensington family. Justice will be served, for all the people she's hurt or gotten killed for her own selfishness."

"Sophie—" Her mother began again, but by then her hands were shaking so hard she dropped the phone, and the call disconnected as the screen shattered.

Her heart pounded and echoed loudly in her ears. Nikki was awake. Her chest tightened, and she was barely aware of Lucas's surprised look as he walked back in at the sight of her, looming over her broken phone.

Her anger was still there, but the fear was quickly consuming her. Her sister was awake, and thanks to her parents, she knew Sophie was back to normal again. Would she try to send someone else to get rid of her? She was hyperventilating, and didn't resist as

Lucas rushed over to her and wrapped his arms around her. She closed her eyes and buried her face into his chest. Her wolf balked inside at this, his scent was all wrong and not what she wanted to calm her fears. Prey couldn't protect her, not like her Mate could.

It was that longing for Korban, as Lucas held her, that finally pushed her over the edge. She burst into a fit of sobs, completely inconsolable.

~*~

He really wished he hadn't turned around to see Sophie one last time that night. He just had to remember that he had packed Sophie's leather jacket in his bag after he'd already headed down to the guest house. All thanks to Mikael startling him back at the garage, he thought bitterly. He had to be there just in time to witness Lucas make a move on Sophie. He was too far away to see her reaction, but she hadn't exactly pulled away, or pushed him away. His mood had soured again, and he stormed back into the guest house and headed for the kitchen, looking for the liquor cabinet. He couldn't find a bottle of gin, and it would take at least a couple bottles to make him forget today anyway, so he abandoned the plan to drink his pain away and instead headed to his bedroom.

He threw open the door and tossed his backpack onto the bed. He paced the room and just seethed for a moment, until he stopped and realized in his fury he'd forgotten something important. He turned to the bed to apologize to Naraka for throwing his stuff at him, but found the bed empty, the sheets still wrinkled and smelling of the other werewolf.

"Naraka?" he asked softly, and searched the room, almost expecting to find him turned back into a wolf again.

The room was empty, and worse, the bathroom door was open and just as vacant as his bed. He sniffed the air tentatively, afraid that the trail would lead out of the room, but no, where it lead instead was even worse.

It went right to the window, which had been left open, and out towards the forest.

Naraka was gone.

11: MEDICATE

Sophie paced, but wanted nothing more than to run far away, and fast. She was being hunted, the unseen target on her back made her itch and growl. The pain had finally been scrubbed away with an unstoppable flood of tears, but now she felt so raw and hollow inside that her anger sought to fill up that emptiness. The one who attacked her and her Pack, and tore apart her family, was awake and once again a threat. "She's awake," she said out loud, her voice hoarse from crying so hard. "She's awake, Lucas."

Her husband nodded, a grim expression on his face. "She can't hurt you here, Sophie," he said softly, trying to reassure her.

"She can't hurt me now, but when she gets out of the hospital, she'll know where I am, and she'll know I turned back again. She could do something worse this time, Lucas. She could hurt Daniel, or... I don't know! I just don't know what to do." Sophie growled in frustration. "My mother doesn't believe that Nikki would do such a thing to me. She thinks I'm the one making it up to ruin the family's reputation. Like what I've gone through doesn't matter."

"It's probably just a lot for her to swallow, honey. It was a lot for me to understand, and I'm Nikki's brother-in-law. Despite all she's done, she's still their daughter, too," Lucas said, but him defending *her* right now was not what Sophie wanted to hear.

"Lucas," she began, but didn't get the chance to tear into him as the flicker of red and blue lights suddenly illuminated the walls.

Lucas headed to the front door as two figures emerged from the police car. Sophie went to the window and recognized them as they approached. "Sergeant McKinnon and Sergeant Ellyk… what are they doing here at this hour?"

The blue and red lights flickered brighter against the darkened sky, and illuminated the trees that dotted the yard, all the way down to the guest house. Sergeant McKinnon was donning his black cowboy hat, but was otherwise in uniform as they stepped up on to the porch. Lucas opened the door before they could even reach the doorknob. "Good evening, Officers. Is there something wrong?"

Both of the men looked grim. "We need to talk to you all. Is Korban here too?"

"He is, as far as we know. The three of them are staying in our guest house. Perhaps we should move this conversation there?" Lucas offered.

"Sure, this may be better news if I don't have to repeat it," Sergeant McKinnon said. "Lead the way."

Lucas ushered them down towards the guest house, following the winding path down dotted with softly glowing garden lights. Sophie followed alongside them, that feeling of dread only growing with every step. Sergeant McKinnon reached the door first and knocked on it. RJ opened the door, and looked surprised to see them all there. "Um, hello everyone. What's going on?"

"Hey RJ. We're here to have a chat. Korban's here right?" Sergeant Ellyk asked, his gaze already searching for him behind the teacher's shoulders.

"Yeah, of course. We just got back about an hour ago, and he went into his room. Come on in, I'll go get him," RJ said, and opened the door wider.

"Thanks," Sergeant McKinnon said, then stepped aside politely to allow Sophie to enter ahead of them.

She walked past them in silence but gave them a nod. Her eyes stung from crying so hard before, and no doubt by the worried looks that the two sergeants and RJ gave her she looked like a mess. She could care less. The forest-like scent greeted her before she saw him, and already she felt a little lighter. The guest house felt more like home than the main house, especially when they entered the living room and found Alex there with a bowl of buttery popcorn on his lap. "Hey you guys came just in time! We're just about to start movie night! The first one involves a group of pets fighting a plague of animal zombies. It's bound to be a cult classic."

"That sounds right up my alley, but I'm afraid we have to pause your movie for a little longer," Sergeant Ellyk said.

RJ joined them, and Sophie almost smiled at the sight of Korban, but the worried look in his eyes, and the sour scent of guilt that accompanied him gave her pause. She wondered before if something was wrong, and now she was certain of it. What was Korban hiding from them?

"There's no nice way to say this, so I'm just gonna give it to you straight. Commissioner DeRusso asked us to come here and make sure that you both were here, and accounted for, and still human. There's been a murder, and right now it seems the suspect is an animal. A Wolven, as far as we can tell," Sergeant McKinnon said grimly.

"Whatever it was tore apart and ate most of poor Judge Affleck, the poor, old bastard. He was a stickler for the rules, but he wasn't all that bad. All they found left of him were shreds of his hair and skin, and enough blood to know he didn't walk away from the attack," Sergeant Ellyk said. "His poor maid found what was left of him."

"Judge Affleck?" Sophie gasped, putting her hands to her mouth. "Oh no…"

"Unfortunately. Yeah, given the good feeling we left the court room in, even the Commissioner doubted either one of you had anything to do with it, but she had us come and check in person just in case. As long as you both have an alibi that checks out for about an hour ago, we'll be on our way," Sergeant McKinnon said and sighed, as clearly this was just the beginning of an even longer night after a long day.

"Sure, of course Officers. We'll help any way we can with your investigation," Lucas offered. "Though like I told you, we got back about an hour ago. We were all in the Mercedes together, and the GPS, dash cam, and my head of security Damion can verify that too. You can even check the security footage of the houses if you need to, but it'll just show you more of the same. We were all here, together."

That only spiked Korban's anxiety, the sharp scent increasing in the air and causing Sophie to glance his way.

"We'll definitely take that footage if we need it. Better to cover your ass than leave it hanging out," Sergeant Ellyk said. "Though I think the dash cam and GPS should cover you."

"We can go get that right now if you'd like," Lucas said.

"All right. As long as that checks out we'll be on our way. Sorry to be the bearers of such bad news," Sergeant McKinnon apologized.

"It is bad news, but I feel worse for the judge's family more than anything right now," Korban said softly.

"Yeah, no one deserves that kind of news," Sergeant McKinnon said, then tipped his hat as he turned to Lucas. "Mr. Bane, if you'd be so kind to lead us to the car, we'll get that tape, and be out of your hair for the evening. You folks have a good night, and be careful. It looks like someone out there isn't too happy with the possibility of change."

They headed out, though Sophie lingered behind while Lucas went over to the car they'd driven up in to assist the police. Korban's frown only deepened and he averted his gaze. The sour stench of guilt had returned and now Sophie eyed him suspiciously.

"Korban, what's wrong?" she asked, studying him carefully.

His amber eyes flashed with a moment of panic her way, but then he glanced away, his gloomy mood returning. "I don't want to talk about it right now," he said.

"Korban, you know if there's something wrong, you can always come tell me," Sophie said gently, reaching to touch his arm and comfort him.

He jerked away, his eyes narrowed in an effort to hide the pain that suddenly was there. "I said I don't want to talk about it. Not now. Maybe you should go and comfort your husband instead."

Sophie flinched at his words, and realized that he must have seen her and Lucas kissing earlier. When he glared at her, she saw through that thin mask of anger. Korban was lashing out because he was hurting, thinking she had chosen Lucas over him. In a sad, twisted way, she already had made her choice, and she hated herself for it.

She wasn't in the mood for his attitude. Not tonight. She was equally in pain, and scared, and now the only thread of hope she had for a better future seemed to have been severed for good with the death of the judge. "Fine. Maybe I will," she snarled back at him, then turned and stormed out of the guest house.

She didn't care if it was a childish retort, she had her own demons to deal with tonight. It only made her feel worse, especially when she saw her words had cut Korban deeper than she meant to.

When would she learn to never look back?

~*~

Korban watched her as she turned and left, his own words haunting him. He instantly regretted what he'd said the moment it left his lips, but he'd been so angry and hurt when he saw Lucas kiss her. It was the cherry on top of everything else that had gone wrong that day. He never should have taken out his anger on her, not after that devastating news. He almost yelled to her, especially when she glanced back, the pain reflected in her eyes before she looked away and hurried towards the main house.

Worse, he caught the worried looks that Alex and RJ were now giving him. After having so many eyes on him all day, he just wanted a moment to be alone and to think, because it was suddenly all too much. Before either one of his friends could say so much as his name, he rushed back into his bedroom and slammed the door. He locked it and began to pace in the room.

His guilt for hurting Sophie was only compounded by the fact that he'd gotten in over his head. He should have never left Naraka alone. Now the man was gone, most likely a rogue Wolven on the loose. Worst of all, someone innocent had lost their life. Judge Affleck, who was an important part of repairing a broken system and supported them so openly, had been torn apart. It wouldn't exactly inspire anyone else to join them in creating change for other infected people out there. If anything this would make people more like General Kane, who saw them as nothing more than monsters. Maybe that was the absolute worst thing, because Korban wondered, too, if maybe he was right.

Not that he would probably live much longer to regret all of this, because no doubt when Mikael returned and found out he'd lost Naraka and maybe blown their cover with a murder, the vampire would do more than just surprise him from the shadows.

If Mikael even showed up again.

He came to a halt as the realization dawned on him. The vampire had promised to reunite him with Ace, but hadn't delivered on his end. What if he'd been duped? What if the two of them had simply gotten what they needed from him, and left? If Ace had been alive all this time, surely he would have come and seen him by now.

Ace was his best friend, and after their last few intimate moments before the attack, maybe he wanted to be something more. Korban would never know, because Mikael murdered him, and Naraka stole his life away from him with a vicious bite. He'd been so blind to trust in two strangers who had hurt him, all the while keeping secrets from RJ, Alex, Tim, Andy, and Sophie; his real friends who actually gave a damn about him. He'd deceived his Pack.

He felt stupid for being so gullible, and the fresh hurt of their betrayal made his rage reach a boiling point. His anger reached a level of fury that he hadn't felt in a long time. Even as distant as the next full moon was, he felt his wolf stirring within him. Great, that was exactly what he needed, to lose control and be thrown back into quarantine again. His heartbeat thundered in his head. He was pretty sure no one got put into quarantine three times, and then got to be free again.

Maybe after all he'd done, he deserved to be locked away and forgotten. He wouldn't be constantly risking RJ's freedom and Alex's happiness with his foolish fantasies of changing the world. Sophie could salvage her marriage with Lucas and live happily ever after with her family. Maybe he belonged in quarantine, where Dr. Hoover could test him all he wanted, until maybe he'd serve some purpose and they found a cure. At least then his painful life would have some shell of a meaning.

Tears sprang from his eyes and streamed down his warm cheeks. He shouldn't be standing here, feeling sorry for himself, when he'd carelessly caused all of this. He could have prevented it if he'd just blown the whistle on Naraka the moment he'd met the man who was stuck as a Wolven. Now all hope he had was gone, and once more he was just alone with his pain.

He remembered the last time he'd felt this way. He'd snuck out of school during lunch to bring his mother the good news. He'd gotten full marks on his global studies exam, and couldn't wait to see her and tell her the good news. She had been the one who helped him study, even when her hands were so frail she could barely turn the page of his text book to quiz him. It was something so small, and maybe could have waited, but he felt this urge to go and tell her. He tossed out most of his lunch tray, but snuck out a cupcake for her, too. Chocolate was one of the few things she could keep down any more, and once she was done chastising him for skipping class, she'd most likely forgive him when she saw what he'd brought her.

He was just fifteen, so his ignorance back then had been excusable. He remembered keeping the hood of his sweatshirt up as he rode the bus over to the hospital, carefully cradling the cupcake in one hand, the folder with his test paper tucked under his arm.

He remembered smiling to the nurses as he walked out of the elevator and onto the oncology floor, headed towards his mother's room. They always smiled back and waved to him. One even teasingly referred to him as her boyfriend and asked if the cupcake was for her. "I'll bring you one next time," he had said and winked, which had them laughing and teasing the young nurse as he headed up the hall.

He walked into his mother's room. He remembered being glad that she had the room all to herself again. Her last roommate had a rasping, hideous sounding cough that still made his skin crawl when he thought about it. He moved the curtain and saw her there, lying in the hospital bed, surrounded by the colorful collection of pinwheels that he'd brought her. Amidst the pinwheels was a collection of get well cards and postcards from friends and even some family, along with a bouquet of bright yellow sunflowers in a blue vase that he didn't remember being there yesterday. Her cocoa-colored skin was so pale from months of being in here without the sun. A vibrant, floral-patterned scarf was tied around her head, the last thin wisps of her once thick, dark hair poking out near her ears. She was laying there, so still and silent. Too still. He went over, his heart in his throat, making it difficult to croak, "Mom?"

He vaguely heard the cupcake land on the ground with a wet slap as he rushed to her side, taking her cold hand in his. Her skin looked even paler and her hands thinner against the contrast of his healthy, tanned colored ones. She was often weak these days, but normally he could see her breathing. She was just too still, and though she looked peaceful, he wanted, no, needed her to open her eyes. "Mom? Mom!" Panic entered his voice, and he hit the nurse call button, giving his mother's arm a gentle but firm shake.

By now her eyes would have fluttered awake, and her breathy voice would tease him for worrying too much. But she didn't move, and she didn't wake up. She didn't die, either. The nurses came, and using CPR, they revived her heartbeat, and she was breathing again. But Maria Diego never opened her eyes again.

Pops came later that evening, after he'd closed the garage up, and took him home. He'd spent the entire day sitting there, alone, feeling stupid over the big and small mistakes he'd made that day. It was later that night when his mother finally slipped away forever in her sleep. She would never see the test paper he'd left alongside that vase of flowers, given to her by someone who didn't even know how much she disliked getting them.

Stupid, stupid Korban, he chastised himself as he began to pace again. His past was filled with endless moments of painful loneliness. This moment would just end up in the pile with the rest. He felt so empty inside, hollowed out from that encompassing anger leaving as quickly as it came. He scrubbed away the tears with the back of his hand. He should be used to this feeling by now.

Somehow, he always ended up alone.

"Korban," Mikael's soft voice snapped him out of it.

He whirled around, his already frantic heartbeat crashing to a halt for a moment. The vampire was perched on the window, giving him a blank look. "What the hell do you want now?" Korban demanded with a growl.

Mikael frowned, his eerie stillness making him even creepier when he gave a small, curious tilt of his head. "I announced meself this time, and ye still give me this kind of welcome. It's not very polite, Korban."

"Polite?" Korban scoffed. "Forgive me if I'm not in the mood to have company right now. It's been a bad day."

Mikael gave him an odd smile. "Are ye that worried that ye lost Naraka, and would upset me?"

Korban tensed, uncertain of how to read that sinister grin. He still couldn't get any sense of what the vampire was thinking. "That's just one crisis of many right now," Korban said softly.

Mikael nodded, and then gestured with his pale hand outside the window. "I suppose having the police show up at this hour does not bode well for anyone either. Rest assured me weary werewolf, Naraka is accounted fer, and he's alive and well."

Despite his earlier reservations, Korban felt a small sense of relief at the news. "He's all right? Where is he?"

"He's just outside here. Wee bit of a problem, though. Seems he got 'imself a bit riled up while we were out, and he's gone and turned himself all furry again," Mikael said, slightly amused.

Korban took a deep breath, and tried to swallow his heart back down into his chest again. He'd gotten upset, and jumped to the wrong conclusions. "Okay. I'll go out and help him turn back once the police leave," he agreed. Maybe by then his heart would calm back down and return to his ribcage. "Just… keep a close eye on him and I'll be out there when I can."

Mikael nodded. "Always," he said, and vanished with another flutter of the curtains.

He went into the bathroom and splashed his face with cold water, then drank a handful of it from his palm. He watched the water swirl down the drain and then gazed up at his reflection. He was a miserable sight, his yellow eyes bloodshot from crying. He grabbed a soft, terrycloth towel and patted down his face. Maybe everything else was falling apart, but he did at least have the ability to help out others. Maybe he did have a greater purpose, other than ending up under the microscope in a lab somewhere.

When he helped Naraka out this time, he could see where he had been all day and most likely it would all be another misunderstanding. He left his bedroom and found the guest house quiet. RJ and Alex were having a quiet conversation in their bedroom as he walked past. He peered outside the window that faced the driveway and watched the red, glowing tail lights of the patrol car vanish as it left the long driveway and headed for the road.

He still waited a little longer before going out there, just in case Tim and Andy returned, but also to calm himself back down again. He could still feel wolf pacing within him, alert and cautious. He remembered to grab the white Styrofoam container with the ribs he'd saved for Naraka. No matter what happened, he couldn't keep hiding these two in this guest house. He'd be willing to help them one last time, but then it was probably best to let bygones be bygones and send them on their way. He couldn't continue to keep secrets from his Pack.

He headed out the back door. The lake was a midnight blue that reflected the darkening night sky. The moon was a sliver of white that was shrinking with every passing day. Normally around this time his senses would be numbed, weakened as the wolf slumbered during the new moon. Yet he felt more invigorated than usual, and his senses remained sharp. He could hear the quiet forest song as he headed into the trees, and could smell Naraka's scent too. It was easy to track them down by this sense alone, but his vision remained clear as he stepped forward through the dark forest. He could see the pair as he approached them: the lean, muscular frame of the vampire as he stood alongside the massive black werewolf with the silver dog tags that glistened around his neck.

"I'm glad to see you're all right. You gave me quite a scare, vanishing like that, Naraka," Korban quietly scolded him as he walked up.

Naraka gave a soft whine in response.

Korban went to kneel down to help him transform back when he froze. There were dark, red dots speckled on the cluster of metal tags around his neck, and larger, dried splotches of something clumped to his onyx fur. His nostrils flared at the sight of it, and for a moment he hoped he was mistaken, but he knew that smell all too well, his dread swiftly returning as it dawned on him.

Blood.

12: AFFLICTION

Korban glared at Naraka, and then to Mikael. "What the hell is this? He's covered in blood!"

"Sorry I didn't have time to drop 'im off to the groomer's fer a bath," Mikael said in his lilting tone. "I prefer givin' 'im a bath when he's back on two legs meself..."

He was tired of the games, and exhausted from the stress of the day. His patience had run out hours ago. "Explain. Before I call my friends who just left and help them escort both your asses into quarantine," Korban growled.

"Whoa now, no need fer threats," Mikael's light tone left him, and his expression turned serious. "Yer awfully serious tonight. Must have been one helluva day."

"A man is dead. Torn apart by a Wolven. That's why the police were here just now. Which is kinda strange, given the circumstances." Korban thrust his finger to the sky at the sliver of moon in the clearing above them and snarled, "don't you think?"

"Aye, I'm sorry t' hear that, but ye don't have t' worry about Naraka. That's animal blood. Not human." Mikael emphasized by tapping the side of his nose with his finger. "I can smell the difference, even if ye can't. Vampires know blood."

Korban wasn't convinced. "So I'm supposed to take your word for it? How can I know that I can trust you when so far you haven't delivered on any of your promises?"

"If yer thinkin' I lied t' ye about Ace, yer mistaken. There's a lot more t' it than we can get into right now, but he's dealin' with it. He will meet up with ye the moment he can, but it's just not as simple fer him to just pop in fer a visit. Besides, can't ye do yer whole wolfy link thing and see fer yerself where he's been?" Mikael asked, emphasizing his words with by wiggling his fingers.

"How do I know you won't bail on me again after I've helped? I'm done with these games. You still haven't told me anything I can verify, and for all I know you are just leading me on. I've had it, I'm calling the authorities and they can sort all this out." Korban pulled out his phone and began to punch in the numbers.

Mikael moved then, so fast he was like a white blur in the night. He caught Korban's wrist, holding him firmly in place and plucking the phone from his open palm. "Hey!" Korban snapped in protest, but the vampire held the phone up as he moved again.

Korban thought for sure when he lifted his arm he was going to throw the cellphone into the nearby lake, but instead he began punching some numbers into the glowing screen. He held the phone up to his ear and Korban could hear someone pick up on the other end of the line. Before they could announce themselves, Mikael spoke. "It's Mikael. I need to speak to the Master. It's urgent."

Korban blinked and frowned.

"One moment," a deep, masculine voice said on the other end, his voice like a boom of thunder over the faint dance music in the background.

Korban stood there, his hands clenched into fists. "I'm not gonna just stand here and let you call for back up."

He took a step forward, but Naraka's ears flattened and he growled as he moved in front of Mikael, blocking his path. Well, this was a fine mess he'd managed to get himself in, and now Mikael held his only lifeline for help.

"Would ye just give it a minute? Damn, all ye werewolves are impatient as 'ell," Mikael grumbled.

Naraka gave a small huff and snorted at that in protest.

"I swear—" Korban began, but never finished.

"Mikael, what's wrong?" An all-too familiar voice came on the other line, one that Korban was sure he would never hear again.

"Yer old friend here believes yer not really gonna be showin' up to our meetin' tomorrow night. Kinda upsettin,' I'm startin' to feel he's a wee bit racist when it comes t' us vampires. Doesn't believe that m' word is bond," Mikael said.

"Put him on the line, I'll talk to him," he said.

Mikael held out the phone to him, and Korban snatched it back. He wasn't sure he could move, and his knees felt weak. He wasn't sure what to think or who to trust in that moment. He brought the phone to his ear, and his voice trembled when he asked, "Ace?"

"Korban." His voice sounded even more authentic with the phone up to his ear. "I thought you of all people would be more open-minded when it came to our kind."

He isn't sure what to say to that at first. It was still difficult to believe that his best friend was on the other end of the line. He opened his mouth several times, uncertain of how to respond, until he finally blurted out, "I thought you were dead you ass."

His laughter was unexpected, but still the same melodious sound that he remembered and his heart swelled. "I am dead Korban, I just didn't stay down." He paused, then added in a softer, more serious tone, "I'm sorry I couldn't find you and tell you sooner. Things have become complicated ever since I woke up in the morgue. That is a very long story for another time. Right now, what I need you to do is trust me when I say that Mikael and Naraka aren't going to hurt you. I know that's a lot to swallow, given our past with the two of them. I know your instincts are probably telling you the same thing as when I first met them. They're definitely dangerous, but they can be trusted, as long as you don't cross them."

Korban glanced at the two men and sighed. "Yeah, I got that feeling from when I helped Naraka. Just… forgive me if I'm still having a hard time believing all of this. Even after everything I've seen it's just… it's so good to hear your voice again. I just hope that I'm not dreaming all this."

"I know. The feeling is the same for me. I cannot talk for long, but we will discuss more soon in person. Man to man, er, vampire to werewolf," Ace chuckled, "what a pair we will make together again. Put Mikael on the line again. We will talk more soon, I promise. Oh. And Korban?"

"Yes?" he asked, his voice still tight with emotion.

"I know this may be difficult, but please do not tell RJ and Alex about this right now. I've already put you in enough risk by talking to you. I swear to you I will explain it all when I see you. But trust me when I say it's better they don't know anything right now when it comes to me. Promise me."

There was an urgency in Ace's tone that made Korban swallow the lump in his throat and he nodded as he said, "I promise."

He reluctantly handed the phone to Mikael, who stepped away quickly and moved out of earshot as Ace spoke to him. Korban kept him in his sights, and saw the vampire tense, then nod as his expression turned grim. "Understood," he said, then pressed a few more buttons on the phone before he handed it back over to Korban. "He wants to tell you one more thing."

He thought for sure that he'd hung up, but he took the phone back, eager to hear his best friend's voice once again. "I'm back again," he said.

"I need Mikael's help, so I'm asking him to come back. I need to ask a favor of you, Korban. I need you to help Naraka out a little longer. He's a bit unstable, and right now it's too risky for him to be in Syracuse. I know this is asking a lot, and I'm sorry I have to be so vague right now. I just need you to trust me like you did back then, and I will fill you in on as much as I can when I see you again."

"When will I be able to see you for myself?" Korban asked, desperately clinging on to that tiny, frayed thread of hope.

Ace was quiet for a moment, and Korban checked to make sure the call hadn't dropped. "I can arrange a brief meeting tomorrow night. I'll have Mikael return as soon as he can after sunset to bring you here. I won't be able to tell you everything, but I can at least catch you up on what we've been dealing with on our end."

It wasn't exactly what he wanted to hear, but it was enough for now. "Sounds good," he said, before adding softly, "See you soon."

"See you tomorrow, Korban," Ace said and hung up.

~*~

Sophie lay awake in bed, unable to sleep. Every time she closed her eyes, she saw Nikki's cruel smile. She could remember her taunts and threats the last night she saw her sister and felt cold. She burrowed under the blankets, cocooning herself into them, but the icy feeling remained inside. She was afraid to fall asleep, because the nightmares that lurked on the corners of her mind were already bad enough. If she was able to keep her eyes closed long enough to fall asleep, she feared what awaited in her dreams.

Her mind was too busy pulling apart the terrible news of the day. The judge being murdered, and the ripples that were left behind with the loss of his life. She felt bad for his family, and bad for her own family. She'd hoped to put the pieces back together, but it was like gluing together a broken vase that had been shattered too hard, pieces were missing and the sharp ones were not fitting the way they used to. She thought of Lucas and his kiss, how she didn't feel anything behind it, except for guilt when she saw the pain it had caused Korban. Her own words echoed in her mind, and the pain reached a terrible crescendo in her chest when the random, fleeting thought entered her mind. *I never even got to see Danny's drawing.*

Enough was enough. She didn't want to fall asleep, and she didn't want to lay there obsessing all night about things she couldn't change. There was at least one right she could make wrong that night.

She untangled herself from the blankets and got dressed, hanging up her old nightgown and pulling on a shirt and jeans. She slipped on some sandals and headed out of the bedroom and went outside. The night was dark, the thin sliver of moonlight above guided her path as she walked down towards the guest house. A cool breeze brushed past her as she walked up the smaller porch and she paused when a strangely familiar scent caught her attention. The scent of wolf that echoed the warm summer forest she knew all too well, but there was another wolf's scent that she didn't recognize.

She frowned when she realized that the trail didn't go into the house, but out and around from it. Curious, she followed the scent, which grew stronger the closer she got to the forest. *Was Korban in danger? How had another werewolf found them out here?*

She quickened her steps, but kept them as quiet as possible as she followed her nose. It wasn't too far into the forest when she heard Korban's voice, along with a man's voice that she didn't recognize. "Do ye finally believe me?" the man asked with an Irish accent. "That not all vampires are bogarts out t' get ye?"

"Bogarts?" Korban repeated.

"Aye, whatdya call 'em? Boogymen," the Irish man corrected.

Vampires? Boogymen? Sophie wondered. *What the hell is going on?*

"I'm not sure you make a good case for that, when every single time I've run into you, you pop up out of nowhere, like a cheap jump scare." Korban said, his voice sounding amused.

Korban didn't seem to be threatened. From what she had overheard, it sounded like he knew this man with the Irish accent.

She moved past a few trees and finally saw them gathered there in a small clearing. She couldn't help but gasp out loud when she realized there were three of them standing there. She hadn't smelled anything but the two wolves, and assumed the Irish man that had been talking was also a werewolf. She hadn't expected the pale man in a long, dark coat standing alongside a massive, black Wolven.

Korban and the Wolven both turned and flinched at the sound she made, but the pale man only smirked. "Seems it's not only a vampire thing, eh, lassie?"

Sophie glanced suspiciously at the three of them. "Who are you, and what exactly is going on here, Korban?"

Korban's eyes widened when she emerged from the trees, and she could see it clearly in his expression that he felt guilty when he blushed, then glanced down. "Yer Sophie Bane. I was wonderin' if we'd get the pleasure of meetin' ye, lass. My name's Mikael, and this fur ball is me Mate, Naraka. He's here t' get a wee bit o' help from Korban 'ere to turn back human again."

So Korban had been hiding something from her after all. She hadn't been sure what to suspect before, but this was a genuine surprise. She couldn't even be mad about it, when she was the one who asked for space, but she folded her arms over her chest and gave Korban a concerned look anyway. "How long has this been going on?"

"Just a couple days," Korban said, though his amber eyes met hers when he added, "I would have told you sooner, but I wanted to respect your request for space. Even if Lucas is not."

She took the small dig in stride, even if it hurt a little. "Okay. I appreciate you listening to me, but something like this is kind of important. Considering that both of us could end up in quarantine if we aren't careful. You could have… never mind. I don't want to argue right now. This has been a long enough day as it is." She kept her watchful gaze on the two strangers. "I'm here now, so why don't you help him transform back, and then we can talk more about it?"

Korban nodded, then turned to Naraka. "Let's get you back on two legs again. Ready?"

The Wolven gave a small nod of his head, his ears perking up.

Korban took a deep breath, and then stepped closer to the

massive wolf. He gently cupped the sides of the beast's face, and tilted his head up to lock eyes with Naraka. In the dim moonlight, both of their amber eyes seemed to glow with a preternatural power. Sophie watched on in amazement as the great, black wolf began to recede, and in his place knelt a toned, handsome, naked man with shaggy black hair and a beard. He stumbled forward, and Korban caught him as Mikael swept over, removing his trench coat and gently lowering it over the man's trembling shoulders. The whole thing took a matter of a couple minutes, and went even faster than when she'd watched Korban help out Spike, Hati, and Blaze return to their human forms. He was getting better at this, and she felt a surge of pride. "Th-thank you," Naraka said, his voice weak but relieved.

Korban nodded, gazing him over in concern. There was an understanding reflected in his eyes that hadn't been there before, and Sophie wondered what had been revealed to him. "When you're ready we'll head back to the guest house so you can rest, okay?"

"Okay," Naraka panted softly in response.

Sophie could sympathize with the pain of the transformation, and that extra twist of agony that came with being forced to succumb to the wolf outside of the full moon. She moved a little closer to the three of them as Naraka caught his breath, and Mikael helped put his long coat on him so he could provide some semblance of privacy to the man. Korban assisted Mikael with getting Naraka up on two feet again, and Naraka winced as he leaned into Mikael's arms. She wished there was something she could do to help, but right now it seemed like they had it under control.

It took them several minutes to get back to the guest house, Naraka's steps slow and stiff. She walked alongside Korban and kept the pair of strangers in her sight. They didn't seem to be a threat, but she was being cautious, and despite their argument earlier and the distance she'd asked for between them, she couldn't help but remain protective over Korban. It didn't help that she couldn't get a sense of the vampire at all. Perhaps because he didn't have a pulse, or any living tissue, he didn't release the pheromones or whatever it was that she could sense from other lycanthropes and humans.

When they got to the edge of the trees near the back porch Korban turned to his two new friends. "I'll make sure RJ and Alex are in their room, and we'll get you inside."

Korban jogged towards the door, and Sophie followed after him, leaving the pair alone for a moment. As Korban reached for the doorknob, she touched his arm. He paused and glanced to her. "Are you sure that this is a good idea?" she asked him in a whisper.

"I can't just leave him out there, you see how weak he is," Korban stated, a stubborn pout curving his mouth.

"I do see. But I also see you have a knack for putting your life on the line for strangers," Sophie said with hushed urgency. "It's incredible what you can do to help others. I won't deny that. But I'm worried about you. If you help the wrong people, Korban… I just don't want to see you get hurt."

Korban's gaze fell at that as he turned away towards the door. "I don't mind getting hurt. Right now it's kind of my default setting."

She flinched and looked down. "I'm sorry. I came over here to apologize for what I said before. I can't sleep, and I keep thinking about it. I was wrong to throw that back in your face like that. It means so much that you have respected my wishes, and gave me some space to sort out this whole complicated mess. But I miss you. I know that isn't fair, because I'm the one who asked for this," Sophie said softly, keeping her hand on his arm as she spoke.

He took a deep breath, and looked to her with guilt in his golden eyes. "I'm sorry, too, for snapping like I did. I shouldn't have been keeping secrets from you. Once we get Naraka settled in, we should talk more about this if you want to."

She wasn't going to sleep tonight anyway, so she nodded and gave him a small smile. "I'd like that very much."

He flashed her a ghost of his usual smile, but it was an improvement. He checked in quickly, and emerged again from the guest house seconds later. He nodded and waved to Mikael and Naraka to signal the coast was clear. In a dizzying burst of speed, Mikael moved across the yard. He set Naraka back down on his feet as he appeared on the porch. Sophie lunged in front of Korban protectively, and a short growl escaped her throat before she could stop herself. The pale-haired vampire smiled and gave her a nod of respect. "Nice reflexes, lassie."

"Please call me Sophie," she insisted. "It sounds like you're calling me a heroic collie when you say it like that."

Naraka weakly chuckled, an amused smirk curving his mouth. "She's not wrong."

Mikael smiled at that, flashing his fangs, but the amusement that shone in his eyes made her relax a little. "As ye wish, Sophie," he said with a playful wink, and then looked to Naraka. "I have t' go back t' the city. Try t' do better today, fur ball, and I'll be back tomorrow night."

Naraka nodded, and then the vampire leaned in, whispering something in a language that Sophie didn't understand, but the intimate tone of it caused her cheeks to warm. Naraka's smile widened at whatever it was, and he pressed a soft kiss against Mikael's smooth, pale cheek, before the vampire guided his arm to Korban for support, and then vanished.

Startled, Sophie glanced around, but Mikael was gone. "He's fast, isn't he?" Korban said, shifting Naraka closer to help lead him inside the guest house.

She gave a nod in response, and followed them closely as they headed inside. Silently they crept up the hall and in to Korban's room. He accompanied Naraka over to the bed, and Sophie went over and pulled the unmade blankets back for him. Once Naraka had settled into the pillows his eyelids seemed to grow heavy, and by the time Sophie pulled the comforter back over him, he went still and his breathing leveled off, slow and heavy.

Wordlessly she took Korban's hand, and they left the room together, turning off the lights and closing the door behind them. She guided him through the dark hall and in to the living room, and the two of them sat down together on the couch. For a moment neither one of them spoke, until Sophie smiled to him and shook her head. She hadn't let go of his hand, and instead gave it a tender squeeze. "Is this going to become a hobby of yours, smuggling in strangers?"

He smiled at that, a soft, short laugh escaping him. "Think it's okay if I keep him?"

"I don't know," Sophie murmured in amusement. "Here I was feeling special that I was the only one you'd rescued, but then you turn out to be some sort of super hero, saving all the wayward Wolven of the world."

His eyes and smile brightened, and he seemed a lot more like his old self again. She missed seeing that spark in him and she felt guilty for snuffing it out.

She reached out and gently touched the side of his face as she rested her cheek against the back of the couch. "I've missed that look. I guess both of us haven't had much reason to smile tonight," she said softly.

His expression sobered at her words, and he asked, "What else happened?"

She inhaled sharply, and lowered her hand to her lap as she curled into herself. "Nikki's awake," she confessed, just above a whisper.

Korban's eyes widened and the color left his cheeks. "She is?"

Sophie nodded, drawing her knees up to her chest. "My mother told me earlier tonight. Before we found out about the judge."

A quiet fell around them, and her vision swam with unshed tears. It was just too much at once.

He moved to put his arms around her, but stopped. "Is it all right if I hug you?" he asked tentatively, uncertain if it would be welcome or not.

Even after their argument, and how she'd isolated him, he was there to comfort her, careful not to cross the lines she had drawn. Warm, wet tears escaped and trailed down her cheeks as she nodded, and then leaned in to him as his strong arms surrounded her. "I hate this," she confessed, the words pouring from her as she wrapped her arms around him in turn. "I hate feeling so powerless and afraid. I hate not knowing what she's capable of doing next. I hate that she tore me from my family. I hate that it feels wrong to try and put it all back together again. I hate her even more for tearing me away from you. I hate pushing you away, when every part of me wants to be with you."

His shirt was damp with her tears, and her body trembled against him as she clung to him. His one arm was wrapped around her still, but his other hand gently stroked her hair. For a moment neither one of them spoke, and then he said softly, "I hate that I have to pretend that I'm okay, when I'm not. I hate that I'm the reason you're conflicted. I hate that I want you, even though I should do the right thing, and let you go. I hate myself, because I can't stop loving you."

She pulled away so she could look him in the eye, her hands gently cupping his face. "I'm sorry," she said softly to him, becoming choked up and unable to finish.

"You don't need to apologize," Korban said, and bowed his head down, leaning into her touch as he closed his eyes to try and mask his pain.

"Stop. Look at me. Let me finish," she demanded, and his eyes flashed open and locked with hers. "I'm sorry I've hurt you. After all you've done for me, and sacrificed for my sake, you've never asked for anything in return but my happiness. I don't deserve it, not if it hurts you. You're my best friend, Korban. You're the other half of my heart. My Mate."

She swallowed down the lump that threatened to choke off her words and soldiered on, her hands clasping together around his large, warm hands. "I've been trying to play my old role, and return to my old way of life, but I can't do it. I can't force myself to live like this, and pretend everything is like it was before. I don't want Lucas, and my wolf wants to tear him apart. When he kissed me earlier, it felt like a violation. It was all wrong. It's never, ever felt that way with you. Even before I was attacked, you've always had a way of making me smile, laugh, and feel safe."

He listened, his breathing shallow, eyes wide with surprised wonder. She held up his hands, interlocked her fingers with his own, their palms fitting smoothly together. "So I know that no matter what happens, whatever hell we face, I'll be ready for it as long as you're by my side."

"Sophie, I—" Korban began, as she leaned forward. He turned his head and glanced away as her lips brushed the corner of his mouth.

She hadn't expected him to move, and pulled back, confusion and a small amount of disappointment coursing through her.

"You know I'll always support you, and stand by you. I love you so much it hurts. But my heart can only take so much," Korban said softly, his voice strained with emotion. "I want to kiss you so badly right now. I want to be with you. But I want to make sure that if I give in to these feelings again, it's for good. I don't want this to be a moment of weakness, because we're both scared and stressed out. It's been a long and emotional day. And I haven't even gotten a chance to tell you half of it."

She recalled how agitated he'd seemed earlier in the day. It had been easy to brush off as a reaction to all the prying questions from the council, but she'd noticed even after the optimistic ending of the forum he'd seemed not like himself. "Tell me," she said.

He hesitated for a moment, but then took a deep breath. "Where do I even begin? You've met Mikael and Naraka, so there's that."

"How did they find you?" Sophie asked.

"Heh," Korban shook his head as he made the sound, "Good question. They've been kind of cryptic about who told them about my ability to help, but you saw it yourself out there. Naraka loses control and shifts into a Wolven, even without the full moon."

She nodded and tensed as the thought clicked, and she gave him a concerned look as she whispered, "Do you think he's the one who killed Judge Affleck?"

"I don't know, but I don't think so," Korban confessed. "He had blood on his fur, but Mikael claims it was from a deer. The things I saw when I helped him transform back though… his mind is very disjointed. I saw a lot of blood, and felt a lot of pain. I saw men die in horrible ways, but it was all happening so fast. I didn't see the judge. Naraka doesn't linger on the memories like Davey did. I think he is trying to forget them, but they haunt him. There's also the memory that I saw, that we share." He shivered a little and paused before continuing, "Naraka is the one who attacked me."

She blinked, and stared at Korban in disbelief. "So you've been helping these strangers, even though that man in there is the reason you're infected?"

He nodded. "I know it sounds crazy, and maybe it is, but I just couldn't leave him stuck like that. I can't explain it, because I also don't fully trust them either. But my gut feeling is to help Naraka, despite what he did to me. I've sensed his regret for what he did, and it felt genuine. And after what I saw tonight, I'm sure my instincts about him were right. He's as much of a victim in this as I was, from the things I saw in his broken memories, and he needs my help. I don't think anyone else can help him. I can't just leave him stuck like that, especially knowing what that felt like. If I can, I want to help him, like I helped you, and maybe I can help others who are stuck as Wolven too. At least then, all of this hasn't been for nothing."

She didn't trust either one of them, and she felt a surge of protectiveness towards Korban. She didn't want those two men taking advantage of his kind heart, especially since she felt guilty for being the one who broke it. She did trust Korban's judgement, which is why she didn't go into the other room and chase Naraka away, but she was going to make sure that he wasn't left alone when it came to those two. She shook her head and gave him a small smile as she leaned back against the couch. "So this is going to be a hobby of yours after all. Rescuing strays like me and Naraka?"

Korban smiled and squeezed her hand. "I've been making the right choices so far. I haven't heard too many complaints."

She sighed and returned the squeeze. "I'm worried you're trusting the wrong people, Korban. I don't want you to get hurt."

"I've been careful, I promise… and there's one more thing," Korban said. "Ace is back. He didn't die the night we were attacked. Well, he did, but he came back as a vampire. I'm supposed to go see him tomorrow."

She gave him an incredulous look. "What? That's almost too good to be true Korban. Did they tell you that?"

"Yeah, and I almost didn't believe it myself, until I talked to him earlier tonight. Right before you showed up. It's still difficult to believe, and I have so many questions, but I'm hoping to get some answers tomorrow," Korban said.

"When are you heading out to meet him?" Sophie asked.

"Mikael is supposed to return after sunset tomorrow and we are going to head to Syracuse together."

Her frown deepened. It still seemed way too convenient for her that his dead best friend rose from the grave, out of the blue, as these two strangers who needed Korban's help showed up. Either way her mind was made up. "I'm going with you. There's no way I'm letting you go alone."

Korban looked uncertain at first, but then nodded. "I'd like for you to meet him. He asked me not to tell RJ or Alex, probably because they'd want to see him, and right now he's living under the radar. I'm not sure what to expect myself. Mikael is the only vampire I've met before and, well, he kind of spooks me."

Sophie agreed with a silent nod, and then went quiet. The silence stretched between them for several moments, and all the while she kept her hands in his. The events of the day and night were finally taking their toll. Her eyelids were beginning to get heavy now that she sat alongside him. "Do you mind if I stay here with you tonight?" she asked softly.

Korban shook his head, and seemed relieved. "I'd like that. If you want I can pull out the couch for you, and I can sleep on the couch over there," he offered, but she shook her head.

"I just want to stay here," she whispered. "Next to you."

"Okay," Korban said.

He rested against the back of the couch, and she snuggled

alongside him, resting her head against his shoulder. He relaxed and draped his arm around her. This close to him, she breathed in and his scent enveloped her, and the fear that had gripped her earlier began to loosen its hold. She was safe here, and she felt better knowing that she was there to protect him, too. Sophie was able to close her eyes without the images of her sister haunting her, and she finally drifted off to sleep.

13: ASYLUM

"Korban. Korban!" Alex quietly hissed into his ear early the next morning. "Wake up!"

Squinting in the darkness, his vision still hazy from sleep, Korban grumbled softly. "Alex?" Korban asked in a disbelieving whisper. He'd never heard the happy-go-lucky mechanic ever use that tone of voice– one of extreme worry and fear. It sounded foreign to him. "What is it? What's wrong?"

Alex's heart was thundering in his ear, and he reeked of anxiety and sweat. His brown eyes were wide, and though he was a shade paler than usual, his face was flushed red as he wildly waved his hands and gestured up towards the hall with a finger. He sputtered incomprehensibly for a moment, then managed to blurt out, "There's a stalker in the house!"

For a moment, Korban blinked sleepily. It was too early for one of Alex's pranks, and he needed a caffeine nudge since he hadn't yet doused his taste buds awake with coffee. "A… what?"

Alex waved his good hand, gesturing towards the hall. "There's a man in your bed! I went to go check on you when I got up, and found some naked creep instead!"

"You like what you see?" Naraka's voice purred seductively from the hallway, and Korban saw the werewolf leaning against the wall, a sultry smile curving his mouth. Naraka winked to Alex and ran a hand down the open flap of his long coat, revealing his toned chest.

Alex squeaked in response and ducked behind the couch, hiding behind Korban. *Well, the wolf was out of the bag now,* he thought. Korban sighed, trying not to wake Sophie, who by some miracle, or through her pure exhaustion, remained sleeping by his side. "It's okay, Alex... he's a friend."

Alex frowned and glanced suspiciously over the edge of the couch from Korban to the stranger in the hall. Naraka's smile widened. "I promise this big, bad wolf won't eat you. Not in a way that you'd mind anyway."

"Okay, well," Korban cleared his throat and interrupted, "Alex, this is Naraka, and Naraka, this is Alex."

"A pleasure to meet you," Naraka's amused expression remained as he spoke.

"Likewise?" Alex said, sounding uncertain, and whispered to Korban, "Who is he? What is he doing sleeping in your bed wearing only a trench coat?"

"He's, well, I—" Korban began.

"Mmm," Sophie murmured as she stretched alongside him before sitting up, "that's a story we should discuss over breakfast, I think."

"Good idea," Naraka agreed, eagerly rubbing his hands together. "I could eat. I'm ravenous this morning."

Alex gave him a nervous smile and Korban reached behind the couch to give him a comforting pat on the shoulder as he said, "I'll go put on some coffee."

~*~

Alex calmed down after Korban explained what he knew over breakfast. Though it was difficult to find Naraka as frightening after the man devoured two stacks of pancakes with such enthusiasm that he didn't notice a smudge of syrup on the tip of his nose. Sophie wondered how long it had been since he'd eaten a home-cooked meal. She was mixing up a new batch to fry up when RJ awoke, and Korban made introductions and filled him in over a hot stack of pancakes and a fresh cup of coffee.

Once everyone had been caught up, they all sat together at the kitchen table, and a quiet fell between them. RJ frowned worriedly and tapped his fingers thoughtfully on the table. He didn't have to say a word to relay his disapproval. It was all in the look he gave, and the way he took a deep breath before finally speaking, "So what's the plan from here?"

RJ's question threw them both off. Korban seemed to be prepared for a lecture, and admittedly, Sophie anticipated something along those lines too. The teacher looked to them, straightening his shoulders as he folded his arms over his chest. "I'd really like to know what your plan is from here on out, because while I understand you're trying to help others, Korban, there's only so much that the law is willing to overlook," RJ added, his expression grim. "I don't want to see you end up in quarantine again, and I certainly don't want to end up in prison. So it would be nice to know there was a plan, at least, so I could decide whether or not it's a good idea to get on board with this or not."

Korban looked down sheepishly. Naraka spoke up first, to everyone's surprise since he'd been rather quiet during breakfast. Of course, he'd mostly been stuffing himself with pancakes at the time. "I don't plan on sticking around long enough to become a burden for anyone here. I just needed Korban's help to transform back, and that's done. He let me stay here because I needed some time to recover, but I'll be on my way soon. In fact, I am headed out tonight. So you won't have to worry much longer about me."

RJ's frown remained, and he seemed unconvinced. Sophie spoke up then, as she gently poked the last remaining bites of her pancake with her fork. "There's something else I need to tell you both," she said softly. "I know there is a lot going on right now but… you should know, too. Nikki woke up yesterday."

"Really?" Alex piped up, the color draining from his face for the second time that morning. "Does she know we're here?"

"I don't know," Sophie confessed, and managed to not wince when Alex delicately touched the neon cast on his arm. "I don't even know what her state of mind is right now, but I figured it was better to let you know to be on guard in case she did decide to say something, now that she's conscious again."

"When it rains…" RJ sighed and trailed off, shaking his head. "I suppose then it's good we have an extra sharp set of eyes and ears around in the meantime, at least."

"All the better to hear you with, my dear," Naraka cracked.

"Great, just what I needed, another smart ass," RJ turned to Korban. "I have to take Alex to get his arm checked this morning. If we're lucky he'll be out of his cast in no time. As long as the three of you lay low here, I don't think there will be any problems. Just… please be careful. All of you." He even spared a glance to Alex, who brightened a little.

Korban nodded. "We will be, I promise RJ."

"And next time, please… let us know before you start sneaking strange men into your bedroom," Alex half-joked. "You nearly gave me a heart attack."

Naraka gave him a small salute. "You don't need to worry, I don't kill civilians."

Before Alex could formulate a witty comeback, Korban stood up and gathered up their empty plates. "Let's go wash these dishes, then get you dressed and ready for the day. It can't be too comfortable wearing just a coat."

Naraka smiled coolly at that and nodded. "I'm comfortable, but if it makes you all uncomfortable… I'll go clean up. Do you mind if I borrow your razor?"

"Everything here is on loan, so just clean up after yourself, and it's yours," Korban said with a shrug, and the other werewolf headed back up the hall.

Sophie watched as Naraka left the room, his movements still slow and stiff, though the look in his eyes had brightened, and he was stronger than when he'd made his way to the table earlier that morning. As Korban scooped up her plates, she stood up as well. "I'll give you a hand with those."

His dazzling smile returned and she was glad. "Thanks. I'll wash, you dry?"

She nodded and they began to clean everyone's plates, followed by the remaining dishes and pans. She realized that Lucas would soon wake up, and start looking for her. She felt a fresh pang of guilt, but what else could she have done? She was thankful that her mind had been at ease, and she'd actually gotten sleep last night, despite everything that had been revealed. She didn't feel anxious or afraid as she finished drying alongside Korban. For a moment it felt like the time when they were alone in the forest, stuck together in the small camper. As if reading her thoughts, Korban turned to her and said, "Just like old times, huh?"

"I remember a lot less space in that kitchen, but otherwise, yes," Sophie said as she looked his way.

"I'm glad that you stayed," Korban said as he rinsed off the plate in his hand.

"Me too," Sophie agreed, taking the plate and drying it before setting it in the drying rack.

Silence fell between them, and RJ cleared his throat and prodded Alex with his finger. "Maybe we should go, and get ready for your appointment," he suggested.

Alex frowned in disappointment but nodded, and the two of them headed out of the kitchen. The quiet stretched around them, but as they emptied the sink she glanced his way. "I wish I could stay longer," Sophie confessed. "I will be by later, but I can come back any time you need me to, if you need help with Naraka or really anything…" She trailed off, uncertain of what she could do, but wanting to offer to help anyway.

"Thanks. You're welcome here anytime… I mean, I'm sure the landlady won't mind," Korban joked with a wink.

She gave a small laugh. "I hope not."

His eyes widened and he held up his hands. "Wait, before you go back, I have something for you. Just wait here a minute."

She blinked in surprise at that, and he turned and headed from the kitchen. He returned moments later with the backpack he'd picked up from the garage. "I found something of yours that got left behind, and I figured you may want it."

Sophie's brow furrowed in confusion for a brief moment, and then he unzipped the bag and she smiled as the scent of leather was unveiled. Korban brightened when he glanced to her and handed her the jacket. "Thank you," Sophie said as she accepted it, and pulled it close to her chest.

She could still smell Valkyrie and her pack's scent embedded in the leather, and breathed in deeply as she cradled it in her arms. She'd earned this jacket, and the respect of their wolf pack. The reminder of what she'd gone through in order to earn it was painful, but here Korban stood with her now, a smile on his face. They were safe, and they'd literally made it through the woods. They would make it through whatever happened next, too.

She pulled on the jacket, which she knew didn't look nearly as cool as it did over the pajamas she wore now, but didn't care. It was comforting to have it back. "I'll be sure to wear it tonight with something more appropriate for our outing," she said.

"Well… I already can't wait until I see you later," Korban reached for her hand, and squeezed it.

She returned the squeeze and held his hand for a little longer before reluctantly pulling away. "Right back at ya. I'd better go, before Lucas comes looking for me and discovers our new friend."

Korban bobbed his head in agreement, but then reached for her hand and captured it. "I mean it. You can come to me anytime you need to, Sophie. I don't want you to feel like you can't do that. I can respect your need for space, even if you're here… if you need me, I'm here for you. No matter what happens."

His touch was warm and welcome and she gave his hand a firm but gentle squeeze. She wanted to say so much to him, but took a deep breath to steady herself, then leaned in to give him a soft kiss on the cheek. "See you later then," she said, and headed out of the guest house before it became impossible for her to do so.

Even as she headed up the walk way, her bare feet cold against the smooth rocks on the path, she felt warm with the leather jacket around her, and the taste of Korban's skin still lingering on her lips.

~*~

Korban watched her go, the soft touch of her lips against his cheek lingering as she went. Damn it all, he couldn't hold back his feelings, especially since all of his control was being used to keep him from running after her. "Aww, I wish she didn't have to go… but it's kinda nice to watch her leave, right?" Naraka teased him from the bedroom doorway, which he leaned against.

"Don't you even disrespect her," Korban growled softly and gave him a warning look. "I don't care if you flirt with me, but Sophie is off limits, understood?"

"Message received, loud and clear," Naraka said, and gave him a small salute.

His hair was damp and faintly smelled of shampoo, and his long, dark strands fell in soft waves down the sides of his face. He looked years younger than she'd originally thought now that his beard was trimmed down, and complimented the angles along his jaw. His eyes seemed brighter than before, and he flashed a dazzling smile. He'd chosen a simple outfit, and wore a pair of Korban's gray sweatpants with a white t-shirt. His toned body fit rather nicely in the plain clothes. Korban sighed. It was difficult to stay angry at the charismatic werewolf. "You know, you clean up pretty nice for a stalker."

"Why thank you, Korban," Naraka purred. "I thought this may be a better look to lay low in. A little less suspected terrorist, and a little more retiring superhero."

"That's one way to put it," Korban said, then gave Naraka a more serious look. "Are you feeling all right today?"

"If you're worried about me going all wolf-y, I think you can breathe easy today. I'm feeling pretty good," Naraka stated.

Korban studied him closely for a moment. After the snippets he had seen of Naraka's past last night during their connection, it was no wonder the werewolf was unstable. He still hadn't made much sense of the jumbled memories himself. So much blood, and pain, that it had disturbed him to the core. He probably wouldn't have slept much last night if Sophie hadn't come over to chase away the nightmares. "Are you sure? Because everything… that I saw last night–" Korban began.

"I don't want to talk about it," Naraka insisted and turned his gaze away. "Not right now. I'm good. I'm calm. Let's keep it that way."

"Fair enough," Korban agreed, and swallowed anxiously. He wondered whose bodies had been left torn and bloody on the ground. He didn't recognize any of the men he'd seen in Naraka's memories, but that wasn't a comforting thought. "You know… if you do need to talk about anything, though, I'm willing to listen."

Naraka tensed for a moment, then nodded, his shoulders sagging as he relaxed. "I appreciate it. I may just go lay down for a nap. I feel better but I also still feel exhausted. Maybe because I usually run on a more nocturnal schedule. Hanging out with a vampire usually results in staying up nights and sleeping during the day."

"Yeah, I imagine that would make things challenging," Korban agreed as they headed into his room. He was going to make sure the window was closed this time just in case, and get some things to get ready for the day while Naraka rested. "So is it true that vampires can't be out in the sun?" Korban asked, curious.

"They don't burst into flames, but the sun makes them really uncomfortable. They get nasty sunburns pretty fast if they don't take precautions, and the sun is too bright for their eyes. Mikael says he can see during the night like it is day, but I think the sun is too intense for them to see anything at all." Naraka went over to the bed and sat down on it.

"And they drink blood," Korban swallowed and touched his own throat subconsciously.

"Yeah, they do. Human is preferable, though in times of crisis, animal blood will suffice. Though Mikael says it's not as easy as they make it out to be in some of those movies. The whole idea of a vegetarian vampire is insulting to the animals. It's not just blood they are consuming, but life and energy. Very different from simply drinking down a V8," Naraka said, then tilted his head curiously to Korban. "Why so many vampire questions this morning?"

"Well… I kind of want to be prepared for when I see Ace tonight," Korban confessed softly, careful not to say it too loud. "We were best friends for so long that… I remember him as he was, and I just want to be ready if… if he's changed."

"Ah, I see," Naraka paused for a moment, and gazed his way. "I knew Mikael before he turned into a vampire."

"Really?" Korban asked, and Naraka nodded.

"He was the only one who showed me kindness as a human, and after he turned vampire, he remained the same. He may not show it to others, but he's still the same man who snuck me water bottles and half his lunch when… well, that's a long story for another time. Being a vampire didn't change him. Though… time, and experiences do change us."

That was definitely the truth. Korban frowned thoughtfully and scratched the back of his head.

Naraka sighed. "Ace is a good person too. I'm sure he was when you were friends, because I see it in you, too. I didn't know him as a human, and I'm hoping that he isn't that changed when it comes to you. I guess we'll see tonight, either way."

"Yeah, you got that right," Korban said. "If you need anything at all during the day, I'll be around."

Naraka settled down on the bed and offered Korban a grateful smile. "Thank you again, Korban. For all of this."

"You're welcome. Happy dreams," he said, then double checking that the window was closed, he left the room.

He had a lot to think about, but as he settled down on the couch he could still smell Sophie on the fabric and he gave a soft sigh.

Maybe Naraka had the right idea about getting a nap. Especially if they were going to have a long day and an even longer night ahead of them. He closed his eyes and listened as Alex and RJ quietly headed out of the guest house, keeping an ear out in case Naraka needed anything, but soft snoring was all that emerged from his room. He dozed off before he heard the car leave the driveway.

14: ALPINE

As they pulled up to The Alpine, Korban wondered just how seedy the Underground really was. A gentleman's club was the last place he imagined they would be headed to that night, but this was the address that Mikael had given to them. The outside of the building was inconspicuous, a plain brick building with a red awning and some simple branding adorning both sides of the building with the logo. There was one entrance opened to the public marked with a small, red awning with the club's logo adorned on it with white lettering. It was a quieter area of the city at this hour during the week, though he imagined it would be pretty busy closer to the weekend.

Sophie raised an eyebrow and glanced to Naraka and Mikael from the rearview mirror. "This is the place?" she asked.

Naraka grinned and enthusiastically nodded, and Mikael sighed and rolled his eyes, a very human gesture. "This is it."

She parked their car around the corner and Mikael and Naraka escorted them over to the door, which was propped open, and a large, powerfully built man stood guard. He was handsome and had the physique of a bodybuilder, wearing a simple but snug fitting black t-shirt and pants to emphasize his powerful frame. The bouncer gave them a serious look when they approached. "IDs?" he said gruffly, glancing down at them through dark shades.

"Aye, I got yer ID right here boyo," Mikael grinned, flashing his fangs and giving the bouncer an intense look.

The hulking man stood there for a long, tense moment just staring him down, then burst out laughing, patting Mikael then Naraka on the arm. "Come on in, the boss has been expecting you."

Korban felt a new flock of butterflies stir in his stomach as they stepped into the dark bar. The counter behind the bar was glowing with a gentle blue neon light that illuminated the bottles and the bartender who was slicing lemons and limes to prepare for the night. She didn't look up as she set about her work, her red hair piled up into a loose but stylish bun on her head. Her pale skin glowed with a blue haze from the bar behind her. There were some tall, round tables set around the empty stage.

The bouncer guided them to the back, which was guarded by two other large men wearing shades who merely nodded to them as they were led past. Sophie moved closer to him when they caught the scent of the bodyguards as they went past. Werewolves.

The short hall was lined with rooms without doors, shimmering purple curtains were pulled in front of each entryway and lined the walls, fluttering as they walked past. They walked past these private rooms and around the corner, and finally came to a dark door. The bouncer knocked twice, and Ace's voice came from the other side, "Come in."

Even as the door opened it was difficult to believe, until he finally laid eyes on him. Ace stood behind a sleek, modern desk with a laptop folded shut in front of him, wearing a sharp-looking but simple business suit. The suit, which definitely hadn't been his style before, somehow gave him the illusion of being older, more mature than his former grunge-rock style had been. He had the same youthful face, and like a photograph his age was forever frozen in time.

He was paler than Korban remembered, no doubt from five years of avoiding the sun. His blond hair was combed back, the pale tendrils falling loosely down his cheek, the same length as the last time he'd seen him. It was his eyes that startled Korban and made him freeze in his tracks. The irises were no longer the sky blue from his memory, but hauntingly blood red, and seemed to glow in the dim light of the club. When he smiled and flashed his fangs, there was no denying that his best friend had become a vampire.

"Korban," Ace said, his voice filled with relief and excitement as they entered the room.

Ace stepped from behind the desk and within a heartbeat he reached Korban with open arms. Korban welcomed the embrace, hugging him fiercely in return. He clung to him for a long moment, until Ace stepped back and they both looked one another over, Ace's hands resting on his shoulders. "Damn I've missed you… and this must be the famous Sophie Bane," Ace said, taking Sophie's hand and shaking it.

"It's nice to meet you too," Sophie said with a smile. "Korban's told me so much about you."

"Hopefully not too much," Ace laughed, the same melodious sound Korban remembered. "I love your jacket, it's definitely not what I would have expected, but you make it work. Of course, not just anyone wears the Valhalla Knight cut."

Sophie blushed, and asked, "You know the Valhalla Knights?"

Ace nodded. "They keep to themselves, but follow the rules and lay low. They sometimes touch base when they are passing through the area. It's nice to have some powerful allies who travel around the country. Please, have a seat. Make yourselves comfortable."

Korban and Sophie settled into the chairs in front of the desk, while Naraka and Mikael sat down on a small leather loveseat that was along the wall nearby. Ace returned to his seat behind the desk. "I still can't believe it's really you," Korban breathed the words in wonder, then blurted the question that had been bothering him the most. "Why have you been avoiding me all this time?"

Ace's smile faded and he gave him an apologetic look. "It wasn't just you I was avoiding, Korban. I was hiding from everyone for a long time."

"What happened to you? You know if we knew you were… that you'd survived, somehow, we'd figure a way to get you a sponsor and get you home," Korban insisted.

Ace only shook his head. "I wish we had more time to get into everything that happened, but the long-story-short version is that I woke up in the morgue, and didn't stick around long enough to find out why I wasn't dead," Ace paused, and glanced over to Mikael and Naraka, before he continued. "I wasn't the only one who woke up a vampire that night, and for a while we looked out for one another. It eventually grew into what we now call the Underground. I find the name a little… derivative, maybe too historic, but it works. Not everyone who was turned can get a sponsor, so we help one another out. We take care of those who need help, we stay under the radar, and we take care of any threats that rise up from the shadows."

"Threats?" Korban repeated.

"There's more than just vampires and werewolves running around this city, and unfortunately not everyone who turns wants follow our rules," Ace steepled his fingers. "When our kind get out of control, we have to do what we can to stop them. Some of us can't be stopped by humans. That's where we come in."

"So… you're helping some, and hunting down others?" Korban asked, swallowing anxiously and resisting a glance towards Naraka.

"It's not easy, but we take care of our own," Ace responded. "By the time I found out that you survived your attack as well, and were out of quarantine because RJ was sponsoring you… I didn't want to risk either of you getting in trouble with the law. It was better if you believed I was dead, than for me to ruin your life."

Korban scoffed and shook his head. "You were afraid of ruining my life? I've been doing that all on my own for years now."

Ace smirked. "Maybe so, but you're still standing. We've always been survivors," he stated matter-of-factly, before unfolding his fingers and giving him a serious look, "which is why I need you to trust me now. We are handling this mess, which you've gotten a little too close to for my comfort. I have my best people looking into Judge Affleck's murder, which is why I need you to lay low and stay out of it."

Korban frowned in confusion. "I wasn't planning on doing anything—"

"Your record in meddling with such matters proves otherwise, my friend. I need you to trust we are handling this, and for you and Sophie to keep staying out of Syracuse until all of this blows over," Ace stated, drumming his fingers lightly on the edge of his desk. "I need you to promise me that you will stay out of it, Korban. I want your word."

Korban knew that there had to be something more about this whole matter, the urgency in Ace's insistence alone gave him reason to wonder what his friend knew that he didn't. "Can you at least tell us what is going on?" he asked.

Ace hesitated for a moment, but then nodded. "I suppose that's fair. We don't know who murdered the judge, but we do know it was brutal. Whoever it was didn't leave much of him behind. Which I suppose isn't too strange, given the possibility of it being a Wolven attack. From what my source at the morgue said, all they found was a lot of blood and bits of skin. Even a Wolven, or Revenants, typically leave behind some bones."

"Revenants?" Sophie asked before Korban could.

"Vampires who have completely lost their humanity, kind of like Wolven to werewolves," Ace grimly explained. "They're vicious, bloodthirsty, and fast. They sometimes devour their victims, too."

Korban felt his stomach churn a little, and he had to swallow before he spoke, "That's awful."

"We're possibly dealing with a very large Wolven, or perhaps a small group of Revenants or Wolven, though we haven't found enough to conclude what is responsible yet. Which is why the further away from the city you two are, the better. The human investigators are leaning towards the Wolven theory, which paints a target on both of you. If you aren't around, then you're safe." Ace explained.

Korban nodded, though this whole thing didn't sit well with him. "Okay, I understand why we need to lay low, and we can keep doing that. But isn't there something we can do to help?" he asked, not wanting to abandon his friend now.

"Actually, there is," Ace said, glancing over to Naraka and Mikael, before his red eyes locked with Korban again. "I need your help to keep Naraka hidden, and away from the city while we investigate. Given his… unpredictable nature, it may be best he stays with you for now, since you are able to help him stay on two legs. If you keep him hidden away, Mikael can stay here with me, and focus on finding who is responsible for the murder."

Korban exchanged a glance with Naraka, who flashed him a sheepish grin, before he looked to Sophie. She stared intently at Ace, studying him cautiously. He wondered what was going through her mind with all of this, but didn't have to think too long about it. "We can do that, if it means you'll be helping the police solve this case," she said, leaning forward in her chair. "The sooner justice is served, the better off we all will be."

Ace's expression went to a careful, neutral mask. "We don't usually get the police involved. It gets messy when humans intervene with these sorts of things."

Sophie pursed her lips. "If the police don't find a resolution to this case, won't that make us look worse in their eyes? I mean… it's one thing to bring vigilante justice from the shadows, but it's entirely another if the case ends up going cold because we don't get them involved. If it isn't solved, then the conspiracy theories will only continue to run rampant and cause more panic, don't you think?"

"Perhaps," Ace said cryptically, then tapped his fingers again along his desk. "What do you propose then, Sophie?"

She frowned thoughtfully for a moment as she considered his question, and then brightened as the answer came to her. "You can take care of whoever is responsible for this, and just leave enough evidence behind to throw the criminal investigators a bone. Let them put the pieces together. They don't need the entire story of who stopped the murderer. They just want enough to solve the case and close it for good."

"That may be possible," Mikael said, "if we are careful, we could leave just enough behind to make sure that investigators get the justice they are looking for."

"If we are able to, I don't see why we couldn't try. But if there is a risk to leave evidence behind that may point them towards the Underground, then it's not something I am willing to take a chance on," Ace said. "But we will see what we can do to help them resolve the case on their side. Especially since you are willing to help us out. It means a lot to me that you are able to provide Naraka and Korban sanctuary. I'd feel better knowing that there were no loose ends involved with this case myself, especially since it's a bit too close for my comfort to you." He gave a meaningful look to Korban that made his face feel warm. "I hate to cut this meeting short, but unfortunately there is a lot of work to be done, and it's better you head back before it's too late."

"Wait… that's all for now? After so long?" Korban asked, unable to hide his disappointment.

"Time waits for no one, I'm afraid, and curfew is coming up for good little werewolves who are following the law," Ace said, and gave Korban an apologetic smile. "Believe me, I wish we had more time, too. We will get together soon to catch up some more, when there isn't some murderous infected running loose. Though before you go, I'd like to speak to you privately, Korban."

Sophie tensed alongside him, and gave him a nervous glance, but he nodded to her. "It's okay. I'd like that."

"Come with us, for a moment, Sophie. I'll buy you a drink

before we go," Naraka offered.

Sophie seemed reluctant still, but then stood up and gave a serious look to Ace, then Korban. "I'll be close by if you need me, Korban," she reassured him, and then headed out of the office with Mikael and Naraka in tow.

There was a stretch of silence after the door clicked shut. Ace smiled and leaned back in his chair, just glancing Korban over with a longing look. "It really is good to see you again, Korban," he finally spoke after a long moment.

"It's good to see you too. I didn't think I'd ever see you again," Korban said. "Dammit, Ace. You could have at least told me."

Ace's smile faded. "I wish I could have, Korban. It was too dangerous to get you involved. It still is. I know the past five years have been tough for you, too. But the things I got involved in… this whole world… it's so much bigger and darker than you can even imagine."

"No, I get it. Especially after what we went through over this summer. I know what kind of darkness is out there. I've seen it first hand, what some of us are capable of," Korban insisted.

"David Bailey was a monster, and I wish I could have been there to end him myself." Ace's eyes narrowed, a distant look in his vibrant, red eyes. "What he did to you and the others… I've seen it before," he said. "The vampire who ran the Underground Court before me manipulated others using his alpha ability too. I've seen that power abused by him. The things he did, and made people do, were vile. Inhuman. Which is why I tried to keep you, Alex, and RJ as far away from it as I could. The Underground is a sanctuary for some, but it's hell for others. A kind of purgatory, where we can exist, but can't be seen. We have each other's support, but we can't reveal ourselves in the public eye. The whole town is buzzing with what you and Sophie were doing for all of us. It's nice to have at least some representation that has the public's attention, in a good way. I'm worried with the backlash of the judge's murder what may happen to all that good will, just as much as you are. Things are challenging enough as it is, without the masses grabbing their torches and pitchforks. The worst part is, whoever is responsible for killing the judge is just one of many things we deal with every day. I didn't want you to get involved, and I still don't. Which is why I need you to promise me you'll stay away."

Korban furrowed his brow and frowned. "I just got you back, and I know how dangerous our world is, but—"

"No, Korban. Please," Ace said, reaching over the desk, and putting a pale, cold hand over his. "I'm begging you. Please stay out of this. I will tell you everything, all of it, another time. But right now, for your safety and mine as well, I need you to trust me. Lay low and stay far away from this. We will take care of it. Then I can tell you the entire story. But I can't… I can't lose you, Korban. I've never seen anything like what this creature has done. The judge was the first human victim, but there have been others. My people. The ones that won't be marked missing, because they already are, technically."

A chill ran down Korban's back. "Wait, so there have been other murders?"

Ace nodded, his mouth a thin, worried line. "We suspect what it could be, but the truth of the matter is that I've never seen something this capable of such destruction. So please, if only for my sanity, I need you to stay out of Syracuse for the time being. Not only to keep Naraka off the radar, and not only because the police suspect a Wolven, but because I don't want anything to happen to you."

Korban met the strange, crimson eyes of his old friend. They were a different color, but they held the same genuine concern that he knew Ace felt. A lump formed in his throat. He wanted to protest, but he couldn't come up with a strong enough argument. He knew he was in over his head as it was, being delegated to babysitting another wayward werewolf, but he supposed at least this way he would be helping Ace out. He sighed heavily, and nodded. "Okay. I'll keep Naraka safe, and try my best to keep him, and myself, out of trouble. I can do that for you."

"Thank you, Korban," he said, giving him a relieved smile.

"But the moment you need help from us, don't hesitate to ask. You know I got your back. Always." Korban put his hand over Ace's cool one, giving it a firm but gentle squeeze.

"Always," Ace gave him a delicate smile, one that hid away his fangs and was more like the one he used to know.

Korban stood up and Ace gracefully followed suit, walking around his desk. He reached out and put a hand on Korban's arm. His hand was around room temperature, but it felt like ice against his feverish skin. "We'll get together soon and catch up some more. I promise," Ace vowed, his voice hushed, almost a whisper.

Korban nodded, but before he reached for the door, he met Ace's eyes again. "Before we were attacked... when you kissed me…" he began, but trailed off, uncertain of what to say.

Ace's smile wavered, and he spoke quickly, "I maybe was a bit hasty back then. I'm sorry. I should have asked how you felt first before making a move like that. You're my best friend. I didn't want to lose you, because I wanted something more, and you didn't."

Korban shook his head. "It's okay, you don't need to apologize. I was taken off guard, and I… I'm still not sure how I feel about it. I never really had time to think about it, with the attack happening so fast, and then believing that you had died. It was painful enough to lose my best friend. I didn't have time to consider what could have been, because you were gone." Korban paused, a small tremor going through his body and another lump forming in his throat. "I've started to think recently that everyone I love leaves me, but then you came back..."

As he trailed off, Ace slid his hand down his arm. "I really am sorry that I couldn't tell you sooner, Korban. I know things would be different between you and if I had at least come back to you before you met her, then I wouldn't have to wonder."

Korban frowned in confusion. "Wonder what?"

Ace patted his arm, and took a step back. "If perhaps I could be your Mate."

Korban blinked at that, and tilted his head. "Sophie's trying to work things out with Lucas," he protested.

"Okay. And who is she out with tonight?" Ace gave him a sly smirk. "I saw how protective she is of you. It's just a matter of time. She'd be foolish to let you slip away, Korban. Sure, the tabloids are going to have a field day when it happens, but at least it will give me new pictures of you to put in my scrap book."

"Your *what?*" Korban blurted.

Ace winked playfully and then gave another hearty chuckle before opening the office door. "I've missed yanking your chain, Korban. I'm kidding. Let's go have a drink on me, before you go."

"We're not talking O positive, I hope," Korban cracked.

Ace rolled his eyes and ushered him out, back towards the bar. "We do serve a killer Bloody Mary that you must try some time," he joked as they headed over to the bar to rejoin the others.

"Really? That's the best you got?" Korban groaned.

"Hey, give me a break. I'm a little rusty. It's been five years since I've had someone much to quip with," Ace said as they approached the soft neon glow of the bar.

Sophie glanced to them as she sipped her mint mojito, and seemed in good spirits too, her cheeks tinged a pretty pink color and the laughter still in her eyes as Naraka finished a story that had her amused. His best friend still knew him better than he knew himself apparently, because even now his stomach felt like butterflies had infested it with her lingering smile.

Ace nodded to the redheaded bartender and leaned in. "One gin and tonic for my old friend, Vicky. Use the 1911, please."

"You got it, boss." Vicky bobbed her head and flashed her fangs, then set to work.

"Wow, breaking out the good stuff. Now I feel really special," Korban said as he slid onto the stool next to Sophie.

"If you're the boss and you don't pull out all the stops for your friends, then what is the point of it all?" Ace said with a shrug.

They finished the evening with another round of drinks before finally parting ways. Naraka wrapped his arms around Mikael, and the two whispered to one another for a few moments. As they said their farewells, Ace touched Korban's arm again. "Be careful out there. I'll be in touch to let you know what we find," Ace said to him, then gazed to Sophie. "It's nice to meet you, Sophie."

"Likewise, Ace," she said.

"At least I know where to find you," Korban said with a bittersweet smile.

"This is just one of my many haunts. I'll show you my other places sometime soon," Ace promised, then pulled him into a brief but firm hug.

"Make sure ye keep a closer eye on me Mate this time," Mikael half-teased, though his expression was difficult to read. "Naraka behave yerself or else."

"Or else what?" Naraka taunted, and gave him a quick kiss that left his question unanswered.

They piled into the car and Sophie glanced to Korban as Naraka buckled up in the backseat. "You all right?" she asked softly.

"I'll be okay. My best friend is back, and I'm here with you," Korban said, glancing back to their charge in the backset. "Are you going to be okay back there, Naraka?"

He flashed a thumbs up as he gazed back to the entrance of the Alpine. "Let's go before I change my mind and drag Mikael back with us. I don't like being away from him for long."

"Hopefully they'll get this thing sorted out soon, for all of our sakes," Korban said.

Sophie drove them towards the lake house, the city yielding to the surrounding suburbs hidden away in green hills and valleys that surrounded Syracuse. He glanced at the city skyline as it shrank in the rearview mirror, before vanishing as the highway swerved deeper into the hills. The sky began to turn orange, pink, and lavender in the twilight as the highway stretched out before them and took them further from home, and closer to their temporary sanctuary.

The thin sliver of moon was visible by the time they arrived to the lake house, a dim glow compared to the hundreds of twinkling stars that glittered above them. The quiet sound of the lake lapping the shore nearby was peaceful, but Sophie couldn't shake the eerie feeling that remained since they'd left the Alpine. Korban and Naraka were quiet as she parked the car. She had so much she wanted to ask, and more questions than answers, but the three of them had remained fairly silent during the ride back. She turned off the vehicle and turned to Korban. "So now what are we going to do?" she asked, wondering out loud what the three of them had to be thinking.

"Naraka can stay with us at the guest house, and I guess we wait," Korban said, unfastening his seatbelt and then rubbing his temples, looking suddenly exhausted. "We can't tell RJ or Alex yet about Ace. It's difficult enough as it is to keep myself out of this mess, I really don't want to get them involved too."

Sophie nodded. "I'm not going to tell Lucas about any of this either. We need to come up with a good reason for you to be lurking around here so you don't have to worry too much if Lucas, Damion, or one of our house staff happens to spot you."

"You mean the fact that I'm visiting my cousin, Korban?" Naraka grinned and leaned forward into the front of the car. "Or maybe I can be his new boyfriend, and we can really confuse your husband."

Korban smirked and shook his head. "As tempting as it is, I don't think that would be nice."

"So you're saying I tempt you?" Naraka teased.

"Let's keep it out of the family, dear cousin. I don't think Mikael would appreciate word getting back to him that you and I were dating. I may be able to heal fast, but I still have a strong aversion to pain," Korban stated. "Did you want us to call you by your name, or an alias?"

"Nathan works. Nate, for short," Naraka answered without hesitating, as though he'd come prepared with this nickname before.

"All right then, Korban's cousin Nate," Sophie said, giving him a steady look. "Before we go in there I want to know why you were covered in blood last night."

"Well," Naraka took a deep breath as he began, blushing and looking down, "I wish I could answer that. From what Mikael said, I must have run into a deer, since that's the kind of blood that was on me. I don't remember too much… you know how it is. Mostly flashes of pictures, and memories of different sensations."

"We really need to work on your control," Korban said softly. "I don't want anyone else to get hurt, or for you to infect anyone else."

Naraka kept his gaze focused down on the floor, a dark and serious expression taking over his playful demeanor, and making him suddenly appear much older, and more tired, than he let on. "I don't want to infect anyone else, either. As far as I know, you are the only one I bit, Korban. I don't attack civilians. I am still not sure why I felt threatened by you that night in the alley. You were just a kid. I have no excuse for what I did to you. You don't owe me anything, in fact it's the other way around. I shouldn't be a burden to you."

Sophie gently reached for his hand and placed her hand over his. "You're not a burden, Naraka. I understand how it feels to be completely helpless, and to lose control without warning. I was lucky, though, that Korban was able to help me. I'm sure he can help you, too. I still struggle, every day it's a battle for control over my wolf. But you don't have to do this alone. We're here to help you, for as long as you need us to."

Naraka looked her in the eye then, and for a second she couldn't breathe. His eyes held intense orange and gold flecks in them, similar but different than Korban's gentle amber eyes. "Okay," he said in a resigned tone. "So, where do we start?"

"I need to help see what happened last night when you were Wolven, to make sure you're completely in the clear," Korban stated. "I think if we know for sure that you were eating venison and not anyone else, that will at least put all our minds at ease."

Naraka nodded. "All right. But not in here. I don't want to be responsible if I lose control and ruin this nice car."

Korban nodded, and glanced to Sophie. "Do you have a little more time to join us?"

She scanned the driveway quickly and then bobbed her head in affirmation. Lucas' car wasn't there, so he must have been at work still, or maybe he went to visit Daniel. Her heart ached at the thought of it, but she didn't have time to linger too long on her own pain. "We can use the safe room in case he loses control. It's just down in the basement of the main house."

"No! Please," Naraka blurted quickly, the air spiking with the scent of his anxiety. "I don't like basements."

"Okay," Sophie said and reassured him by touching his arm. She didn't want to stress him out. "We don't need to go there. Let's go to the clearing, where we were last night." It wasn't the most ideal place, but it would be far enough away to at least warn the others if Naraka did lose control again.

Naraka nodded, and she felt the tension melt away from him as he relaxed. "Okay."

The three of them headed past the guest house and into the forest. The trees were becoming more vibrant and colorful with every passing day, though it was still warm as summer lingered around them. Familiar, quiet sounds of the nocturnal life waking around them began to fill the air. They arrived to the clearing within moments, without incident. Naraka paused in the center and gazed up at the tiny sliver of moon. "It's kinda crazy how much I used to take for granted… not too many moonlit walks these days. At least, not on two legs." He joked, and glanced over to Korban. "I suppose we should get this over with. Clear my name by showing you the truth. I just… hope that you won't see me as even more of a monster when you see all the other things that I have done."

Korban didn't like the sound of that, but he reached out and put a comforting hand on Naraka's arm. "I'll see what I can see, and then we will talk about it, okay?"

Naraka took a deep breath, as though to steel himself, and then looked up into Korban's eyes. "Let's do it then."

Korban braced himself for the familiar sensation to take hold once more, and it didn't take long. He felt oddly weightless and grounded at the same time, as though part of him had left his body.

He felt the night air, and saw the sky, the moon a little brighter and more visible than last night's sky. He felt the rush of his dark paws under him, the freedom of being out of the other wolf's den. No… it was his room he was fleeing from. He could still smell his own scent in the air, in Naraka's nostrils as the black wolf raced into the dark forest. The trees became thicker the more he ran, slowing him down. He soon found a clearing, further from the one they stood in now. There were only animal scents here, and decaying leaves that crunched under his paws. He stopped and listened, a small echo of that crunching sound nearby. His nostrils flared and Naraka– and Korban– caught the smell at the same time. Fresh meat.

Sure enough, a small herd of deer were frozen, their ears pointed up and eyes round. They thought by remaining still they wouldn't be seen, but it was too late. Naraka's stomach was empty, and it had been awhile since he had a decent hunt.

He lunged out of the clearing noisily, and the deer scattered, trying to flee from him as fast as they could. It was too late for one young buck, who gave a good, spirited chase through the trees, but Naraka pounced for him, kicking off a tree for a surge of speed, and then his teeth tore into the back of the young buck's throat. It was a quick, efficient kill. The spray of blood from the slashed jugular vein gushed out and soaked into his dark fur. The buck was dead before he hit the ground, and Naraka tore into him, ravenous, his razor-sharp teeth ripping easily into his prey's flesh. Korban felt his own mouth water, even if his human stomach churned at the thought of raw meat.

It seemed like Naraka was innocent after all. Korban felt a bit of relief and tried to turn away from the scene before him, stepping away from the Naraka in the memory. But suddenly the dark wolf gazed upon him, his golden eyes brighter against his crimson-splattered muzzle. *You must see it all,* the dark wolf said, in a calm, deep tone that was similar to Naraka's voice, but the soft growl of the words was different, more primal somehow.

Korban froze, just like the deer had before its final moments.

I will show you what they did. Why this one continues to run without the moon and protect the one on two legs. The dark wolf's eyes seemed to glow even brighter as his voice boomed in Korban's head, and before he knew it he felt himself falling again, deeper into Naraka's mind.

15: IMMUNIZATION

The darkness was infinite. Korban squeezed his eyes shut, but the murky shadows behind his eyelids frightened him more than the endless void. It was strange to fall like this into another mind, without any idea of where he was headed into the other werewolf's memories. There wasn't even a breeze to signal the direction of his descent. He continued drifting downward, until suddenly cold, calculated voices began to echo around him, adding to his unease.

"Patient Zero remains indifferent to stimuli… will try a new strategy tomorrow to see if prior results can be duplicated."

"Patient Zero unaffected by today's tests. Will resume injections of adrenaline during the next experiment."

"Patient Zero continues to plead for help, but is otherwise unresponsive to our questions. Will continue research into a catalyst to trigger the transformation outside of the full moon cycle."

"Help… me…" Naraka's voice echoed softly in the void.

A blinding light flooded Korban's vision, and he squinted and covered his eyes with his arm. When he lowered it again, he was sitting on the back of a bus as it sloshed and bounced down a rainy road. His other senses returned, the thundering roar of the engine startling him along with the sudden change of scenery, and the scent of perspiration and anticipation filled the air. Korban glanced around, for a moment confused, and uncertain as to where this bus was headed. Figures began to appear in the seats, shadowy and faint at first. Six young men who wore identical tan-colored uniforms came into focus, like spirits materializing from thin air. While their clothing was the same, their appearances couldn't be more different; each man a unique combination of build and skin tone.

During one of the bounces, Korban was lurched down, and suddenly he was sitting on the bus. Feeling nauseous, he steadied himself by extending his arms to the back of the seat in front of him, realizing his arms were thinner, and his hands larger and different.

He glanced to the window and out at the rain, his reflection a younger but familiar echo of the young Naraka. It was odd seeing his eyes a deep brown instead of the intense sun yellow that they were now. He could sense the anxiety building inside of him, the nausea from the bumpy ride, and a growing tinge of excitement. He tried to open his mouth to speak, but found himself powerless to move his lips. Though he couldn't move or speak, the voices around him came in, mid-conversation, like a radio station finally settling into its signal. "Like you'd even know what it's like to be with a woman, Maverick," Naraka's voice spilled from him. Naraka's voice seemed different, younger and brighter, as if something was missing in the man now.

The other boys on the bus burst out with laughter, except for the large, rotund young man who sat diagonally from him, whose ears and face went red. Naraka reached over and pat him playfully on his round shoulder. "Hey, you know I'm just kidding, Marvin. Lighten up a little, big guy."

Maverick glared at him for a moment when called by his real name, but then a grin broke through and he swatted him back. "I know my way around a woman better than you. Ass."

"Hey if you two keep flirting like that we're gonna have to ask you to get a room," a dark-skinned boy sitting in front of Naraka teased. "Just because there's no more 'don't ask', don't mean ya'll gotta be telling, okay?"

"You're just jealous, Walter, that Maverick's with me, and that means I claimed the man here with the best pair of tits," Naraka shot back.

"I'll give you tits!"

Maverick launched himself over to him, wrestling him under his large arm and pressing him into his chest, giving him a rough but playful noogie which only caused them to all burst into a rowdier fit of laughter.

"All right, now boys, settle down." A familiar, authoritative voice came from the front of the bus.

They scrambled back to their seats without hesitation, sitting up at attention. To Korban's surprise, a younger General Kane stood there, the same calculating and cold look in his eyes. His hair was darker and his face not as lined as Korban recalled, but his military jacket was pressed and pristine, even if it was missing some of the many medals that he'd worn during the panel. "We're almost to the training grounds. You've been selected by me for this advanced training. Don't make me doubt my choices now."

"Yes, Sir," Naraka and the other boys chorused, and he settled back against his seat and his gaze returned to the rain-speckled window once more.

Korban's mind was spinning with questions. He remembered the General's attitude in the court room, and wondered if he'd find out more than just about Naraka's past in this deep memory.

The scene shifted, as if ripples of water in the window moved time along. Korban found himself running out in a field, the rain long gone and greatly missed as Naraka kept a steady pace. The sun was unbearably hot and burning down on them from a vibrant, blue sky, but Naraka was in good spirits despite the intense heat. The young men were leaner now, stronger, and faster, moving as a group around the training field, executing the maneuvers like seasoned veterans. Even Maverick's bulky form was more defined, his body transformed into solid muscle. They slowed down their sprint after hearing the shrill blow of a whistle, Naraka in the lead.

"Bring it in boys. Water break before drills," General Kane's voice boomed from a crackling loud speaker.

As they gathered around the water cooler and doused their parched throats, Maverick smirked to him. "You guys got anyone coming for graduation?"

Naraka shook his head. "Nah. Got no one to come."

"Me either." Maverick said, glancing to the others who also shrugged. "You, Tommy?"

"Nope," a red-faced boy with buzzed, blond hair said while flicking his glasses with a few drops of water and attempting to wipe them off with a dry corner of his shirt. "Even if they wanted to, I don't think my foster family could afford the trip."

"Unless one of the sisters from the orphanage shows up, I'm on my own," Walter added.

"Screw it man, forget the nuns. I say we go party it up after the ceremony. Drink until we forget our own names, and that we're all a bunch of orphans stuck together," Naraka said. "We've come this far, so fuck it. Let's celebrate, brothers. We've earned it."

"Hell yeah we have," Maverick gasped out after splashing a handful of water onto his own face. "Shit. I don't even want to wait until then. Let's do some pre-celebratin' tonight. I don't think I can wait another couple weeks to party."

"Now that's the first smart idea I've heard you suggest in a long time," Naraka said, and gave him a playful punch in the shoulder before jogging away. "Last one to finish drills is buying!"

"Hey! First round only! I'm not buying the whole night again dammit!" Maverick's voice faded into another round of laughter.

The scene shimmered again, and to Korban's surprise he watched as Naraka was standing before a mirror and slid his dog tags underneath his collar, smoothing the last button in place that hung from his decorated green jacket. He looked more filled out somehow, and taller. Perhaps it was the way he carried himself. There was a knock on the door and he glanced away from the mirror. "Come in."

The door opened and suddenly General Kane strode in. His cold blue eyes held a lot more warmth and energy, but even still they were intense, demanding perfection. Naraka saluted him. "Sir."

"At ease, Lieutenant." He smiled, and Naraka lowered his hand and slightly spread his legs apart, his cheeks warming a little as he glanced away. General Kane chuckled and said, "Still not used to that title, are you son?"

Naraka released a nervous breath and Korban could feel the swirl of mixed emotions within the man. Honor, excitement, and a deep-seeded worry that he would let the General down, or worse, his brothers. "No, Sir."

"You're the best of the best, and from your class, my class… that's quite an honor. You should be proud," General Kane said and circled around him, clapping a fatherly hand on his shoulder. "So, you ready for the big day?"

"Sir, yes, sir." Naraka answered sharply. "It is an honor to have trained with my men. We look forward to serving our country."

"Excellent. It has been a pleasure working with you and your squad. I feel that your group has maintained the level of control and perfection that our military needs during these difficult times." He paced the floor of the barracks, studying every towel that hung perfectly folded from each bed frame. "In fact, I have a special assignment for you. Something top secret that will be the future of military technology."

Naraka watched him, uncertain of what to say. "What kind of military technology, sir?"

"I'm afraid that's classified for now, Lieutenant, but after the hard work you boys put in, I'm sure you will love it. It's a real, hands-on opportunity that will get you and your boys some field experience. It's what you have been training for." The general turned and beamed proudly. "You boys have done so well, it's time to put that practice into action. It is the least I can do to recommend you for such an assignment. I know you will serve our country well, and with honor."

"Thank you sir." Naraka smiled, saluting the General again, then once the General saluted and left, he quickly began to finish readying himself for graduation.

The ripples happened again across the memory, and time passed by once more. There were flashes of the graduation ceremony where Naraka received honorable recommendation, followed by moments of Naraka and his squad celebrating well into the night. This time when the picture came into focus Naraka was not sitting on a bus but strapped inside a harness on a helicopter, the familiar faces of his team gathered around him. The sound of the helicopter blades were loud as it hovered towards its location. There were some nervous jokes and laughs, but once the helicopter landed after a few minutes passed, they all went from joking college-aged kids to serious young soldiers.

General Kane approached from the cockpit with a metal suitcase in hand. He smiled to them proudly before he spoke. "Boys, you are about to become the first squad we test out with these."

He opened up the case with flourish, and inside there were six wrist watches that seemed fairly normal. The screens along the watch face were tiny but looked advanced, the miniature computer screens detailed, and upon closer inspection looked expensive. "These have everything you will need for the next twenty-four to forty-eight hours. They're equipped with advanced GPS technology that should guide you to where your target is located, using the safest path available. It should change your course if there are any dangers ahead, whether it's the enemy or any natural obstacles that you may encounter. Your mission is to find a black box from a plane that was shot down somewhere in the jungle. This island is uncharted for the most part but not too big, a couple square miles really. These watches will help make a live map that you can navigate with, if the technology works. If not, your packs have a week's worth of rations, and you'll be charting this island by hand. Either way, you are all more than capable of handling this assignment, which is why we brought you here." He paused. "But first, before heading into the dangerous jungle we wanted to make sure to properly prepare you. It turns out that there was a recent warning of an unusual viral outbreak in the area, and we wanted to make sure you boys were properly safe guarded against any and all diseases. The Lieutenant will help me administer the vaccine, and you will depart this helicopter as soon as you are given the shot. Do you have any questions, men?"

"No sir!" they chorused.

Naraka unfastened himself from the harness and went over to the General, who opened up another section of the metal case and revealed six needles that contained a dark looking serum that resembled black blood. Whatever it was it reminded Korban of the same thick serum he'd witnessed before, and it sent a chill down his spine that he couldn't shake. Naraka paused for a moment, staring at the grim-looking liquid, and for a moment was hesitant to inject it into Maverick's arm. General Kane glanced to him. "Something wrong Lieutenant?" he asked.

"No sir," Naraka said, but didn't sound certain.

"It looks like shit, I know, but trust me, it's nothing compared to the virus that is out there," General Kane said and rubbed an alcohol swab on Tommy's arm, and then poked the needle into the targeted spot.

After administering the vaccine to his men, Naraka pushed up his sleeve so the General could pierce his arm with the long needle. Naraka turned away as he winced from it, never having been a big fan of shots. There was a sharp sting, and then a warm feeling ran through his arm from where he'd been injected. His pulse quickened, but Naraka mentally scolded himself for being nervous over a simple shot. He was the leader of his team, he couldn't lose face right now.

General Kane pulled out the needle and patted him on the shoulder. "Good luck, Lieutenant."

One by one they hurried from the helicopter with their gear, ready for the mission. Naraka was the last in line, the general looking grim when he glanced back his way. Low, under his breath, General Kane murmured, "*...and let slip the dogs of war...*" He cleared his throat, then said louder, so they could hear him over the helicopter's whirling blades and booming engine, "Take care and see you in a few days. You're doing your country proud. You're doing me proud." The helicopter started to lift off, and they stepped back as the General clutched the door and started to close it. "Good luck, men."

The helicopter took to the sky, abandoning them to the island. Naraka turned to the men in his squad. "Let's go."

They made their way through the thick, tall grass of the jungle. The air was sticky and wet with humidity, but the sun was hidden away thanks to the thick covering of green leaves above them. They wandered around, poking at the buttons of the watches. Sure enough, they seemed to be able to scan the area and map it out for them, helping them evade pitfalls and even some venomous snakes. Their journey took them through the shade, but they were all sweating in the hot, humid air of the jungle. They traveled for hours together, simply tinkering around with their new toys, until the sun began to set. Naraka gazed up at the orange sky and finally gave the command. They would have to set up camp for the night.

Together they found a secluded stretch of beach along the inlet of the island that provided enough cover for the night. They quickly set up their tents and built a small fire out of driftwood, the flames crackling and sparkling in different colors. They gathered around it and Maverick pulled out a hidden stash of Southern Comfort he'd smuggled, and they all passed it around, taking long swigs. They laughed and joked as the sun sank below the horizon, the group reminding Korban so much of his times with RJ, Alex, and Ace. Korban knew that relaxed, easy feeling that came over Naraka as they reminisced and went over their adventure for the day. These were his men, and he was their leader, but they were closer than friends, and more like brothers.

As stars and a full moon began to glow against the darkening sky, Maverick was the first to complain about the stomach pains. They teased him light-heartedly as the poor fellow clutched his belly, hunching over and looking ill. "Aww, can't handle your own liquor, Maverick?" Tommy teased with a smirk, even though he was also sweating profusely, and wiped the sweat from his forehead away with his arm. "Damn this heat... I feel like I'm burning up and the sun is going down."

It was Walter that fell to the ground first, clutching his own stomach in agony. For a moment there was laughter, as they figured their friend was continuing their game of picking on Maverick. But when his eyes rolled up into the back of his head and blood spurted from his mouth and nose, they realized quickly that something was not right, and that this was no joke.

After that moment, everything seemed to suddenly speed up, as if one of them falling made the rest start to feel ill. Tommy collapsed, his glasses falling off into the sand as he arched and twisted violently against the sand. The blond was screaming, twitching on the ground as if he was being shot at from above. It was all surreal, as if they were all being attacked by the same invisible enemy. Naraka clutched his own aching stomach and witnessed it all. Walter was the first to stop moving, but Maverick began doing something much worse.

His bucking and arching increased, and something started to happen to his friend. His skin rippled like waves, brown and bloody hairs sprouting out of his massive body. The young man screamed and bloody foam began to froth from his mouth, how he found the air to keep screaming Korban had no idea. Naraka tried to crawl over to him but his own pain was too great. To his (and Korban's) horror, he watched as his young friend's face began to melt, the sound of breaking bones and wet blood splattering onto the sand. Maverick threw his twisted and hideous head back up to howl, and suddenly he exploded— flesh, blood, and darker things spraying across the ground.

Korban wanted to look away, but he couldn't, frozen in terror along with Naraka. He'd never seen this before, but knew all too well what it was. This was what happened when the change went bad. This was something that could have happened to him after being bitten five years ago. Korban had been extremely lucky, but Naraka...

To his growing horror he witnessed what Naraka had so many years ago. Watching his men, his brothers, die twisting in agony as their lycanthropy took hold of them. As Naraka collapsed into the blood-soaked sand, knowing his own fate would be the same, he closed his eyes and began to pray, pray for his lost comrades, pray for it all to end... and it did, to his horror, it did.

The screams, howls, and sloshing of blood stopped. On the quiet island he could hear everything else suddenly out of the silence. The rustle of a leaf. The many footsteps of ants in a nearby ant hill. Somewhere in the empty forest island he could hear birds nestling in a tree for the night. His nose stung sharply with the metallic stench of blood, and Korban gagged from the memory sense. He'd never smelt so much gore and death before, not like this.

Naraka saw his hands were no longer his own, but instead massive black paws attached to long, furry black legs. His clothes had been destroyed when he transformed, the fabric in tiny bloody pieces everywhere, covered with Tommy's, Walter's, Maverick's... all of his brothers' blood. All that remained of them were their twisted remains and their dog tags, shiny with fresh blood as they glistened in the moonlight. Naraka sat back on his huge haunches and threw back his head, his howl booming through the night, echoing the agony of losing his brothers to this horrible fate...

When the scene shimmered again, Korban wished he could beg for it to stop. He'd thought his life had been bad, he'd thought what he suffered was unbearable. But watching Naraka's life was like watching a horrible horror movie, the kind that went wrong, and with no turning back.

The island faded away into darkness, and the next thing Korban knew, he and Naraka woke up, not on the beach, but instead naked in a cage. There was a horrible scratching sound around him, like many things were scratching against something at once. The tap that occurred every now and again made him flinch from its loudness. There was heavy breathing all around him, and the juicy sound of heartbeats thudding in many chests. He opened his eyes and the light was so bright around him it took a few moments. He was in a small, white, padded room, where one side of the wall had solid glass. Behind the glass he could see many people in white coats, all scribbling notes and staring at him, then glancing down at their note pads. His throat was raw and dry. His eyes burned under the bright, hot lights of the fluorescent bulbs that burned overhead. He could hear the filaments sizzle and crackle and it made him grit his teeth.

If the glass was sound-proof, it would not have mattered. He could hear everything over there, the scratching of the pens on the many pads, someone popping bubble gum. He shakily got up to his feet, glancing to each of the stark white faces who blankly studied him. "Help... me..." he croaked, his throat aching from disuse. "Please... help me..."

But not one of them could hear him, or chose not to, instead writing and writing...

Naraka stumbled with aching muscles to the window, pressing his hands against the cool glass to sturdy himself. He gazed into the eyes of the scientist that was in front of him, pleading. "Help me."

They stared for a moment, then quickly averted their horrified gaze, trembling a little as they wrote. It was then he caught a glimpse of himself, his reflection catching his vision at that angle. No longer were his eyes the dark brown they had once been. From then and forever more they were a bright, glowing gold. His eyes widened in horror at his reflection and he began to pound on the glass. "Help me! Please! Make it stop! Make it stop!" His heart was pounding furiously, his hands making the glass shudder, the scientists on the other side backing up quickly. All of them looked on in terror as the glass began to crack and give way as if it were an ordinary window pane. "Help me! Please!"

The glass shattered, but by then the scientists were rushing out the door screaming, their pads and notes abandoned. Armed guards rushed in, pointing guns from all directions at him. "Hands up, freeze!" they screamed, and tentatively Naraka obeyed, holding his bloody and cut hands up in the air.

They watched with equal horror as the cuts on Naraka's hands healed before their eyes, small shards of glass tinkling against the mess that was on the floor. They fired darts at him, but the needles broke against his skin, his bare flesh suddenly like armor it seemed.

Naraka stood there, looking at his hands in awe, then down at the darts that had attempted to pierce his skin. He smirked, then laughed, a mirthless and maniacal sound. "What have they done to me?" he asked no one in particular, the guards looking hesitantly at one another.

Naraka lowered his hands to his sides, gazing to the door. He wanted answers. He wanted to know what happened to his brothers, why they died and he... he was suddenly more powerful than when he'd been on that island.

Suddenly the general was there, rushing into the room with a gun in his hand. He pointed it at Naraka's head. "Easy now, Lieutenant. At ease."

Naraka stared at him, a familiar face but with an unfamiliar, cold, and distant expression in his eyes. The look that Korban knew all too well. "Now son, I know you must have a lot of questions... but I think if you come with me nice and peaceful like to the other room, I'm sure we can answer those questions for you."

"Maverick... Walter… Tommy… everyone... that island... this place... Sir... what happened? What's happening to me?" Naraka demanded, his bloody hands shaking.

"We aren't exactly sure, Lieutenant. We'd like to perform some tests to make you better, son." The general was sweating, nervous, that odd look about him still.

Naraka made a face. Something did not smell right, literally. Whatever it was it made him anxious, and he wanted to run. Still, this was his General. Maybe he could set this right. Maybe the inoculation did not work like they thought it did. Maybe he'd hallucinated because of it and had a dream of being a wolf, of howling mournfully at the loss of his friends, his brothers. "Please, sir... help me..."

"I will, Lieutenant." He had that same interested, intense look Korban had witnessed in the court house. "I will."

"Please... no more..." Korban's voice echoed over the memory. "Please..."

The images shimmered away, and suddenly he was back to the present, standing there in the forest clearing, his trembling hands on Naraka's shoulders. Even though that had been a while ago, for the first time he noticed that Naraka had not aged much since then. His amber eyes still focused to his, and for the first time he could understand the deep pain that reflected from those mad, yellow eyes.

Sophie was shaking him from the side. "Korban? Are you all right?" she demanded in a worried tone. "You stopped breathing."

He nodded, regretting the move immediately as he still felt dizzy and light-headed from the memory. His stomach churned as he gazed to Naraka, whose face was a blank mask, though the emotion still swam in his eyes. "I'm going to be fine… Naraka… what the hell?"

Naraka swallowed and stared at him. "You saw it too, didn't you? What happened to me, and the others."

"Yes," Korban said, his voice tight.

Sophie glanced between the two of them and frowned. "What did you see, Korban?"

It took Korban a moment to gather his thoughts, and then he

spoke. "I saw that Naraka isn't the one who attacked the judge. He killed a deer last night, no one else," he paused, meeting Naraka's gaze cautiously. "I saw what happened before you were turned. General Kane is the one who infected you and your men."

Sophie's eyes widened in horror at his words, her hand covering her mouth as it dropped open in shock.

Naraka glanced away. "Yes," he said with a heavy sigh, and the acrid smell of anguish came from the werewolf. "I helped him infect my men. My brothers. It was my fault, they trusted me, and I was foolish enough to blindly trust the general. I can't believe I was that stupid, and they all paid for my mistake. I watched them all die, and somehow survived. I would have stayed locked up, and away, if I hadn't met Mikael. I should never have attacked you and ruined your life. You suffered enough before I came into the picture and made things worse."

Korban had the distinct impression that Naraka had delved into his own painful memories in turn, but he didn't care. His eyes felt damp, wet with tears that he had not yet shed. Tears for the one who had attacked him so violently five years ago, and left him for dead. He could understand this man for the first time, could see he'd also been blinded by his own former prejudice for the supernatural. Too blind to see that Naraka had been telling the truth all along. He didn't kill civilians, and he didn't kill the judge. Naraka had been used as a weapon, betrayed by General Kane just like his men. Everything he had known and trusted gone in one injection, everything he stood for robbed away with one violent experiment.

"No," Korban insisted suddenly, reaching out and gripping Naraka's shoulder again, "you're wrong. It's not stupid to trust someone who you thought was on your side. Someone who should have been there for you no matter what. It doesn't make you weak, and it doesn't make it your fault. He lied to you, twisted your trust, and your men's trust, to do this… awful, unspeakable thing. No one deserves that kind of betrayal. It doesn't make you stupid for believing in someone who ended up hurting you. It makes them the monster, who used your faith against you."

Sophie tensed nearby, the words hitting home for her as well.

A silence fell across the clearing. Naraka's shoulders sagged down, and his eyes focused on the forest floor. "I still need to take responsibility for my own actions, Korban."

"Your men – your brothers – wouldn't want you to live your life like that, trapped in a moment that you cannot change. No one can change the past, Naraka. We can only take steps towards making a better future. What Kane put you and the others through is wrong. A man that can do that… he's capable of doing so much worse," Korban said, and a chill ran through him suddenly that had nothing to do with the autumn air.

"Capable of murder… so the status quo remained the same," Sophie suggested with a grim frown.

Naraka glanced to the two of them, the realization coming into focus in his haunted eyes. "You act as though you've met General Kane before. How?"

"He was one of the representatives on the Council, and he made it pretty clear he wasn't a fan of changing the rules for people like us," Sophie stated.

"He does have motive, and the means to turn anyone into a werewolf," Korban said, his nausea returning at the thought. "What better way to keep things as they are, and not have people go looking into him, then to inject someone close to the judge and have them attack, or maybe inject the judge himself?" After what Ace had said, and what he witnessed in Naraka's memory, either grim possibility seemed plausible, and he felt a little ill thinking about it.

Naraka's gaze went up to the sky as he sighed again. "It's possible. He's far more ruthless than I had known at the time. Him being in town, and being a part of this Council, only to have the judge be murdered shortly after… it is a suspicious coincidence."

"We should warn Ace and Mikael," Korban said. "They need to know if he's involved."

Naraka nodded in agreement. "If he has anything to do with this, we'll know soon enough. And if he is responsible, I won't let him get away with it. Never again."

16: REMISSION

When they got back to the guest house, Naraka headed into the bedroom to make the call, while Sophie lingered in the hall with Korban. She gazed to him, and saw how tired and worn the usually playful and warm man had become. "I'm worried about you," she said softly, mindful that RJ and Alex were sleeping in the other room. "When you use that ability of yours, and connect with others… it takes a toll on you, Korban. You can't see it, but I can. You even stopped breathing for a moment… it's dangerous, and there's still so much we don't know about it."

"I know it's risky," Korban said wearily, rubbing the back of his head. "I just… I just wanted to try and help him."

"I know you want to help others, Korban, but he made a good point out there. Why are you helping him, after all he's done to you? You don't owe him anything," Sophie insisted, reaching and touching his arm.

"I know I don't," Korban said with a heavy sigh, glancing away from her. "After what I saw though, I understand him. I literally walked in his shoes. I saw what he's been through."

"Korban—" Sophie began to protest, but a pained cry from the other room made them both freeze.

The color drained from Korban as he darted for the door to RJ and Alex's room. He flung the door open, Sophie rushing up behind him. RJ was sitting up in their bed, and was whispering comforting things to Alex, who was gritting his teeth and red-faced with pain. Sophie frowned in worry and confusion. "What's happening?"

"It's all right, he just needs a few minutes," RJ explained, keeping his voice calm and steady as he gently patted Alex's trembling shoulders. "He'd be okay faster if he took his medicine, but he's being stubborn."

"It's fine," Alex growled out as he glanced away, avoiding eye contact with all of them as sweat pooled on his forehead. "I don't need drugs."

Korban nodded, though he looked shaken by the scene before him. Sophie remained at his side in the doorway, uncertain of what to do. RJ was comforting Alex, but clearly the mechanic was in agony. "I thought his arm was getting better," she said, looking worried.

"It was, but apparently his body is as stubborn as he is, and it was healing in its own way. They had to do surgery to reset his arm, which is why we ended up spending the day at the hospital. He's only home now because they needed the beds, and they sent him home with some pain medicine. Which he's refusing to take."

"I don't need it," Alex grumbled.

"The doctors wouldn't have prescribed it if you didn't need it, Alex," RJ gently responded. "How about just one? So you can take the edge off and sleep. I hate seeing you hurt like this."

Alex glared at his cast, which Sophie saw was new, a lime-green color in place of the neon pink. He seemed to struggle for a moment with the words, but finally relented with a heavy sigh, "Fine. I'll take half of one."

"That's my tough guy," RJ said, looking relieved as he turned to Korban and Sophie. "Would you mind grabbing a glass of water for him? I'll grab his pill."

"Sure, of course," Sophie said as Korban silently nodded.

They headed to the kitchen, Korban busying himself with getting a glass from the cabinet. Sophie watched him as he went over to the fridge to get ice and finally asked, "Is there anything I can do?" She couldn't help but feel a new surge of guilt, seeing Alex struggling and hurting made her heartache.

Korban glanced to her with a solemn look. "I wish there was something either of us could do for him."

For a second, their eyes locked, and Sophie tensed when she saw a flickering slide-show of images. A young Alex wearing an over-sized ball cap, waving his tiny fists angrily as he shouted in Spanish at some kids who'd been bullying a young RJ. Then it changed to Korban pushing a toy car around as he played with Alex, who was pretending to repair the miniature vehicles in his upside-down shoebox. She could see "CYRUS AUTOS" scrawled in crayon on the box, the R and S's written backwards. The images were as clear as if Korban was showing her a movie, and her brow furrowed in confusion.

It was as if suddenly they weren't in the guest house, but in the garage, like how it had been before the explosion. There was something different about it, and as she looked around, she realized there were two people she didn't know watching over Korban and Alex as they played. The woman resembled Korban in many ways, the same chocolate brown eyes that he had before he was infected gazed over the boys with affection. Next to her was a man who looked like an older version of Alex, an aged Hispanic man wearing a hat similar to the one the boy was sporting, only his fit much better on his head. "It's good for Alejandro to have a friend his age. A lot of kids don't play with him, because he's small, and they think he's younger than 'em. It probably doesn't help that his scary abuelo chases them away when they pick on him."

Sophie stared in wonder. She realized then that this was what Korban had described to her, that link he had where he could see others' memories. The woman who must be his mother, Maria, only smiled to the older man, who must be the fabled Pops they spoke so highly of. "Korban could use a good friend, too. Thank you for hiring me, even if I don't know much about cars, I'm a fast learner."

"I know you are, and I don't mind. It's kinda lonely here, and it will be nice to have a young set of eyes around. You'll be doing me a favor if you field the phone calls and write down the notes. I can't even read my own damn hand-writing some days," Pops said with a shrug, then glanced over to the boys. "It'll be good for Alex to have you around, too. He never got the chance to meet his mother, and he could use a more feminine influence in his life."

"Oh, I'm sorry to hear that," Maria said softly, her expression softening as she gazed over to the small boy playing with her son.

"Yeah, me too," Pops said with a sigh. "I loved my daughter, but she loved the pills more than anything else. She struggled with it most of her life, but in the end addiction took her from me, and Alex. It almost took my grandson from me, he was born with the same addiction his mother had. Which is why he's always been so small. He was born two months early, and spent his first few days of life being weaned off the same drugs that took Mirabel. When I held that tiny, baby boy in the palm of my hand for the first time, just days after he came into this world… I swore then that I'd do everything in my power to protect him."

Sophie stepped back, and the image suddenly faded. While the images seemed to have taken a few minutes to witness, she had the odd feeling that only a few seconds had passed between them. She was back in the kitchen, her eyes locked with Korban's, and a stunned expression on his face as well. "I'm sorry," they both blurted, and Korban's amber eyes shifted to the floor.

"Was that… your ability?" Sophie asked, surprised.

He nodded in response, looking overwhelmed by it as well. Her heart was racing, and adrenaline was pumping through her veins. She felt somehow stronger, as though the brief connection had invigorated her. From the sound of his heartbeat echoing hers, it seemed that the effect had been mutual. They stood there in silence for a moment, then Korban asked, "What did you see?"

"I… I guess your memories of Alex and RJ, when you were younger," Sophie confessed, still mystified by it all. "I saw your mother and Pops, I think, talking about Alex…"

Korban's eyes widened, but he was careful not to connect their gaze this time. "I was just thinking about that, it's one of my earliest memories, overhearing that conversation… I didn't understand it until I was older, but just now… it was like I lived it all over again," he said, swallowing anxiously. "So you saw, and you now know why he won't touch the pain killers. Pops told us when we were older the full story, how his mother got addicted to pain killers, then when those weren't enough she moved on to stronger opioids. He's always been terrified of becoming an addict. We could barely get him to take so much as a Tylenol growing up. He'd rather suffer, even now, to avoid it, and we can't blame him really."

"That's awful," Sophie whispered.

"Please don't tell him I told, er, showed you," Korban said softly. "He doesn't like to talk about it."

"I don't blame him, it's a tragic story to have. I wouldn't want to relive it every time I was in pain either," Sophie said, then reached out and took Korban's free hand, giving it a gentle squeeze. "I won't tell him, I promise."

Korban smiled, relief in his eyes as he picked up the glass from the counter. "Thanks."

They went and delivered the glass of water, and Alex swallowed down half of a pill, looking anxious for several moments afterward, before finally relaxing and gazing over to them. He offered them all a thumbs up with his good hand. "Okay. Back to bed for everyone now, show's over. See you in the morning at breakfast?" Alex cracked a strained smile.

"Of course, we won't miss it for the world," Sophie said.

"Will our new friend Naraka be joining us as well?" Alex asked as he settled back against his pillow.

RJ raised an eyebrow and gave a look to Korban, echoing the question without words.

Sheepishly, Korban scratched the back of his head again as he stepped backwards, slowly, towards the door. "I er… yeah… we'll need another plate for him. Just for a few more days."

RJ narrowed his eyes a little and gave him a scrupulous look, but ultimately ended up closing his eyes and shaking his head. "All right, but you'd better loan him some pajamas. It's crazy enough around here without having people running around naked."

"I'll make sure he's set," Korban chuckled. "Good night."

They exchanged farewells for the evening, and then parted ways. Sophie glanced to Korban once they were alone in the hallway again. "I should head back, I guess," she said it, in hopes that maybe she could convince herself more than anything.

"If you have to," Korban whispered, and tried to keep the sadness from his tone, but she could smell the melancholy in the air.

Her gaze moved down to the floor. "I should… I should do a lot of things… but… I'm starting to question whether or not I should…" Sophie trailed off, and shook her head. "I'm not making any sense right now."

"No, I understand what you're trying to say, anyway," Korban said, then reached up and cupped her cheek in his palm. "What is it that you want? I mean… what do you really want, whether or not you should want it?" He paused, and chuckled at himself. "Now I'm not making much sense, either."

She smiled, putting her hand over his and leaning into his touch.

"I could tell you… but do you think I could show you, instead?"

She bit her bottom lip as she watched the realization flood his expressive, yellow eyes. His cheeks darkened a little, and the unspoken emotions swirled in those golden pools. He'd been cautious not to reconnect with her eyes up until then, but curiosity must have gotten the better of him. "I don't think it works that way. I can only seem to see people's memories. I can't predict the future."

Sophie moved a little closer to him, her gaze locking with his. "I guess I'll have to describe what I wish for." She paused and took his hand into hers, her heart racing along with his. "That is what I want," she said. "I want to finish my degree, and become a lawyer. I want to find some way to make peace with Lucas, and for both of us to be a part of Danny's life. I want a big family, and I want it all with you."

Korban swallowed, quiet for a long moment while his eyes watered. His voice strained when he finally spoke. "I want it, too," he murmured, a guilty look following the words. "More than anything, I want that for you, and for us. I wish I knew how to make it come true."

"I think I know what I need to do," Sophie said, her voice growing steadier as her resolve. "It's not going to be easy, nothing ever is, not really. But… I'm going to make it happen somehow."

Korban opened his mouth, but she put a finger to his lips and smiled to him as she continued, "It's my choice in the end, after all. I'll need a few days, but I need to talk to Lucas. I don't want to hurt him, but I can't break your heart. Not ever again."

He nodded, too stunned to speak. She couldn't help but smile as she removed her finger from his lips, kissing the tip and pressing it again to his mouth once more. "I'll see you in the morning. Be careful. I believe in you, if you saw what you did with Naraka and you trust him, I trust your judgement with him. I'm not too far away if you need me."

"I believe in you, too, Sophie," he said, still looking dazed. "Good night."

"Good night, Korban," she said, giving him another hug before she reluctantly parted ways and headed back to the main house.

It was so dark out now, the quiet of the lake peaceful even with the lack of light. She realized the moonless sky loomed above her, and for the first time she missed its soft, ethereal glow, just as she already missed Korban. The moon's light would return in the next few days, and with it her strength would too. She had a difficult decision to make, but she had taken steps toward it that dark night. She knew what she wanted in her heart, and now it was up to her to make it come true.

~*~

When Korban returned to the bedroom, Naraka was pacing and counting under his breath. For a moment, his good mood was deflated as he worried that the other werewolf was going to lose control again, but his voice was calm as he counted every step. Naraka slowed to a stop, and when he turned to Korban, his yellow eyes were stormy. "I told Ace and Mikael about General Kane being in town. They're going to look into him, but I'm worried. I know what he's capable of, and I'm afraid of what he'll do to them if they underestimate him. If the general is involved, this situation is going to become critical, fast. I keep hoping his involvement is just a theory, but even if they look into Kane, it's a risk. Vampires can get cocky. Their whole mystique and lore from before the virus can blind them to the fact that some humans can be more dangerous than we are."

"Ace and Mikael will be fine; they'd let us know if they were in trouble and needed our help. Right now we need to make sure you're in control, and you're good. You are cool right now, right?" Korban asked, giving Naraka a worried look.

Naraka nodded, pointing a finger towards the window and the dark night sky. "It's a new moon tonight. There's no way I'll lose control," he confidently stated.

"Now who's being over confident?" Korban teased.

"Even at my weakest time, I have never turned during a new moon. Even when they tried to inject me with the serum, it wouldn't drag the Wolven out," Naraka got a haunted look as he said it. "And believe me, they tried."

A cold chill ran through Korban at those words. The memories Naraka shared resurfaced and made him feel uneasy. No doubt there were even worse memories locked inside the erratic werewolf's mind. "I'm sorry," Korban said softly.

"You don't need to apologize for their cruelty," Naraka began, his hand going to the collection of dog tags around his throat. "I know you're not sure what to say. No one does, and that's fine, believe me. There aren't words that exist that would ever make it better. There's no comfort in accepting what happened, only that the more time that passes, the further away from that moment I get. Every day it's different. Some days it's easy to distance myself from the memories, and others… it's easier to let myself slip away and let the wolf out, so I really can forget it all."

No wonder he couldn't control his wolf side, Korban thought with a frown. He understood the feeling. It was easier for a long time to just let the wolf consume him and to slip away from the worries and pain of the world. "You can't keep running, Naraka," Korban insisted. "Losing control like you did could get someone hurt. I know when you attacked me it was an accident, and I felt the guilt you did when you lost it back then. But what if it happens again? If you let the wolf run amuck, someone else is going to end up infected, or worse. I know you are a good guy, I've seen and felt what you did. It's incredible after all you've been through."

Korban paused, taking a shaky breath. "I'm willing to forgive you for attacking me. It was an accident, and yeah, it's not been sunshine and rainbows, but it led me to this moment, and to the woman I love. And that's complicated, too, but… I don't regret it anymore. I accept what happened and I'm making the most of it every day. But I will not forgive you if you put someone else through this, or take an innocent person's life away. There are healthier ways to cope with all you've gone through than turning Wolven. All this transforming has to be taking a toll on you, too. So… maybe words can't make it better. Maybe taking action to find peace for your fallen brothers and doing good in this world will help. You didn't ruin my life. We can't change the shitty things that happen to us, we can only control how we react to them."

"You're starting to sound like a cheesy motivation poster," Naraka said with a sly smirk, "but I'm picking up what you're putting down, Korban. I don't want what Kane did to me to get the best of me ever again. I don't want to spread his infection, and I won't. You have my word."

The sincerity in his tone, combined with the emotions that filled the air, made Korban believe him. "Good. Then maybe we start looking into some ways to help you stay in control tomorrow morning. I'm not an expert, but we have to start somewhere."

"Sounds like a plan to me," Naraka stated, then reached and

patted Korban on the shoulder, giving him a squeeze. "It's nice to go to bed knowing I've got a friend in my corner. Thanks."

"You're welcome," Korban said.

They exchanged farewells for the evening, and Korban headed out to the couch, insisting that Naraka take the bed for the night; partly because he wanted his guest to remain comfortable, but the other half of him secretly hoped that Sophie would return. He sank into the soft sofa and wrapped the blanket on it around himself, breathing in deeply. He smiled as he settled in, the delicate scent of mint and vanilla still lingered where she'd slept.

~*~

The familiar laughter and notes of the beginning of Duran Duran's *Hungry Like the Wolf* were playing from his phone as it vibrated along the coffee table, waking him up. Korban groaned, and rubbed the sleep from his eyes as he rolled over and blindly searched for it in the dark. With everything that had been going on, he didn't remember to change it back. His eyes came to focus on Sergeant McKinnon's name on the screen and he groaned again before answering. "Hey, Tim," he sighed, already expecting bad news at this hour.

"Korban, where are you right now?" Tim demanded, his voice tired and stressed.

"Laying on the couch at the Bane lake house, which is surprisingly comfortable," Korban responded, sitting up and rubbing his temples as a headache began to form. "What's happened now?"

"There's been another Wolven attack. Another body," Tim said, the weariness and sorrow heavy in every word. "Sophie is still there, right?"

"As far as I know, yeah. She's staying at the main house," Korban stated, and immediately leapt up from the couch as a pang of fear rushed through him.

"Cory Carter was just found torn apart in his hotel room. We've notified his family and Senator Hunter." Tim continued on the other line, as Korban rushed to the bedroom door, trying not to fling it open too forcefully.

Naraka was sleeping soundly in the bed, his arms wrapped around one of the pillows. Korban breathed a sigh of relief.

"You sound really tore up about this, Korban," Tim snapped grimly.

"No, it's not that. Sorry. I just… it's early. My condolences," Korban stammered. "No one deserves this."

"The press is going to have a field day. It's a good idea to keep your head low and stay put for a while, even if it's for your own sanity," Tim cautioned him.

Korban watched as Naraka murmured in his sleep and rolled over, still clutching the pillow close against him. "Yeah we won't be going anywhere any time soon."

After they hung up, Korban finally woke up and the weight of what Tim had said finally sank in. Senator Hunter's intern had been murdered, which meant another member of the Council had been targeted. He glanced to the sleeping werewolf, who seemed finally at peace and wondered if maybe Naraka was right about Kane's involvement after all.

17: FESTER

The murders of the two Council members were inescapable. The news made headlines on RJ's morning newspaper, and the nonstop speculation and coverage was running on the television and any time they went online. As tragic as it was to lose a respected, elderly judge, it had been even more upsetting to lose the fresh-faced, young intern with a promising future. The media was in a frenzy, like piranhas who'd gotten a drop of blood in the water. Korban turned off the television when they began showing footage of them hounding Senator Hunter as he arrived at Hancock Airport earlier that morning. He put his head in his hands and rubbed his eyes, unsuccessfully trying to fend off a headache. "This day just keeps getting better and better, doesn't it?" he asked no one in particular.

RJ went over and patted him on the shoulder. "Well, along that vein, we've been invited to the main house this morning for breakfast. It's okay if you aren't up to it."

On one hand, he would be seeing Sophie, but on the other... Korban wondered if she'd talked to Lucas yet. Still, given what had happened last night it was probably a good idea they talked together over breakfast. He couldn't avoid Lucas forever, and on the plus side he'd be seeing Sophie, too. "I'm good, let's go eat."

Alex was unusually quiet as they got ready, then headed up to the main house. Korban glanced and saw Alex's knuckles were white and the circles under his eyes dark as he shuffled along. Alex never embarrassed him by pitying him after the full moon. The least he could do was extend that courtesy to his friend. If he needed help, Alex would ask.

They were escorted at the door by Damion to the dining room. Before the doors were opened, the delicious scents of their meal wafted into Korban's nostrils, and his mouth watered in anticipation. Succulent sausage, sizzling bacon, and buttery pancakes were piled up on platters set upon a long, thin buffet table. There was a colorful arrangement of freshly cut fruit, and to Korban's delight, a rich blend of dark roast coffee percolating in a pot.

Korban was drawn to the fresh coffee like a moth to the flame, and as he savored his first sip, Sophie walked in the room alongside Lucas. She was wearing something fancier than normal at this hour—a simple but stylish black dress. Lucas wore a matching suit and looked camera ready as always. Korban almost dropped his coffee mug, and suddenly felt very underdressed in his faded Syracuse Orange t-shirt and navy blue sweatpants. Sophie offered him a grim smile when her eyes met his. Without words he knew she hadn't talked to Lucas yet, and no doubt this morning's breaking news had been the reason why she didn't get around to it.

"Ah, good, you're here. Glad you three could join us," Lucas greeted them with a smug grin. "We have a special guest who will be joining us this morning, so I figured it may be good to have everyone together. Though… there may be some time to change into something a bit more professional, if you wanted, before he arrives."

Korban felt a sinking feeling in his gut. Lucas was never one to pass up the opportunity to show off, it seemed, but even this was a bit more lavish than usual for him. There was a lot of food for just five people, even with two werewolves present, and the house staff were still bringing out more trays of food.

"Who is this 'special guest' exactly?" Korban anxiously asked, cautiously sipping his coffee.

Lucas straightened his shoulders and lifted his chin up when he answered, as if even saying the guest's name should be done in a formal fashion, "Senator Hunter, of course. He's in town to take care of some dreadful business, as you know. I figured I would extend an invitation for him to join us to escape the paparazzi for a little while."

It took all his strength not to spit out his delicious coffee, and it burned his throat when he quickly swallowed it down. Korban sputtered for a moment, and RJ went over and patted him on the back. Sophie gave him a worried look and approached him. "Everything all right, Korban?" she gently asked.

He nodded as he coughed, and once he could speak again, he tried to play it cool. "Sorry, coffee went down the wrong pipe," he said once he could string a sentence together again. "I think, if it's all the same to you, we'd better just take our breakfast to go. Alex needs his rest, and I'm expecting a call from my cousin this morning, too." He gave Sophie a meaningful look.

She looked a little disappointed, but she nodded. "We'll miss you, but I understand. You'll have to tell your cousin I said hello. Maybe you should bring an extra plate of food, in case you're still hungry later."

Korban offered her an apologetic smile. "I'll be sure to tell him. Thanks."

They quickly piled up food on their plates, Korban grabbing an extra as Sophie hinted for Naraka, and headed back to the guest house. As RJ balanced his and Alex's plates, he glanced Korban's way. "You all right?" he asked.

Korban bobbed his head, concentrating a little harder than normal on the path at their feet. "Sorry to use you as an excuse to get out of there, Alex," he said as they stepped up onto the porch.

"I don't mind, Lobo," Alex replied. "My arm's too sore to deal with that *pendejo* this morning anyway. I'd rather eat breakfast with our new cousin. I just wish Sophie was joining us, too."

"Me too," Korban sighed.

They set the plates down at the kitchen table. "I'll go check in and see if he's up yet," Korban told them before heading back down the hall.

He opened the door and was relieved to find Naraka there, but surprised to discover he wasn't alone. Thankfully this time he didn't outwardly flinch. He was getting tired of giving the vampire that kind of satisfaction. "So vampires are immune to daylight?" Korban asked, proud he kept his shock out of his voice as well.

Mikael, who was sitting alongside Naraka and stroking the werewolf's dark hair, only gave him a slow, mischievous grin that showed off his pearly, white fangs. The vampire looked dressed for winter, wearing a long, white coat over dark pants and matching gloves on his hands. A white hat and dark sunglasses completed his unusual look. "Rumors about our sunlight intolerance are slightly exaggerated. I won't burn t' ash and mess up yer nice carpet, don't ye worry," Mikael said.

"If he does, I promise I'll vacuum him up," Naraka teased.

Korban shook his head but smiled. "Is Ace okay? Did you guys find out anything more?"

Mikael's grin took a very cat-like turn. "Naughty Korban. Ye wolves can't help but diggin' fer answers, can ye?"

"I just wanted to know how my best friend is doing," Korban protested, but quickly averted his gaze when he added, "and maybe just checking in on the investigation."

"Ye both had an intriguin' update for us, even though we turned out nothing ourselves last night. We'll be looking more into General Kane. Even if someone 'ere is giving us a hard time about it," Mikael stated, with a pointed look to Naraka.

"Kane is dangerous, and any pup you've put on his trail today won't know how to deal with him. Not the way I would," Naraka said, worry sobering his expression. "You and I could handle him, I know we could. Anyone else getting involved is putting themselves in danger, and putting us all at risk."

"We do make a good team, but Ace has someone he trusts on the trail. I'm confident they will be extra cautious. They all know what's at stake here," Mikael reassured him. "Besides, there's been a wee change o' plans."

"What kind of change?" Korban asked.

"I heard through the grapevine that the Senator is here to stay fer a few days. Ace and I don't think it's safe fer Naraka t' stick around, not when all his security settles in," Mikael answered.

"Damn, that was fast," Korban swore and scratched the back of his head. "How'd you find out he was coming here before I did?"

"The Underground keeps tabs on everything that matters," Mikael said. "And making sure that me Mate is safe is definitely a priority. I thank ye for keeping him safe, but it seems we're better off relocatin' for a little while. Think ye can keep it under control fer a little longer, fur ball?"

"I'm feeling stronger, thanks to Korban's help," Naraka admitted. "I think I can handle a few days without him."

"You're leaving then?" Korban asked.

"Just fer a couple days, while the Senator is here. I'm takin'

Naraka back to the Underground. He should be able to behave himself the next forty eight hours or so. It's safer fer all of us that we go before he arrives," Mikael said.

A mixture of emotions ran through Korban. On one hand, not having the responsibility of babysitting an unpredictable werewolf was liberating. Yet he also suddenly worried about what could happen if he wasn't around and Naraka lost control again. "Where will you go? Is there a way I can reach you?"

Naraka gave a lop-sided smile. "Aw, Korban, I didn't realize that you cared so much about little ol' me."

Korban's cheeks burned and he offered, "If you want, I can ask Alex if you could stay at the garage for a few days. It's under repair, but I think the insurance is holding it up so you'd have a safe, quiet place to lay low."

The couple exchanged a look for a long moment before Naraka said, "That's not a bad idea. Beats staying on the run."

Mikael nodded. "Aye. If Alex agrees."

"I'll go talk to him. We brought you breakfast, too. Er... some breakfast food," Korban clarified after a wary glance to the vampire.

"Don't worry. I'll get a bite later," Mikael said, flashing his fangs.

"I bet you will," Korban responded. "Come on, let's at least discuss it over breakfast. There should be time for that, right?"

Mikael tilted his head as though listening to the wind, and then gave a small nod. They headed together back to the kitchen. Alex and RJ stared in surprise as the vampire walked in, and an unreadable expression crossed the teacher's face. "Um, hi, I'm Alex," the mechanic warmly greeted the pale man with a welcoming smile. "Care for some breakfast? I think we brought enough for one more."

"Mikael," the vampire said simply with a nod, "and thanks, but I'm on a special diet."

"Gluten-free?" Alex asked.

"You could say that," Naraka snickered and headed over to the table to eat while Mikael smirked.

RJ frowned at Korban. "Do you have anyone else hidden away in your bedroom that we should know about, Korban?"

"No, not in my bedroom," Korban said carefully, which earned him a long, incredulous look from RJ before he slowly lifted his coffee mug up to his lips and took a long sip. Averting his gaze, Korban turned to Alex before he continued, "Would you mind if these two stayed at the garage for a couple days? With the Senator incoming security is going to get increased around here, and it's better they aren't here when that happens."

"I think it should be okay, just for a day or two," Alex said. "Construction has been delayed, and even if they did start it up it wouldn't be until after the weekend. I'd feel better knowing someone was keeping an eye on the place, too."

Mikael and Naraka both looked relieved. "Thank you," Naraka said between bites. "It means a lot to both of us."

"Just don't leave any dishes piled up in the sink, please," Alex said, half-joking, half-serious as he glanced over to RJ, who was still being eerily quiet as he busied himself with his meal.

Naraka laughed. "I promise we'll be on our best behavior. It'll be like we were never there."

RJ remained silent, staring intently at his newspaper as they hurriedly finished their food. Alex handed over the keys to their apartment, and the pair were on their way, Mikael pulling a hood from under his collar and shielding himself further before putting his hat and sunglasses back on, then vanishing out the back door with Naraka at his side, leaving the trio of friends alone again.

RJ cleared his throat, giving Korban a serious, but worried look. "I know you've always been the one willing to help out a stranger. Hell, both of you get that from Pops. It's just second nature to you. I just hope you're not risking everything, to help every lost werewolf who crosses your path."

Korban gave him a sheepish look. "Technically speaking, Mikael was never staying here, he only came to pick up Naraka. And he isn't a werewolf, he's a vampire."

Alex's eyes widened at his revelation. "No wonder he was so pale," Alex remarked.

RJ's frown deepened. "I just hope for all of our sakes you aren't putting your trust in the wrong people."

Korban still wondered that himself, even though he felt that Naraka was trustworthy after his glimpse inside his memories. Mikael, on the other hand... he didn't get a chance to argue, as his phone began to play Duran Duran. He welcomed the interruption at first, then saw who was calling, and the feeling immediately vanished. He answered, afraid of what news was on the other line. "Good morning, Tim."

"Good morning, Korban," Patty's cheerful voice greeted him on the other line. "Sergeant McKinnon is handling a few other things right now, but he asked me to call you. Do you have a moment?"

"For you, Patty, always," Korban said, pleasantly surprised.

"Oh, excellent," she began, the sounds of the busy police station muffled more than usual, making Korban wonder if she was calling him from Tim's office.

She explained why she had called in a gentle, apologetic tone. He listened to the instructions she had for him, his own smile fading as her words sank in. By the time they hung up, RJ and Alex were staring at him. "What'd Patty say?" Alex asked.

"Tim thinks it's a good idea that Sophie and I show up to pay our respects to the judge, and apparently he isn't the only one. The mayor asked if we'd be making an appearance at his funeral, and suggested it may be in our best interest for our cause if we did show up. Maybe it would squash some of the rumors that we are involved in his murder," Korban explained, scratching the back of his head.

RJ exhaled sharply at that and asked, "What do you want to do?"

Korban weighed the options for a moment. "Honestly, I don't want to deal with any of it. I'd rather not go, and be made into a spectacle again," Korban said, then looked to his friend and sponsor. "But people are dying who want to make a change for people like me. I need to do something. If… if this is all I can do right now, so be it. I'll do my part, and hope that maybe it will make a difference."

RJ gave him another long look, pride shining in his eyes. "Maybe it will," he said with a hopeful smile, and shook his head. "I guess we'd better start getting ready. If we're gonna do this, we'd better do it in style."

~*~

When they pulled up to the funeral home, they were greeted by a swarm of paparazzi, hovering around the police barrier like vultures. The cameras were rolling on them before they even stepped out of the vehicle, the mechanical eyes eager to catch a glimpse of whoever stepped out to go into the service. There was something macabre about the entire scene. Pops' funeral had quite a crowd, but it had been nothing like this. The community came and paid their respects to a man who'd served them well. This was all wrong, reporters and photographers trying to catch the perfect shot to publish online or print later.

Sophie and Lucas had taken a separate car ahead of them to escort the Senator, and Korban felt conflicted. He wanted to be there with Sophie, she needed him there, just like he needed her. But to be in close proximity with him… he swallowed anxiously as the car pulled up and he watched as Sophie tensed alongside Lucas' side as they hurried into the building.

Korban wondered if maybe he was making a mistake, but as the security guards opened the car doors, he took a breath to steady himself. He could do this; it was the right thing to do. He could go, pay his respects to the man who tried to help, and then they would be on their way. He climbed out of the vehicle with his best friends in tow. They were wearing their nicest, and darkest, suits. Alex had loaned his black jacket and pants to Korban for the event, and he was wearing Korban's charcoal gray suit in turn. They'd agreed earlier when getting ready it would be important that he was wearing black at the funeral to avoid any of the wrong kind of speculation.

From the moment he stepped outside, it was as if he'd entered a new world. There were journalists shouting his name, pleading for a brief word or interview. His inner wolf wanted to flee, and a new kind of anxiety filled his human side, but there was a small glimmer inside of him. People were asking for his opinion, and still interested in what he had to say. It felt surreal and wonderful, at the same time. He politely declined their offers for now, and headed inside the building with his friends at his side.

Tim and Andy were lingering just inside the doorway, wearing their dress uniforms. "Hey, there you are," Tim greeted him warmly, and they exchanged brief, tense handshakes with one another.

"It's getting crowded out there," Korban said, then glanced around as strangers in black milled around, a lot of them looking more like bodyguards than family members there for the funeral.

"It's a little crowded in here, too," Andy said. "Glad you boys could make it."

"We're just here to pay our respects, then be on our way," Korban said. "I hope that his family won't be upset that we're here."

"Nah, his wife passed away a couple years ago, and any family who did show up is used to the crowd by now. It's been like this since they opened the doors to the public. Mostly security going through since the Senator is here," Tim said.

Korban saw Sophie head into the room where the wake was and put a hand on Tim's shoulder. "I'm gonna take care of business and catch up more with you guys before we leave," he said, then followed her towards the room, leaving his friends together.

He'd attended far too many funerals over the years, and they never got any easier. He braced himself to say goodbye to a stranger this time, but before he even stepped in the door he nearly walked into General Kane, who was stepping out of the room and now blocked his path to go join Sophie. He seemed surprised to see him there, his eyes going round and wide before his expression smoothed to that cold sneer that passed as a smile for him. "Ah, Mr. Diego, you come here to get some more photo ops?" he asked.

Korban swallowed to keep from growling at the man who bared his teeth at him. "I'm just here to pay my respects and honor someone who gave their life to make things better for infected people like me."

"Yes, well," General Kane squared his shoulders as he spoke, "I'm sure he'd be honored to know that a lycanthrope came to his funeral. It's not like one of your kind wasn't responsible for his untimely demise or anything."

Korban wasn't going to rise to this man's bait. He wasn't interested in playing whatever power games that Kane was concocting. "Last I knew, they suspected a Wolven, but they didn't know for sure who or what murdered Judge Affleck. It's not a good idea to go around accusing people without evidence. I thought it was innocent until proven guilty."

Kane's smile turned sinister. "That only applies to—"

"All United States citizens, that's the next line you should be telling Mr. Diego here," Senator Hunter interrupted, walking over and flashing his dazzling smile at both of them. "I wouldn't want to discover that one of our high-ranking Generals, especially one on the Council, is actually prejudiced when it comes to werewolves."

General Kane averted his gaze and his smile vanished. "Of course not, Senator. Pardon me, it's been a rough past couple of nights. Dealing with this mad Wolven on the loose just has me a bit on edge. I didn't mean anything personal, Mr. Diego. I just want to get whoever is responsible and make sure justice is served before anyone else loses their life to this… monster." Kane stated.

"That's what we all want," Korban agreed.

"Is it, though, Mr. Diego?" General Kane glared back up at him. "I mean, if you knew something, or someone that could potentially be a suspect, you'd bring them in, wouldn't you? If a fugitive was behind these murders, you'd be up front and honest, and not… hide anything, would you?"

Korban opened his mouth to fire back at the man, but the words suddenly clicked together and he stopped himself as his meaning became suddenly clear. How did he know about Naraka already? A cold chill ran through him.

"Oh, get off it, Kane," Senator Hunter grunted in disbelief, though his anxiety perfumed the air. "Your bigotry is showing. Come take a walk with me for a moment, Korban. You don't need to deal with this."

Korban blinked in surprise, not sure he'd just heard him right. When Senator Hunter gestured for him to follow, he found himself obeying without hesitation. They headed up the hall and after the Senator had a brief conversation with the funeral director, he graciously nodded and offered his office for them to go sit in. The surreal feeling from earlier returned, only more intense than before. Korban felt like a prisoner in his own body as he automatically walked in and took a seat, while the Senator closed the door tight behind them and went over to stand behind the desk.

The silence stretched between them for a long moment, before the Senator finally raised an eyebrow and asked, "Care to tell me what the hell that was about, Korban?"

He tensed. It was an automatic response, and he hated himself for flinching at the other man's tone. "I have no idea what he's talking about," Korban said in as neutral a tone as he could manage.

Senator Hunter folded his arms over his chest, his frown deepening. "Don't you lie to me," he threatened in a low tone. "I need you to come clean, right now. If you know anything about these murders, or if you're somehow involved, I need to know. I can't deal with a scandal of that magnitude. It's bad enough your name keeps making headlines, without it being printed alongside mine."

Another chill went through him, deeper than before. Korban stared down at the floor. "I never asked for this attention," he stated.

"Really, Korban? Please, you're many things, Korban, but you're not that ignorant." The Senator scoffed. "Like you didn't know from the moment you ran off with Sophie Bane that your name wouldn't appear in tabloids?"

Korban gritted his teeth together. "Don't bring Sophie into this," he growled "She has nothing to do with it."

"You're the one who brought her into it by getting involved with a married woman. Breaking up a billionaire and his wife? Clearly the apple didn't fall far from the tree, if you're following the same pattern as your mother," the Senator snapped.

Korban's heart thundered in his ears and his irritation transformed into anger. His hands clenched into fists and he glared at the Senator as he bolted up from the chair. "Don't you dare talk about her. You have no right to say a damn thing about her!" Korban pointed at him, his unbridled rage making his hand shake. "You can say whatever you want about me. I don't give a shit about your opinion of me. You are nothing to me. But I will not tolerate you bad mouthing mom. She deserved better than a heartless monster like you. The 'good' Senator who was too busy on a campaign trail to be bothered to visit her while she was pregnant. Who couldn't be bothered to come around even when she was dying."

The Senator gave him a dark, stern look. "You have no idea—"

"No! You have no idea what it was like! Watching her cry because you weren't there. Because we were your dirty little secret. She loved you, and you abandoned her when she needed you the most. Twice." Korban felt hot, stinging tears begin to pool in his eyes. "You didn't see how she suffered, or how she wasted away to nothing. You weren't there."

"You have no idea where I was, or wasn't, back then," Senator Hunter stated in a flat tone, his volume rising with his own anger. "I've worked hard to get where I am now, and I've done a lot more for you and your mother than you'll ever really know. I risked a lot, just getting you out of quarantine. I don't want to see you piss it away. You need to stop this crusade now, Korban. You need to stand down and stay quiet, and maybe those jackals will lose interest and leave you alone. You say you don't want this attention, then now's the time to stop being involved in this political mess, before it's too late. Before you ruin the work I've put into all of this. I have spent the past few years putting together a strategy that will work to bring rights back to the infected. Let me do my job as Senator and let yourself be free from this whole ordeal. If you stop now, you could still have a chance at a normal life."

Korban stared at him for a moment, before letting out a mirthless laugh. "Unbelievable. Even now you're just worried about ruining your damn campaign. You honestly think anything about my life has ever been normal? Even before I was a werewolf, I wasn't normal. Mom died, and you… you were never there. If it wasn't for Pops and Alex, I'd be out on the streets. If it wasn't for RJ risking everything for me, I'd be stuck in a cell. You want me to keep my head low? I've done it most of my life, and I'm done with it! I won't be stuffed back into some cage like an animal, to be forgotten, ever again. You may be able to push me aside, but I am not the same boy you abandoned. I didn't have a choice when this whole thing started. All I have done so far is the result of me trying to do the right thing. I saved Sophie, and protected her because that was right. I've helped others like me, because it was right. I'm not going to stop now, just because it's easier. Nothing has ever come easy for me. I've had to fight every step to get where I'm at today, and I won't stop now."

Senator Hunter glared daggers at him. "If you so much as breathe a word about…" He growled again as he trailed off, as if afraid to admit it out loud himself.

"Don't get it confused. This isn't about you, or airing out your dirty laundry. My life has never been about you. You made that clear when you left before I was born. This is about me doing what's right for people like me and Sophie. I don't have any intention of harming your precious reputation," Korban stated.

"Good. I knew you were smart," Senator Hunter began, but before he could say more a gentle knock on the door interrupted.

Korban opened the door, and the funeral director stood there, giving them an apologetic look. "Pardon the disruption, gentlemen, but the memorial services are about to begin."

"Of course. We're done here anyway. Thank you." Senator Hunter offered the man his picture-perfect smile.

Korban couldn't get out of the room fast enough. He was still riled up at the nerve of him when he sat down between Alex and RJ, near the back of the crowd. Sophie spared him a cautious glance from across the aisle, the worry reflected in her eyes. A minister stood up at the front of the room, and recited kind words about the murdered judge, words that he barely heard over his own thundering heartbeat. Alex leaned over and whispered, "You okay, Lobo?"

Korban didn't trust his voice, and gave a small nod instead.

~*~

Sophie struggled to pay attention to the memorial service. Her eyes would stray across the aisle every few moments to check on Korban. He radiated pain and frustration that seemed more than just mourning the loss of the judge, and she wondered what happened.

Lucas gently took her hand in his, cupping her palm and patting the top of her hand with the other. It was a noble attempt to try and comfort her, but it was in vain. She quietly chewed her bottom lip, her stomach churning as she wondered when she would get the chance to go comfort the man she loved, while trying to let her husband down as easy as possible.

She hadn't been able to speak with Lucas about her feelings. She approached him first thing that morning, but then he'd delivered the news that they would have an additional guest joining them, and the next few hours turned into a whirlwind of preparation for Senator Hunter's arrival.

Her heart felt heavy with remorse, knowing she would soon break Lucas' heart. She hung her head, and stared down at the floor. A funeral was a morbidly appropriate setting to think about the end of a marriage. She wanted some kind of sign that what she was about to do was right, then felt guilty for thinking that. Lucas was trying, but she had a change of heart. Her old feelings had returned, but not in the way that Lucas would be happy about. She couldn't be there for her son, who was the reason she'd tried to keep things together in the first place. It hurt that Lucas was genuinely trying to return their lives back to normal, but the truth was things never would be the same again. She was angry and frustrated that she didn't get a choice to feel this way, and Nikki had manipulated the wound in their marriage and made things worse.

Just thinking of her sister made her anxiety spike again, and she was relieved when they finally stood up, a line forming to go pay respects for Judge Affleck in the middle aisle. She leaned over to Lucas and whispered, "I need some air."

He nodded to her, and escorted her out of the room. She hurried across the hall to an empty chamber, most of the chairs gone and in the other room. The stench of decay and lilies lingered in this room, accompanied by so much grief and sadness. She paced in the empty room, trying not to lose her nerve as she stalked in front of where the coffin would be displayed. "Do you want to step outside, honey?" Lucas asked her gently.

She hated that he was playing so nice, especially because she knew it wasn't an act. The feelings radiating in him were pure. She felt like a monster, but what good would it do either of them to continue to play pretend? She steeled herself, stopping in her tracks. She wasn't able to look him in the eye when she spoke. "Lucas, I can't keep doing this. I can't keep pretending it's like it was before. You and I… we had so many great years together. But even before I was attacked, before I was deceived, you and I… we had our issues."

"Of course we did, honey. Every couple does," Lucas said.

"Not like we did, Lucas," Sophie insisted, finally turning to face him. "You have always wanted me to be something I'm not. You mean well, and you're a wonderful man in many ways. But I can't submit to you again, and play housewife. I didn't like it then, and I really don't like it now. Ever since Daniel started school, I have wanted to go back and study for my bar exam. You managed to talk me out of it every time."

"You don't need to, Sophie. I can provide more than enough for you," Lucas protested.

She shook her head. "It's not because I need to, Lucas. I want to become a lawyer. I want to finish, more than ever, and be able to help others. I need to defend the innocent, and be able to bring back our rights."

"If it means that much to you, why didn't you say something before?" Lucas asked softly. "You know you could tell me. I didn't mean to make you feel that way, honey."

He was still trying, and it broke her heart. "I know, and maybe now you would listen. But you know back then you wouldn't have, you'd try to talk me out of it, or change the subject, or Danny would interrupt us," Sophie said, her vision becoming blurry with unshed tears. "But that can't happen now, even though I wish it could. I miss those happy times, but they are in the past. I've changed, and so have you, Lucas. We grew apart, and I think it's time we talked about where we go from here. I can't be there for Danny, not until the laws are changed. But you can, and you should. He needs one of us in his life. If you and I stay together, what will happen to him? My parents can help us for so long, but they're both getting older, and they have to deal with… so many other things."

Lucas went silent, squaring his jaw and getting a stubborn look that she knew all too well. "Of course I will be there for Danny. That doesn't mean I can't be there for you, too." He paused, then glanced towards the door as people began to wander past. "You are right, we should discuss this, but now isn't the time. I'm going to go to the condo and check on Danny, and meet up with you at the lake house later to discuss this more. If that makes you happy."

There was a finality in his tone that she despised. She wanted to talk to him now while she had the nerve, but the crowd outside the door was thickening, and the murmurs were starting to ripple through the hall. Maybe it would be best if they talked more in private, because she felt an argument brewing between them. She sighed and solemnly nodded. "All right."

He turned and headed towards the door. Damion had been lurking just outside and Lucas turned to him. "I may need to arrange for a pick up," he began, but was interrupted when RJ, Alex, and Korban emerged from the other room.

"That won't be necessary. I can just get a ride back home with my friends," Sophie said.

Lucas frowned, but he couldn't argue her point, at least not in public. "All right. I'll see you later then," he responded, and then headed out after Damion.

She watched him leave and guilt swelled inside her heart. Sophie closed her eyes and took a breath, and as she inhaled she caught that wonderful, soothing scent of forest, fur, and a hint of coffee. She felt the knot in her stomach loosen as she turned to Korban. "You okay, Sophie?" he asked her as he approached.

"I'll be fine," she said with a nod. "Let's get out of here."

"Sounds good to me," Korban said, and they headed for the exit together. "Mind if we make a quick stop at the garage? I think it may be a good idea just to pop in and make sure cousin Nate is all set."

Sophie smirked and nodded. "Sure, that's fine by me. I'm not in a hurry to get back."

Especially with the argument that would be waiting for me there, she thought. She stayed close to Korban's side as they headed out the doors, quickly got to their car thanks to Sergeant McKinnon and Ellyk leading the way, and finally relaxed once they were seated and on the road. She took Korban's hand and gave it an affectionate squeeze, which he promptly returned.

As they drove, her thoughts wandered. Cyrus Autos was a few minutes away from the funeral home, so she didn't have a chance to let her mind roam too long. Especially once the car turned the corner, and Sergeant McKinnon cursed under his breath, while Sergeant Ellyk echoed his sentiment with a "What the hell?"

Sophie's attention snapped towards the garage as Alex gasped out loud. The garage was surrounded by police vehicles, including a couple large black vans. Blue and red lights were flickering all over, a dizzying display as dozens of men in dark armor and SWAT gear circled the building, carrying intimidating weapons in their hands. The entire block had become a crime scene, with several officers taping off the area while several neighbors gathered along the edges and speculated what had happened this time.

Korban's heart was pounding hard, the color draining from his face. He couldn't help but breathe out a horrified, "Oh no."

18: CONTAGION

All eyes stared in fear and wonder at the scene that was unfolding before them. Tim pulled the car over and parked it. He was out the door before Korban could even bring himself to unfasten his seatbelt. "Who's in charge here? What's going on?" Tim demanded, and even though he was several yards away Korban's enhanced hearing was able to understand every word spoken.

One of the officers along the caution tape border waved over to another, who headed inside the garage door.

RJ glanced to Korban and Sophie. "Stay here for a moment. We're going to take care of this."

Korban nodded, his heart in his throat and unable to speak in that moment. Sophie reached over and squeezed his hand, which helped comfort him. A dark-skinned, bald man dressed in a black suit and tie emerged a moment later and approached them, peering over his sunglasses. "How may I help you, gentlemen?" he asked in a smooth bass voice, a hint of irritation in his tone.

Tim played it cool and introduced himself and Andy as Alex and RJ hurried out of the car. "Sergeants McKinnon and Ellyk, of the Syracuse Police Department, Preternatural Defense Unit. We were escorting the owner of this establishment home to check on things and are rather surprised to find a Federal Agent like yourself here, Agent…?"

The man pulled out his badge and displayed it for them with a grim expression on his face. "Special Agent Singer," he corrected, and then asked, "You said the owner is with you? We'd like to ask him a couple questions."

"I'm the owner, Alejandro Cyrus," Alex blurted as he walked over. "What's going on here? If you guys are looking for a tune up, I'm afraid we're still closed for repairs."

Special Agent Singer's frown remained as he glanced to Alex. "May I see some ID?" he asked, and Alex pulled out his wallet and handed it to him. The Special Agent glanced it over for a moment, then returned it. "Unfortunately, not every customer got the memo that you're closed, Mr. Cyrus. An anonymous call alerted us that someone broke in earlier this morning. While we haven't found signs of forced entry, our concern is that this wasn't just a simple breaking and entering. We have found evidence that the man spotted here was Nathaniel Araka, an unregistered werewolf we have been looking for. He's been missing in action for quite some time now, and considered extremely dangerous."

Korban's eyes widened. How did they know Naraka was here? It wasn't like their neighbors to call the police, but maybe they were being extra cautious when it came to the garage. Cyrus Autos was the heart of their community for many years, and most of their neighbors were extremely upset after the explosion. Mikael and Naraka were careful, but maybe Mikael's suspicious outfit stood out more than he'd care to admit. Either way it seemed the cat, or rather the wolf, was out of the bag now.

One of the officers, decked out in full SWAT gear, walked over and said, "We've combed the premises, Sir, but with no luck. It seems the suspect has escaped."

Singer's eyes narrowed. "Expand the perimeter and search further. Get every second of footage, from every security camera the next ten blocks over. I don't want to lose him now. Report any and all findings to me immediately." The officer nodded and headed to issue the orders to the others, as the special agent turned back to the small group waiting there. "I'd like to ask Mr. Cyrus some questions about his association with the suspect. Any and all information could benefit our investigation."

"I don't know any one named Nathaniel Araka," Alex stated, looking confused. "I'd like to assist you, any way that I can. Perhaps if we go inside I can see if anything is missing, and that may help?"

Singer nodded and said, "That would be an excellent place to start, Mr. Cyrus. Why don't you lead the way?"

Alex lead the investigators toward the garage, and Tim swore and headed back to the car. He leaned over the open window and stared at Korban for a moment. "You aren't hiding anyone else that I should know about in there, are you, Korban?"

"N-no," Korban lied, shaking his head.

Tim stared him down for a long moment before he spoke again. "I better go call Commissioner DeRusso. She isn't going to like this. Not one bit. Stay here for now, got it? Don't talk to those guys unless I'm there with you too."

Korban swallowed and nodded, trying to push his guilt down.

Tim pulled out his phone and walked over to make the call, while RJ and Andy talked over by the barrier. Korban couldn't see RJ's expression from where he sat in the car, but he was certain he wasn't happy either.

Sophie's purse vibrated, making them both jump. She exhaled sharply and dug through her bag to pull out her cell phone. Korban caught a glimpse of the screen and saw Lucas' name glowing, along with a photo of him and Daniel together. "Hello, Lucas," Sophie said, "Now isn't a really good time to talk, we have a lot going on here at the garage."

"Put Korban Diego on the phone," an unfamiliar, gravelly voice answered. "I know he's with you."

Sophie tensed, and looked at Korban. He frowned in confusion, the emotion mirrored by Sophie when she asked, "Who is this?"

The man chuckled on the other line, but it wasn't a happy sound. "I asked to speak with Korban. I'm not in the mood for an interview. Put him on the phone, before I lose my patience. And when I lose my patience, I start taking parts off Mr. Bane here, and… what's the little one's name? I think you yelled for Danny before, is that right, Lucas?"

"Go to hell you monster," Lucas snarled from somewhere nearby, his voice taut with pain.

"Dad, I'm scared," Danny's voice came, soft and fearful.

Sophie blanched and handed the phone to Korban, almost dropping it in her shaking hands. Korban took it and brought it up to his ear. "This is Korban," he said, trying to keep his voice level despite his rising fear and anger at whoever was on the other line.

"You've been a busy boy lately, Korban. Putting your nose in a lot of things that you really shouldn't have."

Korban swallowed, trying to remain calm. "What do you want from me?"

"I want you to come to the Bane family's condo for a little chat. No cops, or I'll throw both of my friends here right out the window. It's a long drop down below. You have thirty minutes. That should be more than enough time to get here from Cyrus Autos. Even if you need to shake off the Feds."

Korban panicked. "Wait—"

"I've waited long enough. See you in thirty," the man said, and then came a beep and silence as the line was canceled.

Sophie's eyes brimmed with tears, her entire body shaking. "We have to go. Now," she insisted, her voice cracking.

Korban nodded, though he hesitated. "We need to tell someone where we're going, and what's going on."

Sophie's eyes lit up and she unfastened her seatbelt before climbing into the front of the car. He watched her move, Tim's keys still dangling in the ignition. "Oh, they'll know. He said no cops, but they'll be looking for a stolen car that belongs to one soon enough. We need to get there and stop whoever he is from hurting Danny or Lucas," she said, and snapped her seatbelt back in place, turned the keys, and revved the engine to life.

Before he could even think to protest, she had the car in reverse, carefully but quickly turning it around and driving off down the street. Korban gripped onto the back of the seat and tried to think as Sophie sped down the road. The way she was driving, it wouldn't take them too long to get to the condo. He tried to piece together a plan in the precious minutes they had on the ride over, but like cramming at the last minute for a test, nothing was sticking in his mind. He worried about Danny and Lucas, and wondered who was there with them and threatening their lives. Most of all, he wondered how he fit into all of this, and how the hell he was going to resolve this without anyone losing their life.

~*~

Sophie drove to the condo as fast as she could. She knew this could be suicide, running in blind without a plan, but what else could they do? The madman on the other line had given them a countdown, and who knew if he'd get bored and just kill Danny or Lucas before they got there. The thought made her ill. Even with their differences, and the argument they'd last had, she didn't want anything to happen to her husband. She saw Korban's worried reflection in the rearview mirror. *Whatever this stranger wanted Korban for, they wouldn't get him either,* she thought with an audible growl. Her protectiveness was already in overdrive, and whoever it was who not only threatened her family but also threatened her Mate would soon know they'd made a lethal mistake.

A couple blocks from the building, she got caught in evening traffic. Stuck at a light, she kept glancing around, waiting for the light to turn green, and tapping her fingers anxiously along the steering wheel. They were losing precious time waiting for mundane things like traffic jams. High above the city, the waxing moon was fully in view now, resembling a clock face that ticked away every passing moment against an orange sky.

She glanced to the empty spot nearby, with its sign warning that there was no parking, and pulled quickly into it, the tire resting on the sidewalk as she parked and left the keys in the ignition. "Let's keep moving," she said, then threw open the door and leapt out of the car, sprinting up the sidewalk.

She rushed around the corner, recognizing the street name. The traffic was rushing through the street in front of her, but she was faster. She darted into the street, car horns blaring and brakes squealing, but she didn't stop to look back. Instead she rushed forward, leaping up as headlights grew too close and watching as the cars sped by under her feet. She ran through a busy street of shoppers, knocking bags and boxes out of people's arms, getting cursed at but moving too quickly to be remotely bothered by anything they said. She rounded another corner, and there it was, the tall building she had once called home.

Korban touched her arm, his face flushed and his breath coming out in panting gasps. She offered him a grateful look for keeping up, then rushed towards the building with renewed determination. She didn't pause for the door man, practically flinging herself into the elevator, the door nearly closing on Korban as he hurried behind her.

They watched as the light notified them of each passing level, its cheery little bell making her grind her teeth. Every second that passed, her family was in more danger.

The thought made her shudder, and the elevator crept along slower than ever. Korban reached and took her hand, and she gazed to him. His amber eyes held a gentleness to them, and he was trying to calm her down. She wanted to look away, to ignore it, but it felt good. "Breathe, Sophie," he said softly. He didn't tell her not to worry. He knew there was no point.

She nodded, and when the bell and light finally crawled to her floor, she punched the security code from memory, and then rushed off the elevator and onto the floor. She flung open the door and found the living room empty, the lights on and television playing a raucous cartoon in the background. She could hear voices coming from the kitchen, and recognized one of as Lucas. Her heart skipped a beat. They hadn't arrived too late.

She was about to cry out to them, but thought better of it. She listened; over the loud sound system and her booming heartbeat she could faintly hear snippets of their conversation, and the soft, sniffling sobs of her son. "Please, you know who I am… look around, you see my home. Take whatever you like. No questions asked. I can give you whatever it is you want. Money is no object to me. Just let us go, and we'll forget this ever happened," Lucas said as calmly as he could, his voice strained.

"The only thing I want is already on his way," the man said calmly. "Or he better be, for both your sake."

Sophie exchanged a look with Korban, putting her finger to her lips. He gave a small nod, and the two of them crept towards the kitchen to try and assess the situation.

"At least let my son go. He's just a boy. He doesn't need to see this," Lucas pleaded.

"I'm tired of hearing your voice. Maybe I'll do the world a favor and cut out your tongue." There was the tell-tale sound of metal sliding against stone, and someone whimpered.

Peering around the corner, Sophie was horrified to find an all too familiar looking man looming over Lucas and Danny with a butcher knife. Lucas had himself in front of their son as Naraka lashed out with the blade, causing Lucas to cry out in pain.

"Naraka no!" she bellowed, launching herself at lightning speed towards the other werewolf, knocking him into the other room, her hands grasping at his wrists, one hand still clutching the bloody knife.

Korban rushed in behind her, the scent of fresh blood alarming him. He saw Lucas clutching his stomach, bright red blood blossoming from an unseen wound. "Hold on!" He slid across the linoleum and knelt at his side, grabbing a towel hanging from the oven and pressing it to Lucas' wound. He still couldn't believe this. What the hell made Naraka snap this bad? "How bad is it? Do you think you can stand?"

"I… I think so…" Lucas said, wincing, his teeth grating together in pain. He rolled his eyes frantically in the direction where Sophie had vanished. "Sophie..."

"Don't worry. She's strong, she can hold her own." It had taken him all summer to accept this, but it wasn't a lesson he'd ever forget. "We need to get you out of here, and to a hospital." He glanced to Danny, whose face dripped with tears.

The boy's eyes went round with fear as he gawked at Korban, who must have intimidated the boy. He was another strange man, with wolf-like eyes. Korban spoke as gently as possible, trying to soothe him. "My name is Korban, Danny, and I'm a friend of your Mom and Dad. I'm gonna need your help to get your Dad to safety, and I need you to be brave, buddy. We're going to help him walk to the hall, but I need you to help to hold this towel up against him. You need to keep a lot of pressure on your Dad's wound so he doesn't lose too much blood. Can you do that for him?"

Danny looked scared, but Lucas gave him a nod, and then Danny nodded to Korban. Korban scooped up the injured man, letting Lucas lean against him as Danny helped keep the towel against him as they headed for the door. He wasn't about to leave a wounded man in a room filled with more knives. Once he got the two of them out to safety he'd go and help Sophie. He kept moving, focused on his goal. He'd deal with Naraka and his betrayal soon enough.

Sophie snarled as she wrestled Naraka down. He was surprised, dropping the knife as they rolled across the room, Sophie pinning him down by the wrists to the carpet. Her eyes flashed like daggers. "How dare you! Setting us up from the beginning! We trusted you! Korban helped you!"

Naraka's surprised look melted to one of eagerness. An amused smile curved his mouth, that was a twisted version of his usual grin.

"I was hoping you'd show up."

She didn't have a chance to blurt a single word out, as she was suddenly thrown off the werewolf and across the room. She landed hard against the back of the couch, and it tipped over with her on it. She quickly scrambled to her feet again and saw Naraka smoothly stand, with a grace she'd only seen in vampires like Mikael. The thought jolted her, and she glanced around wildly. Where was the vampire? She glared at Naraka. "Where's your bloodsucking boyfriend?" she demanded.

"Oh, don't you worry about him," Naraka said, his voice strange and distant, almost sing-song when he spoke. "And speaking of partners… Korban, Korban, Korban… trying to sneak out on me already?" His yellow gaze locked on him across the room. "But you just got here."

Sophie saw Korban leading Lucas and Danny towards the door. She lunged at Naraka before he could attack them, knocking them both into one of the sofas and causing it to topple over. They rolled a few feet along the carpet, and Naraka pinned her down with a deep chuckle. "You're so feisty! It's kind of a turn on, darlin'."

Korban overheard Naraka's words and suppressed a growl as he reached the door. He opened it up and found the hall empty. He sniffed the air, cautious, but only picked up Lucas' blood and pain, and Danny's determination and fear. There was still no sign of Mikael anywhere, but he would be on the lookout. Lucas moaned in pain as they stepped carefully up the hall. "I'm getting you to the elevator, and then Danny can get the door man downstairs to get you help, okay? I won't leave Sophie alone."

Lucas grunted out, "Thanks."

"You're being really brave, Danny," Korban told the young boy, who was still pressing the reddening cloth against his father's wound.

Danny didn't say anything, his face pale and eyes wide as they reached the elevator. Korban pressed the button and glanced back at the open door, straining to listen for Sophie, scared to leave her alone like that with the crazed werewolf. The elevator had descended back to the bottom floor, and the little light was inching its way up again. It seemed to be moving even slower than when they'd arrived.

There came a loud crash from the living room, followed by the shattering sound of glass. All three of them flinched at the sound. Lucas gripped Korban's arm and groaned, "Go help her, please. I can manage from here."

Lucas leaned against the wall as the elevator continued to ascend at a crawl. Danny kept his small hands pressed against the bloody towel, loyally remaining at his father's side. Korban hesitated only for a moment, then nodded before turning and hurrying back into the condo. Mikael never seemed to be too far away from Naraka's side, and Korban kept his guard up in case the vampire would try to sneak up on him again. Though if he popped up unexpectedly right now, Korban was going to deck him, for more than one reason.

She struggled to free herself from beneath Naraka, his heavy body pressing down against hers. She managed to free her leg and kick out, but it connected not with the werewolf but one of the standing lamps nearby, which fell to the ground with a loud, clattering crash. "Get… off… of me!" Sophie snarled at him.

The corner of his mouth kept twitching, a nervous tick he didn't have before. As he leered down at her, his face seemed to contort, and her heart leapt into her throat. Was he shifting into a Wolven? He didn't even smell like wolf any more, or the cold absence of life that she knew to be vampire. Yet he wasn't human either, but something else that took her off guard. The death-like stench that rolled from him now seemed to make her Wolf squirm, desperate to get away from him as he leaned down and breathed on her. "What's the matter, darlin'? Your fear smells… mouth-watering," he said, bowing his head down and inhaling her scent in deeply before licking his lips. "Delicious."

Alarms were sounding in her head, not that she needed them to warn her she was in danger. A primal fear that had more to do with her being a woman than wolf began to bubble up to the surface. She struggled harder against him, but his strength was incredible. She took a breath to howl out or scream, but suddenly something crashed against Naraka and he was lifted away from her, rolling across the floor, knocking more furniture around in the process. She caught his forest and wolf scent and the fear faded. "Keep your hands off her!" Korban viciously growled as he pinned him . "What the hell has gotten into you Naraka? I thought you didn't attack civilians, and you nearly gutted Lucas for no reason!"

Naraka laughed, a dark and foreign sound. "He's hardly innocent. Do you even know what his company does? I'm doing the world a favor. Just like when I put you down, Korban. You should have just kept your head down and remained another sheep, following the flock. But no, you had to go and start stirring up trouble. You drew the wrong attention this time, pup. You should have just kept your nose out of it."

Naraka rolled him beneath him, and Korban grunted and struggled against the other werewolf. "Out of what? You're not making any sense!" Korban exclaimed.

He had to calm the other wolf, and so Korban reached up, cupping his face, locking his gaze with Naraka's in a desperate attempt to understand what had happened to make him snap like this. This close his yellow eyes were like tiny suns, smoldering down at him. Yet even as he braced himself, waiting for that odd feeling of weightlessness, the sensation never came. Korban frowned in confusion, which quickly turned to horror as Naraka's face contorted against his palms. Korban managed to shove him off as the man dissolved into a fit of manic laughter. "Who are you?" Korban demanded as he scrambled to his feet, Sophie suddenly by his side and glaring suspiciously at the man they had thought was Naraka.

"I'm Naraka, for now," he said once his laughter finally faded, giving a twisted pout. "No fair. You ruined my big surprise."

There was something truly terrifying in this so-called Naraka's expression, especially as his features seemed to morph and ripple as he smirked at them with a sinister grin. Korban took a step back, nearly tripping over one of the fallen chairs. "What the hell are you?"

"That's just the thing, Korban," he said as his face seemed to warp and melt, his features rearranging like a fluid, horrific puzzle. His amber eyes began to glow red, then turned a familiar stormy blue. His jaw thickened and squared, and his dark hair thinned as gray hairs began to appear. There were terrible sounds that accompanied the transformation, the cracking of bones and the wet sound of shifting muscle. Yet even as it happened before his eyes, Korban still couldn't believe it when he was suddenly staring at another familiar face.

Sophie gasped out in disbelief. "Kane?"

19: SEPTIC

"That's General Kane to you," Kane corrected her with a sardonic smile. "Not that it matters, really. I can be anyone that I desire to be. As long as I've tasted their blood, I can morph myself into a copy of anybody. I'll be adding to my collection today, it seems." He brought his hand up to his lips, and licked Lucas's bright, red blood from his fingers, his eyes rolling back in pleasure. "A bit rich for my tastes, but I guess that's to be expected, now isn't it?"

As he cackled at his own bad joke, Korban tried not to lose his lunch. "What do you want with me? You could have just asked, you didn't need to go this far," Korban insisted, and shuddered at his own words as he realized the man's intentions even before he finished his own sentence. "You want to kill me… why?"

"I suppose that's a fair question, given the situation," General Kane said. "I'd want to know why someone wanted me dead, too."

He stepped forward in their direction, studying his hands, which were still smeared with Lucas's blood. "There's so much that can be determined by blood. The tiniest drop can hold so much information about who we are. The color of our hair and skin. The potential of our body's defense against illness and disease. Our genetic destiny, all determined by the tiniest chromosomes, before we even take our first breath. For so many years we simply accepted what we were, a product of our parents' blood. Until the day we began to examine the possibilities, and found out that there are infinite amounts of potential in what it can really do." He lifted his hand up to inspect it closer, a manic look in his eyes. "Our greatest gift as human beings is innovation. We don't settle for what was, and we strive to make a better future. We are constantly looking to improve the world around us, so it was only a matter of time before we began to look into ways we could improve ourselves. Why take steps for a better future if you aren't there to reap the benefits you've sewn?"

"Those are all nice points, but I still don't get why you want to spill my blood," Korban said with a frown.

General Kane leveled his gaze with Korban and gave him a slow smile. The hairs on his arm began to stand on end as he felt that familiar, creeping power crawl over him. Korban quickly glanced away, sweat beading at his brow, and felt Sophie tense next to him. "You've been a naughty wolf, Korban. I'm only doing my due diligence as an American citizen and ending you now. Before you go and stick your nose into more business that it doesn't belong in."

Korban's eyes narrowed, and he braved a quick glance to throw a dirty look in the general's direction. "You mean exposing you for what you did to Naraka and those soldiers?"

Kane gave him a genuinely surprised look. "You really do have a knack for finding trouble, don't you, Korban? Though maybe it isn't all your fault. It's in your blood, no doubt, even after you were infected. Your father is just as vexing as you."

It was Korban's turn to be taken off guard. "My father? What does he have to do with anything?"

"The Good Senator, always playing political games. Did you know that the Council was his idea? He couldn't resist the lure of being able to make a statement that would shine a positive light on his re-election. Unfortunately, your unexpected fame due to your heroics would naturally bring you to the table of discussion. A convenient gathering, which brought most of my enemies together, until he got cold feet and didn't show up. Sending his poor intern instead, when he realized his name would be sharing the same sentence as yours in the headlines. He couldn't risk people looking into your connection, now could he? If he had just shown up like he was supposed to, or maybe cancelled the entire thing completely, then maybe all of this wouldn't have been necessary." Kane paused, then licked the rest of the blood from his fingers before he continued. "You see, it all comes down to blood in the end."

Korban laughed, even as his stomach churned. "You honestly think he gives a damn about me? He's never been a part of my life!"

"That may be true, but he can't ignore your death. Neither with the coroner's report. Once they have to piece you back together, they'll look into your blood. Even if he avoids me forever, he can't avoid the truth. As delightful as it would be to rip him limb from limb, I would be satisfied with eviscerating his career instead. Especially since I'll be silencing you in his place. It's really a win-win for me either way. Though I would prefer to devour him, I mean… imagine the things I could do if I were re-elected as Senator… though perhaps after I've destroyed him on paper, I can put him out of his misery once and for all."

"You keep going on and on about blood. What are you, some kind of shape-shifting vampire?" Sophie demanded.

Kane glared at her. "I am far superior to any of you… weak abominations. Your kind… vampires, werewolves, and the rest… are nothing more than mistakes, while I am… perfection. Allow me to demonstrate."

He suddenly knocked the heavy couch easily across the room with one hand, not even breaking a sweat. "The strength, and speed." He leapt towards them, and in a flash was behind Sophie, his fingers threading through her hair, sending shivers down her spine. His face rippled and his hair turned blond, Kane suddenly leering at her with Lucas's face. She leapt back, glaring at him and keeping her back away from him. He smirked, looking smug. "The ability to be whoever I want, not just a mangy wolf. Every strength you have on two legs, and so much more. The full moon doesn't hold my power. Silver doesn't slow me down, and neither does the sun. I can call upon my power at a whim. Which of course, leaves you at a slight disadvantage. Only..." He moved again, a blur, and got into her face, his breath hot and foul. "Any disadvantage leaves you completely vulnerable, and at my mercy."

Her eyes narrowed. "So you think." She brought her knee up into his balls, shoving him hard away from her. He howled in agony and crumpled into himself, cursing and red-faced.

Sophie rushed towards the exit, but a blur appeared in front of her, Lucas's sneering face once again too close to her face for comfort. "Thought it would be that easy, Sophie dear? Damn, you're more cold-blooded than me to do such a thing to your husband."

"You're not even half the man Lucas is you monster!" Sophie snarled as she threw her arm back to punch him, but he caught her fist, and began crushing her hand with his own.

She cried out and he laughed. "You little bitch, you're going to pay for that."

"Get your hands off of her!" Korban snarled and lunged at him.

Kane released Sophie, but knocked them both across the room with two swift strikes of his hands. Sophie spun in the air and managed to land in a crouching position, but Korban collided with one of the fallen couches. The force of the blow knocked the wind from his lungs even though he landed against the soft cushions. Korban gasped for air, dazed and disoriented.

The general leapt and landed hard on Sophie, sending her crashing down into an end table, smashing the ceramic lamp into a thousand sharp pieces which stabbed her as she rolled through the mess, adorning the pale carpet with red splashes of her blood. Before she could even get up, Kane had her pinned down again, shoving her face hard into the floor. "You see, my little she-wolf? I became something far greater than you will ever be."

"Can't handle a bruised ego, oh Perfect One?" Sophie growled, then bucked, almost throwing him off her but Kane wasn't underestimating her anymore, and suddenly launched his elbow down hard into the center of her back, causing her to arch into the floor and cry out in pain.

"You won't have such smart words coming from your pretty little mouth when I'm through with you, Sophie dear..." He leaned in, using his weight to pin her struggling form down to the ground, grinding her into the shards of the lamp. One of the shards pierced into the side of her breast and she whimpered in pain, which only made him laugh. "Then again... maybe it would be more rewarding to keep you alive to play with some more... in perhaps a more intimate way—"

But suddenly there was a rush of wind, and the weight was gone from pinning her down, and she could breathe much easier again. She got up quickly, the shards falling free from her skin as it healed rapidly, the holes and blood stains on her shirt the only remnants of the attack. Korban had the general pinned to the wall, which now had a crack along it from the force of the blow. Her Mate looked absolutely rabid as he pinned the general to the ruined wall. "Don't you ever touch her again you bastard!"

Korban must have hit him hard, because even he was in a slight daze, but then Kane chuckled again. "So nice of you to join us again, Korban."

Kane moved faster than before, one minute he was there, the next he was gone, and not even half a second later Korban smelled his foul breath, recognizing the sickening smell of blood and decay, and then the next moment he was pinned to the wall, stars flashing into his vision from the force of the blow. Kane laughed, leaning in and his putrid breath making Korban's stomach churn. "Any last words, Korban? I think a final request is worth honoring, as long as it is a reasonable one..."

"Get off of him!" Sophie snarled and leapt onto Kane's back, yanking him ferociously away.

Kane gave a bored yawn and caught her ankle, twisting her leg until it made a disturbing crack. She gave a pained yelp and let go enough for him to throw her across the room, using her to knock the heavy sofa another few yards back until it struck the wall, along with Sophie's head, with an audible crack. Sophie's body went limp on the cushions, her eyes rolling back into her skull as she was knocked unconscious. Korban threw all the force he could into elbowing the general's stomach, pain radiating from the blow as he struck his suddenly stone-like skin. "Foolish mutts. The more you fight me, the stronger I get! Though I must say, this is rather exciting... you're definitely more of a challenge than the usual, mundane human."

He leaned in, shoving Korban harder into the wall, making it suddenly difficult for him to breathe. If he didn't do anything else, he would be crushed to death. He struggled instinctively, but Kane was suddenly a wall, immovable, and slowly crushing the last of his air from his lungs. "I bet your blood is stronger, maybe sweeter too. I suppose there is only one way to find out," he said and leaned in, his foul, hot breath curling against Korban's throat, the werewolf struggling all the more against him.

Korban's heart was pounding against his rib cage, his lungs screaming for air as sharp, wet teeth grazed his skin. He tensed and froze at the sensation, afraid to move. Yet when those blunt teeth began to tear into his flesh he began to struggle harder against the solid man, desperate to escape though his vision was swimming with dark spots as his body screamed for oxygen, for escape, for the pain and degrading dominance to stop.

The wall cracked a little from the pressure of his body against it, or maybe it was his ribs. Korban was in too much pain to tell where any new wounds or breaks began. He heard a scream in the distance, a young boy's cry of surprise. "You?!" Danny yelped out in disbelief.

He'd thought he imagined it, until Kane pulled away from his throat to listen. Korban was vaguely aware of the blood that poured, hot and sticky, down his throat as the friendly stars that danced along his vision were getting larger and darker at the same time.

"Let him go, brother," Naraka's voice came, stern but calm as he demanded in a level tone, "Korban isn't the enemy. He's my friend. You've never been the bullying kind before, Maverick."

20: SHOCK

Korban could suddenly breathe again as Kane stepped back. He gasped in deep breaths, the air that filled his oxygen-starved lungs an almost euphoric sensation.

"Nate," Kane's voice seemed far away, even though he stood right behind him, "is that really you?"

"The one and only, last I knew," Naraka replied. "Though it looks like you've managed to get yourself the ability to really be all that you can be."

Kane chuckled. "How do you know I'm not the real General?"

"Your answer just now. You called me Nate. General Kane never called me by that name," Naraka supplied. "It's been a long time, brother. I thought you died."

"Maybe I should have. Healing piece by piece, bit by bit, is a very slow, and very painful, process," Kane, Maverick, or whoever the hell he was said. "I see the General lied to me about your demise, too. Makes me wonder what else he was lying about."

"So many things, brother," Naraka said, his voice softer, and gentler. "You need to let Korban go. He's helped me through a lot."

"No can do on that, Nate," Maverick said, tightening his grip on the back of Korban's neck and causing him to tense up again. "Your boy here is the best bait I can get to settle an old score."

"No one else needs to die, Maverick," Naraka kept his voice steady, and Korban felt a calm wave wash over him as Naraka's familiar power seeped from his voice. It must have been working for Maverick too because his grip had loosened. "You killed Judge Affleck, and you took out General Kane. Though it seems you did a better job with the General. They never even reported him as dead."

Maverick's body tensed and he tightened his grip again, causing Korban to let out a gasp. "I got angry with the judge, and got sloppy. He shouldn't have insulted me. And as for our long, lost General… I took my time with him. I made him suffer like he did to us. I devoured every piece of him, bit by bit, slowly over days. Finger by finger, toe by toe. He was a big man and it took almost a week for the shock to finally stop his heart, and I couldn't revive him again. Or maybe it was because I'd taken his left arm by that point." Maverick paused, licking his lips at the memory. "No one will ever find his body. There wasn't anything left when I was through with him, so there was no issue when I took over his life."

Korban shuddered at this revelation, and wished he had the room to throw up. The bite mark along his throat felt raw and throbbed in time with his pulse. His body ached and his knees buckled. The pain his body was in was starting to take its toll. He felt dizzy and sick and wasn't sure if he could stand on his own.

"Mav, don't let them win. Don't let them turn you into a murderer," Naraka pleaded.

"I'm a weapon, Nate. The perfect weapon, the perfect soldier, all wrapped into one. They made me into this, gave me this gift, and left me to die. You left, too. You don't know what it was like, the agony of piecing myself back together after days and days of rotting. To wake up in the morgue and find all the bodies everywhere, torn apart, the blood on your hands." Maverick trembled, and Korban felt his fingers dig into his skin as the shape-shifter's excitement grew. "You were the lucky one, Naraka. You were taken in and cared for by our General. You always were his favorite pet, even before you were a wolf. But he abandoned me! Forgot about me! Didn't even recognize me when I finally found him!"

"You honestly think I'm lucky? You think he took care of me?" Naraka scoffed. "He locked me up in the deepest, darkest part of quarantine, where no one could find me. If it wasn't for Mikael I'd still be in that dungeon, poked and prodded until my mind finally snapped and I ended up like you, brother."

Maverick seemed to struggle with that revelation, and a fowl, death-like stench seeped into the air as he shifted again. Korban caught a sidelong glimpse as his flesh morphed and twisted into a new face, one he only remembered from Naraka's vision. Though the young, jovial Maverick from Naraka's memories was no more. This man had been broken and twisted, his face a mass of scar tissue. Patches of red, pink, and white scars covered nearly every inch of visible skin, like some macabre puzzle pieced back together. The man was barely recognizable, except for his voice, which came from a lipless, gaping mouth that was just as scarred as the rest of him. "Enough! I'm already damned, Naraka. I have nothing left now but the thrill of the hunt, and after tasting the blood of the infamous 'werewolf savior,' I'm looking forward to finishing the rest of him."

Korban struggled against the shape-shifter, who laughed as he slowly choked off his air again. Korban grabbed for something – anything – and his fingers caught the base of a nearby lamp. He smashed it against his attacker's side, but he might as well have hit him with a pillow for the reaction he got. He wasn't lying when he said he was getting stronger. The shattered, ceramic shards of the lamp didn't even scratch his skin.

Maverick laughed, glancing from the struggling werewolf he had pinned to the wall to the other challengers. Naraka gave a very dark, low growl, baring his sharp, pearly white fangs. "You're protective of him? Taken him under your broken wing, have you Naraka?" He shook his head. "Some things never change."

Korban dreaded the moment those spots returned to his vision. The dizzy feeling, and then the return of that horrible breath... he couldn't stop it, and suddenly vomited, causing Maverick to let go and take a few steps back in horror. "Disgusting..." He sneered as Korban sank, heaving to the ground.

He kicked Korban hard, the ground spinning beneath him as he struck the entertainment center, causing a loud series of breaking glass as it buckled under the force of his blow. By some sick and twisted miracle, the blow didn't knock Korban out, but left him disoriented instead. The pale shadow that must have been Mikael lunged forward towards the dark form of the soldier. When Naraka joined the fray, the three figures in the room became a mass of colors dancing across his blurred vision. Animalistic snarls and growls filled the air, the occasional splatter of crimson and smell of fresh blood signaling that a nasty strike had landed. Objects and the remnants of furniture were being shattered and smashed. The once immaculate Bane Condo has become a battleground.

His vision finally came back into focus again as Naraka cursed and viciously snarled with the soldier, their muscles straining as they grappled in the middle of the devastated room. "You won't win this one, Mav. You may be stronger, but you're not any smarter than you were back then!"

"That's rich coming from you, you stupid mongrel! You can't stop me! I'm invincible, no thanks to you or your vampire friend!" The soldier threw his head back and laughed.

"Oh, fuck me, I'm tired of ye runnin' yer mouth!" Mikael finally spoke up as he stood, wiping some blood from the corner of his mouth and baring his fangs. "Ye just keep goin' on, and on, about how great and fuckin' powerful ye are. Well so far I ain't impressed by you or yer 'perfect weapon.' If yer plan is t' bore us t' death, yer on the right track. Just because I got an eternity now, doesn't mean I want t' waste it with a fuckin' wanker like you."

Naraka snorted, but the sound quickly turned to a pained moan as Maverick twisted his arm and something snapped. The so-called perfect soldier smirked over to the vampire. "You were saying?"

Mikael's glare became lethal. "No one harms me Mate," he said in a cold, flat voice.

Korban saw the pain in Naraka's eyes, then like a flash the pale vampire leapt upon Maverick, his hand a blur with a glint of twisted silver, and then he leapt off the shape-shifter, who stood there for a long moment, as baffled as Korban was about where the weapon had appeared from. Then it dawned on him. It was the same knife that Maverick used on Lucas, now forced down Maverick's throat. Maverick clutched his neck as he gagged and choked on the lodged piece of metal.

Naraka leapt forward with a wolf-like growl, knocking Maverick onto the ground. The blond vampire moved like a blur past him, this time grabbing cords from the broken entertainment center, so many black cords that snapped from the broken electronics, sparks flying from the tips. Korban's jaw dropped open, then quickly closed as he realized what was going to happen next, too horrified to turn away.

The vampire jammed the wires into Maverick's gasping, open mouth. The man's eyes widened, and then his body jerked and jumped as the electricity ran through him. Korban thought the worst smell had been the man's breath, and that was until the scent of burnt, rotten flesh filled the air, making his nostrils burn. The lights around the room flickered, then finally the fuse must have blown. The power went out, the soldier's body thudded to the ground, and finally went still.

Korban's eyes adjusted to the dark as the two spoke, his vision still hazy. Smoke wafted from Maverick's head, but Korban didn't let his gaze linger. He would already have nightmares from this, he didn't want to remember any more details than he needed.

Mikael stepped away from the body, his face a blank mask again as he approached and knelt alongside Naraka. The werewolf's head hung down and tears streamed down his cheeks. "How bad is it?" Mikael asked gently, carefully studying his wounded arm.

"My arm will heal, soon enough," Naraka said as he rolled his shoulder and winced, looking down at it. "Everything else… that will take time."

Mikael nodded, then wiped Naraka's tears away with his pale hand. "It's not yer fault. He wasn't the same man ye knew anymore."

"I know, but… it doesn't make it any easier," Naraka said. "Seeing him like that. Knowing how much he's suffered."

Now that the dust had settled, he rushed over blindly in the direction where Sophie had fallen, stumbling and tripping over the battle debris of broken furniture. He found her, laying on the couch, her breathing slow and even, her heart still racing in her chest. He touched her cheek, her skin felt warmer than usual. Or maybe he was starting to feel colder. His teeth chattered when he spoke and goose bumps prickled along his arms. "Sophie…"

She stirred and moaned, leaning into his touch before her eyes flashed open and focused on him, surprise then relief reflected in them. "Korban… you're all black and blue," Sophie said softly as she gently reached up and caressed his cheek with her fingers. Her brow creased and she glanced towards the condo's front door. "Danny… Lucas… are they okay?"

"The wee lad was a bit shaken when he saw us come out of the elevator, and his Da is a bit worse fer wear, but gettin' stabbed in tha gut'll do that t' ye," Mikael said.

Somewhere down on the street below, sirens were approaching. Help was on the way, but the sound made Mikael and Naraka tense.

"We'd better get outta here. Are you two gonna be all right if we jet?" Naraka asked.

Sophie sat up, wincing as she moved her foot. "Ow, dammit! I think my ankle's broken, but I'll survive. I need to go check on the rest of my family since I know my Mate is okay."

Korban smiled, though he felt woozy. "Yeah, I'm fine… I just need to sit a moment…" His vision was swimming again and he stumbled. Maybe he lost more blood than he thought.

Sophie caught him before he fell, and he saw the worry reflected in her blue and gold-speckled eyes. "You're so pale," she said, her voice sounding so far away.

Dark spots began to fill his vision, and he felt like he was floating. Sophie called out his name, but it sounded even further away as he slipped into the darkness.

~*~

"Korban!" Sophie cried as he passed out. Her ankle seared in pain as she steadied her hold on him as he slumped in her arms. Before she could blink, Mikael was there, and helped shift Korban's weight, lowering his body onto the couch. Sophie sat down alongside him, gently touching his face. She cradled his head and felt a warm wetness. Tilting his head to the side, she saw the bite mark was still bleeding, and frowned. "He's not healing!"

Mikael frowned and leaned in, causing Sophie to growl defensively, and the vampire to meet her gaze with a serious expression. "I won't hurt him, I just need a taste t' see if his blood's been infected."

Sophie clung tighter to Korban, about to protest, but Naraka looked to her, his amber gaze intense and his voice oddly calming. "He won't hurt Korban, Sophie. Let him help."

Every fiber of her protested this idea, yet she found herself giving a nod, and Mikael leaned down and put his mouth over Korban's bleeding neck. She did give a warning growl that was more animal than human, and after a moment Mikael pulled away, making a face and spitting the blood on the carpet. The dark spray of blood was more like motor oil and Sophie's eyes widened at the sight of it. Mikael coughed and sputtered, shaking his head. "It's worse than I thought. He's been poisoned."

Sophie stared at Mikael, horrified. "What can we do?"

"I got some of it, I'll try t' get more out. I've never tasted anything like it, and hope I don't ever again," Mikael said, then leaned in again, making a face before he bit into his throat.

The wet, sucking sound made Sophie's stomach turn, and Mikael released Korban after another moment, spraying more blood out onto the carpet. At least this time it was more red than black. "I got most of it, the rest will be up t' him."

Sophie could hear Korban's heartbeat steady again, along with his breathing. She felt warm tears slide down her cheeks as she cradled his head in her lap. His neck wound still wasn't healing and he remained unconscious, but there were small signs he was already doing better than before.

Mikael was gagging and sputtering still nearby. He ran his hand through his short, dirty blond hair and shuddered. "Fuck, that's foul. Ye better tell 'im when he wakes up that I saved his arse."

The sirens were getting louder, and Naraka went over and touched Mikael's shoulder. "We'd better move, now. Before the cops come and crash this party."

Mikael nodded, spitting another mouthful and grumbling under his breath in Irish. He wiped the blood away from his mouth along his dark sleeve and the two of them started for the door. "The emergency stairs are down the hall near the service elevator. I don't think you'll have to worry about running into cops this far up, just be careful when you get down to the lower floors," Sophie told them, and then added, "Thank you. For saving us all."

Naraka smiled to her, and patted Mikael's back as they turned to leave, only to freeze a few steps later. A metallic click came from the door. "Don't move or I'll shoot," Damion cautioned. "Are you all right, Mrs. Bane?"

Sophie tensed. She'd almost forgotten about Lucas' bodyguard. "I'm fine, now. Where the hell were you?"

"Sorry, Mrs. Bane, I was parking the car." He paused and glanced around the trashed room, giving a low whistle. "Seems I missed all the action."

"Ye sure did, and no thanks to ye, the one who was actually tryin' to kill everybody is face down on the carpet," Mikael snorted. "If ye don't mind, I'd rather not have t' deal with bullet holes in m' clothes. It's already gonna be a bitch t' get dry cleaned as it is."

Damion glanced to Sophie, who sighed and nodded to him. "It's not a good idea to shoot our new friends, especially after they both saved us from… whatever he was." She looked to the lifeless body on the ground, which had finally stopped smoking. She shivered and drew Korban closer against her, unable to stare for too long. "Are Lucas and Danny safe?"

Damion hesitated, but lowered his gun. "Yeah. Mr. Bane was regaining consciousness when I sent them both down in the elevator. I called 911 and he asked me to make sure you were all right and shoot anyone who was a threat." He gave a sidelong glance to Mikael and Naraka as they started past him, as if reconsidering that order.

"They're not a threat to us," Sophie insisted.

The bodyguard bobbed his head and grunted in affirmation, then started over toward them. "Your foot is black and blue, I'd better take a look at it."

He carefully stepped over the wreckage in his path and headed over to assess her wounds. He avoided the jagged glass of the ruined coffee table and stepped around Maverick's body. Maverick didn't twitch or give any sign of life, so when he grabbed Damion by the ankle and crushed it with a sickening crack before throwing him across the room into the wall, Sophie didn't even get time to scream when the soldier was up again, his burned out eyes and mouth still steaming from the electricity. "YOU THINK I'M DONE? I'VE ONLY JUST BEGUN!" His voice was gravelly and cracked, sounding as monstrous and ruined as the rest of him.

He leapt towards Sophie, his fingers outstretched like claws and his teeth gnashing like a rodent. He was stopped only a few precious feet from where her and Korban were on the couch, Mikael and Naraka restraining him. "Brother, please! You have to stop!"

His hot, foul breath was dangerously close as those jagged, vicious teeth snapped at her. "I'M NEVER GONNA STOP! I'LL TEAR YOU ALL LIMB BY LIMB! YOU CAN NOT STOP—!"

BANG!

It happened in horrific slow-motion. Sophie watched as the vampire and werewolf struggled to restrain the bulky soldier. Watched as his head suddenly exploded like a red water balloon from the shot from across the room. Damion had his wounded arm propped up on one of the broken and bent chunks of furniture across the room, his bloodied knuckles still squeezing the trigger.

Naraka's yellow eyes were round and horrified as he held the ruin of Maverick's skull in his hands, blood splattered all over him and Mikael. His breathing became shallow, quick breaths. Mikael swore and grabbed his Mate's face quickly. "Naraka, breathe. Just breathe, my Mate. Ye can't lose it, not now."

Naraka tensed, and began to hyperventilate. Sophie could smell the strong scent of his wolf starting to emerge. Mikael tried to soothe him, whispering calming things in Gaelic as he clutched his face with his bloodied hands, pressing his forehead up against his. It didn't seem to be helping, the traumatized werewolf already slipping away.

"Mikael, get him out of here! He can't be seen here as a Wolven!" Sophie cried out, her heart in her throat. If Korban was awake, he could have maybe helped calm him down, but the faraway look in Naraka's yellow eyes was too far gone.

Mikael yanked on Naraka's side, trying to tear him away from the scene. As he moved, Maverick's ruined body fell forward in a gory mess and the remnants of his skull remained in Naraka's hands. Sophie would have thrown up but there wasn't enough time. His golden eyes turned to focus on Damion. She felt her own wolf surge forward within her, and she yelled out as forcefully as she could, "STOP!"

Naraka froze, and Sophie's heart thundered in the back of her head as she felt a rush of power rise within her. Her body seemed to thrum with power as she barked out the command with as much force as she could muster, "LEAVE. Now, Naraka. GO!"

He didn't even drop the half of Maverick's skull in his hands as he turned and ran for the hall. Mikael glanced to her, thanking her without words, and then rushed off after his Mate.

Sophie stood there, trembling. The power that pulsed in her body left her feeling light-headed, and rejuvenated, at the same time. Was this how it felt for Korban when he was able to send his power into someone? The feeling was quite a rush. She could see why someone would get addicted to it, and that thought frightened her.

She heard the door to the emergency exit slam in the hall and a strange silence fell across the room. Damion slumped over and panted for breath, pain echoed in his every exhalation. It was a short-lived respite, as the second the elevator dinged and the doors slid open a team of SWAT officers spilled out in full riot gear. She still felt her own power radiating through the air and gently ran her fingers through Korban's hair, sending some of her warm energy into him as she sat there, poised as the team of officers began to take in the decimated war zone of her living room. She was ordered to freeze, and obeyed. She could see her own reflection in one of the plexiglass shields and her eyes were a vibrant, glowing yellow. Amidst all the wreckage and with an unconscious Korban in her lap, she must have made quite a sight.

There was a whooshing sound and a familiar sting in her shoulder as a tranquilizer struck her. Damion was yelling something at them, but the words became nothing more than muddied noise. She watched her reflection, her yellow eyes fading back to blue again. If she had the strength, she would have laughed. A side-effect of the rush of power, the euphoric feeling still thrumming inside of her even as the sedative seeped through her and sent her spiraling into darkness, her body collapsed down and her nostrils filled with Korban's forest-like scent before oblivion claimed her once more.

21: REMEDY

Sophie awoke in the hospital, her wrists once again in the itchy restraints, a mild headache radiating in her skull as her eyes came to focus on that familiar ceiling with its fluorescent lights and white popcorn panels. She sat up immediately, lurching against the restraints and causing them to clang loudly against the metal guard rails of the bed. "No. Not again!" Sophie cried out, banging the metal against metal. "Let me go! I want to see Korban! Lucas! Danny! I need to see that they're safe!"

Remnants of the nightmare she'd lived through flashed in her memory and her stomach quailed. The hospital door opened and Dr. Hoover came rushing in. "Mrs. Bane! Please, Sophie, it's all right. Just protocol. We'll get you out of the restraints in just a moment, okay? Then you can see Korban and Lucas. All right?"

"Damn you and your protocol! Why am I back in quarantine? What did I do wrong? We were defending Lucas and Danny from… I don't know what the hell he was!"

"I understand, Sophie, please," Dr. Hoover held his hands up defensively, his voice level in attempt to calm her down. "You're only here to make sure that your injuries are taken care of. Just like Korban and Lucas. It's just a matter of following the rules. You were both pretty beat up, and the only hospital for infected is, well, here. We're set up to treat you. The restraints are merely a formality. I was just coming to check on you and remove them." The keys jangled in his hand and he offered a friendly smile. "Honestly."

Sophie's hands remained clenched into fists, but she took several deep breaths. In through her nose, then exhaling through her mouth. She watched as Dr. Hoover went to her side, giving her a tentative look, then carefully unlocked her restraints. She examined her freed wrists and watched the redness from the silver-laced rope vanish before her eyes. "I want to see them right now… wait, why is Lucas here, too?"

"He had to be tested, due to his injuries, and yours in case he accidentally became infected in the crossfire. So far, his tests have been negative for lycanthropy, but we may need to run a few more just to be certain that he's in the clear."

"Where's my son?"

"Daniel is out in the waiting room with your parents. And Mr. Jackson is in recovery as well."

She breathed a sigh of relief. Damion would be okay, too, it seemed. They had all made it, by some miracle. "I'd like to see Korban. Please, Doc."

"Of course," Dr. Hoover handed her a robe that was folded on top of the dresser nearby. "I'll give you a moment of privacy, and then we can go—"

She was already up and threw the robe around herself as she headed for the door. "Not necessary, Doctor. Let's go."

Korban wasn't awake when she got to his room. He was still pale and still as he laid there, but she relaxed when she saw his chest rising and falling, and heard his heartbeat. "How is he?" Sophie asked, her gaze lingering on the bandage over his neck.

"He hasn't woken up yet, but his vitals are stable, and as far as I can tell, he should make a full recovery," Dr. Hoover replied, then tentatively added, "Your husband is still in surgery. They are making sure his wound is clean before they stitch him back up. The initial scans show that he was pretty lucky. His intestines weren't perforated, but they're taking every precaution just in case we missed something. He's in good hands."

Relief flooded through her, and she went over and touched Korban's hand, careful not to brush against his restraints. "Another one of your protocols?"

"Just until he wakes, and we see that he's still himself," Dr. Hoover said. "Once we know that, he'll be freed just like you."

"So we aren't prisoners here?"

"No, not this time. Mr. Jackson and your son reported everything that happened, and they have security footage to corroborate their stories. You both risked everything to stop that infected man. I'm still waiting on his autopsy report to find out exactly what viral strand was inside him. It needs to be studied so we can understand what went wrong."

A chill ran through her and she squeezed Korban's hand. There were still bruises along his arms and face. "You shouldn't study him, you should make sure every part of him is destroyed. Incinerate his corpse and put him to rest. Trust me, Dr. Hoover. You don't want him coming back."

"He's been declared dead, and part of his head seems to be missing. I don't think he'll be causing any more problems."

Sophie gave him a pointed look. "Are you really so certain? Vampires and Revenants don't have pulses either."

Dr. Hoover's smile vanished as he considered her words, then gave a small sigh and nodded his head. "I'll go make some calls. We'll see that the remains are cremated. I don't think any of us want him coming back."

She finally relaxed. "Good."

~*~

The hours passed. Nurses in protective gear came in and out, and Dr. Hoover came back later to let her know that Maverick's body had been sent down for cremation. She still remained on guard at Korban's side. He'd barely moved in his sleep, though occasionally his heart would speed up and he would moan until she would squeeze his hand, and that calmed him. She had a lot of time to think, and even more time to worry. She was tempted to sneak out to the waiting room and try to see her parents and her son, to confirm with her own eyes that he was okay, but she couldn't risk it. As much as it hurt her heart, she had to take Dr. Hoover's word for now.

She was pacing alongside Korban's bed when the door opened and Dr. Hoover popped in. "I thought you should know that Lucas is awake, and in recovery. He'd like to see you if you're up for it."

She glanced anxiously to Korban, but he seemed at peace for the moment. "Okay."

Sophie followed Dr. Hoover down the hall, passing rooms that were locked tight. Occasionally she caught a glimpse of someone inside a room, in various states of restraint. She smelled other wolves, the empty, cold scent of vampires, and other unidentifiable infections. Some were just human, and those were the worst. Perhaps they were in there for observation, or to treat what would now be considered a mundane mental illness. She was glad when they reached the recovery wing and Dr. Hoover ushered her inside. Lucas was laying down, his bed completely flattened and his head propped up by two flat pillows. He was naked from the waist up, and bandages were wrapped across his abdomen. Dark bruises peered around the edge of the clean, white linen and were speckled across his pale skin. He smiled as she approached him. She felt a new surge of guilt as he relaxed and optimism rolled off him. "Hey," Lucas grunted in a weary voice.

"Hey," Sophie greeted him in turn, going over to the side of his bed. "How are you feeling?"

Lucas winced. "Like I'd been stabbed in the stomach. I don't recommend it, not even a little bit."

"I'll have to remember that," she said with a small smile. "Dr. Hoover said Danny is in the waiting room with my parents."

He gave a small nod, his motions slow and careful. "He let me know he was here, and okay." Lucas paused and gazed up to the ceiling, closing his eyes before continuing, "Daniel was so brave. I don't know what I would do if I was in his position, at his age. I owe a thank you to your friend, too. Korban helped Danny stay calm."

"Korban has a knack for that."

An awkward silence fell between them. Sophie glanced down to her hands as she gathered her resolve. "I know this isn't the best time to bring this up... but I don't think there ever will be a good time to discuss this, and we need to talk about our future."

Lucas sighed. "I already have a feeling I know what you're going to say. You weren't happy with me, and the way things were going between us. You hadn't been happy for a while, even with anything you could ever desire at your disposal as my wife."

"Lucas, you've got it all wrong. I've been so blessed all my life. I was born into a family that could give me anything I could ever need or want. Not that I'm complaining, I'm so very grateful for that. But the only place I have ever felt like I had purpose was at school."

"You have purpose at home, too, Sophie. You're an amazing mother to our son."

"Yes, having Danny was… is still one of the happiest moments of my life. Being his mother has brought me so much joy. He's growing up, and I love seeing what a wonderful boy he is becoming. We raised an incredible young man together, Lucas."

"Yes, we did. But—"

"But he's growing up, and as time goes by I will still be there for him, but I need to get back my purpose too, Lucas. Danny is my son, and the most important part of my heart. But he isn't the only part of me."

Lucas didn't seem to know what to say to that, so he stayed quiet, staring off as he listened.

"School is the only place I have ever had to earn something. All my grades, making it to Valedictorian of my class, then law school… that was all me. Not my family's money. It was where I could shine and learn and grow. When we did mock trials, or when I was interning at the court house, I felt so alive. Like what I was doing made a difference. I wasn't just boiled down to what I looked like, or my family's fortune. My intelligence and hard work mattered. I mattered."

"You know you always meant the world to me and Daniel, Sophie."

"I know that, Lucas, and you both mean so much to me, too. I love being a mother, and I loved being your wife. My first passion has always been to become a lawyer. Not for any sort of fame or money, but because it gave me purpose. It was an arena where my brain and my heart could serve justice and help others." "I know you think what you're doing is for the best, and maybe it is, for you. Maybe for Danny too. But it isn't best for me. You broke my heart when you asked me time and time again to postpone my dreams, Lucas. You did that all on your own. And Nikki… she manipulated me even further, using that hole in my heart to take advantage. But the truth is, I was already looking for a way out. Not because I didn't love you, but because you were keeping me from something that I loved."

Lucas was stunned. "Sophie, I'm sorry. If you had told me… if I had known—"

Sophie met his gaze with a frown. "I did tell you, Lucas, but you just weren't listening. Everything we argued over and over again. You just had to take control. You couldn't trust me to be more than just your wife and Danny's mother."

"How… how can I make this right, Sophie?"

"You… you can't," Sophie said with a heavy sigh. "I don't love you like I used to, Lucas. I can't keep pretending like things are the way they used to be. You can't keep pretending either. I've changed, and not just because I'm infected. I almost died when I was bitten, and that night when the Wolven was ripping into me I saw moments of my life, the cliché greatest hits of Sophie Bane. I saw our first date, our wedding, the day I found out I was finally pregnant. That day I was so sick, and you actually burned Ramen soup but I pretended to like it. The day Danny was born, and I held him for the first time. But I also saw all the things I couldn't get to do, as time was slipping away so fast. I saw my excitement of finally acing the bar exam. I saw myself in court, all the lives that I could have helped save. I thought that in the moment of my death, I would have felt at least fulfilled from those cherished moments, but from the moment I woke up to everything again, the thing that has stuck with me has been my regrets. I've been given a second chance, and I won't continue to wait for you to say it's okay, or to get anyone's approval to pursue my goals. I refuse to keep on waiting. I'm sorry, Lucas." She paused to take a deep breath and steeled herself. "I want a divorce."

Lucas blinked, then glanced away from her. "This is because of him, isn't it?"

"No, not exactly. I do love Korban, but he's not the reason I want this. This was happening long before I even met Korban." She paused. "I tried to see if this could work between us, Lucas, but it isn't anymore. I loved you, but you haven't changed, and I have. I can't keep pretending that things are the same. I can't live this lie. I need to have the freedom to be who I am, and you need… you need to be with someone who compliments you, not someone you want to fit into a certain mold."

Lucas was quiet for a long moment, then he gave a forced, short laugh. Sophie gave him a concerned look but he just shook his head. "I love you, Sophie, with all my heart and soul. I want this to work out between us. If you feel that we can't fix it, though… I don't want to fight you. All I want is for you to be happy. I can't be too mad with Korban, either. He saved you, me, and Danny. I owe him in ways that even I can't repay."

His cool, gray eyes met hers. "And you… you've been through so many changes lately, Sophie. I know it feels like there is no way to go back to what we had before, but… if you really want this, I won't stand in your way. We will always have our brave and smart son to connect us, and me being your sponsor..." He trailed off and averted his watery gaze, a fresh, deeper pain radiating from him.

Sophie felt like a monster, but she couldn't take back what she'd said, and she couldn't keep hiding what she felt in her heart. "I hope, one day, for Danny's sake, we can be friends. You mean so much to me, Lucas. What I've said… I know it's a lot, and I'm sorry to hurt you. But I couldn't keep lying to you, and pretending I'm something I'm not. I can't deny that my feeling have changed. And it isn't fair to you to try to keep trying to make this work when I've moved on."

"And I thought getting stabbed in the gut hurt," Lucas muttered.

She started to apologize, but swallowed it down instead. Another stretch of silence fell between them.

"If you want a divorce, then so be it. I'll get my lawyer to start filing the paperwork as soon as I'm out of here. Until then… all I can do is hope that you'll reconsider. My heart isn't as ready as yours to let go of what we had. You should go… I need time alone now, please." Lucas couldn't stop his tears from streaming down his cheeks, or the emotion from straining his voice, but he did keep his composure and didn't fall into a fit of sobs.

She fought back her own tears as she stepped back, towards the door. "I hope someday you'll be happy again, too, Lucas. I really do."

She left him there, her heart lighter and pained at the same time.

~*~

When Korban woke up, he found himself alone, his wrists bound to the sides of the hospital bed. Before he opened his eyes he knew exactly where he was, the familiar scents of the quarantine ward making his stomach ache, not that it made too much of a difference as his entire body felt bruised and sore. The wound on his neck in particular still hurt.

He opened his eyes slowly, hoping that maybe it was some weird, sensory memory and he was actually sleeping on the couch at the lake house. As his eyes came into focus in the dimly lit room, he realized what he had already known to be true. He never was that lucky.

He focused on his breathing, and glanced around the room, swallowing down his panic. Compared to his last stay in quarantine, this room was more like a traditional hospital room, with more furniture than a just a bed. There was a couple chairs for guests, and a dresser nearby that had a growing collection of flowers and cards. Included in the arrangement were a vase filled with sunflowers, and alongside it another vase with a rainbow cluster of pinwheels that made him smile.

The door opened, and as if sensing his thoughts, Sophie walked in, wearing a simple robe and slippers. She brightened the moment she saw him. "You're finally awake, sleepy head." Sophie said as she approached him, pulled over a chair, and gently squeezed his hand. "You really had me worried."

His fingers intertwined with hers. "I have a confession to make. I may be a werewolf, but I'm no John Wick. I think I've experienced more than a life time's worth of action, and now I'm definitely paying for it," he grimaced. "In other words, I'm not cut out for battle."

She smirked and leaned over, kissing him softly on the forehead. "You're still my hero for trying. Though I think you could benefit from a few Brazilian jiu-jitsu classes."

Korban's jaw fell open in surprise. "Is that where you learned how to fight?"

"Yes. It gave me a good escape, to go spar for a few hours and take a break from school. It was also a hobby my mother supported, even if it wasn't lady-like, because a woman unfortunately needs a means of protecting herself."

"Something tells me you were born with the ability to convince others. A natural lawyer."

She brightened at the compliment, and gently patted his hand. "Speaking of convincing, I have a couple things to tell you. You've been out for about a day, but a lot has been happening while you were asleep. Once Dr. Hoover clears us and we're out of quarantine, Mayor Varno has asked us to come speak to the remaining Council. She didn't tell me too much, just that it was important and she wanted us both to be there."

Korban's stomach sank. "Do we really have to?"

It was Sophie's turn to offer an apologetic look. "I think it may be a good idea, after what we witnessed. We can leave certain things out, of course, but I think we should let the Council know that we aren't exactly on the top of the food chain either." She winced as she said it, and added, "Maybe that wasn't the best choice of words, but you understand what I mean."

"Yeah, I do. And you're right. We need to tell them, I just wish that… well, I don't know what I wish for any more. Maybe just to be left alone awhile, with you."

Sophie stood up from her chair and sat on the edge of his bed, careful to not lean on his leg. "I talked with Lucas. I asked him for a divorce," she confessed, and reclaimed Korban's hand. "I told him almost everything, but I couldn't tell him the whole story. I can't explain to him what it's like, to be in a room with another human being and want nothing more than to devour them."

"So he couldn't accept that you want to be a lawyer?"

She playfully swatted him for teasing, but her expression softened as he lightened the mood. "Keep it up, and you'll see exactly how I got my black belt. You know what I mean."

Korban grinned. "I do, sorry. I blame the pain, and the fact that right now your smile is the only thing that seems to be helping me feel better. How did he take it?"

"About as good as could be expected," Sophie sighed, leaning closer against him. "I know he's my sponsor. I know it's complicated. But I can't pretend I'm his wife, and everything is the same as before, when all I see him as is dinner. And then there's the matter of you and I. The possibility of losing Lucas hurt, but just the idea of you… I can't pretend to be just friends with you."

Korban loathed the bindings on his wrists, and wished he could wrap his arms around her. She reached up and gently smoothed his hair with her hand, and he leaned into her touch.

She leaned in and whispered the words he'd been waiting to hear. "I love you, Korban Diego. Now, and always."

Sophie pulled him into a sweet, tender kiss.

22: APPOINTMENT

Their stay in quarantine this time, thankfully, was very short, just like Dr. Hoover had promised. After a couple days of recovery, Korban felt more like himself again, though it seemed to his and the doctor's surprise he'd gained a new scar. Dr. Hoover had told him he was thankful he'd taken Sophie's advice, and actually had the ashes stored in a locked iron box that would be too small for Maverick to put himself back together again. He revealed that they had even blessed it with an ordained priest, and a rabbi, just in case.

Things had quieted down when they emerged from the hospital that morning, though a skeleton crew of the media were there to cover their discharge. It seemed that a famous celebrity was claiming to be a vampire, so most of the attention had been drawn away from them for now. The reprieve was welcome, even if Korban and Sophie both had their doubts that the confession was true.

Lucas had already left the hospital the night before. He was still upset with her decision, and didn't say much to Sophie as he left. She couldn't blame him, and it still stung a little, but in her heart she knew it was for the best. Though returning to the lake house was going to be a bit more strained and awkward. Since the condo was now a crime scene, and would need reconstruction before they could return to it, Lucas had told her that he and Daniel would be staying at the main house. Since she couldn't be technically under the same roof, it seemed for the time she would be living in the guest house with RJ, Alex, and Korban. It gave her a small amount of hope to know she would at least be close enough to see Danny. It wasn't much, of course, but it was something. More good news came when they were reunited with their two friends, as Alex relayed that Cyrus Autos passed its initial building inspection, and in the next day or two would be cleared for them to return home.

The following day they were called in to speak with the Council. The ride over had been tense and quiet. Instead of meeting in the court room, this time they were granted a private audience in Mayor Varno's office. As the small group gathered in chairs around the mayor's desk, a somber mood filled the room. Mayor Varno was poised behind her desk, Commissioner DeRusso sat alongside her, Tim and Andy both stood guard at the door. Korban, RJ, Alex, Sophie, and Lucas sat across from her desk.

Two of the Council members were absent that night. Senator Hunter had already returned to Washington, D.C. and was listening in over a video call. Dr. Hoover was on call at the hospital, but would be informed of their discussion later.

The mayor greeted them with an amicable smile as the tension filled the air. "Thank you all for returning on such short notice. I know you've all been through a lot, and I want you to know first and foremost that I appreciate you taking the time to meet with us again."

"Of course," Sophie said.

"I'll get straight to the point. In light of, and despite recent events, we have been discussing different options when it comes to moving forward. The Commissioner, Senator, and I have come to a solution with the help of Dr. Hoover's research. Syracuse has been a historic haven for progressive ideas when it comes to human rights. The Underground Railroad ran through here. Seneca Falls held one of the most important rallies for women's suffrage. For many years, we have been a sanctuary city for immigrant families who needed a safe place to call home. It only makes sense that we would also be a beacon in the face of this new challenge, and hopefully other cities and states will follow our lead once again," Mayor Varno explained. "For all these reasons and more, we would like to try something new when it comes to handling our quarantine process. Dr. Hoover's research, and your testimony combined, have lead us to the conclusion that the best way to help our infected citizens is to give them the opportunity to have a normal life. Through the intervention of an Alpha, such as yourself, we can assist those who are able to control themselves, but do not have a sponsor for various reasons. This will give us an opportunity to help the infected citizens who are in limbo, while also opening up more space in the hospital. We will provide the funding for you to foster these individuals, and in exchange you will protect and provide for your charges, keeping them and the public safe. We're thinking we start small, just one additional werewolf for now, but we may look into increasing the amount as time goes on. We don't want to overburden you. We want this to work for you, and the city. So what do you say? Do you accept?"

Korban blinked. He wondered if he should pinch himself to check if he was still dreaming. "If he's a werewolf, can he legally sponsor another werewolf?" RJ asked.

"Right now, no, but since this is all on a trial basis, we checked the current laws for loopholes and it seems that at least for now, the law doesn't have anything that states a human being can't sponsor more than one infected person," Commissioner DeRusso supplied with a small smile. "At least for now, we can bend that rule a little, as long as you'd be willing, Mr. Martinez."

Korban and RJ exchanged a look. RJ held his gaze for a long moment, then turned to the Commissioner. "Korban has always had my back since we were kids. I knew from the moment I knew Korban was infected that I wouldn't abandon my friend when he was in need. I believe in him, and I will stand by him. Always. If this bends the rules but won't get him in trouble, then I'm willing to do whatever it takes. I'd rather be on the right side of history."

Mayor Varno turned her smile on him. "So what do you say, Korban? Will you accept the role of being Syracuse's first Alpha?"

All eyes and ears were on him. Korban nodded, then stood and extended his hand across the desk to shake on it. "I do."

~*~

"I can't believe it! All hail the mighty Alpha of Syracuse!" Alex howled as they headed out to the car, putting an arm around his shoulders. "Alpha Lobo! Your royal furry-ness, I hope you don't forget us mere mortals now that you're on top!"

"I won't forget to royally kick your mere, mortal ass if you keep it up," Korban chuckled.

"This calls for a celebration! What do you say, fellas? Curfew is a little later tonight, why don't we go sing a couple songs over at Howl at the Moon? I bet Mikey will be honored to serve the Alpha his first official gin and tonic."

"I hope that I'm included in this party," Sophie piped in.

"Of course! We all party tonight!" Alex cheered, though he glanced around. "We seem to have lost a member of our party already, though. Where's Lucas?"

"He headed back to the lake house. He's still not feeling too well." Sophie said with a frown. "He's never been a fan of karaoke anyway, so it's for the best."

Alex accepted this answer with a nod, though he seemed momentarily sad that he wouldn't be joining the fun. He brightened almost immediately though as they piled into the car and headed out for the bar. Korban drove, and Sophie held his hand as they drove to the bar. The euphoric feeling of the pieces finally coming together filled him with indescribable joy. He was thrilled that he had one more surprise for his Mate up his sleeves.

When they arrived at Howl at the Moon, Mikey was ecstatic to see them. "Hey guys! I was wondering when you'd be showing up!"

"You can't keep a good dog down," Korban cracked as he approached the bar and exchanged a handshake that ended in a quick hug with Mikey, patting him on the shoulder before he pulled away.

"The usual tonight?" Mikey asked.

Alex hopped on a bar stool and pulled the karaoke list over. "Yeah, though pour from the top shelf tonight, Mikey. Our little Korban is all grown up and got himself a job!"

"No way! Seriously?" Mikey beamed, his brown eyes bright. "This really is a cause for celebration! Hold up, I got just the thing for the occasion. I'm getting you the special reserve from the manager's office. Don't you dare go anywhere, I'll be right back." He headed to the back of the bar, vanishing behind the curtain that was drawn there.

Sophie sat down between Alex and Korban and slid her arm around his side. "So, you going to be singing tonight, Alpha?" she teased, whispering in his ear and giving his lobe a playful nibble.

A thrill raced through him, and he smiled to her, leaning into her touch. "I think I may be inspired to sing something special, but before I take requests… there's something I want to give you."

Sophie blinked in surprise, the question in her eyes before she even asked, "Something for me?"

Korban reached into his pocket and got down on one knee in front of her. Sophie's heart skipped a beat, and stopped until she realized it wasn't a ring he pulled out, but his phone. The screen glowed as he hit a button on the side. There was an e-mail opened up on his phone, a confirmation sent from Syracuse University for a bar exam review course that started in the spring semester. She had to read it a couple times to comprehend what he'd done. "You… you didn't! That's so expensive, how…?"

Alex waved his hand. "We had to use some of that sweet reward money on something other than upgrades for the garage." RJ flashed her a mischievous grin of his own, and a thumbs up.

Korban kept his gaze and smile steady as he asked, "Sophie… won't you be my lawyer?"

She blinked at him, for a moment too stunned to speak. Then she smirked, and raised an eyebrow. "You're not planning on getting into even more trouble, are you Korban Diego?"

Korban flashed her his trademark, wolfish grin. "Let's just say it will be nice to have a lawyer in the family."

Sophie gazed in wonder again at the e-mail on his phone, then shook her head as she laughed. "Well, I know your type all too well," she said, then slipped his phone back into his hand and caught him by his shirt collar. "So I know when it comes to you, I'll have to demand my payment up front."

As she drew him down closer, his smile burned more seductive. "Really? How much will it cost to have you on retainer?"

She paused when her lips were close enough to brush against his and she wrapped her arms around his neck. "Everything."

~*~

Word traveled fast, and after an evening of celebrating they headed out to the car. On their way, a pale skinned, red haired woman approached them. Sophie recognized her from their visit to The Alpine and tensed, stepping in front of Korban instinctively. The woman only smiled and looked her over in amusement. "The Master wants to have a word with you." She glanced over RJ and Alex with a seductive smile. "All of you."

"The Master?" RJ and Alex echoed in unison, and gave Korban a pointed look.

The redhead looked amused. "You can explain to them on the way over. Drive to this address. It will appear to be closed, but walk in and enter the door with the light over it," she said and slipped a plain looking business card into Korban's hand. "He'll be waiting for you all there. Don't keep him waiting, the curfew clock is ticking."

Just as quickly as she appeared, she was gone, leaving the four of them alone. There wasn't too much time to give all the details, but Korban sighed and gestured to the car. "I'll fill you in. Just… Sophie, can you drive?"

She nodded, and as she drove them over, Korban fidgeted in his seat as he filled in RJ and Alex on everything that had happened the past few weeks. When he finished, Alex's jaw hung open, and RJ had a deep frown. "You want to come clean about anything else, Korban? Because I swear, you'd better do it now."

"Dude, you should have told us Ace was alive-ish!" Alex blurted out, the air souring with genuine hurt. "What the hell, Lobo?"

"I'm sorry, I really am," Korban apologized. "Ace swore me to secrecy. After all that has happened, I wanted to try and protect you. I swear, I was going to tell you when I could. I just didn't get the chance to with shape-shifting cannibals coming after us."

RJ leaned over the seat, meeting Korban's gaze. "Look at me Korban. I want you to promise me, and swear it to me now. The only way this is going to work, for you to be Alpha, and for me to be sponsoring werewolves we don't know… I want your word that there will be no more secrets, Korban. Because I swear to all the powers that be, if I find the Loch Ness monster in our bathtub, or a wendigo playing Nintendo on our couch one day, I'm going to turn you into a throw rug, Alpha or not!"

RJ was pissed, and deadly serious as he glared at Korban. He swallowed and nodded, though after a long, tense moment, Alex suddenly snickered and lifted the mood when he repeated, "Wendigo playing Nintendo?"

"I'm serious," RJ stubbornly insisted, but as the other three burst into fits of laughter, he cracked a smile.

Sophie pulled the car into a parking space near their destination, across from the Landmark Theatre, and they headed over to what appeared to be a closed café alongside a busy restaurant. Only the door was mysteriously left unlocked, and a single light dangling above a side door was lit, as the redhead had stated. Faint piano music floated from beyond the door. When they opened it they revealed a staircase with a Broadway-style sign that announced that they had arrived to The Fitz. They carefully headed down the steps where a muscular, tall, blond bouncer waited by a coat check, glanced over their identification and let them past.

Inside, The Fitz was a stylish speakeasy, with a flair that was something from another era. There was a classic, timeless feeling in the air. There were small groups of people gathered at the bar and around the room, sitting on comfortable vintage chairs and sipping cocktails. The bartenders and bouncer wore outfits fitting the classic vibe of the place, and the piano music completed the aesthetic with a talented pianist playing a jazzy tune. Like magic, the redhead reappeared as she stepped out of the crowd, giving the surprised group a sly, mysterious smile. "Follow me," she said.

She led them towards the back of the club. Alex gawked excitedly as they walked past a huge, steam-powered elevator engine. They reached an inconspicuous door where the hulking, werewolf bouncer from The Alpine was looming outside the door and eyed them all as the redhead ushered them in. The office was just as stylish as the rest of the club, a massive room with a black leather couch that lined one wall. A sleek, black desk and set of chairs took up one corner of the room. RJ and Alex both gasped in surprise when they saw him sitting there. Ace stood up, smoothing his stylish suit, something akin from a classic gangster movie, and offering them an apologetic smile. "I hope you guys weren't too hard on Korban. I made him promise not to mention my existence for your own safety. The vampires of the Underground chose me to be the Master Vampire for the city after the previous Master had to be dispatched… a long story better told another time. I hope you can forgive me for being so secretive, but I wanted to keep you both out of this as long as I could. It seems that effort was made in vain. I should have known it was a matter of time before you all would be in over your heads."

Korban gave a small tilt of his head in confusion. Ace raised an eyebrow. "Oh, come on now. You know exactly what I mean, Korban. With the ability you have, not only are people going to be drawn to what you can do, but other supernatural creatures as well.

Even when I asked you to try and stay out of this, it seems that it's inescapable for you to not get involved with Underground business. Especially since you've been named the Alpha of Syracuse by the mayor. RJ is your sponsor, and Alex lives with you. Of course they'd end up involved in this whole mess."

Korban glanced down, feeling a surge of guilt. RJ folded his arms over his chest. "So you dragged us over here to lecture us? Taking a page from my notes now, Ace?"

Ace smirked, his pale blue eyes lighting up in amusement. "Not exactly. I wanted to reveal myself as a vampire to you, anyway, but I also have a couple friends here who wanted to see you again."

From the shadows, Mikael and Naraka emerged. Mikael was wearing his usual black trench coat and hat, though his hair was now a dark color, clipped short and neat and his eyes a stormy, blue gray. Naraka wore a black, short-sleeved mesh shirt and black leather pants. The pair of them looked like they were ready for a night of clubbing, a look meant to camouflage them in a late night party crowd.

"I'm glad to see you're both all right," Korban said.

"Yes, we're good now. Thanks to both of your help. My heroes," Naraka said, giving Sophie a wink and a thumbs up.

Sophie blushed, and it was Korban's turn to look at her in surprise. "I was able to help keep him from losing control, when you were unconscious."

Korban couldn't help but feel a sense of pride in her. "Damn right you did," Naraka said. "I wanted to thank you both for your help before we headed out on our way."

"Leaving so soon? But I thought we were going to be helping you stay in control." Korban said.

"We'd stick around longer, but it seems that Special Agent Singer has quite the hard on when it comes to capturing me. As much as I love a game of chase, I don't want to risk this getting back to you, Alpha Korban."

"Word really does travel fast," Korban said, then gave the pair a concerned look. "Where will you go? Will you be okay?"

"We'll leave a trail for our new friend Singer to stalk me for a little while, and then lose him before he knows he's gone down the wrong rabbit hole. It's not our first time on the run, but this will be our first time on a mission. I'm going to make sure that the rest of my brothers… I'm going to make sure they are at rest, or at least not lost to madness like Maverick was," Naraka explained, gently touching the small collection of dog tags around his neck.

Korban could see the pain briefly reflected in Naraka's eyes, but as Mikael gently put a hand on his shoulder he relaxed. "We're going to be all right," Mikael said. "We'll be in touch again, when it's safe. Ye know we couldn't stay away forever."

Naraka winked in his direction. "Just don't let your new position go to your head, Alpha."

"You know I won't."

They celebrated their farewell/reunion by going out to the dark bar and Ace treated them to a couple rounds of drinks. As the night died down, Ace pulled Korban aside privately. "I'm glad that you were able to help stop that shape-shifter, but I hope you learned from running head-first into such dangerous business."

Korban frowned. "It's not like I meant to do it. We didn't get much of a choice. He called us, and was threatening Lucas and Daniel over the phone. Sophie wasn't going to leave them like that, and neither would I."

"Just, please let me know first next time. You could have been killed," Ace insisted with a worried look.

Korban let out an exasperated sigh. "How am I supposed to contact you when you don't even trust me to have your phone number? If you want me to be in touch, of course I will be. You're my best friend. But I can't contact you if you don't give me the means to do it."

Ace sighed in return. "You're right. Which is why I want you to have this." Ace handed him an older, flip-style phone. "It's a burner phone, so it's difficult to trace. If you are ever in need for me, or the Underground, you can contact us at any of the numbers on this. It will be forwarded to my phone, wherever I am for the day, or night. That way you can always be in touch."

"I hope it's not for emergencies only. I'd like to spend time with my best friend again, now that I know he's back."

Ace smiled. "Of course. You know that no matter what, we always made a great team. And now you get to be the Alpha in the light, while I am the Master of the shadows." He paused, his expression turning serious again. "I tried to warn you before, my friend, but you didn't listen then. I hope that you'll at least try to listen to my advice now."

"Advice?" Korban repeated.

Ace nodded, his expression grim. "My people call me The Master. They turn to me as a leader of the Underground. Just like you, I never asked for this. I got tangled up in a very messy matter. I defeated the previous man they considered The Master, because someone had to stop him. I was just trying to do what was right, and like you, it bit me in the ass. I've learned a lot since taking this position. You and I remember it from the comics and movies we grew up with. The whole cliché shtick, 'with great power, comes great responsibility.' It may be overused, but there is truth to it."

Korban listened, and nodded when he finished. "I promise you that I'll be careful from now on. Believe me, I've learned my lesson."

Ace reached and put his hand over Korban's, his cool touch sending a chill through him. "I need you to be on your guard, even while not in danger. As a leader people will look up to you for guidance, but there will be others who aren't happy with your new role as Alpha. Some people don't like change. Just… be extra diligent when it comes to who you trust, and who you let into your life. Don't make the same mistakes I've made."

Korban stared at him for a moment. "We have a lot of catching up to do, don't we?"

"You have no idea." Ace said, then offered him a smile as the others meandered back over. "We'll talk more about it later, Alpha."

"You got it, Master," Korban teased back, and they both dropped the topic for now, though Korban wondered when he'd get the chance to find out more about Ace's story.

~*~

She was feeling bold as they walked out of The Fitz, and as they started on their way back to the lake house, she turned to the guys and asked, "Do you mind if I make a quick stop?"

"Sure. We have a little time left," Korban said.

She steeled herself and turned the car towards the hospital. She parked the car in the front and turned to Korban. "I won't be too long. I just… I need to see for myself."

"Do you want me to go with you?" Korban gently asked.

She thought about it for a moment, then shook her head. "I

need to do this, by myself."

Korban nodded. "You got this."

Alex and RJ flashed her a thumbs up and she headed into the hospital. Sophie wasn't even sure if they'd let her go and see Nikki or not, but she had to try while she had the nerve. She approached the front desk. "I'm here to visit Nicolette Winters."

The woman behind the desk frowned. "You and everyone else who follows her on Instagram. Do you have identification?"

Sophie went for her purse, but the security guard nearby waved his hand. "Come on, Karen. You know who she is. Everyone in Syracuse knows. Mrs. Bane, follow me. I'll take you to see her."

"Thank you."

Sophie followed the guard to the elevator. He pressed the button and seemed a little nervous as it climbed up the floors. "Sorry to hear about you and your husband."

She blinked in surprise, but of course the news would get out. Sophie gave him a polite nod. She wasn't sure what to say to him, though he seemed to take the hint and changed the subject. "Your parents have been here quite a lot lately, but I'm sure she'll be happy to see you here. She keeps asking about you."

A drop of sweat ran down her spine and she wondered if this was a good idea or not. She felt suddenly trapped, and was glad when the doors opened and the guard stepped out onto the hospital floor. She clenched her fists at her sides, her nails burrowing into her palms as she followed him onto the floor. Her stomach did a small flip-flop as the elevator doors closed and her chance at a quick escape headed up to the next floor. She took a slow, deep breath through her mouth, to try and limit inhaling too much of the pain, fear, and anxiety that lingered in the antiseptic smell of the hospital.

The guard took her to the last room down the hall before coming to a stop. Most of the rooms here were sterile, with warning signs and extra precautions taken to keep infection from spreading into the patients' rooms. As though he'd read her thoughts, the guard supplied, "Your sister's room was just cleared for regular visitation a couple days ago. She'll be moving to another floor to continue her recovery in the next day or so."

Sophie finally found her voice after swallowing the lump in her throat. "I'm glad to hear it."

He nodded and stepped aside so she could enter. There was still a plastic curtain around the room, and the windows had remained sealed. The television was on, some familiar commercial jingle sounding a little too happy for her current mood, and the soft glow of the screen giving the room an eerie feeling. A green curtain was drawn around Nikki's bed, probably to keep any passing paparazzi from sneaking a picture. The whole room felt foreboding, and even as Sophie walked in, she felt a growing sense of dread. She wasn't even sure what Nikki would say when she saw her. Echoes of her cruel, twisted laughter played in the back of her mind. Still, she had to see for herself that her sister was alive, and awake.

When she turned the corner of the curtain and saw her there, she gasped. Her little sister was laying there in the hospital bed, an IV connected to her thin arm. In the blue light of the flickering TV, she seemed so frail. Dark circles made her one eye look almost hollow on the right side of her face. She didn't have any makeup on, and she seemed both older and younger in appearance somehow, as though her mask being taken away revealed someone so fragile underneath. All this, however, wasn't why Sophie gasped. Her sister was no longer the meticulous, camera-ready model that she had prided herself on for so many years, and it had nothing to do with her lack of eye liner. The right side of her face remained a gaunt ghost of what she had been, but most of her left side was now hidden away with fresh bandages. From the edge of the linens, Sophie could see a hint of the scarred ruin of burned flesh, bright pink even in the dim glow of the room. Nikki's eye was listlessly staring at the screen, though at the soft gasp turned her head slowly to look in her direction. "Sissy?" Nikki's voice sounded small, lost.

Sophie tensed and froze, unable to breathe until she managed to exhale, "Yes."

Tears welled in the eye that wasn't bandaged, and Nikki made a soft, mewling sound. "I missed you, Sissy! I wanted to see you, but Mommy said you were busy. Too busy to come and see me after the accident. I was so scared. I almost died!"

Surely, she hadn't heard her right. Sophie took a step back, as if Nikki had slapped her across the face. "What are you talking about, Nikki? You know exactly why I didn't come visit until now."

Nikki blinked, confusion reflected in her eye. "No, Sissy, I don't. Did we get into a fight or something before my car crash? It must have been a really bad one for you to avoid me, even after this."

Sophie gaped at her in disbelief, and her heart sank. "You… you don't remember what happened, before the accident? You don't remember what you did to me or Korban beforehand?"

Nikki gave a tentative shake of her head. "I can't remember much of anything. The doctor said I suffered a brain injury, and that the swelling caused me to have amnesia. I remember some things, and even today I remembered something new… you remember that time when Daddy tried to take us camping in the woods, and we ended up staying at a hotel because Mommy got mad when the tent collapsed all around us that night?"

Her heart thundered in her head. She couldn't believe this. Nikki smiled with half of her face, and she felt suddenly cold. She hadn't been sure what to expect, but somehow this was worse than anything she had imagined. "Yes, I remember," Sophie said, her back to the wall to keep herself from falling.

She remembered everything, but Nikki clearly did not. She sniffed the air, to see if maybe her sister was lying to her, but the sour scent of deceit wasn't there, only genuine joy, combined with the lingering pain and sadness.

"I'm so glad you're here, Sissy. I was beginning to worry," Nikki prattled on, oblivious to the destruction she had caused. "I'm going to see a plastic surgeon tomorrow, and he's hopeful that in time we'll get the scars reduced. He says even with some make-up and lighting, I'll be able to keep my modeling career. It's just going to take some time, but maybe a vacation will be a good thing. Mommy and Daddy both agreed a break would do me some good, too, don't you think?"

Sophie wasn't sure how to respond, or even if she could speak in that moment. Nikki frowned. "Sophie, are you okay? You seem worried about something."

Sophie struggled to think for a moment, her heart torn in two. She wanted Nikki to pay for what she'd done to her life, but it seemed her sister had ended up ruining her own life, too. She still had a vacant look in her one eye, the bandages covering a ruin that would surely end her career, despite whatever the doctor had told her. She hadn't expected to feel so much sorrow in this moment. Grief for the life she had lost, and even a little sympathy for the life that her sister had lost because of her own folly. Nikki blinked slowly at her, unaware of all the suffering she had caused.

After a long moment, Sophie finally spoke, her voice weary. "I…

I'm just tired. It's been a long day, and visiting hours are almost up. I'm… I'm glad you're doing better." She wanted to scream and yell at her, but this shell that remained of her sister didn't remember what she had done. It wouldn't change what happened, or that Nikki caused it all, but even as much as she hated it, a part of Sophie still wanted to protect her little sister. It made it even more frustrating, and Sophie couldn't stand it.

"Thank you, Sissy," Nikki said, sounding relieved. "I hope you'll come to see me again soon."

Sophie had no intention of ever returning to visit her again, and the conflicting emotions inside her becoming too much. "Yeah. Sure."

She couldn't get out of that room fast enough, brushing past the guard who'd kindly escorted her, and ended up taking the stairs down to the ground level. She didn't catch her breath until she reached the car where the guys were waiting. She sat on the driver's side and just breathed, inhaling and exhaling slowly as she gripped the steering wheel. All three of the men in the vehicle gave her a worried look, and she caught a glimpse of her eyes, which flashed yellow. She closed them tightly and leaned forward, burying her face into her hands as the tears she'd held back began to escape. "Nikki doesn't remember anything. She has amnesia from the crash, and she doesn't remember what she has done!" Sophie blurted out.

Warm arms slid around her and she turned and buried her face into Korban's chest. Her hands grabbed into his shirt as she melted against him, and dissolved into a fit of sobs.

~*~

Sophie felt numb on the way home. RJ ended up driving, while Alex and Korban sat alongside her in the backseat for the ride. She was so upset that even this close, Alex's alluring scent didn't trigger the wolf inside of her. She was thankful to be surrounded by friends, and even took his hand along with Korban's. As they drove out of the city and finally were on the dark, country roads she spoke again, "I can't believe she doesn't remember. After everything she put me through… after she tore my life apart… I can't even confront her about it, or even ask her why she did it. She isn't even aware of how much pain she put me through. To her, it's like it never happened, and for me… it's something I deal with every day."

She hung her head down and let her tears fall silently for a few moments, Alex and Korban gently squeezing her hands. RJ peered at her in the rearview mirror, his brown eyes filled with sympathy. "Even if she doesn't validate it, you know the truth. We know it, and we'll support you. No matter what she says, or what your parents say. They may never get what she did to you, or accept the pain she put you through. But that doesn't make what you went through invalid. You don't ever have to justify your feelings to anyone, and you certainly don't have to justify your pain to the one who put you through hell."

Sophie lifted her head up again as RJ's advice sunk in. Something in his words resonated with her, and calmed her down. While it didn't make her situation any better, she at least knew she wasn't alone. No one could change the past, but she at least had these three with her to face whatever came in the future.

RJ pulled the car into the gate, driving in and parking at the end of the driveway closest to the guest house. Sophie started to follow them, but the front door to the main house opened and caught her attention. Lucas was standing there, in a loosely buttoned shirt and pair of jeans. He called out to her, "Sophie, can you come here?"

She wasn't sure she was up to talking to Lucas. She wanted to just crawl into bed and hide under the covers, but she turned and sighed. "You don't have to talk to him now if you don't want to," Alex said softly.

"I'll see what he wants. I won't be too long," Sophie said, then headed up to the porch.

Lucas still moved stiffly, and offered her a small smile as she approached. It quickly vanished as he saw her in the porch light, concern taking its place. "What happened?"

"I went to visit Nikki," Sophie stated. "She has amnesia."

Lucas's frown deepened. "So she doesn't remember what she did to you, or us?"

Sophie solemnly nodded. "I'm not sure how to feel right now, but I'm not up for an argument."

"I didn't call you over here to argue," Lucas insisted, gingerly touching his side. "I thought about something on the way back from our meeting with the Council. I had an idea, and I think it may cheer you up. Come around the porch, I have a surprise in the back."

She gave him a curious look, but followed him as he slowly walked around the porch. She turned the corner and froze. Danny was sitting on the swing that faced the lake, his favorite blanket around him as he flipped the page of a book in his lap. She glanced to Lucas, wondering what kind of cruel trick this was, but he offered her a gentle smile. "The law only states that you can't 'reside' with him. You're technically 'residing' over at the guest house," Lucas said, and offered her a genuine smile. "I'm his father, and your sponsor. As long as we have that, I want our son to have his mother in his life. If we're already bending the laws, we may as well bend them a little more so that you and Danny can be happy."

Fresh tears filled her vision and she glanced from Lucas back to her son. "Lucas… are you sure?"

Lucas met her gaze. "Just because it didn't work out for our marriage, doesn't mean we aren't still a family. Danny will always be our son. I don't want him to ever doubt that both of us love him."

She brought her hands to her mouth to cover her lip as it trembled. She was crying again, but this time it was because she was overwhelmed with joy. Danny paused his reading and turned to them when a soft sob escaped her. He removed his headphones and immediately dropped his book on the porch with a resounding thud. "Mommy?" He said in disbelief, and leapt from the porch swing, his feet barely touching the ground as he raced toward her. "Mommy!"

She didn't even have to think about it. She sank down to her knees and opened her arms as Danny flung himself into her embrace. She couldn't exhale for a moment as his arms wrapped around her, but she didn't care as she inhaled his scent. Fruit juice, cookies, baby shampoo, and something akin to the baby powder scent he had as a newborn underneath it all. She would know him anywhere, and inside her wolf calmed. This was her pup, too, and finally she could hold him again.

"I missed you so much Mommy. I'm so glad you're back," Danny sniffled as he held onto her.

"I missed you too, baby," she whispered. "I love you so much."

"I love you, too," he said, then after a few moments he pulled back a little to meet her gaze. "You have yellow in your eyes now, it looks pretty. Can you see in the dark now?"

Sophie smiled and nodded. "I can."

"Wow! That's so cool!" Danny beamed, then took her by the

hand. "Can I read you a bed-time story?"

"You want to read to me?"

"Yeah! And then you can read one to me. Okay?"

"Okay."

She let him lead the way over to the porch swing, and he picked up the book he'd dropped on the way, gently wiping the cover onto the corner of his pajama bottoms before he climbed back onto the swing. He patted the seat beside him. "We have a lot of bed time stories to catch up on."

"We do," Sophie said, and sat beside him.

He snuggled close into her side and pulled the blanket over them both, the baby blue fabric more worn than she remembered, but just as soft. She listened to her son as he read her the story, amazed at how clear his voice was, and memorized every detail of this moment with all her senses.

When Danny finally fell asleep in her arms, she glanced over to Lucas, who was standing nearby and leaned against the column of the porch. There was no way he could carry their son up to his bedroom, not with his wound still healing. They exchanged a look without words, and she gently scooped up her son's limp body into her arms and brought him in through the back door. She tucked him into bed with his favorite stuffed animal, a well-loved, plush frog he dubbed Ribbit, and kissed his forehead good night. Before parting ways, she gave Lucas a gentle hug and whispered into his ear, "Thank you."

He gently hugged her back. "Good night, Sophie."

"Good night, Lucas." It was the perfect end to an otherwise awful night, and filled her with renewed hope.

23: REHABILITATION

Cyrus Autos passed its final inspection the following week, and with the early turning of the leaves, and the commercials for the New York State Fair unavoidable, summer was coming to a close. School would be starting, and they thankfully had one last long weekend to celebrate the garage's re-opening. Sophie and Lucas had worked out a schedule for her to come and visit Danny on alternating weekends, and as her sponsor, he'd be there for check-ins before and after the full moon. Things were settling back into a new normal, and the mayor had scheduled some appointments with a realtor to look at some potential houses to start their werewolf fostering adventure. Alex suggested a lot of names for what they were doing, but none of them stuck more than that one had so far.

Before they headed to set-up the grand re-opening party, Korban and Sophie stopped by the graveyard to pay his mother's grave a visit. He was surprised to find amidst the older pinwheels a small pot with wilted sunflowers. He stared for a long moment at the flowers, uncertain of what to do, but then the pinwheels spun despite the lack of breeze on that warm, almost Fall day, and a sense of peace filled him. He left the flowers there, and Sophie gently planted the new pinwheel, which joined the others in spinning as they walked away, hand-in-hand.

~*~

Lucas was all too glad when he saw Dr. Hoover walk in to his doctor's office. "Finally time to get rid of those remaining stitches I see!" The doctor greeted him with a friendly smile.

"Yeah, I'll be glad when I can finally stretch my back properly again," Lucas said.

"Well, we'll get those out of you and get you on your way so you can enjoy all the freedoms of being stitch-free."

As Dr. Hoover began to remove the remaining stitches, Lucas stared over at the posters on the wall. "Tell me, doctor… how has your lycanthropy research been going?"

"Well, progress has been slow lately. We're hoping that with what we find in our studies through the Alpha program we'll be able to learn more. I've got some ideas for a vaccine, but we're still waiting on getting the approval for trials in laboratory mice. As much as we have learned, we still have a long ways to go."

"I see." Lucas said, thoughtful. "Suppose that your program suddenly obtained a rather… generous grant. Do you think that you could make more progress then?"

"With proper funding, definitely. You know how it goes. Money can't buy happiness, but it can fund patents and research, and that's pretty much the same thing," Dr. Hoover chuckled, though as he glanced to Lucas he paused. "What are you offering, Mr. Bane?"

"As much as you need, and more. I want to invest in your research, Dr. Hoover. I want to be more than just the billionaire who innovated an entire industry. I want to be the man who helped fund the cure to the world's worst virus epidemic that we have ever seen." Lucas paused and watched the young doctor's face light up before he continued, "I want you to be the doctor who makes history."

Dr. Hoover grinned, and pulled out the last stitch. He set down his scissors and removed his plastic gloves before extending his hand. "You have yourself a doctor."

Lucas clasped his hand. "And you, Dr. Hoover, have yourself an extremely generous grant for your research."

They shook on it to make it official, and Lucas smiled. "I'll send the paperwork immediately. There's no time to waste." *The sooner they found a cure, the sooner Sophie could be human again,* Lucas thought with a bemused smile. The sooner his wife would be able to return home, this time for good.

~*~

There was a banner hanging from the opened bay doors of Cyrus Autos that read "WELCOME HOME" in colorful letters and it was perfect. The entire neighborhood and many patrons were meandering about as Maggie's famous barbeque filled the air with a heavenly scent, along with an array of delicious dishes that were lined up along the tables Alex had pulled out for the occasion. There was music booming from the new sound system that Alex had added as just one of the improvements to the garage. Alex demonstrated the new lift, and showed off a couple of his new gadgets with the excitement of a kid on Christmas Day. It wasn't just a homecoming, it was a block party. Best of all, the cops had already showed up to join the festivities. Tim and Andy were all too happy to share some beers and barbeque, and as Tim said, "It's nice to finally see you all when you're not in trouble." Even Mikey dropped in before he headed to class.

As the sun sank in the distance and day gave away to night, the three-quarter moon rose over a darkening sky. Sophie and Korban were sitting up on the roof, watching the party below. "I never would have guessed at first glance that the community would come together like this," Sophie confessed.

"To be honest, I wasn't always so sure either. I didn't realize how much it meant to be a part of this neighborhood, until Pops took my mother and I in, and we became a part of it too. I was afraid for so long that because I was infected, I wouldn't be welcome any more. I didn't want Alex to lose the work he loved and his home. I hid myself away so long, and now… I guess now it's unavoidable."

"Are you scared?"

"Terrified, actually," Korban said, nervously chuckling. "I don't want to mess this up. I want to be a good Alpha and help others overcome their lycanthropy. I want this to work, for us, and for everyone who has to deal with it."

Sophie slid her arm around him and nestled closer against him. "I'd be worried if you weren't scared. It's a lot to take on. But you'll do just fine. You helped me gain control of myself, and not lose to the wolf. I know in my heart you're the perfect man for the job."

His cheeks darkened and made his amber eyes look brighter.

"Thanks."

"It's good to be the Alpha, ain't it, Lobo?" Alex interrupted as he plopped down alongside him.

Korban jumped in surprise, which made Sophie and Alex laugh.

"I have a surprise for you two," Alex gleefully announced.

"You mean besides a sudden heart attack?" Korban gasped.

"Please, let him finish. He's been driving me nuts all day on when the perfect moment would be for him to bring it up." RJ said as he joined them, sitting alongside the other side of Sophie.

"Okay, shoot. What's the surprise?" Korban asked.

Alex beamed to RJ, who patiently nodded. "Okay, so… you know how there was a hold up in the insurance pay out to the garage. Well, thanks to the reward money from Lucas, I was able to finish the garage and get some upgrades… but the insurance that Pops had in place, well, it finally came through. I got this check, but it's way too much. I mean, a man like me, I'm happy with what I got, you know. My garage has all the latest upgrades I could ask for, and well… with our family growing and stuff, it may be a good idea to have a bigger place to live anyway. I mean, Sophie and you need a bigger bedroom, and then there's the incoming new fosters–"

"Okay, now you're killing me, Alex. Get to the point," RJ chided, sounding equally excited.

"Okay, okay," Alex said, taking a deep breath for dramatic effect. "I want you to use the money and put it towards the new house for the Alpha project."

Korban blinked in surprise. "Alex… are you sure? I mean… the city will be helping us, and there may be more funding given to us as the project grows."

Alex nodded. "RJ and I talked it over, and we both agree it's what Pops would want. You and I were his sons. He would want to do this for you. Besides, if you move out I can finally get a cat again."

Korban laughed, and pulled him into a fierce hug, still cautious of his arm and its neon green bandage. "You're both the best friends a guy could ask for. Thank you. For everything."

They all exchanged embraces, then Alex winked to them. "I'm going to get another drink to celebrate. You guys want any?"

"I'm good for now, thanks," Korban said.

"Sophie?"

"I'll be down in a moment to get a refill," she said, gesturing to her empty bottle alongside her.

RJ and Alex headed back down to join the party, just as the music switched from something upbeat to something slower, Korban glanced to her and smiled. "How about a dance to celebrate, love?"

"You don't even have to ask," she said, and accepted his hand to get up on her feet. She slid her arms around him and the two of them slow-danced under the stars.

~*~

"As you can see, the living room and kitchen are very spacious, as are the bedrooms, which are right upstairs... there is a den over here," the realtor said and led them into the den, her heels echoing on the hard wood floors as she made her way through the house. "It's already cable ready, so you can definitely get high speed internet if you chose with no problem or hassle from the cable company."

"Very nice," Korban murmured, watching Sophie's face light up with every room. He was excited, but watching her happiness was even more wonderful than seeing this large house, perfect for their plans together. Their life together. "You said how many bedrooms in this model?"

"There are five bedrooms upstairs, and a master suite. Three bathrooms, and a half bath, and a full bathroom with a nice spa tub in the master bath. The attic is on the third floor, you can probably convert that to a bedroom or two with a bit of work if you needed," the eager realtor said with a grin. "Oh, and the basement! I remember you asking about that before. Let me show you, it's entrance is over here, between the dining room and the kitchen."

She walked quickly from the den through the living room, and they followed. The house was perfect for what they needed. Large rooms, tons of space. Lots of windows, so there was lots of air, lots of light. Walking down to the basement they found it huge, and Korban figured if they reinforced the glass on the windows it would be perfect. "The basement isn't finished, but I know the perfect contracting and building company if you would need it finished, or the additional rooms for the third floor too." She turned and smiled to them. "Washer and dryer hook-ups are here downstairs, too, in this little closet," she said and opened the small closet in the far corner of the basement. "These are also brand new, along with the kitchen set." She paused to study the two of them closely. "So what do you think?"

Sophie beamed, and answered her. "It's perfect."

"We'll take it." Korban grinned, putting his arm around Sophie.

The realtor's smile went wider. "Excellent, if you come right upstairs with me, I have the paperwork ready for you. Mr. Bane said he'd take care of the finances, but I have some things for you to sign as well."

"Great, let's get to it," Korban said, and they headed upstairs to take care of business.

After signing a stack of legal documents, it was done, and the realtor handed them the keys. She shook their hands eagerly, then hurried off after quick good-byes. He grinned. Apparently their decision of creating a wayward werewolf house would benefit some human beings out there as well, in more ways than one.

The realtor gone, they meandered through the huge, empty house, Sophie mentally imagining the setup of each of the rooms. They made their way up to the master suite and lay on the floor, gazing up at the skylight window.

"We're really doing it," Sophie beamed, gazing over to him. "Home sweet home."

"Indeed..." The first advertisement would be broadcast on the news tomorrow. Korban smiled to his Mate. "Our home... open to others, but ours."

Sophie giggled and rolled over, pinning him to the floor as her smile turned seductive. "Yes, and who knows how long we'll have the place to ourselves." She leaned down and whispered huskily in his ear, her warm breath curling in the whorls of his earlobe. "So we'd better get to work on christening this place, while we can make as much noise as we wish, my Mate."

"You read my mind," he chuckled, unable to think of a more perfect end of the day, or beginning for their life together in their new home.

~*~

~*~

WANT MORE MOONLIGHT NOW?

Visit the official website taintedmoonlight.com for news, updates, character biographies, interviews with the author, and even more bonus content!

Share *Tainted Moonlight* on your social media with friends and help the Pack grow! Like *Tainted Moonlight* on Facebook and follow @AuthorErinKelly on Twitter to participate in full moon giveaways and contests that feature exclusive rewards for Pack Mates.

JOIN THE PACK TODAY!

~*~

AUTHOR'S MESSAGE TO THE PACK

I never meant for this to happen.

It all began as a one shot, smutty fan fiction written for me as a gift from a friend. A friend who had a knack for bad endings. It was a short, slash scene featuring Remus Lupin and Sirius Black from the now legendary Harry Potter series written by J.K. Rowling. Spoiler alert: at the end of this brief story, Sirius left Remus suddenly and without explanation. It was this open ending that triggered my inspiration. There were endless possibilities, and my mind kept wondering- what happened next? I remember discussing it with my friend, and her shrugging and saying something along the lines of, "It was supposed to be a one shot?" I picked up my pen, and together we wrote the next chapter. Remus, alone and lamenting his lover's absence, fell into a deep depression. He lost his job, which he loved, and Sirius, who reunited with him only to vanish again.

It was then that two characters came into my mind who would help Remus in his time of need. Lobo, who would develop later into Korban (hence his nickname given to him by Alex), and Sophie. Lobo was an American werewolf in London (har, har) who was on a mission to help fight for werewolf's rights, especially after hearing that Lupin was fired for being a werewolf. Sophie was a British werewolf and Lobo's mate, who he had rescued years ago. Together they befriended Remus and helped pull him out of his slump. The story grew legs and we added so much to it, titling the story "Hungry Like the Wolf" and dubbing the stories we wrote around it the "Hungry-verse". The story grew in popularity with readers of the fan fiction leaving great, supportive comments- especially about the original characters. We even had fan art. It was the first time that one of my fan fiction stories had gotten praise for the portrayal of original characters – not an easy feat in fan stories.

As we continued to write, the characters developed even more, and new ones were added. We even had plans for spin offs and sequels, and my friend had a wonderfully dark ending in store for our characters and our readers. It was going great, but then life and college happened to both of us, and so our magnum opus of fan fiction sadly was left unfinished.

Then it happened. My characters, who had gotten so much attention and care for so many years, began to demand a story of their own. Perhaps it was because I couldn't leave their tale unfinished. Perhaps it was because I loved these characters that were developed for so many years, as if they were my own children. Perhaps I'd become a bit of a lunatic myself. Whatever it was, their story kept haunting me, and even after we abandoned their initial story, the idea of monsters helping monsters stuck with me.

I began to write their story again, this time developing a world of their own, from the ground up. It started anew, with anything dealing with the wizarding world being removed for obvious reasons. In the place of magic, I used science. The curse of the werewolf became a virus of unknown origin, and vampirism a mutation of the virus. I drafted strict rules, laws, and quarantine protocols that the infected would have to overcome, and most importantly, that my plucky werewolf rights activist would have conflict with. The more I wrote, the more ideas came to me. I wrote, and rewrote the story about seven times just for fun. I was enjoying the ride of this story for what it was, but as the idea to publish it began to form in my mind, I was anxious at first. There was the usual nervousness about sharing my art, of course, but I also didn't want to hurt my friend's feelings. Our story that we had put so much time and effort into had morphed into my solo endeavor. I talked to her about it, and she eased my worries by telling me that it was okay, because the characters were "still talking to me" after all this time, and she had moved on to other stories and fandoms. With her blessing I went full hog into the story, but without her the story wouldn't exist. Which is why I dedicated Tainted Moonlight to her, as she more than deserved it.

As I edited and rewrote, many major changes were made. I decided to start Korban's story from the beginning, after he'd been infected and dealt with the horrors of quarantine. Originally he started as he did in the fan fiction – he was this social justice werewolf with a pack of his own to protect and they faced the challenges of the world together. I wanted to dig deeper and follow his journey at the right moment, and having his story start when he'd already started helping others didn't feel right. I wanted to explore his story as him struggling as a lone wolf to how he formed his Pack, and finally found a family of his own.

As I explored the idea, Korban's tale unfolded and I discovered even more to the story. I knew it would take at least three books for him to discover his path as an Alpha wolf. There were many characters cut out from the original manuscript, but this was also for the best. It gave me a better chance to develop those characters properly, and to show their introductions to the Pack. As the series continues on, you'll get a chance to meet some of these werewolves and other characters, as well as reunite once more with some characters we met so far. It also gave me the opportunity to show how Korban met Sophie, and the complex relationship they have together. Everything fell into place as I made changes to my story. One little ripple of an idea continued to echo and resonate through me, and still does, even today.

As the first part of Korban's story closes, the real story has only just begun. He now has the knowledge of what an Alpha is capable of doing, but has also seen what abusing his power can do to others. His new beginning starts at the end of Infected Moonlight as he struggles to balance his new role as Alpha of Syracuse, straddling the line of darkness and light.

So ultimately, what can I say? While I never meant for this to happen, I am so glad it did. Buckle up because this story has really only just begun now, and I'm looking forward to the ride just as much as my lovely readers. Thank you so much. Every one of you helps make this journey worth every single step.

~ *Erin Kelly*

LOVE IT? HOWL IT OUT!

Your reviews help so much! If you're loving this series so far, please leave a rating on Amazon.com! Your opinion matters and may even appear in a future novel!

Don't have an Amazon account? No worries! You can leave feedback on Good Reads or on any of my social media, all links are available for easy access on taintedmoonlight.com
Please share your thoughts today!

The Pack will return, and continue to grow. But as their family grows, new complications will arise that will change everything for Sophie and Korban.

Their adventures will continue in the fourth book, Awakened Moonlight, coming in 2020!

THE PACK COMES BACK IN 2020 WITH AN ALL NEW STORY YOU WON'T WANT TO MISS!

Check out taintedmoonlight.com for news, updates, and more!

ABOUT THE AUTHOR

Erin Kelly lives in Syracuse, New York with two loving cats, and her dogs Winchester and MacManus. When she is not writing about werewolves, vampires, and other things that go bump in the night, she is often drawing, reading, planning her next traveling adventure, swimming at the gym, or can be found at several local karaoke bars belting out ballads by the Backstreet Boys with her friends.

Tainted Moonlight is her debut novel, with *Captured Moonlight* and *Infected Moonlight* only the beginning of a series with many more stories to come.